# Two Guys, a Girl, and a Tripod

## FOR THE LOVE OF CORN
### BOOK 1

# SARA SITWELL

# Contents

*For anyone whoever thought Simon Says could be more than a children's game. Enjoy this porn with a plot.*

# Trigger Warning

This book contains sexually explicit descriptions as well as descriptions of violence and other things which may be disturbing to you, the reader. If any of the following is triggering for you, please do not read this book.

Abuse

Alcohol consumption

Anal sex (consensual)

Anxiety/panic attack during porn scene

Attempted sexual assault

Bondage (consensual and non-consensual)

Cheating (past)

Choking (consensual)

Domestic violence

Gun violence

Home invasion

Hidden cameras

Impact play (consensual and non-consensual)

Invasion of privacy

Jealous partners

Kidnapping

Knife violence

No-contact with family (parents)

Non-consensual sex (alluded to)

Revenge violence

Rim job/ass eating - (alluded to, not explicitly said)

Safe word needed (respected and the scene stops)

Sexual violence

Snuff film (alluded to, doesn't actually happen)

Stalking

Violent ex-boyfriend

# STI Disclaimer

Hey kids–I hope no actual kids are reading this. Let's talk about STIs, shall we? I know. It's not fun. No one wants to discuss that kind of thing. It's been stigmatized. It gets a bad rap, even just talking about it with your partner. Schools teach abstinence-only, thinking that'll cure it. Yeah, sure. Ok, Karen.

A big part of being an adult performer is getting tested regularly and ensuring your partners–on- and off-camera–do the same. How do performers go about that? There's a database that creates adult industry-standard testing policies and operates a digital clearinghouse for work availability data.

What that means is it allows performers–even amateurs, like me–to keep track of our own tests and our co-stars' tests. Directors or companies that wish to hire us can also use this database to ensure that everyone on set has been tested recently. The database only shows yes/no 'cleared to work' results and not actual results for any individuals.

The industry standard tests include HIV, Hep B, Hep C, Syphilis, Trichomoniasis, Gonorrhea, Chlamydia, and Mycoplasma genitalium–MGEN for short.

The latter is fairly new and if you ask your regular doctor they may not have even heard of it. If they have, they may say you don't need to be tested if you don't believe you've been exposed as it's not prevalent.

You'll never hear or see me use the word 'clean' to describe STI testing results either. Using that word indicates that someone who does contract an STI is unclean and that's simply not the case. Contracting an STI of any kind–curable or not–is not something to be ashamed of. I won't go into your options if you do test positive for something as I'm not a medical professional. Just know that there *are* options.

If you do test positive, it's also important to let a partner–or partners, depending on your activity–know about potential exposure. This helps to keep the infection from spreading to someone else before it's caught.

I know the sex education in this country leaves a lot to be desired. Abstinence-only *has* never and *will* never work and yet it's still being pushed. So if you've never been tested, if your partner has never been tested, if you haven't even considered it, please do so–preferably before becoming sexually active with anyone.

Your health is important, as is that of your partner. Or partners, as is the case in this book. If you have any concerns, or even if you just need more information, contact a medical professional with questions.

Please stay safe out there, folks.

# 1

## Brody

Shit.

Shit, shit, shit.

I've read the same five lines of code at least three times without processing anything. Now I have to re-read them because of my stupid roommate and his stupid determination to finally get me laid.

*"I'm making you sign up for one of those dating apps."*

Miles said this with the same determination as when he claimed he'd kick my ass in high school for failing to realize Amanda Sheridan was into me.

He didn't kick my ass, but only because we'd been interrupted by the algebra teacher as he shouted at us to get to class. For the record, Amanda was into Miles. Not me.

I've been thinking about those words all goddamn day because I know—I just *know*—he means them. He means every single word.

It's not that I hate women. I fucking love women. Really, I do. Unfortunately, they've always intimidated me more than I care to admit. When Miles and I go out, they gravitate toward him because he flashes those charming smiles and has those brown eyes that women want to fall into. That they want to look into while they scream his name.

I grunt and return my focus to the monitor in front of me.

The new system update for Harp Solutions has been on the fritz—likely because I wasn't the one who created it. I keep telling Mel not to let other specialists touch my stuff.

I keep telling her they aren't qualified, but she keeps bringing them in and I have to clean up their messes while doing my own job. The computer screen glows black, a result of the dark mode I have enabled on every product where it's available. While the long strings of code look like gibberish to many, to me, they're the inner workings of one of our more important systems.

Harp Solutions prides itself on privacy—for our clients and within the company. It's probably for the best. Otherwise, I'd end up throttling the programmer who fucked this up. I run my hand over my face and rub my eyes. The only sound in my small office is the cracking of my neck as I twist it side to side, breaking the silence.

Before I can return to the task in front of me, a notification pops up on the top monitor to my left. The background on this one isn't mine. It belongs to a client's wife. The conniving bastard wants to catch her cheating and it turns out that, despite her deceit, she trusts her husband implicitly. She downloaded the program that's been spying on her simply because he suggested a new virus protection program.

The stupidity of some people.

The notification I've been waiting three days for is finally there, in the bottom right corner of the screen: *Email from Grace Harden deleted.*

It's not hard to find a recently deleted email. Most people never empty their trash, though some providers automatically delete things older than thirty days. Mrs. Rawley is indeed one of those people. You'd think someone who's trying to hide an affair would be more careful, but not this woman.

I save the file and use our secure system to send it to the definitely-cheating husband because he's paying our company to catch his definitely-cheating wife. It's going to be a nasty divorce, but that's none of my business.

An impatient message comes in from Mr. Rawley. I reply, asking if there's anything else he needs and his response is similarly short. I'm done with him for the day.

I return to the code but get distracted again when a notification comes through from Mel. A new client referred to only as C-120483 has been assigned to me. The information within the file pertains to a company they intend to either disrupt or fully destroy. It's obvious that whoever their target is, they're shady as fuck. This company is into something serious and it's the kind of thing that makes me wonder just what else Mel is hiding from me.

Harp Solutions usually focuses on jealous spouses, adult children in a hurry for their parents to die, business partners in need of dirt for blackmailing purposes, and corporate espionage. Am I happy that the company I work for exists solely to destroy dignity and invade privacy? No, but I made my peace with it. None of the people involved are innocent, I learned quickly. Besides, if we don't do this, another company will.

Mel Ashcroft has always been a shrewd businesswoman and we've run under the radar for nine years, serving clients in their less-than-savory activities. We rely on word of mouth to gain new clients. The scum of the world really do seem to know each other.

This new target for client C-120483 is a little worse than usual. Part analyst, part not-so-ethical hacker, part software engineer, my first step is to determine what their shipments contain. My initial guess would be either drugs or weapons. Human trafficking doesn't seem likely and Mel has never dealt in that, as far as I'm aware.

Then again, people change.

A notification flares on the bottom right corner of my main screen as I scan the new documents. An email just came through to my personal inbox, inviting me to create an account, and it's from...

"*KinkRink*?" I snort.

My text to Miles is more for his benefit. I don't need to click the link to know where it'll take me.

Me:

What the fuck kind of site
is this?

Miles:

You don't HAVE to use it.

I will. No one knows how to pull the guilt strings like my best friend, so why fight it?

Turning to my personal laptop, I quickly open the email and click the confirmation link. It pulls up a white screen with red and black writing all over it. "*KinkRink*" is in bold along the top left side and I'm prompted to create a username and password.

Miles:

Just don't use something
stupid like loverboy69

Me:

Damn, I thought that was
a good one.

I stare blankly at the laptop screen. I hate creating usernames. BrodyTorrence30 just won't cut it–I need to be anonymous. I sigh and my fingers twitch over the keyboard for several minutes before typing out the only thing that comes to mind: technerd94.

"Very creative," I mutter to myself, but it's done.

I quickly create a password and am provided access to the site. Immediately, it prompts me to upload a photo–yeah, right–and input profile information such as my gender, sexual orientation, relationship status, and more. I can't focus on the *About Me* section now.

Me:

I'm not doing this right
now.

Miles:

Now or tonight, but you're
gonna do it.

Yes, I'll do it because damn it, Miles will find a way to make me. I won't meet anyone. I won't go on a date. I've been on dates. I've tried to meet women, both organically and on dating apps. It never works. They never want to see me again.

What makes this site any different?

—————————

You'd think he grew up having to fight for every scrap, the way he scarfs down his food, but I know that's not the case. I've been slowly, almost carefully, stabbing at the pasta dish Miles made for dinner while he's been shoveling enormous bites into his mouth. I'm not even sure he's paused to take a breath.

"You know," Miles says through a mouthful of food, "you're going to have to-"

"I'm know," I interrupt and send him a sideways glance.

"You don't have to show your face," Miles urges.

"I wasn't going to." I was never going to. I don't have co-workers I worry might recognize me on the site–though that would mean they're on it too, I suppose–but I still don't want my face on it.

"Just run the photos by me before you add any." Miles means well, wanting to make sure I show my best side, but I'm self-conscious all the same. "You can be fully clothed," he adds.

"I don't think that was ever in question." I shudder at the thought of posting nude photos, even faceless ones.

"What are you gonna say in your profile?" The question has to make its way through another mouthful of pasta.

"Computer nerd looking for love?" I ask. "I don't know, this is fucking weird. I hate writing about myself."

"Want me to write it?"

The offer startles me and I meet his gaze. He's still chewing, his brown eyes indicating he's sincere. He swallows, waiting for my response, and my eyes drop to his Adam's apple as it bobs beneath his inked skin. The man is fucking covered in tattoos.

"Er, yeah, ok." I look down at my plate and use my fork to move the bowtie pasta around, creating a trail through the creamy pesto sauce. I stab a piece of grilled chicken and pretend to examine it, though my eyes won't focus. "What-what would you say?" I can't look up, can't meet his gaze.

"I'll text it to you later."

*Great.* I'm in for a treat, I'm sure. He's either going to make me sound like a bad boy who finally wants to settle down or some reclusive computer nerd who can't find a girlfriend without his best friend's help. While the latter is true, I really hope he doesn't go that route.

For several minutes, the only sounds echoing through the kitchen come from Miles' fork stabbing at his pasta and hitting the plate below. I continue to stare at my own meal, not feeling particularly hungry. Abruptly, I stand from my stool, muttering something about having a lot of work to do before rinsing my plate and setting it in the dishwasher.

"Leave the other dishes and I'll take care of them in a bit." I disappear into my office before he can respond.

Miles has his side of the house and I have mine. My office and bedroom are connected by a bathroom so that, if Miles is working from home, I don't need to venture into the main part of the house and risk overhearing his latest project. His studio has its own ensuite bathroom and there's a third one accessible from the hallway outside his bedroom. When he came house hunting with me five years ago, we knew immediately that the place was perfect. At the time, he'd only had his then-side hustle for a year, but in the years since it has become a full-blown career.

*Talk about ironic.* My roommate's an amateur porn star and what am I? *A goddamn loser.*

The room is well-lit with floor and desk lamps. I never use the harsh, overhead lights. I'm not even sure the last time I turned them on.

In addition to four monitors and my personal laptop, my office is also home to a few game consoles and a huge television mounted on the wall opposite the desk. I'd once thought about joining the trend of people who live-stream themselves playing video games, but I'm not entertaining enough for that. Instead, I sit alone in my office, pulling the Nintendo Switch controllers from their perch. It's time for an evening of solo adventuring in a fantasy world.

# 2

## Sophie

Sophie

Shit.

Shit, shit, shit.

"Where is it?" I mutter to myself, digging through my laptop bag. Everything is in there–my laptop and charging cord, the books I brought to read on the plane, the external hard drive that I travel with, the snacks I bought in the airport–except for one very vital thing. My phone charger is missing. How did I forget my fucking phone charger? I used it at the airport. I know I did.

I freeze, my mind running through the events from my layover this afternoon. I unplugged my phone as they announced pre-boarding and must have forgotten to grab the cord before standing up and moving to gather with the rest of the passengers. The crowd was restless, so I was more focused on not jostling people as I passed them.

*Cool.*

Having already showered and readied for bed, I now have to go to the front desk and purchase one of the cords from their little shop. I groan and grab my key and wallet, slip on my aged flip-flops, and hurry out of my room, and down the hall.

My nipples harden in the cold hallway, showing beneath my thin, oversized t-shirt. The soft slap of flip-flop against foot is louder than I would like it to be as I speed walk to the elevator. I jam my thumb against the button and cross my arms over my breasts to hide my traitorous nipples, knowing there's a camera somewhere, but not wanting to find it.

The elevator dings and the shiny, metal doors slide open to allow me to enter. How is it even colder in here? I shiver and press the button for the lobby, still muttering to myself about how stupid it was to just walk away from the damn charger in the airport. Some lucky fucker got a new one for free. I bought it yesterday, specifically for the trip. The one I keep on my bedside table at home is a little worse for wear.

The elevator reaches the lobby, but before I can squeeze through the barely open doors, I'm nearly bowled over. The man, who doesn't seem fazed by the collision, is older with only a rim of white hair at the back of his head and gray stubble on his face. It's August and hot as hell outside, but he's wearing a huge coat, holding it tightly closed. He mutters an apology as he presses a button for his floor and I slip out before the doors can close again. Why can't people just look where they're going?

I round the corner and my eyes fall on the little shop, if you can call it that. It's more of an alcove right by the front desk. There's an assortment of candy bars, a few first aid items and toiletries, a small refrigerator with drinks, and a freezer with meals and ice cream. At the end is a group of chargers next to some earbuds. I hurry over and grab the right charger for my phone, but when I turn to the front desk, no one is there.

"Fucking great," I groan.

I can't let my damn phone die, so rather than return to my room, I sit on one of the couches that face the front desk. I really hope it doesn't take too long.

This wasn't the plan. I should've gone to bed earlier. Hell, I should've *arrived* earlier, but my second flight out of Chicago was delayed due to storms in the area. The Midwest still won't leave me alone, it seems.

Footsteps approach from the hallway and I glance up to see the front desk employee who checked me in. She's a petite older woman with dark hair and somewhat wrinkled, tan skin. Her dark eyes are warm when she smiles at me.

"I'm so sorry, were you waiting for me?" she asks, eyes falling to the cord in my hands.

"No, you're fine!" I exclaim. I hop up and meet her at the desk so she can scan the item. "I just realized I forgot my charger at the airport," I groan dramatically.

We make the transaction quickly.

I start to pry the container open as I head back to the elevator, crossing my arms after I press the button. My nipples need to calm the fuck down. Still messing with the plastic, I sway side to side as I wait for the doors to open. There's a spectacularly comfortable bed waiting for me in a probably too-cold room—just the way I like it.

The elevator ride and trek back down the hallway take no time at all without someone trying to knock me over. My phone, sitting on the bedside table, is at three percent battery. That's the lowest I've let it get in a while. I can't remember the last time I even let it get below forty.

I quickly plug it in and turn on my alarm. I always wake up at least half an hour before I think I need to and that's still probably far earlier than most people would. It'll be my luck that I get to my destination with an hour still to go before I'm supposed to be there, but that's my burden to bear. Early is on time and on time is late.

I yank the covers back and crawl beneath them. With a sigh, I turn off the light, flop my head on the pillow, and hunker down in the sixty-five-degree room. Perfect sleeping temperature.

My alarm would piss me off if it weren't for the fact that I'm excited for my collab today. Tony Gerth is someone I've wanted to work with for a while, but we haven't been able to align our schedules until now. The excitement doesn't make me any less tired as I reach to turn off the noise and turn on the bedside lamp.

I go through my normal routine for a shoot day. Body shower, quickly curling my hair, and the full face of makeup. Happy that I don't need to dress nicely only to strip the moment I arrive, I slip on a pair of cropped joggers and an old T-shirt. After placing my laptop on the desk, I empty the rest of the contents from its bag next to it. To the bag, I return a variety of items I'll need for the shoot, including release forms, my costume, and a pair of shiny, black heels. The pumps have been featured in a lot of my content recently and are looking a little worse for wear, but I don't see them getting much screen time today, if any.

The heat out on the street wouldn't be overwhelming if it weren't for the humidity that comes along with it, even at nine in the morning. August in New York City isn't going to be on my travel list again, but it was the only option if I wanted to get here this year.

My Uber driver waves as he pulls up and I slide into the back, placing my headphones on before we even pull away from the curb. I don't want to be mean, but I can't be bothered to answer questions about my trip.

I like being aware of what's going on, so rather than playing loud music and zoning out, I pull up the map on my phone and follow our progress to the location in silence. We take no detours and as the hotel comes into view, I let out a sigh of relief.

The hotel lobby is gleaming and bright with tall white columns and a grand chandelier hanging in the center. I pass through and head for the elevators, trying not to attract attention. Tony's a local, but his apartment is having some major work done. Since he has my collab and a few others scheduled, he splurged on a room for the week. I admire the professionalism. I can think of several performers who simply would have canceled, despite knowing I came here for them. Not everyone is consistent and reliable in this business.

I'm thankful I don't have to worry about how clean he keeps his apartment. My brain calls forth a rather nasty memory of a recent collab. I shudder as I step onto the elevator and press the button for Tony's floor. My body trembles with pre-filming jitters. As the elevator doors open to let me out, I work my jaw to keep it from locking up with anxiety.

*Breathe.*

The hallway extends to either side of the elevators and I check the sign to figure out which direction to take. Room 521.

As the door comes into view, my anxiety skyrockets. I shake out the arm not holding my bag, pull off my headphones, and knock. The sound of my knuckles colliding with the hard surface is jarring in the silent hallway. A muffled shout comes from the other side.

"One sec!"

The door swings open, bringing me face to face with a man I've only ever texted. A man whose body I've seen a whole heck of a lot more than his face because, well, that's the nature of the job. I could probably pick his cock out of a lineup.

"Honey?" Tony's voice is deep and full of excitement. His brown eyes are warm with fairly pronounced crow's feet in his tan skin when he smiles. He's wearing a white tank top that shows every gorgeous muscle and baggy, black pants. The absurd thought occurs to me that he's taller than I expected.

"Yep! Tony?" Even if I didn't recognize his face, the tattoo on his right bicep is one I've seen many times during my self-care sessions. My cheeks warm at the most recent memory.

"Good to meet you, come on in." Tony steps aside and allows me access to the room.

It's much larger than my home for the week. The king-size bed juts out into the room next to a stiff-looking couch. An armchair, coffee table, and desk round out the 'living space'. The curtains are flung wide open to allow as much natural light as possible to hit the furniture. His tripod is set up, angled toward the bed.

"How was your flight?" Tony asks, closing the door behind me.

"Not bad, I got delayed out of Chicago," I say absently, still examining my surroundings.

"Does it meet your expectations?"

"It'll do," I tease and set my bag against the wall furthest from the bed.

The first step is always administrative stuff, which includes signing each other's release forms and taking ID photos for our records.

"Can I get you anything?" Tony asks as I strip near the desk in the corner.

"I forgot my water bottle," I groan, pulling my shirt over my head and tossing it onto the chair next to me. My bra joins it seconds later.

"I've got extras." He places a bottle on the desk next to me.

Four years in, two of which have included working with co-performers, and it still feels bizarre to change in front of a person who's going to see me naked in five or ten minutes anyway.

The lingerie I chose is easy to pull off so that, when the time comes, it won't require us to pause or cut anything from filming. When I'm finished, I turn to face my co-star whose back is still turned.

"Ready?" I ask. He's still fully clothed.

Tony turns and grins, his eyes freely roving my body. His tongue darts out to lick his bottom lip and I'm pretty sure he doesn't notice his own sharp intake of breath.

This part, I like. I may be a bigger woman, but my ability to make a man stare in awe is a power I'll never take for granted.

"Let's get to work." He removes everything except his boxers, so quickly I barely have time to register his movements.

Before beginning, we each take a couple of selfies for social media–another basic requirement, though not for legality or safety. Marketing is a huge part of the job. We place our phones in their tripods and angle them so that neither will pick up the other, while still getting as much of the room as possible. It's always best to get multiple angles, not just for variety, but in case one phone or camera fails.

There's no intro into the scene, no scenario to set up. It saves me from having to act, which is something I've never been good at. Some adult performers lean into the ridiculous, bad acting, but I haven't quite reached that level of confidence.

Tony stands in front of one of the cameras, far enough away to be seen from the shins up. I sink to my knees, the carpet rough on my skin. I've got to start using a pillow or even a couple of towels for a cushion. My knees hate this position, but it gives a great angle for the viewer. Tony's eyes meet mine and he brushes a hand down my cheek before gripping my chin. We keep eye contact for another moment before he speaks.

"Get to work." It's an order, but his voice is soft and gentle.

Looking up at him through my lashes, I slowly lower his boxers. His cock, thick and curved slightly upward, falls out and I lick my lips as my eyes drop to stare. The act is only half for the cameras. I've been looking forward to this.

Tony uses the hand opposite the camera to grip my hair gently and guide me forward. Swirling my tongue across the tip brings forth a moan from Tony's throat. Taking him into my mouth pulls another from him. I smile around his cock and move my head, using my hand to stroke in time.

He allows me to set the pace, his grip light in my hair. I bob back and forth and my free hand finds his thigh to steady myself. Every few pumps, he pulls me forward, forcing me to take him down my throat as far as I can, but he lets go almost immediately each time.

Before long, my face is a mess. Tears have caused streaks of mascara to make black paths down my cheeks and there's a fair bit of mucus and saliva covering my chin and his cock. Tony glances at his phone, the one nearest to us, to gauge the time we've been filming. Judging that we've been in this position long enough, he pulls me off and I gasp for air. Tony bends and his lips find mine, his tongue forcing its way into my mouth.

"Get on the bed," he orders with a growl.

Tony removes his boxers completely, kicking them away. He moves the tripod while I slowly stand. I crawl onto the bed and he lands a firm smack on my ass, making me giggle. I flop onto my back, lying sideways across the bed for the sake of the cameras. His hand grazes my skin before he crosses the bed and rounds the corner.

Tony climbs up and reaches for the waistband of my panties. He slides them down while I lift my ass up to help and then tosses them toward one of the cameras, just missing it. The bed shifts with his weight as he settles between my legs, hands going to the backs of my knees to lift them. He shifts so that the camera behind him has the perfect angle. My eyes flutter closed and I moan as he slides inside me.

I love the stretch. One of the best things about porn is the size of the dicks I get to fuck. I wouldn't change it for the world. I hadn't realized until working with other creators that I even had that preference. None of my partners outside of the industry had been well-endowed, so I wasn't exposed to it until then. Turns out I'm a size queen.

While Tony continues to fill me, he pulls down one cup of my bra to bare my tit and lowers his mouth to my nipple. I raise my far hand to grip his hair and moan again as he fully seats himself within me.

When his tongue swipes over my nipple, I whisper a curse. His hips pump back and forth, picking up speed. He's forced to remove his mouth, but his hand replaces it. He massages my breast, pinches and pulls on my nipple, all while pistoning in and out. He leans forward to kiss me aggressively, his tongue practically attacking mine.

After several more minutes of some seriously intense fucking, Tony pulls out, slapping his cock on my clit. The contact causes me to twitch and whine. He sits back on his heels, grasping my ankle and adjusting me so he's no longer between my legs.

"On your knees," he says with a grin.

I roll over and get on all fours, then feel his hand gently pressing my upper back. He forces me to lower my head and chest to the bed. My ass is still in the air and Tony angles my hips for the camera before he slaps himself on one buttcheek. He enters me again with a deep thrust and I cry out.

"Fuck, you're so tight," he grunts, pulling out and landing another, harder smack on my ass.

This slap jars me, causing my chest and my pussy to tighten. Tony grunts and speeds up. He grips my hips and starts a punishing rhythm. My arm furthest from the cameras flies up above my head to keep my body from moving forward with the power of his thrusts. My other hand grips the comforter next to my shoulder.

I have to fight to keep my eyes from closing. I want so badly to focus on the pleasure he's causing. Even though I doubt I'll see an orgasm during this scene, I can't deny it's fun.

"Roll over," he orders with urgency, pulling out.

I move as quickly as possible to get into the final position. He half straddles me with one leg over my torso, but his foot is on the bed so his weight isn't on me. He fists his cock while I lay with my mouth open and my eyes closed. It's better than flinching every time I think this stroke will be the finishing move.

He grunts and I feel the warm, wet, stickiness cover my face and tongue. After just a few seconds, the shower stops.

Naked, sweaty, and with a face covered so that I can't open my eyes, I smile while Tony grabs his camera to take an 'after' picture.

"One sec," he chuckles, straddling me while he rubs his softening cock between my breasts for the photos.

I giggle, feeling silly just lying here, unable to see what he's doing. I don't even realize I'm biting my bottom lip until he groans and swipes a thumb over it. He surprises me by leaning down and kissing me. The only thing going through my mind as his tongue presses forward into my mouth is that this will definitely be a hot way to end the scene.

Tony pulls away but tells me to stay put. A minute later, he returns with a damp cloth, wiping his cum from my eyes. When he seems to have most of it removed, he presses the cloth into my hand to allow me to finish up.

"You ok?" he asks. "I'm stopping the cameras."

"I'm good," I chuckle, finally feeling that I've done enough with the cloth to open my eyes. Tony did his best, but it never hurts to be thorough. My lashes are sticky with damp mascara.

"That was great." Tony's still naked, searching through the footage on his phone to see if anything got messed up. It's better to know now than in a few weeks when we're editing the content.

"Absolutely," I agree.

I slide off of the bed and take my phone from my tripod, imitating him in reviewing the footage. The angle I have shows more of my face at the end until Tony grabbed his phone for the final shots. Not only is this going to be a great video, it's *long*. We took over an hour which means I'll be able to split it to sell in two or three parts.

I'm so focused on reviewing the footage that I forget I'm not alone. Tony's voice startles me.

"You hungry? We could grab something before you go."

My eyes flick to him, then back to my phone noticing it's near noon.

"I'm actually gonna head back," I say with a grimace. "It's going to be a long week and I want to get as much rest as I can when I'm not working."

Tony smiles.

"No worries. Are you doing any touristy things while you're here?" He picks up his boxers and slips them on, but doesn't make a move to find any other clothing while I dress.

"I hadn't thought of anything. I still have a couple of shoots that are up in the air," I add.

"Well, make sure you take some time for yourself while you're here. Every work trip needs a little pleasure."

"I thought that's what we were just doing?" I wink and Tony laughs.

"You know what I mean."

"I do," I giggle. "If you have any recommendations, I'd appreciate them."

"I'll text you."

I wipe away as much of the mascara beneath my eyes as possible and, a few minutes later, I head back down to the lobby to wait for another Uber. While standing on the curb, I fire off a text to my roommate.

Natalie doesn't travel as much for work as I do but tries to get something in each quarter.

Me:

First collab done!

Bestie:

Ooo how was Tony? It was Tony, right? Or is he tomorrow?

Me:

No, you're right. He was great, supes professional. I'd definitely work with him again.

Bestie:

Wooooooooooo! And another wooooooooo! Rad! Ok, so who's tomorrow?

Housekeeping has come and gone. My bed is perfectly made, fresh towels on the racks in the bathroom, trash emptied. I scan the room, hoping I remembered to put away anything remotely damning.

No dildos in sight.

My phone buzzes with a text from Tony. It's a list of restaurants he says are close to my hotel. I shoot him a response, thanking him and telling him I had a great time working with him.

My stomach rumbles angrily, reminding me that I'm absolutely famished. Sex takes a lot out of you, even when you *don't* achieve orgasm. After showering and reapplying just a touch of concealer and a thin coat of mascara, I throw on one of my walking-around dresses, along with a pair of bike shorts to avoid chub rub. I've got one of the restaurants on Tony's list in mind, a Thai place he says has been around for over a decade and produces the "best motherfucking spring rolls you'll ever put in your mouth". Lucky for me, it's only three blocks away.

Teeny Thai-nee is one of the most ridiculous restaurant names I've heard of, but the place lives up to it. The line is out the door, but I can see through the window that there are just six tables inside the busy little restaurant and every one of them is full. Most customers are taking their orders to go.

*No nice, easy sit-down lunch for Sophie.*

I walk at a brisk pace to get back to the cool room waiting for me. The temperature in the lobby instantly dries the sweat on my skin, turning it sticky rather than slick. I'm never traveling in August again unless it's to a tropical beach where I can drink daiquiris in a bathing suit all day.

I yank out the two containers from the plastic bag, one containing the spring rolls and the other the pad see ew. The plastic utensils look sturdy enough for the meal, but the first thing I focus on is the container of spring rolls. They came with a brown dipping sauce that has scallions floating in it and smells delicious.

I can't wait any longer. Taking one of the little parcels, which looks almost burnt, I dip one end in the sauce. It's thin, soaking into the crunchy wrapper. I take the first bite and I don't know if it's that good or if I'm just famished, but I swear to god, it's fucking orgasmic. I pull my phone across the table and take a quick selfie, mouth still full, holding up the remains of the spring roll. I send the picture to Tony with a quick thank you before devouring the rest of the food.

# 3

## Sophie

Sophie

I feel more refreshed when I wake up on Wednesday, no alarm needed. The shoot today isn't scheduled until noon. I don't film with women often, but I do enjoy it. There's something about the relaxing environment women create that makes me excited to get down to business.

It's common in the industry for straight women like me to film with other women and for gay women to work with men. It's one of the many double standards in porn and one reason I'm thankful to be an amateur, with control over who I work with and when.

The pressure just doesn't exist for straight, cisgender men in the industry. This means they can be much more strict about the genders they work with, but that's their mistake. Who knows what they'd discover if they just opened up a little? Literally and figuratively.

I take my rolling carry-on instead of my laptop bag today, knowing I'll need to change clothes a couple of times, reapply makeup, and have a few toys on hand. Penny and Vera, roommates who both work in the industry, invited me to their place in Williamsburg.

I asked the concierge last night for the best way to get to my destination. She provided a few options, but my midwestern ass wants the easiest. Not wishing to chance the subway, in case I get lost or end up running late, I decide to take another Uber.

The wall by the front door to the building has a list of names next to buttons to buzz the apartment and I search for Penny and Vera's real last names. *Stinson, Young* pops out at me and I press the buzzer.

"Yeah?" comes a female voice a few seconds later.

"It's Honey," I reply, realizing I haven't given either of them my real name yet. It's not unusual for co-performers to simply call each other by our porn names.

"Come on up!"

A loud buzz fills the air and I open the door before it stops, stepping out of the heat and into an only slightly cooler lobby. It's nice, all white and sterile. There's a line of mailboxes along the left wall and two office doors to the right. Ahead of me is a stairwell and next to that is an elevator.

Not wanting to sweat any more than necessary, I move to the elevator and press the button. I repeat the apartment number in my head while I wait for the doors to open.

The nerves are rearing their ugly head. Head? Sure, head. Whatever, the anxiety is back. The stress monster is making its presence known. A stress monster would have a head. See? Full circle.

My thoughts are all over the place as I step onto the elevator and press the button for the fourth floor. I close my eyes and take deep breaths. I've spoken with both women on the phone and the conversation flowed well. They made me feel like they truly wanted to work with me. It makes sense since they were the ones who reached out to me and not the other way around, but it still feels nice.

I still can't find it in me to do the reaching out yet, especially when the creator–or creators, in this case–has a significantly larger following than I do. I'll follow performers on social media in the hopes they'll follow me back and even message me. Even after four years, I don't feel that I've earned the right to ask someone to work with me. Natalie tells me, and I know full well, that these thoughts are ridiculous because new performers are constantly doing that to me. Specifically men.

*Men and their audacity.* My anxiety momentarily lifts and I roll my eyes.

The doors open and I take a tentative first step out, looking left and right. To my right is just one apartment door. To my left are a couple more before the hall turns sharply. Seeing that the visible doors aren't the one I'm looking for, I head toward the corner. Just as I round it, I see a woman's head pop out from an apartment a few doors down. She looks my way, her short, pale purple hair swaying with the movement. There's a big, beautiful smile on her face as she waves her arm wildly.

"Down here!" She doesn't have to shout too loud in the small space.

I smile, realizing as I approach why she didn't fully step out. All Penny Pepper is wearing is a red lace bra and a matching thong. It takes me a moment to find my voice, but I stammer a greeting.

"It's lovely to meet you." I hold my hand out like it's not awkward standing here fully clothed while she's barely covered in her lingerie.

Penny pulls me into a hug against her tiny frame.

"Come on in, girlie! I'm Penny." Her voice is musical and light, filled with excitement.

"Wow, this is beautiful."

I enter the apartment through the kitchen and stare around at the space with its crisp, white walls. The kitchen countertops are gray and look like they might be marble. The stainless steel appliances are sleek and simple. Further in is a living room with a slightly off-white sectional couch and wicker coffee table. By the window in the corner is a matching wicker chair with a huge, round back and a black cushion. A television is mounted on the wall opposite the couch and beneath that is a long bookshelf made of dark wood.

None of it matches except for the wicker furniture, but it feels homey. The endless number of plants that are, quite literally, everywhere really add to the aesthetic. There are five hanging in front of the window that looks out over the street below. The bookshelf below the television has more than I care to count–a few large creeping vine plants, but mostly smaller ones. There's an enormous rubber plant by the wicker chair and another by the couch. Still more are sitting on a small table between the couch and a hallway that I assume leads to the bedrooms. Even the kitchen has a few low-light plants on the counter which stand out against the white backsplash.

Natalie and I have quite a few plants, but I aspire to this level of green thumbery.

"It's a work in progress," says Penny. I gape at her.

"Oh my god, it's perfect. Do you film out here on the couch? 'Cause the light from that window is–" I make a chef's kiss motion and Penny giggles.

"Yeah, it's one of our favorite filming locations. The bedrooms have some good lighting too, but you're right about the light out here."

A woman appears in the hallway wearing a long, dark green, satin robe, cinched tight around her waist. A smile spreads across her pink, glossy lips.

"Hey Honey, I'm Vera." She holds out her hand as she closes the space between us and this time, my smile is a little easier. I've gotten over the shock of the basically naked greeting I received from Penny.

"It's so nice to meet you both. I was just telling Penny how much I love your place."

"That's sweet." Vera's voice is a little deeper, sultry. The two women make a powerful team, on- and off-camera.

"Can I get you anything?" asks Penny, moving back into the kitchen. "Water or...?"

"Oh, water would be great, thank you." I set my purse on top of my suitcase and Vera eyes the luggage.

"You came prepared," she chuckles and quickly adds, "I like it. Penny and I were thinking we could sit for a few minutes and chat. Just to make sure we're all comfortable. Is that ok?"

"Honestly, I'd prefer it," I admit. I'm always game to jump right in, but when I'm outnumbered, it's easier to sit and talk first.

"Wonderful."

Penny hands me a glass of ice water and I follow the women over to the sectional. Vera isn't quite as heavy as I am, but she's definitely got some curves to her. She's similar in size to Natalie, though her weight is distributed a little differently, held more in her breasts and thighs in a way that suits her. Her pale skin is perfect–neither of the women has tattoos, unlike the way my arms and thighs are covered in random designs–and her hazel eyes are absolutely glowing. I can tell just how much she loves this job.

"Can I ask how you two met?" I can't stand it. I know from their social media that they've been friends for a while and people speculate that they're in a relationship together, but I'm not sure.

"Penny was the videographer on a shoot I did a couple of years ago," says Vera, easily using her friend's stage name. "We connected and hit it off. We even went to dinner right after the shoot." She grins at Penny who returns the smile.

*Oh, they are so dating.*

"We talked about how much we love the industry and I said I wanted to try being in front of the camera. Vera helped me with the confidence required to show off my body." Penny shrugs. "I've never felt so at ease with someone so quickly."

"That's kind of how I met *my* roommate," I reply with a warm smile on my lips. I fucking love friendship. Real friendship is so wholesome and sweet and pure and I just love to see it. I could give a TED Talk about my favorite TV show friendships. "But it was at a convention about a year ago instead of on a shoot and she was already involved in the industry."

"So not at all like how we met," Vera laughs.

"Ok, maybe not, but we clicked instantly. That's what I meant."

"Kind of wild how that can happen," Penny muses.

"Yeah, I moved out to LA about six months ago and stayed with her and her boyfriend at the time. When she dumped him, we moved in together for real and the rest is history."

"Your roommate is Sapphic Emerald, right?" asks Penny. I nod.

"She's... a character." A crooked grin spreads on my lips.

"Love the name," says Vera.

"She used to think it was a mistake because she boxed herself into basically only making lesbian porn before she branched out into findom too. She loves it though and she's good at it and she's hella gay. Her words, not mine," I add.

"Oh?" Penny's confusion is evident.

"After dumping her ex, I think she finally realized that men ain't shit." I shrug.

"But you're straight," Penny clarifies.

"Unfortunately."

The three of us converse for several more minutes or so before I let them know that I'm ready to get started. As I did with Tony, we sign our documents and take photos of IDs. Selfies can wait until I'm in costume. I wheel my suitcase into the corner and unzip it.

"Ooo that's a pretty color," says Penny.

She's standing over my shoulder and pointing at a pale yellow pile of lace and straps. It's a lingerie set that I bought specifically for this trip. In addition to it being a great color with my overly tan skin, I realized that I needed yellow clothing to add to my collection. I grab the lacy undergarments with a nod.

"I have some toys," I offer. We haven't discussed the scene we'll be doing. "Not sure how we should play this."

"Oh we have quite a few toys too," Vera assures me. I know she'd prefer to be the one calling the shots in our scene, which will be second. "How do you feel about monster dildos?" She smirks. Mischief dances in her hazel eyes.

"Like size or style?" I laugh. "Because it's a yes to the latter. I haven't trained for crazy big toys though." It's a goal, to be sure. I know videos of women with ridiculously huge dildos sell well. I just haven't tried it.

"Both, but we'll stick with style. Pen, do you want to grab the strap and that new dragon toy?"

Penny's eyes light up and she races off toward the hallway, her bare feet slapping loudly on the floor as she disappears.

"Penny really loves to use a strap," Vera explains. "And god, she's good." I can see some kind of delicious memory flashing in her mind as her eyes glaze over for a moment. I grin.

"Bring it on."

The scene begins with me watching television, fully clothed in what I wore over to the apartment. Penny rounds the corner from the hallway and when her eyes fall on my relaxed form, she grins. We're roommates in the scene, and her plan for months has been to seduce me.

My character isn't sure at first, biting my lip and scanning her all but naked body. I admit that I've thought about her too. In bed, when I'm alone, with a toy in my hand, I picture her body and the things I'd do to her, the things I'd have her do to me.

Our lips crash against each other, fervent and passionate and seeking so much more. My hands remain on her face, mostly because I, Sophie, feel weird groping women I don't know. Men? Fine. Women? Intimidating.

Penny's touch finds my neck, my breasts, my ass. She slides a hand over my pussy, on top of my clothes, and pulls her head back. She slowly peels my clothing off, my pretty lingerie totally wasted on the scene. I forget about that as Penny trails kisses down my body, which comes alive beneath her lips. I'm on fire now, my pussy aching to be touched. *Really* touched.

We continue, all hands and fingers and mouths on each other before she brings out the strap and orders me onto my knees. As I maneuver into position, my elbows resting on the back of the couch and my ass sticking out, I hear Penny tightening the harness around her hips. She grabs my hair and pulls back gently until her lips are next to my ear, her breath tickling my cheek.

"I'm going to fuck you so hard you'll see stars."

The words send a shiver down my spine and I moan, wiggling my ass, enticing her to move quickly. She grabs the bottle of lube on the table beside the couch and squirts some onto the toy. Once ready, she pulls my panties aside and slides the dildo over my slick center, teasing at first. I moan when she eases inside, stretching me with the bulbous head. Each groove forces another moan or whimper from my lips as Penny moves. When it seems that the toy is about halfway in, I moan with abandon and try to thrust backward. Penny's hands on my hips force me to remain still while she sets the pace.

She picks up speed, thrusting in and out. One of her hands slides up my back to tangle in my hair and she pulls lightly. My eyes close as my head tips back. The noises coming from my open mouth rise higher in pitch as I feel an orgasm building. I likely won't get there, but the pleasure is real.

"Such a greedy girl," Penny murmurs. "Come for me. Come while I fuck your sweet, wet pussy just like you've *always* wanted."

I come apart–or pretend to–stiffening my body and crying out louder than before, which is an accurate imitation of my real orgasms. Penny slows as I let my body relax and her hand lands hard on my ass.

"Good girl."

A few seconds pass while I try to catch my breath.

"And cut," says Vera, startling me. "Say cheese!" she shouts and I turn to face her.

She has her back to us, holding a phone up for a selfie. Immediately, I perk up and throw a peace sign up while winking and sticking out my tongue. I don't know what Penny is doing, but the dildo is still half inside me when Vera snaps a few pictures.

"Oh, that's a good one. I'll send them to you."

I lower my head to my forearms, my ass still sticking out while Vera comes around to take a few close-up photos of the toy inside me. Penny pulls the toy from me and removes the harness. A thud follows as she drops the whole thing onto the waiting towel.

"You ok?" She places a gentle hand on my back, but all I can manage is a thumbs up. She giggles. "Need a minute?" I nod.

Ten minutes later, having fixed just the slightest error in my makeup and cleaned up a little, it's Vera's turn. I've changed into a light blue bodysuit. This scene is far more sensual and romantic, but there's no lead-up or preparation before we begin.

Vera and Penny lead the way into a bedroom down the hall, each carrying a tripod while I carry mine. Just like the living room, the bedroom is mostly white with off-white or wicker furniture and I wonder if this space, like the garage and extra room I have with Natalie, is strictly a studio.

We set up the tripods with the understanding that Penny will just duck in for a couple of close-ups now and then. The wide angle is going to benefit this scene more. The white comforter is soft beneath my hands and knees as Vera and I crawl onto the bed and wait for Penny to make sure the two phones in tripods are recording. She gives us a thumbs up and we dive into the scene in which Vera plans to sit on my face.

When the scene ends, Vera rises up and swings her leg over to allow me my freedom. I sit up and run a hand through my hair, not bothering to wipe her from my mouth and chin yet.

"That was amazing," Vera breathes. "Who taught you how to do that?"

"My roommate and I have filmed together a few times," I say with a shrug. I'm not sure why they're surprised. "She's a good teacher." I giggle and Penny smirks.

"I wish we had time for another scene," she says. "But maybe if I'm out in LA, I'll look you up. I might need a piece of that action."

I laugh, full and loud, feeling completely at ease with these two.

"Deal," I agree. "If you come out to LA, just give me a call."

Penny offers me a damp washcloth while Vera goes around to stop the cameras. I clean myself up and then carry my tripod and phone out to the living room to begin packing my things.

"We have plans tonight," says Penny, pulling on a robe. "But we'll get you the footage by the end of the week."

"No rush." I wave my hand and pull off the bodysuit to begin putting my regular clothing back on. "I'll get mine to you by Sunday night, but I won't be editing anything for a hot minute."

"Sounds good." Penny grins.

"You're here until Saturday, right?" asks Vera as I pull on my shorts.

"Yeah, I fly out early that morning."

"Do you have any plans tomorrow night? Maybe we could get drinks or something. I know how hard it is to take a moment for yourself when you're traveling." Her smile is warm and I find myself wanting to accept because she's right–it can be damn near impossible sometimes.

"I'd love that. I'm filming early afternoon, but I should be able to meet you guys somewhere after five."

Vera claps her hands together with glee.

"Awesome! Ok, we'll text you an address and we can plan for six. Does that work?"

"That'll work." I grin, glad to expand my list of friends in the industry by two.

# 4

## Brody

*LA native, computer nerd, and a lover of nature. When I'm not working, I spend my time playing video games, trying and failing to learn to cook, and hiking or hitting the gym. Not a major fan of crowds, but I'll brave them for the right person. My best friend would say I'm pretty fucking cool, but take that with a grain of salt. I'm still discovering what I like and what I'm looking for in a partner. Would love to meet someone to spend time with and get to know, develop a connection, and find something real.*

Miles sent me the blurb last night, but I was hesitant to read it, afraid of what he might have said. I stare at the words. Shakespeare, he is not, but it's better than I could have come up with. My best idea was to write 'just ask' in the About Me section. He saved me from that, at least. I copy the text and log in to the *KinkRink* app, which I reluctantly downloaded this morning.

I paste the information and click the save button, officially publishing my profile.

*Great.* Now I have to fill everything else out. I quickly add my relationship status, my sexuality, and what I'm looking for: single, straight, long-term relationship. I glance apprehensively at the *Kinks* section. My lips press tightly together while I stare at the little screen as if I can magically make the words appear. Should I add something? Surely there's something on the tame end of the spectrum that I can include.

I take a look, in search of the most popular terms. I'm surprised to find some pretty tame options. Anal sex is basically mainstream in porn now, according to Miles, as are some rougher acts. I scan the terms and stop on one that makes my heart pick up speed.

*Domination.*

Miles has talked about how he prefers to be more submissive when he films with men, a relatively new experience for him. Those discussions piqued my interest and sent me down a rabbit hole of kinks and fetishes, discovering that I find a few things related to domination to be... rather exciting. But Miles has never mentioned that he enjoys submitting outside of his shoots. Maybe it's just porn where that happens.

I'll fill out the kinks section later. I scroll through my phone and try to find a few photos that I can crop my head out of before posting. Everything is a picture of me with Miles or with my sisters. I can't put my sisters on this app, even blurred or cropped. And adding Miles to my profile, with a relatively well-known face and–let's face it–body, isn't going to help me remain anonymous.

I send a text to my best friend, asking for help.

> Miles:
> PHOTOSHOOT! 📷 📷

*God damn it.*

His thundering footsteps echo across the house and he bursts through my office door, breathing heavily. There's a huge grin on his face and his eyes are practically sparkling with delight.

"Yes!" He yells, a little too loud for the small room. I wince. "Sorry, yes," he whispers.

"Can it wait until tonight?"

"No, we need natural light. Get out here."

Running a hand down my face, I stand and follow him to the living room. The blinds are open, allowing the afternoon sun to spill onto the couch and glint off the glass in the center of the coffee table. Miles points to the side of the couch in the sun.

"Sit."

"Bossy," I mutter, but do as I'm told. "Do you really want me in jeans and a T-shirt?" I ask. "Shouldn't I be, like, dressed nicer or something?"

"Do you own something nicer?" He cocks his head, pausing halfway through raising his phone.

"I have a suit." It's a suit I haven't worn in years, but I'm sure it's fine.

Miles rolls his eyes.

"The suit you wore to Raegan's wedding like eight years ago? Absolutely fucking not. I'm sending you shopping later. If you're gonna date, you're not going out looking fucking homeless."

"I don't look homeless!" That was a little too loud.

"You do. Just sit down, shut up, and look pensive or something."

"Pensive?" I raise an eyebrow.

"Yeah, like you're thinking about something deep. Imagine what the love of your life looks like or something. What's the meaning of life? Where do we go when we die?"

"Why? I'm not even going to show my face."

"For when you *do* share a face pic before meeting someone. You can crop the ones you post. Just do it."

"Sure."

I try.

I fail.

I can hear Miles' frustrated grunts, though he's trying to be silent as he moves around me, getting just the right angle.

"Dude, fix your face. You look angry," he says with an annoyed huff.

"Fix my face?" I repeat, utterly confused. "What does that-?"

"Like this." Miles drops his expression, softens his eyes, raises his eyebrows just the tiniest bit, and looks to his right, toward the window.

I start to wonder why he's so good at this and then I realize it's his fucking job. I take a deep breath and let it out slowly.

"Ok."

I try.

I think I do better.

Clearly, I don't.

"Ok, ok. Let's try..." Miles looks around but doesn't seem to come up with anything. "Maybe we *should* wait until you can dress a little nicer."

"That makes me feel great."

"Shut up. Women are gonna flock to you with or without clothes." He waggles his eyebrows suggestively and lowers his phone to begin searching or typing. It's hard to tell while his thumbs move quickly. "Let me send you the name of this girl I worked with last year. She works part-time on adult sets, but her main career is styling B- and C-list celebs. Trust me, she'll deck you out."

"Oh god, are you sure?" I hate being the center of attention. Trying on clothes with some woman I don't know might break me.

"I'll come with," Miles assures me, glancing up to send a supportive smile my way. He taps his thumb once more with finality and I hear my phone chime in my office. "That's her contact info. I texted her to let her know you'd be reaching out. See if she's free Friday. I'm working tomorrow."

My lips form a tight line, but I nod.

"You'll thank me. I swear." He taps his phone a few more times and my phone chimes again. "I just sent you the pictures I took. I know they're not great, but please just post one for now."

"Why not just wait?" I ask.

"No one is going to interact with a profile that doesn't have a single picture," he shoots back.

I raise my hands in surrender and stand from the couch.

"Am I dismissed?"

"I want you sending three messages a day. I *will* be checking your work."

"Homework. Great. *Now* am I dismissed?"

"Fine." Miles rolls his eyes. "But call her. Moira is rad. You'll like her."

"Is this a setup?" I raise an eyebrow.

"You're not her type." Miles waves his hand, dismissing me. When I continue to stare at him, he adds "You have a dick."

"Got it."

"Go. Shoo. Back to your cave." Miles tries to wave me out of the living room of my own house, but I grin and smile before turning away. "Post *one* picture and actually try to connect with someone!" he shouts after me.

I disappear into my office and close the door, leaning my back against it. I take a deep breath. And another. And another.

I'm going to kill him.

Hasn't he known me long enough to know what I can and can't do? Like... socially? I've tried going on dates, I've tried flirting. I suck at it all. Miles knows it just as well as I do and yet he's pushing me into this. I owe him, though, having practically begged him to move in with me five years ago.

I needed him here. I couldn't live alone anymore. I was too fucking depressed. I needed someone to pull me out of my room and make me feel human. Make me touch grass now and then.

Pushing myself off of the door, I walk back to my desk. I don't have set hours. I have projects I complete, client discussions, information to share, code to revisit when people fuck up. I can work whenever the hell I want as long as the work gets done, but I still try to keep normal business hours.

I look at my phone like it's going to bite me. It's just sitting there on my desk, mocking me with the texts from Miles. The contact information and the photos. Needing to get this over with, I pick up the phone and open the messages with a dejected sigh.

None of the photos are great. Maybe I can crop this one of me with one ankle on my knee. My right hand is on the opposite knee and the sunlight emphasizes the black and gray geometric ink running down my arm. Women like tattoos, right? If Miles' body is any indication, I think so.

I edit the photo, cutting off my head, and quickly post it to *KinkRink* as my profile photo. No need for a caption. I'm not that witty.

I return to the messages from Miles and open the contact information for Moira Hall. The accompanying text says 'stylist to the stars' as if that's going to convince me this is a good idea. I take a deep breath and call the number.

It rings.

And rings.

And rings.

Finally, halfway through the fourth ring, someone answers.

"Hello?" The female voice is chipper and light.

"Er, hi, my name is Brody Torrence. A friend of mine gave me your number. He says I need a stylist." I mutter every single word, half in embarrassment and half in shame.

"Oh, yes! Lance said you'd be calling. Nice to hear from you so quickly. He said it might take you a while."

"Yeah, well if I didn't call now, he'd keep asking."

She giggles.

"Yeah, he's intense sometimes, isn't he?"

"You have no idea." I roll my eyes. "Would you be free for..." What is it called? "A consultation on Friday?"

"Hmm, I think I have the morning free. Would that work?"

"Yeah, that's perfect. Where should we meet you? Do you have an office or-?"

"I'll send you the address, but Lance knows where my shop is."

"Shop?"

"Yes, I operate out of a storefront, but I have loads of designer options and I can custom order. I have tailors available as well. Lance says you're kind of tall?" she asks.

"Six foot six." My height is half the reason I don't buy anything better than jeans, cargo shorts, and T-shirts.

"Definitely taller than most of my clients," Moira chuckles. "Not to worry. I'll have you looking suave and debonair in no time. See you at nine on Friday."

"Thanks, Miss Hall."

"Oh, call me Moira!"

I feel marginally better after speaking with her. She's nice and warm and friendly and she knows Miles, even if she only calls him by his stage name. This is going to be fine. I'll be fine. It helps to know she wouldn't be interested in me. It feels less judgmental somehow, given the reason for this shopping spree.

Still holding my phone, I see a text from Moira with the address before another text comes through from someone else.

> Isla:
>
> Uh Miles says he's forcing
> you to date?

He *would* tell my sister. I groan, but it could be worse. Isla and I are closer than I am with our older sisters. Raegan and Henley would immediately tell my parents who would ask me a million questions, the answers to which, I definitely wouldn't have.

> Me:
>
> He made me create a
> dating profile on a weird
> app. And no, I'm not telling
> you what it is.

I don't need to worry about accidentally stumbling upon my sister on a site like *KinkRink*.

> Isla:
>
> Is it Grindr? Is there
> something you want to tell
> me?

Me:

It's not Grindr

Isla:

It's Grindr

Me:

Not arguing. Did he also tell you he's making me shop for new clothes?

Isla:

FINALLY! I've been telling you to lose the stupid Star Wars tees for literal years. Send them far, far away.

Me:

You want to come? It'll be Friday morning. No need for space travel.

Where did that come from?

Isla:

Let me see if I can switch shifts at the cafe, but I definitely wanna be there. Text me the address.

Great. More company. I only have myself to blame.

---

Miles makes dinner again, something he's been doing since he moved in because "If you won't let me pay rent, at least let me do something for you." I'm not upset by it. He's much better than I am and it's healthier than eating out every day.

When I walk out to the kitchen, he's not there. There's a chopping board with sliced red onions and a bag of burger buns sitting out, but nothing else. While I stand there, wondering where my best friend has disappeared to, the back door opens and Miles walks in holding a plate of cooked burgers.

"I wanted to fire up the grill," says Miles with a shrug.

"Four?" I ask, looking down at the plate of cheese-covered patties.

"Protein, man. You saying you won't devour two of 'em?" He raises his eyebrows, setting the plate on the kitchen island.

"No one said that."

"That's right. It's leg day tomorrow. Get the lettuce and the tomatoes out." Miles points with the spatula toward the fridge. "Top shelf," he adds when I open the door.

I grab the plate of tomato slices and the bag of washed lettuce. After setting them on the island, I turn back to find the pickles, mustard, and ketchup. Miles pulls plates from the cabinet and sets one at each of our usual stools at the kitchen island.

We work around each other to build our burgers. I avoid the tomatoes but go for the jar of pickle slices while Miles avoids the pickles with a face of disgust.

"How, man?" He asks the same question every time he sees me pile them onto my sandwiches and burgers, but I grin and pop a single one into my mouth. He shudders dramatically and sits at his spot. "I guess *someone* needs to eat my pickle." He pauses and closes his eyes, not turning to face me. "I mean the pickles that come with my sandwiches."

"Mmhmm." I nod and take a bite of my burger. "I don't swing that way," I say with a mouthful. Something crosses Miles' face that I can't recognize.

I'm barely finished with my first burger when he pops the last bite of his second into his mouth. He stands and sets his plate in the sink.

"I'll clean up." I don't know why I say it. It's our system. He cooks, I do the dishes.

"Thanks, I've gotta get back to work." He practically runs back toward his studio.

I take my time with the second burger, sitting with my thoughts. I haven't opened *KinkRink* since I posted the photo, afraid of what comments I might get. I don't have the notifications on, so I have no idea if anyone even reacted at all. The consultation on Friday—Moira didn't correct me when I called it that—looms like a storm cloud in my mind. I have never liked pulling focus in a room and now, not only will Miles be there, but I invited my sister.

*Fucking idiot.*

I finish the burger, still swallowing when I stand and take my plate to rinse it off in the sink. I clear the burger toppings, saving the excess, and bring the cutting board and knife over to rinse off. I finish the rest of the cleanup quickly. Easiest cleanup in weeks. Miles gets to clean the grill.

Instead of returning to my room, I sit on the couch and open up Netflix, looking for something to take my mind off of my impending doom. Nothing. I go through the different apps on the TV, but nothing jumps out at me. I switch to the movies and shows I digitally own, hoping something familiar will be enough.

I land on *Parks and Rec*. As the episode starts, I bite the bullet, unable to wait any longer. I pull my phone from my pocket and open up *KinkRink*. Sixty-seven notifications await me and I notice my inbox has a little dot next to it too. My hands feel clammy as I tap the notification button.

People liked the photo, I see. It's not even impressive, but fifty-three of the notifications are just people having *liked* it. They actually went and clicked the little heart below the photo to show some love. Another dozen notifications show that people followed my profile. Finally, the last two are comments.

> sexisub (F, 27):
>
> omg i love your tattoos!

> handoverheart (F, 38):
>
> i need a new necklace

*A necklace? What does that even mean?*

A smile spreads across my lips at the responses, even if one of the comments is unintelligible. I click the heart icon to 'like' both of them and click on the envelope icon for my inbox. Six messages await me.

One is a man asking if I'll fuck his wife. Nope, deleting that bad boy.

Another is a woman whose profile says she's located in England. She's traveling to the US and wants to hook up. Also no. Even if she wanted more, I'm not doing long distance.

A second woman tells me she wants to ride me into the sunset. That makes me crack another smile, but there's no way I could contend with that level of confidence.

Another man, but this one wants me to- Nope, can't even finish reading that one.

Another woman who only says one word in greeting. Since I don't have anything to go off of and her profile is emptier than mine, I ignore it. I don't want to be rude, but if I'm going to force myself to interact with people, I'd like to be able to do my research.

The last message just has an emoji with no photo and no gender even listed. Yep, that'll get a response. I see what Miles means about no one interacting with profiles that have no photos.

I shake my head while Leslie Knope starts up her well-meaning shenanigans and decide to start on my homework. Since I'm not sure where to begin, I explore the site. There are groups I can join, some focused on specific kinks, some on locations, and a variety of other things.

There's one called *Los Angeles LTR*. The group description tells me it's for people looking for long-term relationships. I decide to join and start scrolling through the discussion posts. Many of these people don't actually seem like they're looking for a relationship, but what do I know?

One post catches my eye. Her username is sweetashoney and, unlike some of the users in a group meant for people in LA, she's actually located here *in LA*.

> sweetashoney (F, 28)
>
> Haven't been on this app or in the city for long. My roommate says I need a love life, so here I am, looking for a connection. I enjoy long walks on the beach, the LA sunsets, and an ice-cold beer. I work a lot, but I'd love to find a reason to work less. So be yourself, ask me something interesting, and give me a shout if you're interested!

Ok, Miss Sweet As Honey. I glance at her profile. No face pictures, but I can't judge. Her curves are more than enough to pique my interest. I feel like a caveman, ogling her body, but I suppose that's why she posted the photos she did. Some are tasteful in black and white, but none show *everything*.

Her skin is darker than mine, but not by much, covered in a variety of black and gray tattoos with some flashes of color. I can see some soft, light brown curls hanging past her shoulders in a few photos as well. God, I'm dying to know what her face looks like. I'll bet she's a knockout.

Her profile confirms she's looking for a long-term relationship and her list of kinks and fetishes is more than a full page. I can't focus on all of the words, so I scroll quickly, catching random things like 'butt stuff' and 'group sex' and 'public play'.

I get the sense she's going to be too much for me to handle, but something makes me open up a new message to her anyway. Time to see if her suggestion of being myself is enough. I remember a question Miles asked me the other day during dinner and decide to use it to sound interesting.

Is that cheating? I hope not.

> **technerd94 (M, 30)**
>
> Hey, sweetashoney, I saw your post that you're looking for a connection. I'm new to the app, but not the area. I do have a question you might find interesting.
> At what size does a pebble become a rock and (2 for the price of 1, here) at what size does a rock become a boulder?

I throw my phone to the couch in a panic, something I've never done in my life.

That was a dumb Miles question. She's not going to respond to that. My heart pounds in my chest. Or is it in my throat? I can't focus on the show at all, even when Leslie falls into the pit during a 'fact-finding mission'.

Should I turn on the notifications so I know when she responds? *If* she responds.

*Oh god, oh god, oh god.*

I still have two more messages to send today because Miles is a dick.

# 5

## Sophie

### Sophie

I stare down at my phone with a crooked grin, amused by this guy's message. His profile is mostly bare, but he's new to the app. I'll give him a pass.

sweetashoney (F, 28)

Well, that's a new one. I can't say I've ever wondered about the size differences between those. Do you know or are you genuinely asking?

technerd94 (M, 30)

Genuinely asking. I don't know the answer.

sweetashoney (F, 28)

Come up with an answer and I'll keep chatting.

My phone is silent for a while and I stare, waiting for the little dots to start jumping, indicating that he's typing.

technerd94 (M, 30)

Turns out a pebble is a rock fragment usually between a few millimeters and a few centimeters in diameter. A boulder is basically just too big for a person to easily move. A rock is everything in between.

sweetashoney (F, 28)

Impressive. A+
Maybe your roommate's right about you being pretty fucking cool.

technerd94 (M, 30)

You shouldn't believe everything you read. What if I'm actually incredibly lame?

sweetashoney (F, 28)

Are you calling your friend a liar? That's not very nice. Maybe you are lame. Suppose I made a mistake responding to your message.

technerd94 (M, 30)

Can I confess something? He's the one who wrote my profile. I never know what to put in those things.

sweetashoney (F, 28)

Ah, that explains it. Is your friend single?

He doesn't respond for several minutes. Did I piss him off? Sheesh, I forget how touchy men can be. I roll my eyes and move to set my phone down on the bed next to me when his response appears.

technerd94 (M, 30)

Serially so

> sweetashoney (F, 28)
>
> Then I should probably steer clear. Serial singleness can be a red flag. Since it looks like we might be looking for the same thing, why you don't tell me about yourself?

We continue to exchange bits of mundane, only mildly personal information. The conversation is enjoyable, even though it feels like it's not going anywhere.

> technerd94 (M, 30)
>
> I'd love to help you explore LA. I know a really good brewery near the fashion district. Would you want to meet when you're back in town?

> sweetashoney (F, 28)
>
> Boy, you don't waste any time! How can I say no? I'll be back late Saturday, but maybe Sunday or Monday?

> technerd94 (M, 30)
>
> How about Monday? Six?

Very few men make a plan so quickly after connecting online. Most beat around the bush or end up ghosting after six messages. This guy got straight to the point. I have to admire that. I chew the inside of my cheek for a minute, wondering if I should send my number, but instead, tell him I have to head to bed. 'Big meeting' early tomorrow.

My legs are in agony when I get back to my hotel on Thursday afternoon. I wish I hadn't accepted Vera and Penny's offer. We agreed on meeting at a little Mexican place near them that has a special on Thursdays in addition to Tuesdays to get a second weeknight crowd. Apparently it works.

I shower with a cap on my hair so I don't have to wash it, taking a little longer under the hot water in the hopes that it will relax my sore muscles. I pull my hair up into a high ponytail and swipe my lashes with mascara then order a ride.

The trip to Williamsburg takes longer than it did before, but that's what I get for trying to get anywhere during rush hour. The traffic here is nearly as brutal as LA's.

Vera and Penny are standing on the sidewalk outside when we pull up to the restaurant. There's a small crowd gathered, but it doesn't look too bad. Penny waves when she sees me and Vera follows her gaze with a grin.

"You made it!" Penny squeals, pulling me in for a hug.

"Thanks again for inviting me. I hadn't realized how much alone time I was getting in that hotel room."

"The threat of cabin fever is *real*." Vera's eyes go wide to emphasize her words. I smile and nod my agreement.

"Sometimes I think I've got the hang of long-distance travel for work, but then I have a busy week like this and I realize I've got a long way to go."

"It takes time," Vera assures me. "I still fuck up now and then. Forget a crucial toy or, shit, *lube*."

"Oh my god, that happens to me all the time," Penny interjects. "Thank goodness I have you now."

"So this place has drink deals on Thursdays?" I ask, changing the subject.

"Yeah, Taco Tuesday is one thing, but Thirsty Thursday is where it's at." Penny giggles just as her phone vibrates. "Oh, our table is ready. Perfect timing."

Penny leads the way to the hostess stand and I see just how *packed* this place is. Wondering if they might be violating a fire code, I follow my newfound friends to the table the hostess is gesturing at. She hands us menus, quickly spouts off the margarita specials, and then disappears.

"I didn't catch any of that," I say to Penny and Vera when she's gone.

"Dollar margs," Penny says with a wink. "That's all you need to know."

"Works for me."

Less than ten minutes later, we alternate between stuffing our faces with chips and queso or salsa and drinking our fruity margaritas. Penny chose a watermelon margarita, but claims there's no real flavor. Vera and I are perfectly happy with our choice of strawberry.

"So," I say through a mouthful of chip and salsa, "forgive me if this is asking too much, but are you two... like...?" I raise my eyebrows and leave the question hanging, unfinished.

It's been nagging at me since yesterday and they seem nice enough that I doubt the question will offend. The tequila helps by providing a sense of bravery. Penny giggles. Vera just smiles.

"No, we're just good friends," says Vera before taking a sip of her margarita, which I notice is almost empty.

"Good friends who fuck," Penny adds as the waitress comes up to ask for our order.

When she disappears again, having written nothing down–a feat I remember doing in my waitressing days, but still marvel at–I turn back to the women across the table.

"Single?" asks Penny.

Whatever question I was about to ask disappears entirely from my brain. There's no way they miss the color draining from my face. It's been six goddamn months *and* Natalie just made me join a kinky dating app *and* I just started chatting with someone who already asked me out. I'd say that's progress. I quickly reach for my frozen drink and suck it down until my head hurts. Squeezing my eyes at the pain, I set the huge glass down.

"Yeah," I finally respond, grunting with the effort to open my eyes again. "Single."

"Touchy subject?" Penny studies my face with concern.

"Just a little."

*That's an understatement.*

"Moving on," says Vera. "Why LA?" she asks. "Why not up here or down to Florida or, hell, Texas or Chicago?"

"Emerald was already out in LA and I didn't really have time to think." Because I was running from an abusive boyfriend and LA is a big ass city where I could lose myself. They don't need to know that.

"Oh yeah, why didn't she join you this week?" asks Vera.

"She was just here a couple weeks ago for a pro shoot," I explain, only mildly jealous of that success. I still haven't gotten to work with a serious production company.

"Damn, we missed her?" Penny is visibly disappointed, but Vera chuckles. "Well, tell her to get in touch with us before she comes again."

"I think you guys might make it to LA before that happens." It's my turn to laugh. "She kind of hates it here."

"Why?" Poor Penny looks offended. Vera places a hand on hers.

"You'll have to ask her," I reply. "I'm just relaying her opinion."

Originally from Albany, I still wonder why Natalie claims to hate the city. Sure, the humidity sucks, but that's only during the summer. She hates crowds, but she handles it in LA, so that can't be it. One of these days, she'll tell me.

———————

The next morning, I wake up with a headache of my own making. Why did I drink that last margarita? Did I have three? Or was it four?

I slowly sit up in bed and follow the sliver of light from the curtains so I can open one side and let some light in.

"Oh, noooo," I grumble, turning away from the bright light pouring into the room and hissing like a vampire burned by the sun.

Muttering about Jose being a dick, I go to rustle through the contents of my laptop bag for some pain meds. I toss two into my mouth and then add a third one for good measure. Just one more scene today and then I'm done here. I can make it through. I *have* to make it through.

I move back to find my phone on the bedside table. My stomach drops when I see the most recent text. My collab for the day is canceled. I can't focus too much on the words, but there's something about a family emergency. I know it happens, but I'm still a little annoyed.

Despite the pounding in my head, I bring my phone with me to the bathroom and start scrolling, looking for something to interact with. I send out a tweet saying I'm in New York City and a gig fell through, asking if anyone is tested and ready to film. I doubt I'll get any takers. In LA, it's always my luck that I see those posts a day late.

I scroll for a few more minutes before standing and cleaning up for the day. I'm not putting on makeup until I have a plan. If I don't come up with a plan, I'm staying in my room and nursing this damn hangover.

Halfway through brushing my teeth, my phone vibrates loudly on the bathroom counter. I wince at the sound, but when I glance at the notification, my jaw drops.

@SaraSitwell:
Hey Honey! We follow each
other and I saw that something
fell through. I'm in town with a
free day. I can't film today, but
would you want to be a last
minute guest on my podcast?
It's called Hide the Sausage, if
you want to take a look at it.
Oh! And do you eat meat?

*We follow each other.* As if I wasn't aware. Sara's another plus-size adult performer who has built her brand over the last few years. I admire her. We've interacted under her posts, but never via direct message. A spot on her podcast would be amazing for my career.

I type out a quick response, thanking her and asking when and where, adding that I do, in fact, eat meat. Sara responds with the address and we set a time that allows me to get ready at my very slow pace. Stupid margaritas.

My head still pounding, I clean up and throw on a sundress, but then I pause, and study myself in the mirror. Do I wear something sexier? Shit, I don't know if this is a video interview or just audio. I'm not sure why it wouldn't be done on video.

I Google the podcast and find that it's both. Some of the guests are fully clothed, some are scantily clad. The latter, I realize, only have thumbnails with no trailers or teasers. Those must be behind a paywall.

*Sexy, it is.*

I change into some cut off shorts and the black lace bustier I was going to wear for my scene today. It's acceptable for the public but would fit better at a bar on a night out. Still, it's a happy medium. I put on a full face of makeup like I would for a shoot, then grab my purse and order another Uber. The pain meds start to kick in just as the elevator doors open to take me downstairs.

Sara is staying at a vacation rental apartment. Smart. More space, a kitchen, sometimes there are laundry machines. I make a mental note to look into that next time, though maybe in cheaper cities. She buzzes me in when I arrive. I don't have time to marvel at the absolutely gorgeous lobby of the building. It's full of colorful marble and there's even a grand staircase leading to the second floor.

I hurry to the elevator across the lobby and hit the button before checking my phone for the floor. Fifteenth, got it. But instead of an apartment number, Sara gives me a code to input. Frowning, I memorize the four-digit code and enter it once I get into the elevator.

When I step out, my jaw drops. The whole goddamn floor is a single apartment. Now I get the lack of apartment number in her message.

"I'm coming!" Sara's voice echoes from somewhere to my left.

The apartment is sleek and modern, all white and shiny with enormous windows. The light spilling in makes me incredibly jealous even though my apartment back home gets great natural light. It bounces off of the surfaces of the white leather couch, the white coffee table, the shiny white marble tile floor. That's when I notice that not a single lamp or overhead light is on. It's all lit by the sun.

Something smells amazing, making my stomach growl.

Sara comes jogging in, her cheeks slightly pink from whatever she was just doing. She smiles from ear to ear and her blue eyes shine with warmth. It's infectious and I feel a grin spread over my face as she approaches with a pale hand held out.

She's wearing a short black dress that fans out when she moves. It's simple and cotton, covered in a floral pattern, but it's definitely not the skimpy clothing I've seen in some of the thumbnails for *Hide the Sausage*. I suddenly feel overdressed. Or underdressed, depending on your view.

"It's so nice to meet you."

"Thank you so much for this." I grab her hand and shake it a couple of times before dropping it.

"Oh of course! A few fans have requested you as a guest, but I just hadn't gotten around to reaching out. This is pure luck!" She claps her hands and rubs them together with glee. "So, you might be wondering why I asked about your diet."

I nod and chuckle as Sara waves for me to follow her back the way she came. I know her podcast gets listeners and I've seen thumbnails, but I haven't actually listened to or watched an episode yet. I feel a little guilty for not at least listening to part of one on the way over.

"Yeah, that was a little weird," I admit.

"I was trying to think of something silly, but wholesome so that we could do it for the regular *and* the premium episodes. My guests and I try different sausages and bratwursts and things like that. I try to go local and if my guest is vegetarian or vegan, then I work around it and find meatless sausage. Just three different ones," Sara continues as we enter into a large sitting room.

There are a couple of legitimate, professional cameras set up on tripods. The studio lights are turned off, aimed at light two very comfortable-looking white armchairs. Microphones are set up to swing toward the occupants of the chairs and over on a side table are two plates wrapped in foil.

"Ok, so feel free to have a seat over there," Sara says, pointing to the chair on the right. "I'll grab your plate and I have a bottle of water for you, just in case any are terrible. I make no guarantees."

"Hey, you're in charge." I set my purse near the doorway and take a seat in the chair she indicated.

"That's right, I am!"

Sara hands me the plate and a labelless bottle of water. A couple of utensils stick out from beneath the foil. When Sara returns to grab her plate, she pauses to start the cameras and taps a few buttons on a laptop I hadn't noticed on the coffee table. I try to get comfortable with the plate on my lap.

"Ok, are you ready?" Sara sits and grins at me.

"Absolutely." I'm nervous as fuck. Heart pumping, hands trembling slightly. This might be worse than when I meet new co-stars.

"It's going to be ok," she says in a softer tone. "There's no pressure to answer anything you don't want to. If there's something you're not comfortable with, we'll skip it. Just say the word. That's what editing is for."

I take a deep breath and nod.

"Let's do this."

"I try to ask everyone this because I find it fascinating," says Sara. "How do you separate work from genuine pleasure? How do you *not* develop a crush on someone you're working with?"

I've practiced this one. People ask me all the time.

"For me, it's a matter of flipping a switch in my brain. These are colleagues, co-workers, so that's how I see them. It's all a performance, right?"

"I'm sure a lot of people believe it's all real and many of us are friends, but sometimes it really is just a one-and-done thing. No real connection."

"It's just work," I agree. "That's not to say I don't have fun, of course." I wink, playfully. Sara grins before moving on.

"This might be hard, but do you mind sharing your *worst* experience since starting collabs?"

"I worked with someone a couple months ago," I start, fighting the urge to look down at my hands. I maintain eye contact with Sara. "We'd discussed the basics. Paying me because I was driving a full day just to get to him, a couple scenes we'd do, all that stuff. When I got there..." I trail off, not wanting to go on a rant, but not wanting to leave out the important stuff. It's easy for women in the industry to be demonized for speaking out against men or studios. The thought of losing everything I've worked so hard to build is terrifying.

"You don't have to," Sara offers.

"No, it's ok." I started the story and it deserves to be finished. I take a deep breath and continue. "His place was absolutely disgusting. I don't mean untidy. I can handle untidy, but my socks were black after just a couple minutes. But on top of that, his specialty is rim jobs. And, well..."

"No." The horror in Sara's blue eyes tells me she knows exactly what happened.

"Yeah, that was the first *and last* time I will ever do that."

"What an ass." She pauses. "No pun intended."

"Yeah, and afterward, he called me a bitch, didn't pay me, and blocked me." I shrug.

"Are-are you serious?"

"Yup."

"Jesus." Sara shakes her head. "I can't believe he had the gall to stiff you. Literally and figuratively."

"I should've driven right back home as soon as I arrived," I mutter. It's true. My intuition was screaming at me to run away. That it was a bad idea to continue. "I stayed because I thought I had to."

"I've been there." Sara reaches out and places a hand on mine. "It's hard to know when you can say no. When you can just turn the car around. Plus if you're hurting for cash, it gives you even more incentive to stay."

"I learned my lesson though."

"At least there's that."

I look down and Sara pulls her hand back, then speaks in a low voice.

"Hey, if you want me to cut that, I will. I don't want you to feel uncomfortable."

I meet her eyes and I can see in those blue depths that I'm not alone. It may not have been the *same* thing, but she's been through similar trauma. Pressure to perform, the feeling that you have absolutely no choice, not wanting to anger someone–specifically a man–by saying no to something. It's a terrifying situation to be in.

"No, it's ok. Those stories matter even if just one person benefits from it."

Sara smiles and takes a deep breath to continue.

"Let's end on a high note, shall we? What's been your *best* experience?"

"You know, despite that last story, I really have worked with some amazing people. I can't pick just one, but this week I worked with Vera Connor and Penny Pepper. They're such amazing women. We even met for dinner last night. It's the kind of support and friendship that I think women need in this industry."

"Oh, I love them. I worked with Vera a couple years ago and I just met Penny recently."

"Yeah, it was a lot of fun working with them. I almost forgot the cameras were even there!"

"Well, thank you so much for joining me today, Honey." Sara grins at me, speaking into her mic. "Tell everyone where they can find your content and services."

I rattle off a list of my sites, smiling into the camera.

"And that's all she wrote, folks. Thanks for joining us for another episode of Hide the Sausage. Make sure to check out my website where you can subscribe to gain access to premium stuff like behind-the-scenes content and our extra steamy episodes."

I smile and wait for Sara to indicate that we're finished. A few seconds later, she nods and I deflate.

"Thank you again." I divulged a lot more than I had expected to, but it's so nice to talk about my experiences and feel seen.

Sara stands and moves to stop the recordings and turn off the studio lights.

"You were great." She taps on the laptop a couple of times and then stands, meeting my gaze. "Hey, I'm here in New York for a bit longer, but I have a house party in a few weeks in LA. If that's something you'd be interested in coming to, you'd be able to mingle with more creators. I'm happy to add you to the list."

My eyes go wide and I sit up straight.

"Really? Oh my god, that would be amazing. Yes, thank you!" I want to jump up and hug her, but I'm not sure how she feels about getting embraced by strangers.

"Great! I might forget if I don't add you to the list today, but don't hesitate to remind me if I haven't sent you the info by Sunday."

"Thank you so much." I sound like a broken record.

"Don't mention it. It'll be fun." She winks. "You seem to have your head on straight and I can safely say you're in the minority there."

# 6

## Brody

I know damn well I'm running late when I step out of the shower, but I can't say I feel all that guilty. An image forms in my mind of Miles pacing by the front door. I took an extra half hour at the gym this morning, forcing him to stay and continue working out. I really don't want to do this stupid shopping trip.

Wrapping the towel around my waist, I crack the bathroom door and turn on the fan. Then I go through my post-shower routine and finish by running a comb through my hair before tousling it slightly with my fingers. I watch the way it falls, longer on top, shorter on the sides.

I throw on a pair of jeans and a black T-shirt that has an image of a tardis on the front left breast. On the back, in large, faded, white letters, it says 'Wibbly Wobbly Timey Wimey Stuff'. Slipping on my tennis shoes, I grab my wallet from my dresser and head out to find Miles doing exactly what I expected him to be doing.

"Bro." The annoyance in his voice is obvious, even in that one syllable. His eyes roam down my body and back up. "Really?"

"The whole point is to get new clothes today," I say with a shrug, leading the way out the door and leaving Miles to grab his keys. If he's making me do this, I'm making him drive. "I figure she should know what she's working with."

Miles groans when he sees the back of my shirt, even though he's seen it a million times. He locks the door behind us and meets me at his jeep. I check my phone to see just how late we are, knowing that with LA traffic, it's going to take longer than a map tells us.

Miles pulls into a parking lot half a block away from Moira's shop in Glendale. All the street parking was full, which we figured out after spending a solid ten minutes trying to find something, so we end up in a paid lot.

The shop, simply called *Moira's*, has a sleek storefront. The outside is all matte, black, metal finishes with a gigantic window next to the front door. The only thing visible through the window is a waiting room with a plush, leather couch, two dark blue, velvet armchairs, and a reception desk. Behind the desk, Moira's name is set in a beautiful, gold script. Lights behind the sign illuminate it, making it stand out from the dark wood behind.

The bell above the door dings when Miles and I walk in, catching the attention of the man sitting at the desk. He glances up, the overhead light glinting off of his shaved head and thick-rimmed, black glasses. He studies me with something akin to disgust. Actually, that's exactly what it is. The look he gives Miles is only slightly better.

"We have an appointment with Moira," Miles says, confidently sidling up to the desk and slipping his hands into the pockets of his coral shorts.

"For…" The man looks down, possibly checking a calendar. "Brody Torrence?" He looks back up at Miles and then at me.

"That's the guy," says Miles, waving his hand toward me.

Without acknowledging the answer, the man lifts the receiver of a phone to his ear.

"Miss Hall, your nine o'clock is here." He pauses, listening. "Yes, ma'am." He hangs up and stands. "Follow me, gentlemen."

Miles shoots me a look with his eyebrows raised to silently say 'Get a load of this guy'. I press my lips together, fighting a grin, and follow Miles around the desk and through a dark blue, velvet curtain that matches the armchairs out front.

On the other side of the curtain is a room with a similar vibe. Centered against one wall is another leather couch with a gold side table at either end. The tables are topped with a black disc that looks like it might be marble. Off to one side is a raised, circular platform with a three-sided mirror. To the other side are three curtains and directly to my right is a door of dark wood marked 'Private'.

"My name is Luca," says the receptionist. "Can I get you anything to drink? We have several rare whiskeys, wines, or-"

"Just water, please," I interrupt. I don't want to be rude, but I definitely can't drink with my nerves this way.

"Two," says Miles.

Luca nods and disappears through the private door while Miles sits on the couch and spreads one arm out along the back.

"This is way too fancy," I mutter, taking another visual scan of the room.

"You can afford it," Miles assures me. I know he's right. He knows he's right.

"That's not the point. This isn't me."

"It could be," he offers. "Man, I know how much you hate this whole attention thing, but I promise you that your dates will thank you for looking like you give a shit. They'll thank *me*." He holds a hand over his chest for emphasis.

Luca reappears and hands each of us a glass bottle of water.

"Moira will be with you shortly. Make yourselves at home."

As he walks away, I call out.

"My sister may join us. Her name is Isla. She can come back whenever she gets here."

Luca doesn't turn, but I see him nod. I suppose that'll do.

"You invited Isla?" asks Miles with genuine shock.

"I didn't mean to," I grumble, taking a seat next to him and while I open my water.

"So, why did you?"

"Should I tell her not to come?"

"Oh no. We need her opinion. I'm just surprised." Miles shrugs, completely at ease in this space. Jealousy forms a knot in my throat.

A few minutes later, the private door opens again and I glimpse a short hallway behind a petite woman with short, curly black hair. She grins when her brown eyes land on Miles, her dark red lips standing out starkly against her pale skin.

"I cannot *believe* you got him here," she laughs, approaching us.

Miles and I both stand. I hold out my hand, opening my mouth to introduce myself, but Moira—I assume it's Moira—pulls me into a hug stronger than I would expect for someone her size. I grunt as the air is pushed from my lungs, my hand stuck awkwardly between us.

"Down, girl," Miles laughs.

"Sorry." She backs away and I smile timidly. "I'm Moira. Obviously," she adds. "Miles has told me a lot about you."

I turn to raise an eyebrow, but Miles shrugs and focuses his gaze on the woman in front of me.

"Where's mine?" He holds his arms out, but Moira walks past him to a table beside the mirror.

"You haven't joined us for Sunday brunch in a month. No hugs for brunch dodgers." She glares at Miles, but a smile plays on her lips.

"I've been busy." Miles falls back onto the couch.

"Excuses, excuses." Moira turns her eyes on me. "So, what are we doing for you today, Mr. Torrence?"

"Call me Brody." I look to Miles for help. "Er, I don't- I'm not sure."

"I'm forcing him to start dating," Miles says. "So casual outings all the way up to, like, eight-course meals."

The gleam in Moira's eyes is the most enthusiastic look I've ever seen. On anyone. Especially when looking at me.

"Free reign?" she asks, speaking mostly to Miles, though she keeps her gaze trained on me.

"I'd say floor it, but maybe just eighty percent," he laughs.

"If I pull back twenty percent, will you let me style you for the next awards show?"

I always forget about the awards in the adult industry. Miles has gone to events for the last two years, but I never thought about people hiring stylists for it.

"Deal."

The bell in the front of the store dings and Moira frowns.

"I don't have anyone else scheduled until this afternoon."

"That might be my sister," I say. "Isla."

Moira's expression instantly returns to one of delight.

"Oh yay! Another woman's opinion. She'll still have better taste than that bozo." She hooks her thumb at Miles who looks hurt.

"Bozo?" he repeats just as Luca leads a woman through the curtain.

She's got the same brown hair, tan skin, and green eyes as me. Anyone would take one look at us and know we're related by those features alone, but that's where the similarities end. Where I'm a giant in any room, she's barely five foot two and–without being offensive–she's never been skinny. She does hit the gym, though, and it looks like she just came from a workout, standing there in her athletic shorts and tank top, hair in a messy bun.

"I've got it from here, Luca," says Moira. He disappears and she smiles at my sister. "I'm Moira and you must be Isla." She grins.

"Sadly, yes. I'm related to string bean over there." Isla nods at me.

"Can I get you anything? Wine, champagne?"

"Oh, champagne!" Isla's eyes light up with excitement as Moira disappears to get her drink.

"Glad you could make it, kiddo," says Miles. Isla sits beside him on the couch and crosses one leg over the other.

"Have I missed anything?" she asks, looking between us.

"I just negotiated for Moira to take it a little easy on your brother," says Miles. "It was practically a hostage exchange." I roll my eyes.

Moira reappears with a glass of champagne as well as a bottle in a bucket of ice.

"Oh, I like her," Isla laughs, thanking Moira for the glass before taking a sip.

"So, Brody," says Moira, turning back to me, "I'm going to take some measurements first and then I'll bring out some items that I think will look good for your skin tone and size. Some pants may be too short, sleeves too. You're taller than most of my clients. But this is for looks first. I have in-house tailors who can ensure the clothes you *do* purchase fit you perfectly. Any questions?"

"Is it too late to run?" It isn't a joke, but the room fills with laughter anyway.

"Way too late," says Miles. "You'll live."

Moira sets her tablet down with the screen unlocked and beckons me onto the platform.

"Shoes off," she orders. I do as she says and step up. "Ok, just hold still and breathe," she instructs. "This is going to get a little personal."

Miles snorts behind me and I glare at him in the mirror. I know what this is going to entail and while I don't enjoy the awkwardness, I don't shy away from Moira's touch. Even when she measures my inseam I remain still. After each measurement, she types the number into her tablet to keep track.

When she's done, she disappears through the private door again, telling me she'll be back with clothes to try on.

"Think she got swallowed up in the clothes?" asks Isla after about fifteen minutes.

"I'm sure there's a lot to go through," says Miles. He stands to bring me my bottle of water. "You good?"

He places a hand on my upper arm, looking up at me from the floor while I remain on the platform.

"Just want to get this over with," I say with a tight grin.

Miles nods and rejoins Isla on the couch.

Moira finally reappears, propping open the door and rolling a rack of clothes out to us. My jaw drops when she turns the rack so I can see just how many items she pulled.

"I know," she says, seeing my face. "I know, but you obviously won't like all of these. You might not even like half. I just need a baseline to start."

"So there's more after this?"

Moira winces.

"Let's get this party started!" Isla exclaims, raising her glass. "What's first?"

---

"I'm never taking your advice again." I leave Moira's shop around noon with Miles and Isla in tow.

Most of the items Moira made me try on were simply so she could see the cut or color on me. In between each item or set of items, Moira would show me images of the real clothing she was picturing. Her shoppers would go out and get what was needed over the weekend, though some would have to be ordered and that would take time. We settled on a lot of items. In fact, I'm no longer sure how many I even agreed to. But I'm due back on Monday to try some of them on for final touches. Moira insisted that she would have several outfits for me by then, wanting to get me ready for the dating scene as soon as possible.

"Because it was expensive or because it was stressful?" asks Isla. She pats my back gently a few times.

"Yes."

Miles snorts.

"I'm telling you, you needed it." He walks ahead of my sister and me.

"Speaking of," says Isla, grabbing my arm to bring me to a stop and turning my body toward her. Miles pauses and spins around. "Dating?"

"I signed him up for a site," Miles offers, rocking back and forth on his feet. He looks like a kid proudly telling his parents about a perfect report card.

"There's a spot in heaven for you," says Isla.

"Not likely," he mutters. Isla rolls her eyes. She knows about his job, but she has never judged.

"Whatever it takes to get you out of the house and out of those stupid Doctor Who shirts." She lightly backhands the logo on my chest.

"Yesterday, it was Star Wars," says Miles.

"I like what I like," I shoot back, glaring at my friend.

"Like what you want, but can you maybe wear something that isn't faded and falling apart?" Isla points at a hole on my shoulder just big enough for the nail of her pinky to fit through.

"That's *one* hole," I correct her. "In *one* shirt."

"Uh, Brody?" Miles cocks his head, his eyes on my side.

I drag my hand over my face. They might be right. I could use a new wardrobe, but I'll never fully admit that.

"I can buy new shirts."

"You just did," says Isla with a grin, turning to continue walking. "Let's do lunch. Do you guys have time?"

"Anything for my favorite little sister," says Miles, wrapping an arm around Isla's shoulders and pulling her roughly to his side.

"Let go," she grunts, pulling out of his grip.

I smile at their backs. Despite the attacks on my sense of style–or lack thereof–I'm glad to have people like them in my life. I just wish they'd let me be the hermit I want to be sometimes.

"How about Mendo?" asks Miles.

"That's a little out of the way, isn't it?" Isla turns to me. "Brody, don't you have to get back?"

"It's fine. Mel won't miss me." And neither will the system I'm trying to debug.

Isla agrees to follow us to the restaurant.

"So have you matched with anyone yet? Or talked to anyone or however this app works?" asks Isla.

"I've gotten some messages." I rub the back of my neck, looking down at the sidewalk. "And I've been doing my homework," I shoot at Miles.

"No one interesting?" He raises his eyebrows.

"I didn't say that."

That stops them in their tracks. Eyes still downcast, I nearly run into Miles before I realize they've halted.

"Wait, really?" asks Isla. She and Miles are staring at me again and I force myself to meet her eyes. There's way too much joy there.

"It was just a conversation," I say. If this is their reaction to a simple connection, I'm afraid of what they'll say when I mention that we already have a date planned.

"That's a step!"

"Any signs she's crazy?" asks Miles, arms crossed over his chest, looking defensive. I can't figure out why that would be. This is a step in the right direction, isn't it? It's his goal.

"Not yet." Do I say it? "We're meeting for dinner on Monday." I said it.

I'd forgotten Isla could squeal that loud. Ears ringing, I stare at her in shock while she bounces on the balls of her feet in front of me. Her hands are balled into fists in front of her mouth.

"A date?" she asks with a muffled squeak.

"Just dinner at a brewery."

"That place over on Wilshire?" asks Miles.

I chose what we both consider to be our place–his and mine. We go there for each other's birthdays or other celebratory dinners, like when we first moved in together.

"Yeah, I thought it was nice but not *too* nice. No pressure, you know?" I ask, still trying to figure out his expression.

"I think that's great," says Isla. She's still bouncing. I can almost feel the vibrations from here.

"Can we please go to lunch now?" I just want to get home and get back to work.

# 7

## Sophie

Sophie

Lost in my book—a paranormal romance about a demon and a very stressed-out woman in need of a good fuck—I don't realize that we're descending until the plane jostles, hitting the ground in Burbank. I've been reading for six straight hours with no pause. Not even to drink water, I realize with guilt.

Even with a layover in Chicago, it's still early in the day. As the plane slows and we taxi to the gate, I lean forward to pack up my book and my headphones. I turn off airplane mode and send a quick text to Natalie that we've landed so she can hop in the car. Flying into Burbank instead of LAX means that Natalie and I live a whole lot closer, making it significantly faster to get checked in and through security as well as home at the end of a long trip. Driving all the way to and from LAX would take half the day.

Without my headphones, I'm forced to listen to the sounds of the plane. A kid a few rows behind me is asking their mother why they have to remain seated. Mom says it's because it's not safe to get up until we stop, just like in a car. A man a little further away is already on his phone and it sounds like a business call. I roll my eyes, but at least he doesn't have it on speaker for everyone to hear.

Most of the window shades are up, allowing in more light than when we were in the air. I reach up to turn off the overhead light and open up the air vent. I can see the heat rising from the asphalt outside. I didn't check the forecast, but it's a safe bet that it'll be ninety degrees or more today. August in LA or August in New York City. They're both sweltering, but one's a dry heat. That means it's not as bad, right?

I've never understood that. *Yes, it's ninety-five degrees, but it's a* dry *heat.* Ok, so the humidity isn't sitting on you and suffocating you. But it's still hot as balls. Why did I move here again? Oh right, I had no choice.

I'm not the first to reach the baggage claim carousel for our flight. The metal slabs are still, taunting me with their serious lack of luggage. I try to block out the sounds around me as the crowd grows. I'm too tired to listen to the screaming children or the one teenager who's complaining to their parents about something inane.

The red light over the carousel finally spins, telling us that the metal slabs will begin to move and our bags will soon arrive.

When I finally have my two very large suitcases in hand, wishing I wasn't traveling alone, I make my way out to the arrivals area where cars are driving in circles, waiting for friends and family. Stepping over to one side so I don't trip anyone, I pull my phone from my pocket once more and call Natalie.

"Hey, where are you?" I ask when she answers.

"Two minutes. You out?"

"Yeah, I'm wearing gray sweats and a hot pink tank top, about halfway down. I'll wave when I see you."

"Cool, stay on the line just in case."

"You got it, dude."

We're silent for a moment while I scan the approaching cars with my eyes. No, that red sedan isn't her. Neither is that one. Or that one, although the pink dice make me do a double-take.

"I see you." I wave at the red sedan with the fuzzy pink handcuffs hanging from the rearview mirror.

"Gotcha! I think I see a spot just a little further down."

I follow Natalie's car until she pulls up to the curb a few spots away. She opens the trunk with the push of a button and I quickly shove the suitcases in. I slam the trunk and set my carry-on bags in the back seat before sliding into the passenger seat.

Without speaking, Natalie pulls away, glancing back to check for oncoming cars. I fasten my seatbelt and wait for her to get us out of traffic, knowing that she'll snap at me if I speak too soon.

"So," she says when she finally feels at ease, "how was the trip?"

"It was amazing!" I exclaim, startling her with my enthusiasm. "Vera Connor and Penny Pepper want you to text them if you're in New York any time soon. They'd love to work with you."

"Wait, really?" Natalie's eyes go wide, but she keeps them on the road. "Those girls are *goals*. I'd love to get my hands on them." In the space behind her glasses, I can see an impish gleam in her warm, brown eyes.

"Yeah, you want their numbers?"

"Are you seriously asking me that?"

"On it, boss." I salute and quickly send her their contact information before sending hers to them and letting them know she's interested in working together. Natalie's phone makes a noise I haven't heard before and I frown. "Did-did you change your ringer to someone moaning?"

Natalie's pale, freckled face splits into the widest grin and she giggles.

"Yeah!" She full-on laughs as we pull to a stop at a red light.

"Who's voice is that?" I barely get the question out, caught between shock and amusement.

"Mine, obviously. Sophie Larson, are you telling me you don't recognize it?" She feigns shock and disappointment as the light changes to green.

I burst into laughter alongside her, rocking back in the seat as we surge forward.

"Why? Why not make it, I don't know, someone you've worked with? Or your dream girl?"

"I *am* my dream girl."

"Fair enough." I wipe a tear from my eye before it can spill down my cheek and take a deep breath. "If I ever lose an ounce of confidence, remind me to come straight to you."

"I won't let it get that far."

Natalie reaches over and pats my thigh before turning onto our street. Less than a minute later, we pull into the driveway between two townhouses. The path leads to two more nearly identical structures behind the first row. She pulls her car to the side, next to mine. There's just enough space between our townhouse and the one in front of it to park two cars with room to get in and out. Rather than using it for its intended purpose, we converted the garage on the first floor into a second studio space.

Natalie helps me with my bags and we haul them to the front door. I find myself once more annoyed that we rent a place with stairs as soon as you walk in. There's another small bedroom and bathroom on the first floor that you can access from the garage, but it's too small to be an adult's room. I lead the way up the stairs, hauling the first large suitcase while Natalie carries up my smaller bags.

"So, tell me about this podcast." She says, breathing heavily.

"*Hide the Sausage?*"

Natalie snorts.

"Yeah, that."

"It was fun. Did you know Sara Sitwell has her guests try three different sausages as part of the episode?" I reach the top and roll my suitcase out of the way, pausing to catch my breath.

"Really?" Natalie laughs as she reaches the final stair and sets the bags down to one side. "What did you try?" She backs away to allow me to return to the car for the second large suitcase.

"I can't remember all three," I say as I breeze past her, still out of breath, "but one was a bratwurst with pockets of Swiss cheese." My mouth is watering just thinking about it, but when I glance back up, I see Natalie scrunching her nose.

"Ew, no thanks."

"You'll have to warn her about your aversion to Swiss if you're ever on her podcast," I chuckle, standing a third of the way down the stairs.

"*If?* You think she wouldn't invite me?"

I shrug and retrieve the last piece of luggage from the car.

"Home sweet home," I mumble, rolling my suitcase across the floor when I reach the top.

I shiver as a thin layer of sweat dries on my forehead and back. Natalie and I like to keep the apartment fairly cold, even when we aren't filming.

My unpacking is methodical and I take an hour to separate clean from dirty clothing, replace my toiletries, and put my toys and accessories back in their storage spots. When I finally open my bedroom door again, Natalie is tossing a few of my things into the washer.

"I was just about to do that." I swipe the maid costume she's reaching for from the pile of clothes I left and toss it in a mesh bag.

"I'm allowed to help." Natalie crosses her arms over her chest and leans away.

"You are," I acknowledge, nudging her to the side with my hip so she no longer has access to the clothing. I add the remainder of the costumes and lingerie. Everyday clothing will get its own cycle.

"You wash mine sometimes," Natalie points out. "You should let people do things for you." She turns and heads toward the kitchen as I reach for the detergent.

"You picked me up from the airport." I fill the machine and start it up, then find Natalie around the corner making a peanut butter sandwich.

"I have to run to the grocery store later," I say, opening the fridge even though I'm probably just going to imitate her late lunch. "Care to join?"

"Nope, I went yesterday."

Natalie leaves the peanut butter, bread, and a plastic food storage container of broccoli florets on the counter and sits at the table a few feet away. It's an old, hand-me-down dining room table from her parents. The current tablecloth is floral with colorful plants and bright green leaves covering it. It's one of those waterproof ones and just looking at the material, I can hear the sound it makes when someone scratches it with their nails. At the end of the table are chairs that match and there's a backless bench on each side.

"You couldn't have waited a day?" I ask, shutting the fridge.

"Nope," she says through a mouthful of sandwich, shaking her head. "We were out of peanut butter."

"Rude."

My phone chimes from somewhere in my room. I ignore it for a few minutes while I prepare my lunch, but after setting my plate on the table, I return to where the phone sits on the bed.

It's a message on *KinkRink*.

> **technerd94 (M, 30)**
>
> Hey, I know you said you were flying home today. Have a safe trip!

> **sweetashoney (F, 28)**
>
> Thanks! I actually just walked in the door a few minutes ago.

> **technerd94 (M, 30)**
>
> Oh, awesome! Love it when travel doesn't take all day. Got any plans this evening?

> **sweetashoney (F, 28)**
>
> Errands, laundry. Adult things.

Literally.

> **technerd94 (M, 30)**
>
> Ah, yes. The monotonous adult things. I'll leave you to it, just didn't want to be that person who doesn't text for days. I'm Brody, by the way.

> **sweetashoney (F, 28)**
>
> Sophie. Looking forward to meeting on Monday.

It's not the chattiest conversation and it doesn't really show me who he is, but it was sweet of him to reach out, given how little we've spoken so far. I wonder when I should send him a photo of my face. My body is visible on my profile. There aren't any photos of me that are fully nude. I don't show my face because I don't really want to be identified that easily. I've never felt like my tattoos would be the thing that someone would recognize. I suppose if anyone is truly obsessed and memorizes every single bit of ink, they can figure out it's me, but that would be insane. I doubt Caleb ever paid that much attention to the artwork I put on my body.

I chew on my bottom lip, still staring down at my phone. I take a deep breath and let it out in a loud raspberry, my lips vibrating loudly.

> **sweetashoney (F, 28)**
>
> Hey, there's no pressure on your part, but I don't have a photo of my face on my profile. Figured you should know who we're meeting in a couple of days.

I send the text and then share a photo. It's a selfie with Vera from dinner the other night, but I cut her out. I posted the full thing on my social media profiles the same night, but unless he does an image search, he won't know that.

I wait with bated breath. I know I'm beautiful. I've been told a million times and even *I* find myself staring at my amber eyes when they catch the sunlight in photos. I get the draw. I still feel my heart pounding when I see the notification on the screen that he's typing a response.

technerd94 (M, 30)

You're gorgeous. Way out of my league. Hope my picture doesn't make you change your mind

My jaw goes slack. If I'm gorgeous, this man is... well, I suppose beautiful is at the same level, but good god. His brown hair has streaks of gold that catch in the sunlight and his green eyes, which stand out against his tan skin, are shining as he looks off to one side. His hand, attached to a heavily tattooed arm, is up near his mouth, but it doesn't hide his full lips. I'd love to know what they feel like on mine. To top it all off, there's a hint of dark stubble on his cheeks and chin. I wonder if that's his usual look or if he likes to be clean-shaven.

sweetashoney (F, 28)

I'm not sure if you're fishing for a compliment or if you're just that self-conscious, but I can assure you that I will not be changing my mind. Not for a handsome chap like you.

*Handsome chap?* What am I, a British socialite in the fucking Victorian era? That's enough time on my phone for the day. I don't wait for a response, sliding my phone into my pocket and searching out the sandwich I made.

"Who was that?" Natalie has finished her sandwich and is dipping her broccoli in a puddle of ranch on her plate.

"Just a boy," I reply in a silly, singsong voice.

"Oh, really?" Natalie plays along and I chuckle at her raised eyebrows.

"Yeah, we have a date Monday. He was just wishing me safe travels. Didn't know I was already home."

"Where's the photo?"

I pull up the app and show Natalie. Her jaw drops just like mine did and she looks from the phone to me and back before settling her eyes on me once more.

"Girl, I'm strictly for the ladies now, but that man is *foine.* Just be safe when you jump his bones." She winks and bites into a piece of broccoli.

"Good to know you're not about to cock-block me," I chuckle.

"Why would I need to when you're so good at it on your own?" She pauses and thinks for a minute. "Are you really being cock-blocked if you make porn?"

"I guess not."

"Love-blocked," Natalie muses. "Love-cock-blocked."

"As if I need reminding of how unlucky I am in love. Thanks."

"What are best friends for?"

"Best friends are supposed to be uplifting," I argue. "Like non-sexual fluffers."

"Someone's gotta bring you down to earth. Your adoring fans sure won't."

She's got a point there. With thousands of followers on social media, it's a wonder I don't have a huge ego. I'm confident in my body, but I don't think that confidence is overinflated. Perhaps it's the struggle with my weight that I've dealt with since puberty. Perhaps it's the mother who encouraged me to lose weight by saying when I did so I'd have to "beat the boys away with a stick". Whatever the reason, I try not to let my popularity go to my head.

When I don't respond, Natalie grins.

"You can't stay mad at me, boo."

"I can when you call me boo."

# 8

## Brody

"Mr. Torrence." Luca nods when I walk through the shop door on Monday morning. I swallow and smile, tight-lipped, returning the gesture while he waves toward the curtain.

"Miss Hall is waiting for you."

"Thanks," I mutter and walk quickly toward the back.

Moira stands next to a rack of clothing beside the little fitting rooms, her hands flying over the hangers. She's mumbling to herself and I'm not entirely sure she heard me walk in. When I clear my throat, she jumps, confirming my suspicion.

"Oh!" Her hand clutches at her chest as she spins to face me. "Brody, sorry. I was making sure I had everything." She waves at the clothes. "Well, everything I'm supposed to have today."

"Didn't mean to startle you," I say with a warm smile.

"Oh no, it's my fault. One track mind and all." Moira picks up a pair of tan slacks and a short-sleeve, beige, button-down shirt. "Here, put these on."

I take the items and turn toward one of the three dressing rooms, but Moira stops me and hands me a dark brown belt with a gold buckle.

"Now go." She nods and I do as I'm told.

The clothes feel foreign on my body. I'm used to denim jeans, cotton shirts—things I can throw in a washing machine without a second thought. This stuff probably all has to be dry-cleaned. I step out from behind the curtain, fighting the urge to shake my head when I see my reflection. I don't look like myself, but I have to admit that I do look good. Maybe Miles was right.

Moira contemplates the clothes, leaning to one side, her hip popped out. One arm is crossed over her stomach, the other elbow resting on it while her chin rests on her hand. It's the ultimate studying pose. She hums as she thinks.

"Please tell me what's going through your head," I groan. "Awful, right? I knew this was a bad idea."

"No, it's good!" Moira waves her arms when I try to retreat into the dressing room. "This is perfect, I was just thinking what else we can do with-" She cuts herself off. "Never mind, I think the length of those pants is perfect. How does the shirt feel?"

"It feels," I wiggle my shoulders, "good, I guess?" I like the way the soft material flows against my skin.

"Good." Moira turns to the rack and hands me another pair of pants, black this time, and a light blue button-down shirt. This one looks more fitted. "Next."

We go through a slew of clothing, including eight pairs of shoes for which Moira gives me express instructions. Wear the brown leather tennis shoes with these pants, not those. Never with that shirt. This shirt would look even better with these pants and this belt. A few pairs of pants and two shirts still need tailoring, but the rest are perfect. She has more coming in over the next couple of weeks, but we'll set an appointment to try those on.

I'm going to need a chart for all of this.

When I leave Moira's shop an hour later, it's with the knowledge that my items will be delivered this afternoon, except for those in need of alteration. Those will arrive on Wednesday. I have to hand it to Moira and Miles. The clothing does look really good and the speed with which much of it is going to be delivered is nuts, though I guess that's part of what I'm paying for.

I lean my head back against the headrest, closing my eyes. My phone vibrates in my pocket and I take a deep breath before pulling it out to check.

> We still on for tonight? My roommate is making me try on clothes, so I want to know if I have to go to that trouble.

I smirk at the screen, glad to know we're going through the same thing. Images flash in my mind of this woman's body in various outfits, trying on sun dresses and short skirts and shorts and low-cut tops. I have to stop thinking like that in public.

I respond quickly and apologize for the fact that she'll need to placate her roommate, but that we're definitely on. I just tried on a million outfits myself, so it's only fair. I pray the clothes will be delivered in time for me to wear something new tonight. Miles' and Isla's comments from the other day have me feeling self-conscious about everything I've ever worn. Ever.

When I get home, Miles is sitting on the couch, staring at the television. His head whips around as I walk through the door, but his face falls when he sees me. I grin, reading his mind.

"They're delivering the clothes in a few hours."

"Oh thank god," Miles sighs. "I thought you'd changed your mind."

"After everything I went through on Friday? Absolutely not. You and Isla would kill me."

"I can neither confirm nor deny that your sister and I have a murder pact."

I roll my eyes and join him on the couch.

"Don't you have to work?" Miles eyes me.

"I'm on call. I needed a mental health day if I was going to try on a hundred and one outfits I didn't even want in the first place."

"Decided what you're wearing tonight? On your *date*?" Miles draws out the last word with his trademark, shit-eating grin.

"You'll be here all day, right?" I ask.

"No, I thought I'd leave you alone before your first date in like three years."

"Two," I mutter.

"Brody, you'll be fine." Miles ignores my lack of confidence and pats my thigh roughly before dropping his hand between us. "Hey, I have to cancel our movie Wednesday."

"Why?" I don't hide my disappointment and Miles winces.

"I've got a shoot. I tried to get him to reschedule, but he can't."

I can't stop taking deep breaths, inhaling as much air as possible, and then exhaling slowly, through pursed lips. My mind runs through everything that could go wrong and I drag my hand through my hair again, letting it fall slightly lopsided. The first outfit I tried on in Moira's shop was Miles' favorite, paired with the brown oxfords.

*Am I already sweating?*

I lift my arms, but there's no moisture visible.

I leave the studio–Miles wanted me to see how I looked in the full-length mirror–and head out to the living room where my roommate is waiting with his arms crossed, leaning against the back of the couch. One corner of his mouth lifts in a lopsided grin as he looks me up and down.

"Last looks." I hold out my arms and turn slowly.

"This girl's not gonna know what hit her," Miles chuckles. "Have fun, man. Don't do anything I wouldn't do."

"How long's that list? Three things?"

"Four." Miles is still grinning as I walk past him to grab my wallet and keys from the kitchen counter.

"See you later."

"See you tomorrow!" he shouts as I close the door behind me.

The brewery isn't far and when I pull into the lot around the corner, I'm still fifteen minutes early. How long do I wait? Is Sophie like me? Does she arrive early everywhere she goes?

I scan the lot, but it's more than half full. I can't see every car, every driver's seat. There's no way to know for sure if she's doing exactly what I'm doing now. I hope she's not. Feeling her eyes on me as I walk in would definitely make me stumble.

Five minutes pass before I decide I can't wait any longer. I quickly slip from the car and walk at a brisk pace to reach the front door of the restaurant with its dark, industrial vibes.

The hostess grins up at me from behind the wooden podium, her eyes shining from beneath dark bangs.

"Welcome, sir. How many?"

"I actually have a reservation," I mumble, then clear my throat. "Torrence, for two at six o'clock."

The young woman looks down at a list in front of her, scanning it with her eyes and her index finger until she lands on what she's looking for.

"Would you like to be seated now or wait?"

"Now is fine. Is it possible to have a view of the front door?"

"Of course, one moment."

The hostess marks my name off of the list, grabs menus and utensils, and leads me to a table. I sit facing the entrance and she hands me the menu with a smile, saying the server will be right over.

The minutes tick by, with no server appearing, and I try to keep my breathing steady. My eyes don't stray from the door, willing Sophie to walk through, hoping I won't be stood up. I know it makes me sound superficial, but I pray she looks like her photos.

*Is catfishing a real thing?*

My heart nearly stops when I see her. Her tawny skin, covered in an array of tattoos, glows in the evening sun. Where the light hits her soft, brown curls, glints of gold are visible. Even her amber eyes are shining when she walks in. The white, floral sundress swishes around her thighs and it occurs to me that it's a good thing I didn't choose a place near the coast. The wind could easily cause a Marilyn Monroe moment.

I stand and wave her over. When Sophie's eyes land on me and she smiles, I swear I feel my entire body warm, a tingle running down my spine. Half of me wants to bolt, to run from the feeling. The other half is desperate to please her, to make her smile at me like that all the time. I haven't even heard her voice yet, but I want to make her laugh, to listen as she says my name.

Fuck, I want to make her *moan* my name.

# 9

## Sophie

My breath catches. Does he have to be even more alluring than his photo? The tattoos peeking out from his shirt are already something I'm dying to trail with my fingers. I can tell he works out too. I'm a sucker for muscles, always have been. His hair falls loosely to one side, just brushing over one eyebrow. His brilliant green eyes could easily become addicting and if I stand here long enough, I just might drown in those emerald pools.

I'm cooked.

I smile and wave with only the slightest hesitation as I make my way to the table. You'd think a porn star could act a little more calm and collected around a stupidly attractive man, but nope.

*Stay frosty.*

"Sophie?" He asks hoarsely.

"That's me, which makes you Brody."

He doesn't seem sure of what to do, so I make a move to hug him. Oh god, why did I do that? He's chiseled. I can feel it through the flowy shirt and I'm almost tempted to lower my hands a little and see if his ass feels as good as I think it will. I resist and pull back quickly with a smile.

*I'm no better than a man.*

"It's lovely to meet you." Brody's voice is a little stronger than it was a moment ago. "Have a seat." He steps forward and pulls out my chair for me.

I do my best to get my dress firmly between my thighs and the wooden chair, but there are a couple of inches of skin that will stick to the polished wood when I stand up. I seriously regret wearing a short dress. That's what I get for being a slut, Natalie would say. She'd mean it with utmost respect for my slut status, of course, considering she's in the same boat.

"I hope this is ok," says Brody, returning to his seat. "I've been here a lot with my roommate for birthdays and things, but I wasn't sure if it was nice enough for a first-"

"It's great," I cut in. *Damn it.* I have to stop doing that to people. "I mean I'm still new and still figuring out where to eat and what places are *actually* good versus what's more of a tourist attraction. My roommate has lived here for a couple years, so she helps, but we both work a lot." *Stop rambling.* "It's nice to find new places though, you know? And I commend you on making a plan. Not everyone would be so quick. It's an admirable trait."

*Admirable trait?* First, a British socialite and now I sound like a professor.

I can't think straight. His forearms are resting on the table and I don't know how I'll be able to keep my eyes off of them—one covered in ink, the other tan and veiny. I take a deep breath and hold it for a few moments like I do when trying to get rid of the hiccups.

"I've learned that over the years." Brody doesn't seem to notice my miniature stroke.

"Your many years in the dating pool?"

"Oh, no, this is my first date ever." The serious expression doesn't fool me and I giggle. "I've barely even spoken to a woman before," he continues and a smile tugs at one corner of his–*Jesus Christ*–perfect mouth.

"Even your mother?" I play along.

"Why do you think I haven't been on a date before?"

"Fair point."

"To be clear, I love my mother."

"Good to know," I respond with a solemn nod, barely containing my smile.

"It's been a while, though," Brody mumbles softly and I see the cheery expression falter. "You know how it is, bad experiences make you want to quit dating." He's trying to brush it off. I have a feeling there's something deeper, but I don't press the issue.

"We've all been there," I agree. "I haven't been out with anyone since I moved here in February."

"Is there a reason? Don't answer if you don't want to. I don't want to pry."

"Honestly," I maintain my smile, "bad relationship. It was hard to trust anyone. Still is. I've been on dating apps for about two months now, but nothing. I want to find someone who adds value to my life."

"And you haven't found anyone who does that?"

"Not enough value to offset some of the shit I've uncovered before we even met." The venom in my voice is hard to miss and I hate myself for the words the moment they fall from my lips. If he doesn't stand up and run now, that's a major green flag. Or maybe it's a red flag because he'd be delusional to think he could be the one to change things.

"I don't blame you."

"So you've met other men."

Brody lets out a deep, hearty laugh.

"Yes, I have met other men. Several, in fact."

The server approaches us then, a young woman with a messy, blonde bun piled on top of her head. She smiles warmly at Brody as she speaks.

"Good evening. I'm Alexis, would you like to hear a bit about our seasonal beers on tap or have you already decided on drinks?"

She doesn't even look in my direction, but Brody only stares at me.

"Lady's first," he says and Alexis finally turns to me.

"I haven't had a chance to look," I admit. She smirks and I decide to bring out the big guns–literally. I lean forward, allowing my cleavage to be on full display. It's one of the few things about me that makes other women jealous. I have great tits. "Do you have any good dark beers? Like a milk stout?"

"I think we do. I can ask the bartender what the best one is."

"Would you? That would be amazing, thank you." My tone isn't sickeningly sweet or threatening in any way. Brody doesn't know me well enough not to be put off by that.

Alexis turns back to my date.

"I'll take this Wild West IPA," he says, pointing to the menu.

"Perfect, I'll put that in and be right back." Alexis turns on her heel and all but runs to the bar.

"I knew there was something about you," Brody chuckles when Alexis is out of earshot.

"What's that supposed to mean?" I raise an eyebrow and cock my head to the side, my heart fluttering with worry. Does he already want to end the date?

"I have three sisters. I've seen the tactics women pull out when they're jealous, but this was different." He leans back and crosses his arms over his chest. God damn, those veiny forearms. How would they look wrapped around my body?

*Get a grip, Sophie.* I breathe a little easier.

"First, of all," I glare across the table, but am unable to hide my grin, "I hope you don't think I'm jealous. Second, different, how?"

"I didn't say *you* were the jealous one. Your confidence is stunning."

"Careful what you say next."

He doesn't back down.

"I didn't say surprising. I wasn't lying when I reacted to your photo on *KinkRink*, but you know that. You know you're gorgeous."

"Of course I do. Men say it enough. Women, too." I refuse to hide my confidence. If he sees it, I'm going to flaunt it.

"I don't doubt it." He sits up in his chair. "So what made you respond to my message on *KinkRink*? I can't possibly have asked the most interesting question."

"It *was* the most interesting question. Most people just ask where I'm from or make it sexual. I liked your profile too." I smirk. "Tattoos just do something to me. I had to give you a chance."

"Are you glad you did?"

"Jury's out. Ask me in a couple hours."

"Deal," he chuckles as Alexis returns with his beer.

She sets it down in front of him and turns to me.

"The bartender said the Spitfire is a good milk stout."

I glance down at the menu and see that the Spitfire is a sour beer and not remotely what I was asking about. I scrunch my eyebrows, teetering on whether I should be petty or accept the suggestion—a raspberry sour beer isn't the worst choice and it's probably refreshing in the summer heat.

"Sounds great," I finally respond with a smile.

Alexis smirks as she walks away.

"Intriguing," Brody says softly, his finger on the menu in the general area of the sour beer selection.

"I don't mind a sour and if it gives her a win," I shrug instead of finishing the sentence. "I've got the guy." I wink and then immediately flush.

"You've got me," he agrees, but his tone has more weight than the flirtatious vibe from before. He clears his throat and shifts the conversation. "So, you said you were traveling for work? I don't think you told me what you do."

"Marketing and production," I answer robotically. It covers a lot and isn't *technically* a lie.

"Ah, but you said you made a sale or something?"

"Closed a deal," I respond with an innocent smile. "I'm freelance, so I have to make connections and presentations myself. It's hard work, but I love it." *That's* not a lie.

"That's what matters, isn't it?" He holds his beer up in a toast only to realize I don't have my drink yet. His cheeks flush and I grin, one side of my mouth lifting as he turns to look for Alexis who just so happens to be on her way over.

"Your *Spitfire*," Alexis says, setting a very pink beer down with a flourish.

"Can't wait to try it," I reply with a grin. She doesn't seem like she's going to walk away immediately, so I lift the drink to my lips and take a sip. I hum as I set it down. "Delicious."

Alexis' face turns a satisfying shade of pink, similar to my beer before she turns on her heel. I screw up my jaw and suck on the inside of my lower lip to keep from laughing, but Brody stares in awe nonetheless.

"I think I love you." His lips part in shock, the color draining from his face, and he stammers to walk it back. "I just mean-" but I'm already laughing.

"At least wait until the second date to profess your love."

Brody cracks a timid smile.

"Yeah, that's usually my rule. Or at least until the *end* of the first date."

"A good rule to have. I personally like to wait until date number three, just to give an air of mystery."

"Oh, so you play hard to get, huh?"

You have no idea. Even though this is the *first* first date I've been on since Caleb, I stand by the rules from before. No fucking until I see a full STI test.

I've mentioned this to other men on KinkRink before, when still in the talking stage. I like to see their reactions because nine times out of ten, they throw a tantrum. Imagine. A grown man getting angry that I want to make sure it's safe to have sex. Absolutely insane. I don't even have a chance to explain what I actually do for a living, which would probably be the final nail in the coffin.

I'm not sure why I let Brody get this far without mentioning either. Something–Natalie would say it's my intuition–tells me he'll react differently. Something tells me he won't judge me for my job. I hope I'm right. I hope this won't blow up in my face.

"I can't be *too* easy," I throw back.

"Easy is boring."

"So," I take a sip of my beer, "three sisters? What was that like?"

"What, are you an only child?"

"Yup." I nod, making the movement large and dramatic. "Only child with parents I rarely talk to anymore. So if you want a big family, it's gotta come from your side." Parents who rarely talk to *me* is more accurate.

"I'm sorry to hear that." Brody's expression falls and he reaches out to brush his fingertips on the back of my hand where it rests beside my glass. Sparks explode along my skin where he makes contact.

"It's ok." Is it? No. But can I change it? Also no. "But stop distracting. Three sisters. Go."

"Well I like to think I have a better understanding of women, having been one of the middle kids, but that's probably not true."

"Uh oh, what does that mean?"

"I think I repressed a lot of memories."

I have to laugh at that. Natalie has an older brother and I've heard horror stories. I haven't had the pleasure–or misfortune–of meeting him yet since he lives back in New York, but Natalie paints a vivid picture when she takes a stroll down memory lane.

"Are you sure *you* weren't the problem?" I ask with raised eyebrows.

Before Brody can respond, Alexis returns.

"Are you ready to order?" She has dropped the customer service voice, I notice, suppressing a smirk.

"You know, we haven't had a moment to even look at the menu," Brody admits. "Sorry, we've been talking. Can you give us a few more minutes?"

"Sure thing." She turns again and dashes away.

"We should probably order before she gets pissed and spits in our food." I grimace at the thought.

"Good idea."

We peruse the menu in silence, but I already looked online to prepare. The place has some amazing food, a lot of which uses local ingredients, but the nerves of a first date will always win out. I need something easy and familiar.

"What looks good?" Brody asks.

"I'm gonna be boring. Caesar salad with chicken."

Brody eyes me skeptically, as if uncertain whether to call bullshit or accept my decision.

"You sure?" he asks. "This place is good. They've got a lot of great stuff." He's treading lightly.

"I promise, a salad actually sounds really good. I spent last week eating like crap because I couldn't cook. I feel like I'm still recovering." One reason I hate traveling for long periods for work is that it messes with my diet and as a woman who does butt stuff regularly on camera, I can't afford for that to happen.

"So you cook?"

"I love to cook, but I find I'm too busy a lot of the time or too tired from work."

"I'm not the best. My roommate's better, but I have a few recipes I can do pretty well. I actually thought about offering to cook for you tonight, but... Well, I didn't want to send the wrong signals or make you uncomfortable."

He looks back down at the menu and I smile. He's clearly nervous, so perhaps he won't even try to invite me over after dinner. I can't decide if that's disappointing or if I should be relieved. We'll go with relieved. God, how cynical am I that I automatically assume I'll have to say no to an invitation?

"I can't tell you how refreshing that is." I meet Brody's eyes when he glances back up. "Seriously, you made a plan, you thought about my comfort." I squint at him. "What's wrong with you?"

"I have a roommate?"

"You mentioned that. It's LA. I think most people do. Next."

"Do *you*?"

"Of course. *Next.*"

"I don't have much of a life."

"So?"

"Well, how often do you go out with friends?"

"Once or twice a week, but it's usually with my roommate. What about you?"

"Once or twice a *month* and it's *always* with my roommate."

"Ok, fine. *One* thing and it's not even bad. You're an introvert. That's not a hanging offense." I push, "So what's your actual flaw, here?" A shadow passes across his face. It's fleeting, barely noticeable. I'm dying to ask what it means, but I refrain. It's way too early to trauma dump.

"I think I'll let that remain a mystery."

"That bad, huh?"

"Ready?" Alexis saves Brody from answering, notepad out and pen at the ready. She's going to make us order now, whether we're ready or not.

"Er, yeah," Brody stammers. He meets my gaze and gestures to me. "After you."

I politely give my order, looking up at Alexis who seems not to hate me anymore. Her expression isn't quite as icy as before. She jots down a few words and looks at Brody.

I watch his expression as he orders his chicken dish, trying to penetrate his mind and figure out what it is he wants to hide. I'm not getting the warning bells I would expect from that kind of exchange, so maybe it's only something *he* thinks is bad. Maybe it's not even a flaw in my eyes. Maybe he has a big dick and he's worried it'll scare me.

Alexis disappears again and in the awkward silence that ensues, I go for another sip of my beer. Brody matches my movement, staring at me over the glass with those deep, green eyes.

I could get lost in those eyes.

I could get into trouble for those eyes.

My phone rattles in my purse and I have to tear myself away. It's Natalie's emergency call. I'm usually the one calling her for it, even though she ignores ninety-nine percent of them.

"Do you mind?" I ask though I have already decided to silence it. "It could be work."

"By all means." He knows. He has to know. He has sisters and how many women have used this sort of tactic on him? Depending on the answer to that question, *that* could be his flaw.

I smile when I see the screen and confirm that it's Natalie. With a quick tap, I silence the vibrations and slip the phone back into my purse. I want to see where this goes.

"Not work?" asks Brody when I turn back to face him.

"Nope, just my friend. I'll call her back later."

"Wait, you grew up here?" I ask in shock. He doesn't seem like an LA native, but I guess I don't know what LA natives are like. "I thought that was a myth! People only ever move *to* LA, they're not *from* here." Brody laughs, the corners of his eyes crinkling.

"Yeah, I grew up here," he says, a little out of breath. He downs what's left of his beer. "My roommate and I went to the same middle and high school. We moved in together a few years ago."

"I've been here 6 months and I hate it. How do you do it?"

Brody shrugs and looks around for Alexis, I assume to order another beer. I finished mine several minutes ago and have been sipping on my ice water, hoping to avoid a hangover in the morning. When he catches the server's eye, he holds up his glass to save her the trip to the table and I see her nod.

"I don't know," he says in answer to my question. "I just... I just like it here."

"You don't have seasons," I point out.

"True, but I travel when I want seasons."

"How do you get through a dry, boring Christmas with no snow?"

"There are plenty of places in the world with no snow at Christmas. Hell, the entire southern hemisphere." He's right.

"Ok, but it, like, never rains here."

"I don't want to live in the rainforest," he counters. "Or Florida."

"Well, who does? It's Florida."

"You get it."

"But... *LA*," I say again with an exaggerated shiver. Brody chuckles.

"Well, what makes Oklahoma so great?"

"Who says it is?" Sure I lived there for nearly 28 years, but I never *liked* it.

"Have you lived anywhere else?"

"No."

"Every place has its pros and cons."

"But you've always lived here," I remind him. "How do you know there's not something better out there?"

"I don't." He shrugs. "But I'm happy here. I've got my best friend living under the same roof, a good job where I get to work from home, and now I'm on a date with a beautiful woman." I feel my face flush.

"Oh, you're good." I squint at him and lean back just as Alexis silently sets down another round on the table and clears our empty glasses.

"I'm well aware." Another wink.

"*There's* the flaw." I shake a finger at him. "Arrogance. I found it."

"Damn it, you discovered my secret." Brody feigns frustration, but I see the smirk on his face. "I guess I shouldn't have ordered another round. You probably want to just end the date now."

"I can chug this if I need to," I tease, but raise the glass to my lips and only take a normal swig.

"You do that and I'll have to call you a cab." He raises his glass to his lips.

"Or take me home yourself." I catch myself before my eyes widen but stammer my next words. "I didn't mean- I just meant- Take me to my *own* home."

Brody tries not to laugh, but I catch his eyes as they darken, the pupils dilating just the tiniest bit. Barely anything, but I notice. I know that look. Shit, maybe *I* messed this up.

"Enjoy yourself, Sophie," he assures me with a warm smile. My name sounds good on his lips. "If you need help getting home, I'll make sure you get there safely."

Full.

On.

Blushing.

I can't stop the heat in my cheeks and it's not the alcohol. I trust this man not to take advantage if I end up in a mental state that wouldn't allow me to consent. I feel safe with Brody.

"I'm going to slow down anyway," I finally respond, grabbing the ice water.

"Good girl."

*Fuck.*

Brody realizes what he said. I see it on his face, but he doesn't take it back, doesn't stammer like me. He lets it sit there, hanging between us, and I try to focus on how to bring the water to my lips. I think I've forgotten how to swallow.

"You mentioned something about streaming." Brody is the one to break the silence.

*Shit.*

"Did I?"

"Yeah, I mentioned watching video game streamers when I'm bored." He looks a little embarrassed by the confession. "You said you like doing live broadcasts."

"Oh, yeah. I do some streaming. Not much," I'm quick to add.

"I'd love to watch you play sometime."

*I'll bet you would, pretty boy.*

I have to make a different suggestion or he's going to ask for a link to my Twitch, which doesn't exist.

"Or maybe we could just play in person." *This word play is going to be the death of me.*

"Sure, what's your go-to?" He seriously has no clue that my mind is filled with entirely different images of 'streaming'.

"How silly does it sound if I say I like the Lego games?" At least I can pivot with something truthful.

"Silly?" Brody repeats. "I love those. Low-stress, perfect for relaxing."

"Exactly!"

I haven't played video games in years, but Natalie's ex had a console of some kind and he made me play one of the Harry Potter Lego games with him. He wasn't great, so I'm glad he didn't stick around much longer, but at least he provided me with a good answer to this line of questioning.

"I have a couple on an older console," Brody muses. "Maybe I should get some updated ones."

"If you're going to have a pro like me playing with you, then you probably should." *Really, Sophie? A pro?*

"I'll be prepared."

"Besides video games," I say, moving on, "other hobbies?" Please say something that gets you out of the house. I need an extrovert in my life.

"I travel," he says slowly. "One of my favorite things is touring vineyards wherever I travel. I'm not an alcoholic," he adds quickly and I nod. "I just like to try local places and no matter where I go, there's always a vineyard with a view."

"Always?" I ask, fixing him with a gaze that says I'm unconvinced.

"Ok, 99% of the time."

"I find that difficult to believe." I cross my arms over my chest only to immediately realize my mistake. Brody's eyes drop to my cleavage. Damn, he was doing so well.

"Name a state or a big city." He drags his eyes back to my face.

"Missouri."

"There's one near Colombia that's on a bit of a hill, so their patio looks out over a lot of fields and trees. Stunning view on a sunny day, even in October when I was there." He smiles, lost in thought, before coming back to the conversation. "They had live music, too."

"Florida," I toss out.

"A little harder because I only went to a couple, but there's one just north of Jacksonville that I loved. You can look right out over the vineyard and you're just surrounded by nature on all sides."

"Uh." What other states are there? Brody's eyes are hypnotizing me into speechlessness and I find myself wanting to be in one of these places with him. As if we're not already on a date.

"Just two states?" He smirks.

"I believe you," I finally say, going for another swig of water.

"That was too easy," he shoots back. "What's on your mind?"

"I wish I could travel for pleasure more often," I admit. One could say I already do, but there's a distinct difference between porn and sex.

"Workaholic?" Brody asks. I nod. "My roommate is that way too. I'd say on average, the guy works 60 hours a week or more. He needs a life."

"He and I would get along well. The plus side of freelance work is I can work when I want, but the not-so-great thing is that I end up working a *lot* because I don't have a set schedule."

"Yeah, that's more or less what he's said. We were supposed to see the new Marvel movie on Wednesday, but he's working in the middle of the day with a new c-... client." It's as if Brody has to correct himself. I brush off the feeling. His roommate is not important. "Don't get me wrong, I'm not mad. I just think he needs to take more time for himself."

"My friend would say the same about me."

"Is she single? Can we set them up?" Brody chuckles.

"Single and has basically sworn off men for the foreseeable future."

"Ah."

"You know, I'm having a great time. I want to be clear about that. But," I cringe, "I have to work tomorrow and I need some rest."

Brody looks down at his watch.

"Oh shit, yeah. It's getting a little late, isn't it?" He glances around for Alexis. "You should have told me sooner, I could've asked for the tab when she brought the last round."

"I honestly wasn't thinking about it," I admit. "Like I said, I'm enjoying myself."

"Well, that's good." He catches Alexis' attention and she hurries over. "Would it be possible to get the check, please?" He smiles warmly at her.

"Absolutely." Is that a hint of a smile on her lips? "Together or separate?"

Brody silences me before I can offer to help with the bill by covering my hand with his.

"Together."

I watch Alexis walk away before I speak.

"Ten bucks says she writes her number on the bill." I grin. "Thank you for dinner, by the way."

"No trouble at all and you're on. There's no way."

I shrug and take another sip of beer. I'm not going to be able to finish it and part of me feels guilty about that, but the safety-conscious part of me knows it would be a very bad idea to drink the last two-thirds. The tingling in my fingers has decreased a little, at least.

Alexis brings the bill, folded into a little black booklet, and smiles at Brody. She doesn't spare a single glance at me.

"I'll be back in a sec." She dashes off.

I stare at Brody's hands as they reach for the check. A knowing smile spreads on my lips. He slowly opens the booklet and I watch his expression change to one of utter disbelief. He holds up the paper, discreetly in case Alexis is watching. Along the top, in cutesy handwriting, is her phone number and a heart.

"I win," I chirp with a big grin.

"I won't be underestimating you again."

*Sure, you won't, pretty boy.*

Brody pulls out his wallet and after setting a credit card down in the booklet, he pulls out a ten-dollar bill.

"I was kidding." I hold my hands up. "You don't have to pay up. You already paid for dinner." But Brody continues holding out the money.

"You won, fair and square." Then he pauses. "Well, maybe not fair. You're a woman, you have experience here. But still, a bet is a bet."

"I'm not taking your money, Brody." I cross my arms over my chest yet again and this time, when his gaze drops, I see a sharp intake of breath. His eyes meet mine again.

Brody leads the way out of the restaurant and holds the door for me when I follow.

"Are you parked in the lot over here?" He motions to his left and I nod.

We walk slowly and I steer us toward my car. This is the most awkward part of any first date—do I expect a kiss? A hug? Is he going to invite me home with him or expect me to invite him over? Just because I said I have to work tomorrow doesn't mean I'm off the hook here.

I swiftly pull out the keys and unlock the door, but as I reach the driver's side handle, I turn to face Brody. He's closer than he was just moments ago and I gasp. My eyes are at chest level and I have to crane my neck to meet his gaze. Sitting at dinner, I forgot just how tall he is. I swallow hard when our eyes lock because those emerald depths are definitely staring down at me with something akin to lust. Even in the near dark of the parking lot, I can see it.

Brody brings his fingers to my chin, tilting my head up just the slightest bit more. My lips part and he leans down, his lips just ghosting over mine. He doesn't kiss me, instead touching his forehead to mine, and this is somehow far more intimate. My eyes close and I feel his warm breath on my chin.

"Sophie," he breathes my name and it sounds like a prayer. "Can I kiss you?"

In response, I move just enough to bring our lips together. The kiss is a lot more chaste than I intend it to be and lasts just moments. What I really want to do is wrap my arms around his neck and pull him tight against me, but I hold back.

When Brody pulls away, I can feel the hesitation. His breathing is ragged as he stares down at me.

"I had a great time," I say with a grin before lifting on the balls of my feet. I give him one last quick peck on the lips and turn back to open my car door. He holds it for me while I slide in.

"Let me know when you get home safe," he says. "You're ok to drive?"

"I'm good." I force myself to sound normal as if I wasn't about to jump his bones seconds ago. "Drive safe Brody. I'll text you."

"Good night, Sophie."

The whole drive home, I can't wipe the grin from my face. Parking my car, standing from the driver's seat, rounding Natalie's car next to me to get to the front door. Smiling the entire time. Grinning like a goddamn idiot.

My smile falters when I see the front door. Stuck to the dark green wood with a small steak knife, is a piece of paper with two large, crudely written words.

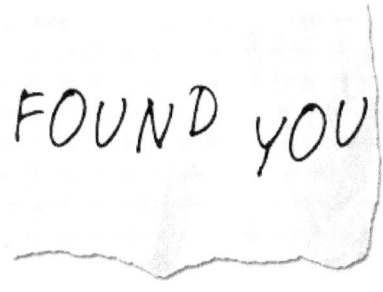

My heart stops. Or does it speed up? I don't know. I can't hear anything. My world is spinning. Nothing else exists except that door and that note.

I can't touch it. If I don't touch it, it's not real. If I don't touch it, he was never here.

I have to touch it, though. I have to take it down.

My whole body trembles and I reach up to pull on the note, ripping it the rest of the way through the blade. The paper shakes in my hand as I study the letters, trying to glean something from them, but I know who did this.

Caleb is in Los Angeles.

He knows where I live.

He's coming for me.

He wants me terrified.

# 10

## Sophie

### Sophie

The realization, the panic, the sheer terror. It all threatens to drown me. I crumple the paper and pull the knife from the wood. I nearly drop my keys in my haste to unlock the door. Once inside, I press the buttons to turn on the alarm and wait for it to chime, indicating it's activated.

My breathing is ragged and my eyes stare vacantly, even as I reach the top step. Natalie is nowhere in sight. Stomping over to the trash can, I step on the lever to lift the lid and it smacks the wall behind it. I toss the cursed items into the mostly full bag. Before letting the lid fall, I grab the paper towels from the side and cover the note, shoving the knife down between other bits of garbage.

As if I can scrub the evidence of Caleb's arrival from my life, I let the hot water run over my hands in the kitchen sink. Even when the soap is gone, I keep them there long enough for steam to obscure the window above.

"How was the date?" Natalie's voice makes me jump and spin while drying my hands. Her footsteps must have been too quiet to break through the fear. *Fucking ninja.* "Sorry," she laughs. Her smile fades when she realizes I'm not laughing with her. "What happened? Are you ok?"

She rushes forward, grabbing my hands still holding the soft tea towel. My mouth opens and closes several times, trying to form words, but none come.

"What did he do?" Her expression turns angry.

I shake my head, still attempting to speak.

"N-nothing," I choke out. "He didn't- It's-" I can't form the words.

"Soph, what happened? You have to tell me or I can't help." She reaches up to cup my cheek before pulling me into a hug, my arms trapped between our bodies.

A sob bursts forth, causing me to convulse and I squeeze my eyes shut against the tears that burn and threaten to consume me. I can't stop shaking my head. I can't stop the thoughts, the memories, from flooding my mind.

"H-he's here."

My voice, barely a whisper, is enough to get Natalie's attention. She pulls away, holding my upper arms. She doesn't ask who. The answer is in my eyes, staring back at her in the overhead kitchen lights.

I can't think, can't function. Somehow, Natalie gets me ready for bed, guiding me through the motions. I can't even be sure if it's Natalie's hand or my own that holds my toothbrush. I end up curled on my side, beneath the covers, in Natalie's bed. She plays the big spoon, her hand smoothing my hair.

"I was hoping you'd have a fun story to tell me about your date tonight," she says softly. "But that stupid fucker had to go and ruin it. I swear to god, if I ever see his fucking face, I'll-" she grunts in frustration, but her hand remains gentle. "Fucking twat waffle."

A laugh escapes through my nose and I feel Natalie tense.

"It was a note," I croak. "On the front door. He stabbed it into the wood with a knife."

"What? When? Where are they?"

"I threw them away," I whisper.

"Hang on, why didn't it trip the doorbell cam?" Natalie's hand disappears from my head. She's silent for a moment. "Fuck, there's a whole three minutes of nothing from earlier. How the fuck did that happen?"

I shake my head. Caleb's no computer whiz and there's no way he just got lucky. If there's footage missing, it means he had help. That makes him even more terrifying. How far do I have to run to escape him? Fucking Mongolia?

"Sophie, we need to do something," Natalie urges. Her voice is still gentle, still soft and low like I might break if she's too loud. "File a police report or-"

"And tell them what? Here's a crumpled note and a knife that now has my prints. Oh, and no one is visible in the footage? Yeah, that'll really get us somewhere. I don't need a grippy sock vacation, thanks."

"No one would send you on a grippy sock vacation," Natalie groans.

"There's nothing I can do." It's an admission of helplessness. I shake my head and sit up.

Natalie studies me, those hazel eyes seeing deeper into my soul than any one person should be able to. The concern is evident, but I have nothing more to say about Caleb. I can't just up and move. I can't run again. I only just got settled.

"It was a good date." I meet her gaze. A small smile plays on my lips.

"Well, that's something. But don't change the subject-"

"I'm not talking about it right now." I shake my head. "Shit, where's my phone? I told Brody I'd let him know when I got home safe."

"Really? Your cunt nugget-"

"That's a new one."

"-of an ex just stabbed a threatening message to our door and you're worried about letting this new guy know you're safe? Which, bee tee dubs, you're *not*."

I swing my legs over the edge of the bed and flip the blankets off of me in one swift motion. Natalie follows me into the kitchen to find my purse sitting on the tiny island which has become more of a catch-all than a prep space. I pull my phone from the outside pocket of my purse and unlock it to see that Brody has messaged me on *KinkRink* three times.

> technerd94 (M, 30)
>
> Hey Sophie, I had a really great time getting to know you tonight. I look forward to doing this again soon.

> technerd94 (M, 30)
>
> Hope you got home safe. You seemed good to drive, but I want to be sure.

> technerd94 (M, 30)
>
> At the risk of coming on too strong, I just want to check and see if you got home ok. Let me know.

Props to him for not reacting angrily, at least. I quickly type out an apology, using Natalie as an excuse for not responding sooner. I hope he's not upset. If Caleb's fuckery fucked this up for me, I'm gonna fuck up his fucking life.

I need new curse words.

Brody's response is immediate.

technerd94 (M, 30)

I'm just glad to know you're safe.
Have a good night.

My lips tighten into a thin line. I should share my number. I really should, but there's still a part of me that knows how easy it is to find all kinds of information with just a first name and a phone number.

I message him good night and look back up at Natalie. She's been staring the whole time, arms crossed over her chest, her expression one of expectation. Expecting a debrief of the date? Possibly. Since I shut down anything to do with Caleb.

"I'm going to bed."

"I'm asking about the date tomorrow."

I just wave a hand before disappearing into my room, utterly exhausted.

Am I going to dream about Brody? Maybe. Will I feel remotely guilty for imagining those muscles beneath my fingertips? Absolutely not.

Just as I'm about to drift off to thoughts of a certain handsome face between my thighs, my phone vibrates. Thinking it might be Brody again, I shake myself awake and reach for the device on my bedside table.

The notification is a direct message on Twitter. Frowning, I open the app. The sender is a creator I've been following for months, since discovering him through another creator we've both worked with.

@LanceKixxx:
Hey Honey! It looks like
we've been mutuals for a bit
and I just noticed you're
based in LA. I'd love to collab
with you if you're interested.
We could make some really
hot content. Hit me up!

Lance Kixxx has been around longer than I have with hundreds of videos under his belt. Of fucking course I want to work with him! It doesn't hurt that he's hot. And hung. And tall. And tattooed–literally covered, save for his face and a few spots on his legs.

> @HoneyDeeVine:
> Hey Lance! You caught me right
> before bed, but I'd love to discuss
> a collab. Let me know if there's
> something specific you have in
> mind and when you're available.

Fuck now I'll never get to sleep.

> @LanceKixxx:
> Wow, that was fast! Are you free
> tomorrow?

*Ohmygodohmygodohmygod.*
Tomorrow? Yes!

---

"I'm only allowing you coffee access if you tell me about your date last night."

Natalie is standing in front of the drip coffee maker when I walk out into the kitchen the next morning. How long has she been waiting there like that?

"He was really nice," I say weakly, but her face breaks out into a grin.

"Define nice." She grabs my arm to steer me toward the couch and away from the precious caffeine.

We fall onto the huge sectional and I set my feet on the table, prepared to sit here for the long haul.

"It was so easy to talk to him." I'm still surprised by it, actually. "He was flirty, but not too forward and-*and*, he didn't even try to come home with me." I say the last detail with a grin and look over at Natalie who sits up a little straighter.

"Wait, he *didn't* try to get in your pants?"

"Nuh-uh, and the kiss was sort of innocent." I'm not sure if that's the right word.

"What does that mean?"

"No tongue." I shrug. "Not even a hint.

"But the kiss was hot anyway?"

"Look, I can't explain it. But he was so worried about me getting home safely and not at all angry that it took me so long to respond. A lack of tongue isn't really a red flag."

"Sophie, you're a fucking porn star and you just went on a date with someone who didn't want to fuck your brains out."

"Who's to say he wasn't just being a gentleman?"

"He's a man. If he was a masc lesbian, then I'd say he was being a gentleman."

I snort.

"Nat, I've gotta have coffee and then get ready. We can break this down more later. Really get into the psychology of it all."

"Fine." She rolls her eyes and lets go of my arm so I can stand. "The *moment* you're done filming, we're talking. I want to know more about this Brody if he's going to date my daughter."

It doesn't take me long to prepare, going through the motions like anyone else would prepare for a day at the office. Except my typical day includes wearing very little clothing–possibly *no* clothing–and sex.

"I'm headed out for a wax, but I'll make sure to be quiet when I get home." The unmistakable jangling of keys echoes through the apartment just before Natalie's footsteps sound on the stairs.

Today's makeup style is going to have to be girl-next-door. I don't have the energy for vivacious vixen. Once I'm finished, I run my hand through my hair one last time, separating some of the soft curls that have clumped together. I'm wearing a tank top and pajama shorts but nothing underneath, assuming Lance and I can discuss costumes when he arrives.

I hate choosing outfits for scenes and broadcasts. It has always felt odd to me to put something on, only to take it off within minutes. Photoshoots are the only time where I feel it makes sense.

There it is again–the anxiety. My hands tremble just enough for me to notice. There's a fluttering in my chest that I now associate only with moments like these. I focus on the next steps.

The bed in the studio is made. Our rule is that used sheets are to be removed and washed, then replaced quickly so that the next person doesn't have to wait. It's a system that has worked for us so far.

I stare around the room with my hands on my hips. The tripods with their ring lights are in place, plugged into power strips. We keep the power strips off when not in use, so

I quickly switch them on. Toys, lube, costumes, and more are all readily available in the closet and the long chest of drawers opposite the bed, but there's no reason to get anything out just yet.

My phone chimes with a notification of movement out front and moments later I hear the doorbell ring. Taking a deep breath, I turn on my heel and make my way to the front door. As I descend the stairs, I can see him through the window. He's looking around, standing about a foot from the door. I nearly miss a step in shock.

Even through the dingy glass, I can tell this man is far more attractive than his pictures. Why can't cameras seem to capture what the eyes see? His hair is dark and just long enough that I can tell it's curly, though the curls aren't super tight. There's a hint of stubble on his face that's a shade lighter. His brown eyes are striking. I imagine they'd bowl over any mere human without the protection of a dusty window. I'm about to find out if that's true. I know there are plenty of tattoos covering his perfectly tan skin and that there are *no* tan lines anywhere on his body. I may or may not have done some *research* when I first discovered him.

I jump the last step, the sound catching his attention. When I open the door, Lance is grinning down at me.

"Hey, come on in!" Did I just squeal?

Lance thanks me, stepping inside. He brushes against me as he does so and heat sparks between us, both familiar and foreign. I swallow audibly. I've never had a reaction like that to a co-performer's touch.

"Sorry, it's a bit tight here." I lead the way up the stairs, knowing he's got a perfect view of my ass.

"Nothing wrong with being a bit tight," Lance chuckles, his voice deep and husky.

"Yeah, yeah," I giggle. "Good to know you're not shy."

"No reason to be shy," he replies when we reach the top of the stairs. "We both know why we're here. I want to make this as comfortable as possible."

"I appreciate that. I'm sure your other collabs do too."

"I hope so."

Even his smile is enough to make me weak in the knees. *Me.* I like to think I'm hard to impress anymore, given the life I lead, but fuck if I'm not genuinely fantasizing about this man.

"So this way is where the magic happens," I say, directing us deeper into the apartment and toward the guest room. I glance back in time to see Lance running a hand through his dark curls as he looks around at the space.

"I've seen your content. Definitely magical."

"Thanks. Yours is amazing. I seriously aspire to that level of production."

"I don't have the lighting you do," Lance points out the sliding glass doors on the opposite side of the room. "I'll bet the balcony would make for a hot video."

"Yeah, too bad I have neighbors," I mutter.

"Good point. Let's not get you kicked out of your place."

Ready to get to work, I motion to my closet and the dresser opposite the end of the bed.

"I have plenty of lingerie and costumes and toys and all that. Did you have a scenario or something in mind?"

"I've found that first-time collabs seem to be best when we just experiment." His eyes fall to mine as he speaks and my cheeks flush with the intensity of his gaze. "I'm all about bad porn acting," he adds with a smirk, "but it's easier when you already know someone."

"I agree." I turn toward the chest of drawers and open the top left one. The left side is mine, the right side is Natalie's. Unfortunately for us, I'm about three sizes bigger than her, so sharing isn't really possible. "Maybe lingerie or a sundress or-?"

I stop when I turn around and catch him staring at my ass. He drags his eyes back to mine and grins.

"Sorry." Lance doesn't sound remotely apologetic. He grabs the strap of his backpack and sets it on the floor. "Wear what you feel is comfortable. If you want to start on the bed, we can get some shots of just you first." He bends down to dig in the bag, pulling out a tripod. "I have a few things. Toys, cuffs, a skull mask." He smirks when he looks up.

"Let's pass on the mask this time."

"You got it, Honey. Can I call you that?" He stands and begins extending his tripod.

"It's my name." I shrug, my tone casual.

"Well, not your *real* name, I'm sure. I always find it weird being called Lance." He's not looking at me and I realize I haven't moved, still holding something lacey in one hand. I drop it and dig around for a specific lingerie set.

"At least mine is kind of a pet name, so I guess it's less weird."

"Yeah, a little different than your roommate, right?" he asks. "Don't you live with Sapphic Emerald?"

"Yeah, she typically goes by Emerald or Em." When my fingers finally find the lavender set, I face Lance once more.

"Makes sense."

"Or Sapphy," I add with a laugh, remembering when someone called her that on a shoot I was helping with. "Although, I don't think that one's going to stick."

"Actually, that's not bad." With the tripod set up, he seems to be waiting for me. "Does *Sapphy* ever film for you?"

"Sometimes, but she's running errands today. Tripods should be fine."

"We don't need a camerawoman. I was just curious." He runs his hand through his hair again and I wonder if he's nervous. "Lucky for you to have someone in-house though. Or lucky for her," he adds.

"A bit of both. Do you have a roommate or someone who helps?" I lean gently against the dresser. The afternoon sun is shining brightly into the room, reflecting off of his eyes, turning them gold. The effect is striking.

"Nah, my roommate, he, er-" Lance chuckles. "He's not as comfortable around all this as we are. He doesn't judge though. We've been friends more than half our lives, but I wouldn't subject him to this."

"I'm sure your friendship has survived worse than him seeing you naked."

"Oh, definitely. But I care about his comfort. I'm not sure he'd want to see me naked with a woman, much less anyone else."

"That's right," I say with sudden realization. "You recently started filming with men, didn't you? It's kind of refreshing to meet a straight guy who doesn't get hung up on that. Most men don't even want to be naked in the same room as another man, let alone touch them. A lot of amateurs would run screaming."

I stop. Lance isn't looking at me anymore and I wonder if I hit a nerve. Instead, his eyes are unfocused, aimed at the bed.

"Er, so releases and IDs first?" I ask. "I've got copies if you need one."

"Nope, I'm covered." He recovers and bends down to reach for his backpack again.

"Is it weird that I find that level of professionalism hot?" I ask, stifling a laugh.

"It gets all the women wet." He winks.

The paperwork and ID photos are quick. When we finish, Lance claps his hands and rubs them together.

"Ok, how can I help?"

I have to swallow the nerves. Usually by now, I'm fine. I'm comfortable. Something about Lance has me amped up in a wholly unfamiliar way. It doesn't feel like a warning bell, but I still can't figure out what it means.

I strip so I can change into the lingerie, speaking while doing so.

"Any limits?" I ask.

"I don't think we're going to encounter any during this scene unless you intend to stick a needle in me."

I snort.

"Definitely not."

"Kissing?" asks Lance and I nearly drop the pair of panties as I pull them on.

"This is going to sound weird," I mutter as I pull up the underwear. Taking a deep breath through my nose, I confess, "No forehead kisses."

Lance stares in amusement. He crosses his arms and leans back against the door frame.

"No forehead kisses," he repeats. "But I can stick my tongue down your throat." I nod.

"Look, I don't know why. I can do the nastiest, freakiest things, but," I point at him for emphasis, "you kiss me on the forehead, you better be prepared for the consequences."

Lance's bark of laughter startles me. His eyes are shining with mirth. Maybe even a bit of mischief. They're practically sparkling.

"Noted. The last woman I filmed with, her partner didn't allow her to kiss her co-stars. I don't mind, but it kind of takes away from a scene if you want it to be intimate."

"I totally agree." I'm glad he doesn't push on the forehead kissing thing. I don't know if I'm just weird or if it's something a lot of women would agree on, but it makes me feel things, and feeling things can be dangerous. "I would have a hard time imagining letting a partner dictate what I can and can't do on camera."

Caleb tried. When he realized I would only compromise on a few things, he got angry. I shake my head to clear the unwelcome thoughts. Lance doesn't seem to notice.

"Have you dated since you started making content?" he asks. We're just standing and conversing now as if we aren't about to fuck on camera.

"I had a long-term relationship for a while, but that ended when I moved out here about six months ago." *When I ran.* "Since then just a single date."

"It's kind of hard to find people who understand, isn't it?" Lance's gaze has turned more observant as if trying to figure out what I'm not saying.

"Very." I don't want to be rude, but I'm so *not* about to divulge all of my secrets to a stranger. I'll fuck him, but I won't tell him all about my ex.

"Oral?" he asks and I start to worry that he can read my mind.

"Good with giving and receiving. You?"

"Love both. Is there something specific you like when receiving?"

I hesitate. No one, on- or off-camera, has made me come. It doesn't particularly matter on camera as long as I'm convincing–and I always am. But Lance is waiting for my reply and I know he notices my pause. I clear my throat.

"Just do whatever is easiest," I finally say. "I'm a good actress," I add with a wink when I see that he's about to protest.

"Does it always have to be fake?" he asks, cocking his head to one side and eyeing me.

"Of course not. But if you want it to be real, we could be here all day."

That earns another sharp laugh.

"I'm not sure if you doubt my abilities or if you're just that cynical from years of neglect." *Neglect*. The word hurts, but it isn't exactly incorrect.

"Can't it be both?" I ask. "What about you? Do you want to instruct me in the scene or tell me now if there's something you like?"

Most men hate being vocal, even in porn. It's a serious oversight, but I'm sure it's a vicious cycle. Men in porn just grunt and barely speak. So the men watching think they have to be silent too.

"You do what you think is best and I'll teach you in real-time," he says with a grin, closing the door and stepping further into the room. "If you need it."

I bite down on the inside of my lips, trying not to gasp at the look in his eyes. Co-stars are excited to work with me all the time–it helps to be somewhat attracted to the person you're filming with–but the look in those brown eyes is *hungry*. He drags his gaze down and then back up, but when it meets mine once more, his expression softens and he grins.

# 11

## Miles

Shit.

Shit, shit, shit.

Why? Why, when Honey told me what a forehead kiss would do, do I want to place my lips right where she doesn't want them? It's an innocent enough gesture, but I know that my reason for doing it is less so. I thought maybe an extra hour at the gym last night would help me work off the jitters. It didn't. Not even a little bit. This is ridiculous. You won't get far in porn if you fall for every performer you work with.

Standing here with her, with Honey Dee Vine, is about as close to a dream come true as I'll ever have. The afternoon light reflects off of a few golden strands of her hair, the glow amplified by the coral color of the walls. There's warmth in this room and it's not just the color scheme. It's her. She lights up the whole fucking space. She's the sun and I'm a flower waiting to bloom in her presence.

*A flower?* Ok, sure. A flower.

"How do you want to start things?" she asks. "My tripod is the tallest I could find, so if you want to start with oral, we can get a good shot from above of you eating me out. If that's ok to start." Pink tinges her cheeks.

"Are you kidding?" I blurt. "If we didn't have to get it all on camera, I'd have thrown you on the bed already to get between those thighs." I worry I've just put my foot in my mouth until Honey laughs.

"Well, you get an A for enthusiasm."

"Can I get extra credit, Miss Dee Vine?"

"Oh, we are definitely doing a teacher scene at some point."

I clear my throat, bringing myself back to reality rather than allowing my mind to wander to thoughts of her in a tight button-down shirt, short pencil skirt, and thick-rimmed glasses with a ruler she can use to-

"I'll take some closeup stuff of you on the bed." My voice is strained, but if she notices, she doesn't say anything.

Honey hands me her phone and I slip mine into my tripod, focusing it on the bed so I can get her whole body. I begin recording with her phone while she turns away and crawls up the bed from the end. It takes every ounce of focus not to let the phone drop and instead watch her luscious backside move away.

*Keep your breathing under control, dumbass.* I can't be salivating for this woman while I film. How creepy would that be?

Honey slowly turns to sit, smiling seductively at the camera. I don't hide my growing erection. It's obvious beneath my shorts and her eyes twitch in one quick, singular downward motion before landing back on the camera lens. Her eyes are bright as she lifts a hand and curls a finger, beckoning for me to join her.

I lower the phone and move the camera up her legs, toward her belly and her breasts. She grabs one, massaging it, and bites her lip when she knows her face is in the shot.

"Come join me, baby," she breathes, making my dick jump.

I have to fight the urge to take a deep breath with my face so close to the phone's mic. Blood rushes to my growing erection while I pull back down her body and then mount the phone in her tripod, making sure that it has a view of the bed without the other one getting in the frame. Once it's in place, I turn my eyes back on Honey and see the same fire that burns in me. She slowly scoots further up the bed to allow me room as I kneel between her legs. I gently trail one hand up her shin, over her knee, up her thigh. Goosebumps erupt along her skin beneath the tattoos scattered across her flesh. I can't tell if the slight tremor is acting or if she's as excited as I am.

"Lay back, baby."

*Is that my voice?*

I've never heard it so full of longing. I slide her panties down and toss the offending garment to the side before spreading her legs a little further so I can settle myself between her thighs. I have the perfect view of her cunt, glistening with need.

"Lay back and close your eyes for me. I want you to feel every single thing I do to you. Every brush of my fingers." I use two fingers to spread her glistening folds and she moans softly. "Every flick of my tongue." She's not prepared when I lean forward and briefly slide my tongue softly against her clit. "Every vibration as I moan against you."

She said not to worry about her orgasm, but I intend to pull at least one from her pretty pussy. More if I can, but let's start with one. She smells so fucking good and I want to really taste her, not just the passing flick of the tongue from a moment ago. First, I'm going to tease.

Propping myself up on one elbow, I use my free hand to draw a line down her center with one finger. Her hips move down, trying to tell me what she wants, following the path my digit just took.

"Ah, ah," I breathe. "I want to take my time with this perfect cunt." She shudders at the last word and I grin up at her, but she's not looking down. Her eyes are closed just as I ordered. "Such a good girl, following instructions."

She feels too good not to slide a finger in, wet and waiting for me, so that's exactly what I do. As the last knuckle disappears, I hear another moan escape her throat. I wish I knew if it was real or fake, but I'm going to do my best to make sure it's the former.

"Do you want another?" I ask, my voice coming out in a growl. "Use your words, babygirl."

"Y-yes," Honey whispers. "Yes, please."

"Good girl."

As I speak, I slide a second finger into her dripping slit and curl upward. The movement makes her hips squirm and I grin, working her harder. Honey's thighs try to close around me, but I push on them with my elbows.

"Oh no, I want full access to you."

"Please."

I'm dying to taste her and her begging isn't helping my resolve.

"Please what?" Maybe if I keep talking, I won't want to use my mouth for other things.

"I need-" She gasps when I push a third finger inside, stretching her before I press my palm to her clit.

"Come on, baby, use your words."

"Oh god, I need-" She ends with a moan instead of a fully formed word.

"I know what you need." That's it. My resolve has crumbled.

Sliding my fingers from her causes her to whimper, but I use both hands to spread her thighs wider. I don't particularly care how visible her pussy is for the camera. I'm going to taste her. I'm going to drive her wild and I *will* make her come undone.

A moan rumbles in my chest as I lick her first before closing my mouth around her clit. She tastes so fucking good and my cock is dying to sink into her warmth, but not yet. Sucking and using my tongue to swirl around her is clearly doing something. I moan, sending those vibrations through her before licking her again. She writhes before me while I work, whimpering and moaning, lost for words.

"I can feel you shaking, baby," I mutter against her. Her hand slams onto my head, fingers threading themselves into my hair.

"Oh, keep going," she whines when I slip two fingers back inside.

I can feel her walls beginning to tighten. Just barely.

"You gonna come for me, baby?" I ask. I can hear the movement of her hair on the pillow as she nods, but her belly is blocking my view. "Come on my mouth. That's it. Fucking come all over my face."

I flatten my tongue against her clit before raking my teeth over her it. The sounds of pleasure rising from Honey get louder, her movements more frantic, until her body tenses. Her fingers dig into my scalp, but I don't stop my onslaught. If she's acting, she's doing a damn good job and if she's not, I'm not going to stop until she begs me to pull my mouth away. Her thighs overpower my grip and clamp around my head, holding me in place.

Every muscle tenses around my fingers. If she's making noise, it's muffled by her thighs on my ears. Even though I can't hear her, I feel her begin to convulse, taking my head and fingers with her as she tries to roll over and away from me, but I still won't stop.

Eventually, she relaxes, her thighs dropping to either side as she pants. Her hand falls from my hair. I can see her breasts heaving with the effort of bringing her breathing back under control. I remove my fingers and raise my head, my tongue wanting to stay on its new favorite meal. She's not looking at me, her eyes still closed.

"I'm gonna ask you something that I think we're both going to cut in editing."

My own breathing is nearly as heavy as hers. I crawl up her body, trailing kisses over her belly, her breasts, up her throat, until I'm eye-to-eye with her. Her eyes flutter open and her gaze is just as fiery as ever.

"Don't ask questions," she pants, "you don't want to know the answer to."

*Liar.* She knows it. I know it. I'm sure she has her reasons for answering that way, so I won't argue. For now.

The taste of her arousal is heavy in my mouth and I'm going to share it with her before I fuck her senseless. I lean down and kiss her. Honey's lips part to allow my tongue inside and she moans against me as she rolls her hips.

"Fuck me, Lance," Honey breathes against my lips.

There's no way I could last through a blowjob at this point. I yank my shorts down, pulling them off awkwardly before Honey's hands fly to the bottom of my shirt, pushing it up. I allow her to remove it and toss it aside. My eyes meet hers while I line myself up with her wet and waiting entrance. She cups my face and nods.

I slide myself gently through her folds and my god, the feeling is divine. Dee Vine, if you will. I smirk down at her.

"Is this what you want, baby? You want this big cock to rearrange your guts?"

This is the worst dirty talk ever. There are so many other things I'd rather ask her, say to her, whisper to her. The phrases and words I choose now are meant for a porn audience. They're the things I know people expect to hear.

"Fuck yes," she whines, closing her eyes and wiggling her hips as if in hopes it will make me move faster.

"Tell me," I growl, lowering my face and running my nose along her jaw. Her hand slides through my hair as I do so. "Tell me you want me to fuck you."

"Please, I want you to fuck me."

I slap my cock against her clit a few times, causing her to twitch and moan beneath me. But then I return to the movement from before, sliding up and down instead of in. I want her absolutely wild with need before I fill her.

"Tell me you want to feel," I breathe against her ear, "this thick cock sliding into your wet cunt." Honey shivers and I grin, chuckling as I lower my face further and bury it in her hair.

"I n-need," she gasps when I slap her with my cock again. "I need to f-feel your thick cock in m-m-my cunt." The last word is a high-pitched whine as I thrust myself deep inside her in one go.

Raising my head, I stare down at her, holding still to allow her to get used to my size. Her eyes are shut tight, though I don't see any indication that she's in pain. I've seen what many of her co-stars are packing and even though I'm bigger than most in every sense of the word, she handles it well. Honey takes a moment to open her eyes, but when she does, I think I might die from the sheer lust staring back at me.

"Fuck." The word comes out in a growl.

Propping myself on one arm, I use my free hand to slide up her thigh, over her belly with a squeeze, and then to her breast. I bring my forehead down to rest against hers as I pull out, almost all the way. Honey whimpers, but seconds later, I push myself back inside. My movements are slow as I roll my hips into her. My lips graze hers before I kiss her gently.

"That's it, baby," I breathe. "That's it, you're taking me so fucking well."

Curses fall from my lips as I speed up, her wet heat spurring me on as she writhes and squirms beneath me. One hand still in my hair, Honey runs the other down my side before her nails dig into my ass cheek. I imagine the crescent-shaped marks they're going to leave and I want her to mark me further.

"Pull my hair," I whisper, still nose to nose, sharing air with her. I lift up and away from her, just a few inches, to watch her face before she acts.

Her grip tightens and when I moan, higher in pitch, I see a mischievous grin playing on her full lips. Her other hand releases my ass then slides up to my chest. She wraps her fingers around my throat, a question in those beautiful brown eyes. One nod is all it takes from me before her delicate fingers squeeze the sides.

"Just like that," I choke out. "You're so good to me, Honey. Fuck, you're so good."

I speed up, thrusting harder as I feel Honey's fingers gripping me tighter. She doesn't have the strength to cut off blood flow completely, but it has the desired effect.

"You want this cum inside you?" I grunt, knowing I won't last much longer.

"Fuck yes," she moans. I drop my hand between us to play with her clit.

"I want you to come with me, baby. Come with me."

She's tightening, her walls spasming around me. Her grip falters on my throat, but it doesn't matter because I'm so close now. Panting and whimpering, I know I'm about to reach my own orgasm, but I desperately want her to get there first.

"Come all over this cock," I growl. "Be a good girl and come all over this cock before I fill you up."

Honey gasps, her eyes shut, and that's when I feel her lose control. Her hand squeezes my throat again, nails digging in, as her pussy tries to milk everything from me.

"That's a good girl." I grunt every word before my breathing stops as my release floods her. "Fuck," I hiss. "Good girl, good fucking girl." I repeat the words as I convulse with pleasure.

With my last remaining ounce of strength, I roll off of her as I come down from the high. This woman might just be the death of me.

Without looking at the phones that are still recording, I have no idea how long we've been filming. I try to catch my breath, panting and sweaty, lying beside Honey who's doing the same. Our hands are next to each other on the bed and every place our skin touches seems to bristle with electricity.

I should get up and get a final shot of the mess we've made as it leaks out of her, but I just cannot gather the strength. The way she drained me...

"Think we should stop the recording?" Honey asks with a laugh.

"Probably." Neither of us moves to stand, though. I reach up to pat her thigh with a few light slaps and then leave my hand there, rubbing circles with my thumb. "That ok for a first scene?"

All Honey does is make the ok sign with her hand, letting loose a breathy chuckle. I match the sound as I roll onto my side to face her, propping myself up with one elbow, and holding my head in my hand. There's a sheen of sweat covering her and a few wisps of hair are stuck to her temples. I didn't have the patience to take off her bra, so her breasts are still half hidden beneath the lace. Her eyes are closed as she tries to control her breathing.

"What do you usually do after filming?" I want to reach out and trace her tattoos with one finger, but I resist.

Honey hums with a faint smile playing on her luscious lips.

"Usually get fast food and veg out for a couple of hours. Especially after an exhausting scene."

"Would you let me join you?"

Her brown eyes snap open and find me. I hold her gaze and reach out, pushing my fingers over her stomach, around her waist. Then I pull myself closer to her. I'm not sure what's driving me to react this way to her, what's making me break my usual rules. I just hope I'm not crossing a line.

Honey's throat works hard as she swallows, unanswering. I can't read her expression, but she's not pushing me away. My fingers press gently into her soft flesh and I try to hold her gaze, but when she catches her bottom lip between her teeth, I fail. My eyes drop to the movement and I'm lost.

My lips descend, crashing against hers in a kiss unlike any we shared in our scene just minutes ago. She reaches up to grip my neck, the other is caught between our bodies with my torso halfway on top of her. When Honey moans into the kiss and parts her lips, I slip my tongue inside. This definitely isn't like the ones we shared previously. I can feel a sense of urgency in both of us that wasn't there before. My fingers on her waist dig in further. I don't want to spoil this, don't want to ruin whatever spell has been cast on us. I don't want to cheapen it, despite the fact that we've already fucked.

Honey pulls away just far enough to speak, her warm breath fanning my lips.

"I'm sorry, I can't."

"Fuck. No." My response is immediate. "I'm sorry, Honey. I shouldn't have-"

She shakes her head as I lift mine so that I can meet her eyes again.

"No, it's just- I mean, I don't- With co-stars, I don't-" Her lips form a tight line and she falls silent.

I sit up next to her, allowing her space. The realization of what she's trying to say is like a bucket of ice water. There's a rock in my stomach, weighing me down. I force a smile.

"Let me, er, get my stuff." I roll over to scoot off of the bed and begin searching for my shorts. I think I threw them off toward the door.

"Lance, I'm sorry." She sounds so vulnerable, embarrassed, even.

*Fuck.*

I stand, shorts in hand, holding them over my waist as if I need shielding from her gaze. She's sitting up now, cross-legged on the bed, completely at ease with her nakedness. I want to sink back onto the mattress with her. Crawl up her body, trailing kisses, tasting her, showing her just how much I want *her*, not Honey. I suppose addressing her by her legal name would be a first step, but I didn't pay attention to our release forms.

"I overstepped." *Understatement.*

I have always made it a point to make sure co-stars feel comfortable. I know how much trust it takes. I've heard the horror stories of women in the industry, but like a fool, I pushed her boundaries. I thought I saw something that clearly isn't there.

Honey bites her lip again and drops her gaze. Her hands are clasped in front of her.

"It's just- When I work with someone new," she says, not lifting her eyes, "I have to flip that switch in my brain, you know?" She looks at me again, begging me to understand. "I have to think 'this person isn't a viable romantic partner', you know? Not that that's what you were wanting or that I- I mean, I don't even *play* off-camera with the people I work with. I try to keep things professional."

I feel one corner of my mouth lifting into a supportive smile. I wish I'd known. I wish I'd met her under different circumstances–in a bar, at a library, *anywhere*. I wish I could convince her to give me a chance.

I take a deep breath and smile, hoping it reaches my eyes.

"Got it. Professional from here on out." I salute and then slip my shorts on before grabbing my shirt from where it landed on top of my backpack.

"We could still grab food," she offers as if trying to placate a child after telling him he can't play with his friends. "If you want."

Her voice is so small. Does she think I'm mad at her for turning me down? It would break my heart if that's the case.

"I want to," I say as I move to stop my phone and take it off of the tripod. Oh great, I caught all of this awkwardness on film. "But I don't want to push you. Rain check." I'm still smiling, even though my eyes are on the tripod as I shorten it.

"Rain check," Honey confirms. I see her nod out of the corner of my eye when I squat to pack up the tripod.

She turns and scoots to the far edge of the bed, bending over to open a drawer in the bedside table. She pulls out a package of wipes and, realizing what she intends to do, I turn away. I should've offered to grab her a towel or something. Moments later I hear the drawer shut and turn to watch as she stands, walking to the dresser and taking a robe from one of the hooks on the wall nearby. It's a simple black, cotton robe, but it cuts off above her knees and hugs every single curve of her body when she ties it around her waist.

"I'll walk you out."

---

I wonder how Brody's date went last night. We haven't seen each other since he left in that fancy new outfit of his. When I pull into the driveway, his car is in its usual spot–not that there's any reason it shouldn't be. The man works from home and the only time he goes anywhere without me is... Actually, except for errands or a workout, he almost never goes anywhere without me. That's why I'm forcing him to try to date.

Walking into the quiet house, I make sure to close the door without slamming it like I've been known to do in the past. I tiptoe away and look down the hall toward Brody's side of the house. His office door is closed.

I chew on my bottom lip debating on whether or not to interrupt him. He was so nervous, but the excitement was there too. It's nice to see him enthusiastic about something as simple as a date. Usually, he only gets amped up about new tasks at work, maybe a video game.

I've never understood the computer stuff, but I listen to every word he says when he talks about it all. I'm not entirely sure he's figured out why, but I came to terms long ago with the idea that he never will.

With a sigh, I turn away from Brody's half of the house and walk down the hallway to drop my backpack off in the studio before heading to the bathroom. I peel off my clothing, which still smells like Honey's apartment. A part of me wants to hold it to my nose and inhale deeply, but I resist the creepy urge.

*That's stalker shit, Miles.*

Stepping into the shower and turning on the water, I move through the motions robotically. As my hands spread the body wash over my stomach, they drift down further. Without thought of actually cleaning myself, visions of Honey appear in my mind. The way she tasted–sweeter than her name if truth be told. The way she moaned for me. The way she moved beneath me. The way it felt when her walls tightened around my cock the first time I thrust inside her.

"Fuck," I growl. I actually growl, like a goddamn animal. For her, maybe I am an animal. A caged animal in need of rescue or a predator in search of its prey, I can't say which.

I slowly stroke my cock as it hardens. My head falls back, lips parting as the water cascades down my back. I'd give anything to have Honey right here, right now, her hands all over me. I haven't gotten to feel her mouth on my cock, but I'm looking forward to that. I know it'll be better than anything my imagination can cook up, but I'm still going to try.

A knock at the bathroom door startles me, ruining the fantasy.

"Hey, man, how long you gonna be? I need to start laundry."

*Really, Brody? Really?*

"Five more minutes!"

After switching the water to cold, it takes less than that for me to finish up and step out of the shower, using the towel to try and dry my hair as much as possible before I wrap it around my waist. I grab the dirty clothes from the floor and leave the bathroom to get dressed.

"Done?" Brody's voice drifts from the living room where our washer and dryer are hidden away in a closet.

I shout a confirmation and disappear into my room. When I reenter the hallway, I can hear that the washer is already going.

"You done for the day?" I ask, running a hand through my damp hair as I round the corner. Brody is sitting on the couch, one arm spread out along the back, his other hand holding the remote as he scrolls through Netflix.

"Yeah, I started a little early this morning." He checks his phone when it buzzes on the couch next to him.

"Who's got you smiling like that?"

"The girl from last night. She was nice." He shrugs.

"Nice doesn't have you grinning like an idiot at your phone less than twenty-four hours later." I point at the device in his hand for emphasis. "Nice is 'hey, I'm also seeing someone else and it's getting serious, so I don't want to lead you on, but I don't think this will work out.'"

"Is that what 'nice' is to you?" He raises an eyebrow before returning his focus to his phone while he types out a message.

"Are you gonna tell me how last night was?" I would have thought it would be the first thing out of his mouth. Unless it was bad. Was it bad? Do I want that? No... right?

"I thought you'd never ask," he chuckles, turning to face me as I round the corner of the couch and sit on the opposite side.

I turn to face him slightly, propping one knee up on the cushion. Brody grins, his green eyes shining. I'm not sure I've seen him this happy in a while. That's what I want, isn't it?

"Well? Don't keep me waiting."

"She's amazing." Did he just sigh? "I mean, she's beautiful, man. She sent me a picture before we met, but fuck, it didn't do her justice."

I grin at him because I know exactly what that's like. A certain amateur porn star just about knocked me over when she opened the door. Her smile was so dazzling, I think I stopped breathing for a moment.

"You haven't been on a date in years," I remind him with a chuckle. "Don't fall for the first girl you meet just because she's beautiful."

Brody shakes his head.

"There was barely a second where we weren't talking," he goes on. "I'm not saying I'm in love or anything," he adds with a laugh when he sees my expression of concern. "I just didn't expect my first date in years to go... so well, I guess."

"I'm glad it did." I lean sideways, against the back of the couch. "Anything happen?" He knows what I mean, but Brody's face doesn't change, doesn't betray any sign of insecurity.

"I kissed her, but..." He trails off, but it looks more like he's lost in thought than that he doesn't know how to finish the sentence.

"And she didn't run away screaming?"

"I'm surprised too," he laughs. "Think she'll go out with me again tomorrow if I ask?"

I raise my eyebrows in surprise.

"Brody Torrence," I muse. "A man with absolutely *no* chill." He laughs again, shaking his head and looking down before his eyes meet mine again.

"Zero," he says with something like pride in his voice.

"Have you talked at all today?" I ask. "Texted her or anything?"

"I said good morning, but she told me she had a busy day with work."

"The ol' brush off, huh?" It's a tease, no hint of truth, but I regret my words instantly. A shadow of doubt flits across Brody's face. I scoot closer and pat his shoulder gently. "I was kidding. I'm sure she can't wait to see you again." His phone buzzes in his pocket. "Ask her about tomorrow. Go see a baseball game before the season's over or something. I'm sure you can find tickets."

"Is that what you'd do?"

The question surprises me. I keep forgetting Brody's not used to this. He's been on maybe five dates in his life, including high school. I doubt anything happened in college, given that he graduated a year early. I'm sure he always had his nose in his books or his eyes on the computer screen.

"I, er, I'd probably do some kind of activity. Not just watch a game, but I don't know, that wine and painting thing we did one time?"

I wave my hand toward the two nearly identical paintings hanging on the wall by the front door. For his birthday three years ago, I gathered a few of our friends and we rented out the whole studio for a class. None of the paintings turned out well, but we display ours with pride anyway.

"That's not a bad idea," Brody says with a nod. I can see the confidence coming back, at least.

"Then do that. Done."

"Oh sure, easy!" Brody rolls his eyes. "What if-"

"Brody, shut up. Just call her." I stand from the couch. It might be too early to start dinner, but I have to do something to stay busy.

"What if she expects-"

"Most women don't want to have to say no to going home with you on the first few dates," I say, answering the question I know he has in his head. "I promise she'll be relieved that you're not moving too fast."

"But when-"

"Brody," I cut him off, turning to face the couch. He is twisted around to watch me. "I will absolutely help you when the time comes, but there's no use panicking about it now, ok?"

No use asking me how to broach the subject of never having had a woman in his bed when I know damn well this is going to end up the same way.

"Look, if you *really* think you'll take that step, be prepared." I sigh when Brody just stares. "Go get tested. I have condoms if you want them." I shrug.

"Tested?"

"Bro."

"No, I just mean, is there- Do I just ask my doctor?"

Jesus, I hate the American education system. It would benefit everyone if schools just taught *actual* safe sex instead of abstinence.

"I'll send you a link to the clinic I go to. You'll be all set." I pull my phone out to type out the info. "You can usually get results within a day or two. Go tomorrow morning if you can."

I press send and Brody's phone vibrates on the couch. I almost want to celebrate this moment. He's never asked me about STI testing before. He must think this woman is worth it.

"You gonna tell me how your shoot went?" Brody asks after a beat.

He knows I filmed with someone for the first time. He also has a vague idea of just how obsessed I was with Honey before I even reached out to her. I wouldn't shut up about her, though I haven't shown him her content. I guess I want to keep her to myself.

"I'm in trouble. She's fucking perfect." I throw my head back with a groan. When I don't elaborate, Brody remains silent, staring me down when I drop my head. I may be able to read *his* mind, but it means he can do the same with me. It's annoying. "I'd ask her out if we'd met under, you know, *normal* circumstances."

"I thought all you did was fuck them and dip." He doesn't mean it as an insult. It's a simplified explanation of the process and not incorrect. "How is she perfect?"

"She's funny and charming and her touch just-" I shake my head, not sure how to continue. "It sends electricity through me. I'm talking major sparks."

"Are you writing a romance novel?" Brody laughs.

"Brod, I'm serious. I wanted to *cuddle* afterward. Cuddle. Me."

"Lance Kixxx doesn't do cuddles."

"Exactly!" I shout, throwing up my arms in frustration. "And neither does Miles Corning."

"I mean, if she's *perfect* like you said, what's the harm in asking her for a drink? Getting to know her? Maybe you'll find out you don't like her after all. Maybe she's the worst person alive."

"She's not Donald Trump."

"Touché. Seriously, though. Why not try?"

"I've told you how careful women in the industry can be," I remind him. I haven't tried to date anyone in my line of work in two years, but I've heard stories from the women I've worked with. I've seen how jaded they can become.

"Yeah, but you're not an asshole."

"Oh, thank you."

"You know what I mean. Ask her or don't. But my recommendation is that you do. Maybe you won't be so grumpy anymore."

"I'm grumpy?" I press a hand to my chest, feigning shock and indignation.

"Yeah, you're a big grump. I want my friend back. You need to get laid *off*-camera."

I suddenly realize that he's right. Not about being grumpy, of course, but about my sex life. Almost all of it recently has been for my fans, on-camera. I've been with women outside of filming, but only a few and not in months. Other than my time with Honey, on-camera orgasms just don't hit the same.

"Fuck, you're right."

"Yes, I know. Now do as you're told and ask her out."

"Let's grab a drink. I need a distraction." I do a double finger gun gesture and grin when Brody rolls his eyes.

"Miles, I-"

"Just let me get some of this footage uploaded and then we'll go. And call your sister."
I had nearly forgotten Isla's sixteen texts to me since yesterday. "She wants an update."

"An update?"

"On your date, dipshit."

---

My eye twitches while I wait for the footage to upload and I lean my head from side to side, cracking my neck.

How long has it been? Two hours?

Nope. Seventeen minutes.

"Think I can leave my phone here?" I shout through the open door, hoping Brody is still in the living room.

"Up to you, man. Don't you like sharing stuff on your pages when you're out?"

"Fuck!" I do. A non-zero number of my fans like paying for my dates, nights out, trips, and just about everything else one can think of. All I have to do is make a post about it.

After another ten minutes of muttering and glaring at the computer screen, the upload has finished. I race from the room to find Brody in another one of his new outfits. The light blue button-down is tailored perfectly to his torso and the sleeves are rolled up to reveal a third of the tattoos on his right arm. His fitted tan pants would make anyone's ass look good and I feel the eye twitch return.

"You dressed up for me."

"And you..." Brody raises an eyebrow.

"You don't like the shorts?" I throw my arms out and spin to give him a good look at the pastel, blue shorts that stop mid-thigh.

"Ready?" He ignores my little fashion show and grabs his keys on his way to the door.

The sports bar is one of our usual haunts, having left the club scene behind when we entered our late twenties and realized it wasn't fun anymore. We're lucky to nab a couple of seats at the bar, directly in front of the Dodgers game. They're losing to the Kansas City Royals in the bottom of the fourth inning, but there's still time.

Brody and I order our beers and a basket of pretzel bites with an extra side of spicy mustard.

"What did Isla have to say?" I ask, bringing the beer to my lips.

"She asked if the girl I met is crazy." He snorts.

"Well, she did go out with *you*."

"That's exactly what Isla said."

"So, *is* she crazy?" I raise my eyebrows. "Because I mean-"

"She went out with me because I'm obviously an amazing human being."

"Ah, yes. How could I forget?" I pull out my phone and hand it over. "Can you?"

Brody doesn't need any explanation. He snaps a photo of me holding my beer and staring at the camera without smiling. When he hands the phone back, I take a few minutes to create a post.

"What's the caption this time?"

"Get on your knees and beg," I reply without looking up.

"Clever."

"I don't need to be clever. I need to be hot." I look up and grin. "Which I am."

"Your fans need to get glasses."

"Probably," I snort.

Part of my online persona includes financial domination, though not the most extreme kind that some women, like Honey Dee Vine's roommate, get into. It makes me uneasy to really do what are known as wallet drains–an entire session of texting or a phone or video call where I demand more and more money. When I first started posting, several fans wanted to send me their hard-earned money, to worship me, so I went along with it. Six years later, those kinds of tributes account for a big chunk of the money I bring in.

As the bartender sets down the basket of bready goodness with two huge cups of spicy mustard, I set my phone down. I'm the first to reach for a pretzel bite, dipping it in the mustard and popping it into my mouth. I instantly regret it. I forget just how *spicy* the spicy mustard is here. I love it, but my mouth is already on fire.

"What's your schedule like this week?" asks Brody.

I have to finish chewing the enormous doughball in my mouth before I respond and Brody takes a moment to pull his phone out for photo evidence of my shame.

"We can't just forget that happened?" I choke once the pretzel is gone.

"Nope. I'm sending that to Isla later." He slips his phone back into his pocket. "Schedule?"

"Mostly filming this week, so I'll be out a lot during the day."

"You know I don't mind it when you work from home, right?" Brody asks, taking a pretzel bite and picking up only a small amount of the mustard. *Smartass.*

"You spoil me."

# 12

## Sophie

Sophie

"Holy forking shirt balls." Natalie is sitting on the couch, staring at me and trying not to gape. "He actually made you come?"

"Yep." It's all I can say. I'm still in shock myself.

"And you lied. Why didn't you tell him you came all over his stupid face?"

"He's kinda hot," I mutter.

"Why didn't you tell him you came all over his hot, stupid face?"

I shoot Natalie a stern look, but she doesn't back down.

"Because," I sigh, "his hot, stupid face was already really smug and I didn't like it. I was about to stroke his cock, I didn't need to do the same to his ego."

"Girl, if any man had been able to make me see stars-"

"I didn't say I saw stars."

"-the first time we were together, I'd still be dating men."

"No, you wouldn't," I counter.

"No, I wouldn't," she admits. "But I might've had a tougher time giving them up."

"He kissed me after," I add.

"Like... off-camera?"

"Well, no, but we'd definitely finished the scene."

Her demeanor changes entirely.

"Sophie, that's not-"

"I know," I say, cutting her off with a raised hand. "But I let him. He wouldn't have-"

"He's a man. If he had wanted to, no matter what you were doing, what signals you were sending out, he would have." Natalie's tone is full of rage. I haven't seen her like this outside of traffic in a while. "Maybe don't work with him again."

If working with Lance was a mistake, it's not the first one I've made. It likely won't be the last. I didn't even check the man's references, looking for performers he's worked with in the past who would vouch for him.

*What the fuck is wrong with me?*

"You're probably right."

"Of course, I'm right."

"If he reaches out, I'll be really mean to him."

"Tear him to shreds."

I giggle. Natalie will always encourage me to destroy a member of the male species.

"I wonder if he's the type to enjoy domination," I muse.

"He probably wants you to tie him to a breeding bench so you can whip and peg his ass, then make him clean the dildo."

"That's an image." I fake an eye twitch, but grin.

"You've seen worse."

"Fair enough," I sigh. "I promise I'll be cold and calculating."

I lean back on the couch and turn my attention back to the adult cartoon we've been binge-watching since Lance left. Natalie took her time getting home after her wax, so she missed him by half an hour. She joins me in focusing on the show once more.

"What time are our appointments tomorrow?" I mutter. One of the characters in the show is refusing a numbing shot for dental work, reminding me of how much I hate needles–when they aren't stabbing ink into my skin–which reminded me that Natalie and I have our bi-weekly STI test tomorrow.

"You're horrible with your calendar, you know that?" She sends me a sideways glance. "Mine's at ten. Yours is at ten-fifteen."

"Got it."

"Did you text you know who today?" Natalie doesn't look at me, but I notice the smirk on her lips out of the corner of my eye.

"Just something quick this morning. Told him I had a busy day."

"I thought you liked him."

"I do," I laugh. "But he doesn't know what I really do. I should probably tell him in person, but I wanted to wait, see if there are any red flags first."

"Good call." She laughs to herself. "Unless you want to send 'I make porn' flowers."

"And what kind of flowers would those be?"

"Clitoria mariana, obviously."

I turn my head and frown, but Natalie doesn't elaborate. Rolling my eyes, I pull out my phone to message Brody. Perhaps I should go ahead and give him my number.

> sweetashoney (F, 28)
>
> Hey, how's your day been?

*Really?* How boring can I get?

It only takes Brody a few minutes to respond.

> technerd94 (M, 30)
>
> Hey! Pretty easy. Are you already done with your busy day? How'd the meeting go?

> sweetashoney (F, 28)
>
> It went well. I'm just glad to be done. Is it Friday yet?

That's what normal people say, right? TGIF and all that.

> technerd94 (M, 30)
>
> Hah! Unfortunately no. I know it's a little fast, but if you're not opposed to another weeknight date, I wondered if you'd be interested in seeing me again tomorrow night?

Well, that's adorable. *Simp for me, Brody.*

Nothing like a second date in three days to let you know a guy's into you. I try not to let my mind wander as I walk down the street from my parking spot. I hate parallel parking, but it was that or park another six blocks away and that was absolutely not going to happen for this chubby chick.

Everywhere in Los Angeles always seems to be busy. It doesn't matter what time of the day, week, or year I try to go somewhere. It's busy. Everything is busy all the time, always. *Fuck LA.*

The shop front says *Paint & Pinot.* I like the alliteration. The building is separate from the others along the strip and it's mostly brick with just a few small windows, above eye level. The front door is all glass, but it's been painted from the inside with flowers. They're beautiful, not like a beginner artist might paint them. Not the way I might paint them. There's shading and flow and it's breathtaking.

"Wow." Brody's deep, rumbling voice startles me and I turn to face him as he steps up behind me.

"Give a girl a heart attack," I chuckle, my hand on my chest, and glance back at the door. "Yeah, the flowers are gorgeous."

"Not the flowers."

When I look at him again, his gaze is roaming me from top to bottom and right back up to my face. My cheeks flush. I've been studied like this many times, so many that I've lost track, but this is different. Those green eyes are fiery, melting me from the core outward. I swallow, hoping the movement isn't actually audible, and smile. Time to put those awful porn acting skills to work–this man puts me off my game and I can't have that.

"Aren't you a charmer?"

Brody lifts one corner of his mouth in a crooked grin and closes the distance between us, using one hand to catch my chin beneath his thumb and index finger. Tilting my head up to his, he leans down to gently kiss me. It's just as chaste and innocent as our first kiss, but I feel that spark again anyway.

My knees threaten to buckle in that brief moment and I reach out for him. One hand lands on his elbow, his fingers still holding my chin. The other grabs at his chest, wrinkling his spectacularly pressed shirt–that beautiful collared shirt that looks so good with the sleeves rolled up over his forearms.

When he pulls his face away, I inhale sharply and bite my lip.

"Let's go paint some really shitty art," he laughs, dropping my chin and trailing his open hand down my arm.

I realize I'm still holding him, so I drop my hands and smile once more.

"How do you know I'm not a pro?"

"Are you?" Brody asks with a grin as we turn toward the door.

"No, but it's rude to assume."

The walls of the studio are maroon and the gold ceiling is made of those tin tile things you see in old buildings. There are paintings hung all around the room, but they're not real works of art. They're examples made by the instructors. Some are Christmas-themed, others have meadows of flowers. One is a mountain landscape with a crude cabin in the foreground.

A small desk like a checkout counter sits off to the left, behind which is a wine bar with plastic glasses.

"Which one are we doing today?" I ask, looking around. We're the first ones here, I notice.

"Which one do you want to do?"

I frown at him, but he just motions to the paintings on the walls.

"I don't-"

"I rented out the studio." Is that pink tingeing his cheeks?

I'm so focused on the fact that he's blushing that it takes me a moment to realize what he said. I can barely get out a sound. My mouth opens and closes. Then opens and closes again. When it's clear I'm unable to form a coherent thought, Brody speaks.

"I wanted to-" he breaks off, muttering something I can't understand while rubbing the back of his neck and looking down.

"Brody, this is sweet." Now *I'm* blushing. Fuck.

His eyes flick to mine, searching my face for any sign of sarcasm or ridicule.

"It's ok?" he croaks.

"It's sweet." I nod and grin. "Let's have some fun."

A smile spreads across his face and he motions toward the desk so that I can lead the way.

"Good evening, Mr. Torrence," says the short redhead behind the counter. Her eyes move from my very tall companion to me and her smile remains warm.

"I'm Sophie."

"Welcome to Paint and Pinot. My name is Tilly. What can I get you to drink?"

"Yeah, you're definitely not a painter," Brody snickers, glancing over as I finish the last stroke on my painting. Hues of blue bring a lake to life, surrounded by a rainbow-colored meadow.

I nudge him with my elbow.

"You're one to talk." I nod at his painting with raised eyebrows. "Are those trees or some kind of monster?"

"Hey, I thought this was pretty good!"

"Oh, it's lovely!" I laugh. "Just a little, er-" I grimace.

Brody's eyes are sparkling while he watches me drop the brush into the cup of very dirty water.

"You'll be able to pick these up tomorrow," Tilly says. She takes the paintings and sets them on a cart next to the counter where she poured our wine. "They need time to dry."

"Thank you so much." I stand and head to the sink at the back to wash my hands before undoing my apron.

Brody imitates me and we hang our aprons on the wall.

"Thanks again, Tilly," he says with a grin. "I'll be back for the paintings tomorrow."

"Are you going to hold mine hostage until I see you again?" I ask with a raised eyebrow.

"Maybe." He shrugs and opens the door for me. "Are you up for some dinner?" The door closes behind us and we're out in the LA heat. The sun is still well above the horizon, so there won't be a break from it for a couple more hours.

"I could be convinced."

"There's a little cafe just down the street. It's nothing special, but it's good."

"Lead the way."

We walk without touching intentionally, but his fingers brush mine on occasion. Those sparks return, shooting up my arm and down to my core, with every graze.

"So, tell me-" I start, but Brody speaks at the same time.

"How was-"

We stop and I chew my bottom lip, waiting for him to speak.

"Sorry," he mutters. "What were you going to say?"

"Oh, no, it's fine."

"Well, I was going to ask how your day was."

"I had a good day," I say with a nod. "Nothing special." Just edited content and scheduled a few posts in between sexting sessions. I can't say any of that. I wonder if I should tell him. Just bite the bullet and admit it.

"Good, good."

Brody stops at the front door of the Carmine Cafe. Below the name, painted in flowing script on the window, are the words 'Italian Delights'. I glance up at him.

"Italian delights?"

"It's delightful." He shrugs and enters, holding the door behind him.

It's a quaint little place with just a handful of two- and four-person tables, but I can see, straight out the back, a fenced-in patio that looks much bigger. All but one of the indoor tables are taken and the couple I can see outside look full as well. There's an enormous display case with baked goods–breads, pastries, cakes, cookies, and so many more, all of which look perfect and identical. On the board behind the counter, I see a list of teas, coffees, soups, salads, and sandwiches.

"So much better than Panera," I mumble, more to myself.

"I wouldn't mention Panera to the owners," Brody warns, but when I glance up at him, he's smiling. "Sore subject."

"Noted." I nod. "Only Italian delights."

"You got it."

We order from the teenager behind the counter and head out the back to the patio with our sandwiches and drinks. There's a table in the far corner, right up against a wall that's covered in what I can only assume is fake ivy. It's too green to be real, especially for August in LA. Even new to the area, I know that.

Once situated, I take a bite of my caprese sandwich, immediately closing my eyes with a moan. It's quite possibly the most delicious sandwich I've ever had. Brody's deep, rumbling laughter causes my eyes to snap open.

"That good, huh?"

"Delightful."

I return my attention to my sandwich and we eat in silence for several minutes. The conversation around us is light, but I can't really hear. Normally, I'd enjoy eavesdropping, but all I can think about is the man across from me and how it's difficult for me to focus, just being this close to him. Even with a table between us.

A couple of the tables closest to us empty just as I finish my sandwich, leaving just the one near the door, a good twenty feet away.

"I'll have to come back here." I glance around the patio. "Maybe bring my roommate. She'd like it. We're both suckers for baked goods."

"Did you want to get something to take home?" He jerks his thumb toward the door, his expression genuine.

"No, no. I was just thinking. Complimenting your good taste, I guess."

"Well, I'm out with you. I have impeccable taste."

"Smooth."

"I try." Brody shrugs, but there's a stiffness to the movement.

"This has been really fun." Maybe if I confirm that it's been a good date, he'll relax. "Even if you're a worse artist than me."

"I'm a tech nerd," Brody reminds me. "Not great with a paintbrush."

"Security consultant, right?" I ask, trying to recall the exact words he used on *KinkRink*.

"Cybersecurity specialist."

"What does that entail?"

"Have you heard of ethical hacking?"

"Like in the movies?" I ask, frowning. "When they hire thieves to break into a museum to test the security?"

"Kind of like that," Brody chuckles. "But less spandex and fewer lasers."

"Well, that's boring."

"I like it." He shrugs. "It's a challenge trying to break into different systems and find the weak points."

"Remind me not to piss you off." That should scare me, shouldn't it?

"I only use my powers for good."

"Do you like your boss?" It's an inane question, but I just want to keep him talking. I want to draw this out.

"I do. She hired me right out of college and I've been working for her ever since. And the job is stable, allows me to save for the future and all that."

"The future," I repeat. Who wants a future with someone in porn? Doubt creeps into my mind.

"Yeah, you know," Brody continues without realizing I've gone cold, "I want kids, but not anytime soon," he adds in a rush. "When my partner and I are ready."

"Kids would be great." There's no enthusiasm in my tone. I used to want kids. Maybe I still do, but I can't focus on anything more than six months out right now. I'm finally finding consistency. I feel like I've only just begun.

"Are you ok?" Brody reaches up to caress my cheek and warmth spreads across my skin at his touch. "I'm not scaring you, am I? Talking about kids on the second date feels kind of heavy, now that I think about it." He blushes, but I smile at the worry on his face. "Is there anything I can do?"

*Pin me down and make me scream your name.*

*Horndog.*

I really need to stop thinking about my job so damn much.

"I'm good." *Great response, Sophie.* I cross my arms over my chest and scrunch up my nose briefly.

Brody stays focused on me. There's something going on behind those green eyes. I'm not sure what storm is brewing in his mind, but do I want to? Maybe now is the time to tell him about my job. Save him some time down the road.

I've always wondered when most people in the industry tell a new partner about their job or side hustle. I can't imagine most just blurt it out on the first date. The fifth feels too late. Maybe there's no right answer either.

The two women seated near the door stand and walk into the cafe, leaving us alone.

"I've got a confession," I mutter, looking down at my hands and clasping them in my lap. I force myself to take a deep breath before meeting Brody's eyes again. The worry in them causes my jaw to clench. "It's-it's nothing *bad*," I stutter. "Not really. It's just something I- Well, not everyone is ok with it. If that makes sense."

I sigh and lean forward, resting my elbows on the table and holding my forehead in my hands.

"Sophie, it's ok." Brody reaches out, gently brushing his fingertips along my wrist. "I think you'll find I have a pretty open mind."

I chance a glance his way. His expression is sincere as if he wants to support me while I tell him something that's definitely going to make a guy like him run for the Hollywood Hills. I stare back down at the table.

After a few seconds, I can't stand it anymore and I blurt it out.

"I make amateur porn."

# 13

## Brody

I'm married.

I have kids I didn't tell you about.

I'm a convicted felon.

Porn wasn't on the list of things I expected her to admit to. She looks like the most innocent woman I've ever seen with her cute, flowy sundresses and her hair falling in soft curls around that angelic face. I almost laugh with relief, but something stops me.

"Please say something," Sophie whispers, not looking up.

I reach for her wrist and pull it away, forcing her to lift her head.

"I'm not going to say it's no big deal," I warn her, letting go of her wrist. "But I have a... friend who does the same thing."

"You don't hate me?" Her eyes are wide with shock.

"Hate you?" I scoot my chair around the table and place my hand on her forearm. "Sophie, you're gorgeous. You're funny and clearly intelligent. You're confident in who you are. Make your living how you want."

She squints, waiting for the other shoe to drop. How could she think I would hate her? Do other men really feel so insecure that they would rather see their partner unhappy than in a career they love?

"I work with other people," Sophie says slowly. "Men, women, transmen and women, nonbinary people."

"As long as you're safe. Sophie, of all the things I thought you were going to admit, this wasn't on my radar, but it's not a deal breaker. It's not-"

I almost said it's not a big deal, negating the very words I said moments ago. It kind of is. She said she works with other people, all genders, just like Miles does. She's fucking other guys. A man like me, inexperienced to the point of ineptitude–how would I measure up?

My face falls, my stomach churns. She'd never want me.

Before I realize what's happening, Sophie leans in to kiss me, her lips soft and supple. I deepen the kiss, turning it hungry as my tongue slides into her mouth. Her hand reaches for my thigh. As it slips higher and I feel those sparks heading straight for my dick, panic mode kicks in. I pull back.

"I have to go," I blurt, standing quickly.

"What?" Her eyes are round and I can see the hurt there, but I can't breathe, can't think. She's looking at me with those beautiful brown eyes, amber in the soft light as the sun finally begins to set.

"I just-" I turn and race toward the door, leaving Sophie sitting at the table.

I'm not going to live this one down.

Miles is in the kitchen, filling the dishwasher when I walk in the door. He does a double take, then looks at the clock on the stove. It's still not dark yet. I definitely shouldn't be home already. He leans against the counter, eyes studying my face while drying his hands on a tea towel.

"The fuck did you do, man?"

I take a deep breath to tell him, but then deflate, letting the air out in a *whoosh*. Miles frowns and crosses his arms over his chest, still holding the towel in one hand.

"Seriously, what happened?"

"Why am I like this?" I blurt.

"Gonna need context."

"The longer I go without-" I can't say it, but Miles nods. "The weirder I get when there's a possibility of that changing."

"Still not sure how you fucked up. Is it because you don't bang every girl you meet?"

"Am I broken?"

Miles is taken aback by my question. Frankly, so am I. I've had the thought before, but I've never said it out loud.

"Fuck that." Miles frowns and circles the counter before his fist makes contact with my shoulder.

"The fuck was that for?" I shout, rubbing the spot of impact.

"Not having sex with someone doesn't mean you're broken, dumbass."

"Not with *anyone*, though?" My mouth is dry.

"You're not broken. Now what the fuck did you do?"

"It just isn't going to work," I mutter and attempt to walk past him to my bedroom. He reaches out a hand to grip my arm, stopping me.

"I thought you liked her."

I swallow, then slowly turn my head.

"I did," I say, then quickly add, "I do. I just can't."

"If you screwed this up-"

"I'm sure I did," I grumble, pulling out of his grasp, but turning my whole body toward him.

"Can you fix it?"

"Probably not."

Miles sighs and runs a hand through his hair, messing up the curls even more than they already were.

"Anything you want to talk about?"

This is why he's my best friend. Sure, he blamed me first and he's right. But he's more worried about how I'll handle my fuck-up, helping me get on with things. He cares about me.

"No, I think I'm just going to..." I trail off. "I'll be ok."

*I won't be.*

"Just give me a shout if you change your mind." He calls as I leave him, "And remember your homework! If you're not seeing her again, I want you sending three messages a day!"

"Brody."

I barely register Mel's voice.

"Brody!" she tries again, quite a bit louder.

It's enough to bring me back to reality. I shake my head.

"Sorry," I mutter. "Yes, customer C-022749. I haven't heard from him since last week."

"And this new file I sent you?" Her voice is shaky and I can't seem to figure out why.

"I'm still working through it," I admit. "There's a lot of information."

Mel nods. Though I can't really tell through the video call, I know those hazel eyes are studying me. Even the little beauty mark below the left corner of her mouth seems to be judging me.

"I know it's a lot, but you're the only one I feel I can trust with a project of this size."

"Do I have a deadline?" I ask, leaning back in my chair. I'm dying to ask for details, but it's not my place.

"As soon as possible."

"The fewer clients I have to deal with, the sooner I can finish it."

"I'm not taking away any of your clients," Mel says with finality.

I shrug.

"Worth a shot."

"That's all for now. I don't think I'll have anything else before our lunch next week."

"Talk to you then."

I end the call and close the video conferencing window. Every program used by Harp Solutions is custom-built, mostly by Mel and me. When she recruited me out of college, I had been about to accept a job in software engineering for a cryptocurrency company. Her dream sounded far more interesting and I'd get to work from home once we'd established things.

Everything from the communication with clients down to the video calls within the company—all of it is encrypted, pathways hidden so that even if one layer of defense falls, we'll be safe. Our clients will be safe. All of our payments are routed through a dozen different banks or more. My own salary doesn't even go to an American bank. It was in my contract. When I signed it, I felt like I was joining some kind of spy ring. I didn't realize I'd be helping knock-off Bill Gates catch his wife cheating.

I scroll through my emails, flagging things for my to-do list—running reports, tracking a few bank transfers, checking internet searches. It's mindless work, but it takes most of the morning just to get through the emails that came in after I left for my date last night.

*Sophie.*

I really fucked that one up. It was going so well until she told me and I had to go and be a spaz. Miles is the most understanding, open-minded person I've ever met in my life and it's mostly thanks to his job. I find it hard to believe Sophie isn't the same. Honestly, if anyone is going to be up for the challenge that is my lack of sexual history, it will probably be her.

*Would have been,* I have to correct myself. *Could have been* if I wasn't such a moron. With a groan, I stand from my chair and stretch, twisting my neck from side to side. Maybe I need to move on. I haven't checked the new messages that have come in on *KinkRink.*

Twenty minutes later, sitting at the kitchen island with a salad in front of me, untouched, I scroll through the messages. I've gotten more than I would have expected, given that my profile has nothing more than a fully clothed photo that doesn't even include my head and a very brief 'About Me'.

> **hotyoungthing22 (F, 45)**
>
> I'd love to feel your hands around my throat while you-

Pass.

> **hotyoungthing22 (F, 45)**
>
> I'd love to feel your hands around my throat while you-

Nope.

I scroll through message after message from women and a few men being overly aggressive. After another half-dozen, I swipe up on the screen, ready to close the app. But something gives me pause. I should reach out to Sophie one more time. Attempt to apologize, beg forgiveness.

"Whatcha got for lunch?"

Miles slaps my back as he walks up behind me before rounding the island to go to the fridge.

"Salad," I mutter, still staring at my phone.

"Oh, did you use the last of the ranch?" He opens the fridge to scan the shelves.

"Still in the door," I say quickly and watch his head whip around to find the bottle.

"Sweet!" Miles grabs more ingredients to throw together as well as the cold grilled chicken he made on Monday morning, ready for the week. "Hear anything from paint girl?"

"Paint girl?" I raise my eyebrows and then my eyes widen. "Oh shit, the paintings."

"When are you supposed to pick them up?" Miles takes a large bowl from an upper cabinet and sets it on the island to begin preparing his salad.

"Today," I groan, running a hand down my face.

"Use it as a peace offering." He's not looking at me when my gaze finds him. "See if she'll forgive you for... whatever you did."

"I ran out," I mutter.

"What?"

I'm not sure if he didn't hear me or if he doesn't believe what he heard, so I repeat myself.

"I ran out." My voice is a little louder, if still weak.

"That's what I thought you said." Miles nods with a sigh. "Have you considered therapy?" He studies me with a gaze that I know penetrates far deeper than I want it to at this moment.

"Well, that's not what I expected you to say." A breath of laughter forces its way through my nose.

"It would probably help." Miles shrugs. "But if you don't want to talk to a stranger about it, you know I'm here."

"I know, man, I know."

*Do I even try with Sophie?*

She deserves better than to have someone run out on her.

"Peace offering," Miles says again, pointing at me with the knife he's using to cut onions.

"Fine," I sigh, holding my phone up to type out a message I hope she'll read.

It takes me several seconds to get started. What do I say? *Sorry, Sophie. I flipped my lid, but I'm good now. Can we go out again? I promise I won't freak out.*

"Yeah, that'll work," I mutter sarcastically.

"What'll work?" Miles asks.

"I don't even know what to say." Before Miles can open his mouth to offer assistance, I add, "I'll figure it out."

"Will you, though?" The skepticism is evident on his face.

"I don't need any lip from you, Mr. Falls In Love With a Co-Star."

"I'm not in love," is all I hear him mutter under his breath.

Returning to my phone screen, I take a deep breath and begin to type.

technerd94 (M, 30)

Sophie, I know you may not read this and I wouldn't blame you, but I hope you'll allow me to apologize properly for last night. I panicked and I have no right to ask your forgiveness, but I'd like to make it up to you. After all, I still have that painting.

Hitting send is the most nerve-wracking thing I've done, second maybe to meeting her in the first place.

She responds almost immediately with her phone number and two words: *Call me.*

I nearly jump from the bar stool to go to my bedroom, leaving a rather surprised roommate and my uneaten salad in the kitchen. I quickly dial the number as I close the door and wait with bated breath, my heartbeat racing faster with each ring.

"Hello?"

Just hearing her voice creates goosebumps on the back of my neck.

"Sophie, I'm so sorry." The words tumble from my mouth so quickly I'm not sure she can catch them. "I just-"

"You're the first person I've been on a date with since moving here," she interrupts me. "I wondered if I should wait to say something about my job, my *career* because I know how hard it can be to accept."

"Sophie, that's not it."

"I'm talking."

My mouth snaps shut.

"You ran away." She pauses and I'm not sure if she's waiting for me to apologize again or if she's trying to think of what to say next. "My roommate told me to move on because I deserve better than someone who bolts at the first thing that doesn't fit into a perfect, picket-fence life. You're going to have to have a pretty solid excuse for me."

I take a deep breath, letting it out away from the receiver. What do I even say to that?

"Did I do something wrong?" The hurt in her voice is like a dagger to the heart.

"God, no." My voice is too loud. "I swear, you're... you're perfect."

"Is it my job?"

"No." My throat hurts, my mouth is dry. Why can't I find better words? "I wasn't lying. That's not a problem for me." That sounds fucked up. "I mean, I'm not a big sharer, but this is different." Still not right. "You can do what you want." Shit.

"Then what is it?"

"Can I explain in person?" I croak. "I know you don't owe me that. We've only been on two dates," as if she needs reminding, "but I want to show you how sorry I am."

"Show me?" Sophie asks and I can hear the skepticism. There's no rage, though. No frustration. Fuck, she's not mad. She's disappointed.

"I'm not the best cook, but I'd make you dinner if you'd let me," I offer. I'll have to ask Miles for help, but I'll do it. "And if you want to leave before we even eat, that's fine too."

"Brody, I don't even know why I told you to call me."

"You want your painting back?" I ask, hopefully. She chuckles. I can hear her try to hide it, but it's there. "You pick the day. I'll go get the paintings this evening and be ready to earn that forgiveness."

"Next week," she says after what feels like the longest pause in history. "Tuesday."

"Tuesday," I agree. "Perfect. I'll send you my address. Any allergies?"

"None. I'll see you Tuesday at six."

"Thank you."

I'm not sure if she hears those last two words before she hangs up the phone. It sounded like I was beginning to soften her, but maybe she just really values that painting she created. Who knows?

Tuesday. I have a whole weekend to freak out about what I'm going to do. What I'm going to say.

Before I set my phone down, an email comes through from the clinic Miles referred me to. My STI test results are in. I know there's nothing to worry about, but a part of me panics when I click the link until I see the green *CLEARED* bar next to my name. The clinic is part of a network for performers, so it shows when they're cleared to work.

I open up the full list and stare at the capital letters *NEG* next to several of the listed infections. A few read as a number on a scale, but it must be all good or that green bar would've been red. I run a hand through my hair and sigh with relief. It's not as if I expected to test positive for anything, but the little green bar allows me to breathe easier.

I recall Miles refusing to use the word "clean" when referencing his results to a fellow performer. He believes that perpetuates the stigma, the way society views STIs. Anyone can get them, even the most careful people. "Clean" and "dirty" only contribute to the problem people have with speaking up or speaking with a partner if something does show up on a test.

I'm not "clean", I'm negative.

# 14

## Sophie

### Sophie

"You were supposed to wait for me." I sound more annoyed than I actually am.

Natalie is in the living room doing morning yoga when I emerge from my bedroom for breakfast. Standing on one leg, using one foot to prop the other leg up on her knee, Natalie ignores me. Her hands are together, palms facing each other, in front of her chest and I assume her eyes are closed, but she's facing away from me.

"You snooze, you lose," she says after a minute or so.

I turn away to start making a bowl of oatmeal. While it cooks in the microwave, I pour my coffee and then lean against the counter to wait.

"So, when are you seeing Brody again?"

Natalie doesn't turn to face me. I chew the inside of my cheek, trying to decide how much to tell her. She'd call me an idiot for giving Brody another chance. Her bullshit threshold with men is rather low, given how her last relationship ended. One could say the threshold is below sea level.

"Tuesday," I finally admit.

"Gonna tell him?"

"Not sure yet."

"Tell him soon. The longer you wait, the more likely he is to run away screaming."

*Not screaming*, I think bitterly.

All I do is hum just as the microwave stops.

"Busy day?" I ask as I stir the oatmeal and then restart the microwave. I return to my spot, leaning on the counter and holding my very hot mug of coffee.

"Yeah, I'm working with someone new over in Van Nuys." She turns to face me and sits on the mat, indicating that she's near the end of her exercise. "She's a cute little sub. Can't wait to get my hands on her."

The mischief dancing in those eyes makes me smile. I've enjoyed watching Natalie grow as a creator, even before we lived together. We were mutuals on social media for over a year before we met in person.

The microwave stops again, but I ignore the loud beeping. I blow on the coffee and bring it to my lips, keeping my eyes on my roommate. The microwave beeps again. She closes her eyes to breathe slowly, in and out as a third round of insistent beeping fills the air.

"Please open the microwave. I can't handle verbally abusive kitchen appliances today."

After breakfast, I set to work. I angle the tripod ring lights toward the bed in the studio, one at each corner. I attach my webcam to one and plug it into my laptop. The rolling desk that we keep in the corner of the room goes beside the bed with my laptop sitting on it, facing toward the bed so I can read the chat.

I quickly change into a red lingerie set, then slip on a floral, silk robe. I lay out a waterproof blanket, not wanting to dirty the sheets for this activity, and set a few toys on it, off to the side. I've chosen a clit sucking toy, three dildos of varying sizes, and a vibrating wand.

Connecting my phone to the Bluetooth speaker on the bedside table, I search through the playlists I use for my cam sessions. Some of the lists are more playful while others sound more like what the internet lovingly refers to as *baby-making music*. I choose playful, then get settled on the bed and drape the robe over my breasts, just barely covering them. My belly button is visible through the opening.

I cross my legs and prepare to start the broadcast. First, however, I grab one of the dildos and suck the tip into my mouth, taking a selfie to share on the social media platforms and let my followers and fans know that I'm about to go live.

After a deep breath, I tap the button to begin and plaster a smile on my face.

I raise my hands over my head and stretch, wiggling my torso so that my breasts and belly jiggle. This movement causes the robe to fall open further. I hear the chime indicating that someone has sent a message in the chat and I glance at the computer, humming in disappointment.

> **sxyboy2205**: ur so sexy i wish i was there
> with u

"No tip, no response, babes," I chirp.

> **cumgetit**: *Tipped 20 tokens - Take off
> clothing* take it off

I smirk and slip the robe from my shoulders. The material glides down my tawny skin, revealing my hodgepodge of tattoos as it moves. I lick my lips and then catch my bottom one between my teeth, attempting a seductive look. I'm sure I succeed, but I always feel a bit like a moron when I do that sort of thing.

"What can I do next?" I moan.

> **handsomemav27**: *Tipped 1 token* where u
> from bb?

I require at least one token for a response, but a single token is only worth ten cents. Still, it's better than nothing. I fight the urge to roll my eyes and respond that I live in LA.

> **handsomemav27**: me 2! We should meet up ur
> so sexy

> **cumgetit**: *Tipped 30 tokens - Play with
> tits* play for us baby

I bring my hands up and play with my nipples, ignoring the message about meeting up. I moan as my fingers tug and pinch, but I can't do this forever. I hope to see something else pop up soon.

> **handsomemav27**: y r u ignoring me bb

I continue playing, but I'm getting bored. Most cam sessions start this way, so I'm not worried. The longer I'm online, the more viewers I'll get. The higher the viewer count, the further up the main page I'll be listed.

> **handsomemav27**: ur a bitch i'm out

Now, I roll my eyes. There will always be people like him who want something for nothing, but the chat begins to fill up with comments. Most don't accompany tips, so I just watch. One viewer tips enough for me to begin playing with my clit over my panties and I oblige, leaning back on the pillows and moving my legs to give the camera the right view. My fingers rub and circle while I moan, despite it being only vaguely pleasurable.

Another tip comes through for the menu item requesting that I shake my ass for the camera. I roll over and raise onto my hands and knees before shaking my backside. This only lasts a few seconds before I roll over to lie back down.

Each tip escalates after that. Once my clothes are on the floor, the broadcast is a whirl of toys being requested for use in all of my holes. I follow along, attempting to give each tipper several seconds of fun, if not more. The direct messages begin to light up, but I don't check. While the main chat is being filled with tips, there's no reason for me to break off into a solo cam session.

After a couple of hours, I find myself lying on my side. The vibrating wand is tucked between my legs, focused on my clit, but without so much pressure that an orgasm is anywhere nearby. I have a small dildo in my mouth and a slightly larger one in my asshole, gently fucking myself as the tips continue to roll in.

> **dlju19284**: *Tipped 500 tokens – Cum for
> me, Honey*  i wanna see u cum

I pull the dildo from my mouth momentarily and grin at the message.

"You got it," I purr, speeding up the movement behind me and closing my eyes. I return to sucking on the toy in my mouth.

I let my head fall back and, as pleasure builds, drop the dildo from my mouth to focus on what's happening below my waist. Putting more pressure on my clit with the vibrator is what sends me over the edge as I shove the toy all the way inside me. Knees bent, my toes curl and I cry out as the orgasm races through me. I milk it for all it's worth, moaning and whimpering to put on a show.

When the waves subside, I slide the dildo from my ass, suppressing a shiver as the length leaves me, and hold it up for the viewers. I simultaneously turn off the vibrator to keep it from overstimulating me.

"Who wants to clean this up for me?" I ask with a smile. Several messages come in from volunteers and I laugh. "Oh, you boys are so wonderful to me. But I think I have to end this broadcast for now. I'll see you all next week. Bye!"

I wave and use my clean hand to stop the broadcast.

"I can't get up," I mutter, lying back on the waterproof blanket and dropping the toys, eyes fluttering closed. There's a knock on the door. "Come in," I sigh.

Natalie opens the door and I can feel her eyes on me as a chuckle escapes her throat.

"Good show?"

"Pretty damn." I nod. "Give me a couple minutes and I'll get all this cleaned up."

"You're fine, just wanted to let you know I'm home. I was thinking about going for a hike if you want to join me."

"How do you have the energy for that after filming?"

"It's nature. I always have time for nature. Come on. Clean up and let's get moving!"

With a groan, I sit up and scoot to the edge of the blanket, careful not to get any excess lube or bodily fluids on the sheet beneath. Cleanup doesn't take long. Once finished, I join Natalie in the living room. She tosses a water bottle to me before heading down the stairs and I barely catch the damn thing before it can hit me in the face.

The drive to Griffith Park is peaceful, despite the traffic. No outbursts from my roommate. I'm still not overly familiar with all the trails in the area, but Natalie has her favorites. She leads the way from the parking lot and we begin the slow climb.

I'm out of breath before we've gone fifty feet.

"I'm taking you on hikes more often," Natalie chuckles when she realizes how difficult this is for me. "Just let me know when you need a break."

"How about a break where we go home?" I ask, my voice annoyingly breathy and weak.

"Nope. Gotta make it to the top, fat ass."

I roll my eyes. I have no problem with my weight and she knows it. The words don't hurt, just the fact that she's going to make me walk this whole stupid trail. We pass a couple walking a golden retriever who looks very happy to see us.

"Oh, can I pet her?" Natalie asks.

The man nods and grins, tight-lipped. He's tall and skinny with circular glasses and ginger stubble on his chin. The young woman's dirty blonde hair blows in the breeze as she holds tight to the dog's leash.

"This is Oakley," she says with a smile as Natalie kneels. I join her.

"Aw, such a good girl," Natalie coos to the dog whose entire back half is wiggling as her tail wags.

We both love on the pup for a minute or two before letting the couple continue on their way with a wave. Then it's back up the mountain we go.

"I have," I pant, "a confession to make."

"Uh oh," Natalie laughs without looking at me. She's a couple of steps ahead of me on the trail.

"Before you get mad," more panting, "just know I'm going with my gut here."

"Yeah, yeah. Just make sure it's actually that intuition of yours. It's on point, but sometimes you follow a different... instinct." She glances back at me with a knowing smile, but I just shake my head.

"Brody," I continue, still huffing, "he sort of ran off on me the other night." Natalie stops and turns to face me.

"He what now?"

"I asked you not to get mad."

"No, you said 'before you get mad', which is totally different."

I ignore the fact that she's right.

"I already told him about my work and I thought he was ok with it for a sec, but then, *boom*. He just ran."

"Like, knocking over tables, ran?"

"No." Laughter comes out through my nose in a huff. "But he got out of there as fast as he possibly could."

"So what's the confession?"

"He wants to apologize." I bite my lip and look down at my shoes, unable to meet Natalie's eyes. "So I said I'd see him on Tuesday." When I look up again, she's scowling. That's understandable. "He's got my painting from the other night!"

"You and I could do the same thing at home for cheaper *and* we could drink more because we'd already be home." She turns and continues the hike.

"Remember when I said I'm following my gut?" I ask, trying to keep up.

"You're following something," I hear her mutter. "But I think it's a little lower."

"Sigh, Nat."

"Did you just *say* the word sigh?" She laughs. Either her annoyance at my forgiving a man I just met is forgotten or I'm just that funny. I choose both.

"Yes, I did. I didn't think an actual sigh would be enough." Were I standing still, I'd cross my arms. Instead, I continue swinging them as we walk, trying to give myself some momentum. "Your prejudice against men isn't enough to influence me."

"Oh fine, but at least let me do another emergency call. Just in case."

"Deal."

My phone rings on the way home.

"It's Lance," I say with a hint of surprise.

"What is it with you and these disrespectful men?" Natalie grumbles as she spins the steering wheel, turning just as the light changes to red.

I ignore her and press the button to answer the call, lifting the phone to my ear.

"Hello?"

"Hey Honey, hope it's ok that I called," says Lance. I can hear the worry in his voice. He clearly knows he screwed up the other day.

"Sure, what's up?"

"I wanted to apologize for Tuesday," he says quickly as if the words need to be said before he loses his nerve. "I shouldn't have kissed you like that after the scene. I took advantage."

"It's ok," I hear myself saying. Mostly because I'm not sure how else to respond. I'm not mad about it, not remotely. That's Natalie's department.

"It wasn't professional," he continues. "I'd love to work with you again, but only if you're comfortable with it."

"Lance, it's ok. We're good. I appreciate you apologizing." I lick my lips, knowing Natalie is listening to every word. "I've got some free time Sunday, if that works for you."

"Sunday afternoon ok?" He's perked up.

"Yeah, that'll work. Your place or mine?"

"I'm happy to come over again if it makes you more comfortable."

I bite my lip. Yes, of course I'm more comfortable in my own space.

"Let's do mine then. Let me know if you have any thoughts on a scene. I'll try to come up with something."

"You got it. See you Sunday. Thanks for giving me another chance."

After hanging up, I look over at my roommate. She's not meeting my gaze, but that's probably good since she's driving.

"So judgey today." A faint smile plays on my lips.

"I love you," she sighs. "But you don't have the best track record."

My smile falls. It's a low blow, but she's right. It's less about my experience with male co-stars and more about the men I date. She's the only person who knows everything that happened with Caleb.

# 15

## Miles

We've already worked together once. Honey didn't seem angry when we spoke on the phone Friday. I really shouldn't be nervous to see her again, but I very much am.

I raise my hand to ring the doorbell and hear it echo through the apartment.

"Hey, Lance." Honey's voice is light and airy when she pulls open the door to let me inside.

"Thanks for giving me another chance." I repeat my words from Friday, but Honey just smiles and nods, closing the door behind me.

"Well you said yes to a scene I've really been wanting to do," she says with a giggle.

I recall how excited she was when I agreed to her idea.

"Anything to put a smile on that face," I reply, almost without thinking.

"I thought we'd work in here today," she says, opening the door right beside the one I just walked through. It swings out to reveal the garage, which has been transformed into a second studio space.

Against the far wall is a set of bookshelves. The individual shelves are mostly empty except for a handful of books and some decorations. In front of the shelves is a long, light gray couch, and off in the corner is a circular wooden table with two chairs on either side. Along the wall next to me are a couple of studio lights. Some natural light comes in from the tiny row of windows along the top of the garage door, but it's obvious that more would be needed.

"Wow, I don't know that I've seen someone use a garage this way," I muse while Honey closes the door behind us.

"Yeah, my roommate and I wanted to make sure there were two spaces in case we both needed to film or do a live show at the same time."

"Good thinking. So, this scene," which already has my blood pumping just thinking about it, "is there anything you want to discuss first?"

"Safe words?" She looks uncertain and I wonder if she's done this before–filmed a scene in which safe words might be necessary or even had a discussion about them. I doubt we'll need to worry for this one, but it's good to be ready.

"Cucumber," I reply with a smirk. "If I need a hand signal I'll tap your shoulder or hip with two fingers."

"Traffic light system for me," says Honey. "And the two-finger tap."

We angle the tripods toward the couch and I take a seat on one side, ready to play the part of the adoring boyfriend. Honey starts the recordings and closes the door at the back of the garage. She stomps into the shot, looking frustrated.

"Hey, what's wrong, baby?" I ask, frowning when she flops down a few inches away.

"It's that stupid bitch, Courtney," she mutters.

"That bad, huh? When's she going to be fired?"

Honey just sighs, her arms crossed. I reach out and slide my hand over her thigh with a sly smile. She matches my grin, slipping from the couch and getting on her knees, her hands gripping my thighs.

"I think I know something that'll make me feel better," she says softly.

My mouth is dry as she undoes my buckle, then the button and zipper of my jeans. I keep my hands beside me while she slips her fingers into the waistband of my boxer briefs and pulls them down. I was already half hard for her before we even started, but watching her undress me like this has me straining against the thin fabric.

When Honey takes me into her hands, she swallows, looking up at me through her lashes. Her pink tongue darts out, wetting her lips and I don't even try to stop the moan that the sight pulls from my throat.

"You think my dick in that pretty little mouth is gonna make you feel better?" I ask, reaching forward to grip her chin. She nods. "Then what are you waiting for?"

Nothing can tear my focus from Honey as she leans forward, eyes still on mine. Her lips part, but all she does first is kiss my leaking tip like I'm not dying to feel her mouth around me. I fight the urge to buck my hips as she grips the base of my cock and leans down before swiping her tongue all the way up the underside.

"You taste so good," Honey moans.

She opens her mouth and sticks her tongue out again, lightly slapping my cock against it and earning another moan from me. When she takes me into her mouth, it's all I can do not to explode right then and there. I close my eyes and lean my head back while she hollows out her cheeks. She pulls me from her mouth and spits, allowing her hand to glide easily up and down my length following the movements of her mouth.

My hand sinks into her hair and I begin to take control, pushing her head down a little further with each bob. When I look down at her again, her eyes are closed, but she's only taking me about halfway into her mouth. That won't do.

I growl and pull her head down, feeling her throat stretch while she chokes. I don't keep her there long, letting her remove me entirely from her mouth. When her head lifts, there's saliva dripping down her chin and I lean forward to kiss her. I taste the slightest hint of my saltiness in her mouth when my tongue explores her. Her eyes are closed when I pull back and relax against the couch again.

"You're not done," I growl.

Honey grins and returns to work, sucking and forcing herself to deepthroat me. My breathing comes in faster with each constriction of her throat and I have to pull her off me.

"I think," I pant, "it's your turn to take control."

Honey grins, raising an eyebrow, and when she speaks, her voice is lower, velvety smooth.

"So you want to be a good boy?" she asks. I nod enthusiastically. "You want to make me happy?" I nod again, and she stands to allow me to take her place.

"Yes, ma'am."

She moves between me and the couch but doesn't sit. Instead, she hooks her thumbs into the waistband of her bike shorts.

"You want to make me feel good?" she asks, slowly pulling down, revealing herself.

My mouth waters and I nod. When her shorts are around her ankles, Honey kicks them off and then pulls off her shirt in one smooth motion. Without allowing me to fully appreciate her tits, she turns to kneel on the couch, facing away from me.

"Show me," she orders. "Use your mouth and make me feel better than I did when I got home."

"Fuck," I breathe, the sight of her making my cock ache to be inside her.

I crawl forward until I can kiss the backs of her thighs, then trail up to her ass. My throbbing erection is still hanging from my pants and I can smell her arousal. I inhale deeply through my nose and sigh, salivating. When I press my tongue to her clit and lick upward, I don't stop until my tongue reaches her puckered asshole. Honey moans in front of me.

"Good boy."

I like praise. I've known that for a while, but the words from Honey's lips have me dying to sink my cock into her. I shove my face into her pussy, devouring, lapping at her. Honey reaches back and grabs my hair tightly, trying to pull me further forward. My nose is practically in her ass when I slip my tongue inside her and she gasps.

I want to make her come on my tongue. I use it to swirl around her clit, not stopping even when her hips try to pull away. My arms wrap around her thighs, pulling her back toward me so I can torture her more. She whines my name, wiggling her hips as much as she can while I hold her. I want desperately to talk to her. I want to praise her like I did before, but I worry if I stop, she'll lose the momentum. I won't be the reason her orgasm eludes her.

I continue my attack until she cries out in beautiful agony, her back arching, pussy gushing and soaking my face. Without stopping, I wonder in the back of my mind if she can squirt. I'll have to try to find out next time.

When her orgasm subsides, I pull away from her, trying to catch my breath. She turns to grin at me.

"What are you waiting for?" Honey asks with a grin. "Be a good boy and fuck me."

"I thought you'd never ask."

I'm on my feet in seconds, practically tripping in my haste to pull off my jeans. I don't want anything in the way. I grab her hips, burying myself in a single thrust. Honey cries out again, her head thrown back while I begin a punishing rhythm. The sound of her wet pussy taking every inch of me fills the studio, loud and wet and lewd. If I wasn't rock hard already, I surely would be just by listening to those sounds.

"Oh, god, Honey," I grunt, my release closer than I want it to be already. "Use me," I beg. "Fucking use my cock."

"Don't you dare stop," she pants. "If you stop, I'll have to punish you."

"Maybe I want that," I retort, continuing to piston into her.

She can't keep up the banter, moaning when I sink my hand into her hair and pull her head back slightly.

"Good boy," is all she can whimper. "My good boy."

*Fuck.*

"Yes," I moan, my voice rising. "I'm *your* good boy."

I've been hers from day one. Hers from the first time I saw her, standing there in the doorway. She may look like the girl next door, but the woman is a fucking demon–respectfully.

Honey pushes herself back into me with each of my thrusts, meeting the movements in a way that has me near the edge. It's too soon. I can't finish already.

"Wait," I whimper. I slow my movements, but Honey doesn't let up. "Please, Honey."

"You begged me to use you," she reminds me fucking herself on my cock. "You wanted to be my good boy."

"Fuck." My voice has risen in pitch, my breathing ragged. I'm desperate, holding on by a thin thread.

*Baseball.*

*Grandma.*

*The feeling when your Uber is way more expensive than it should be after a concert.*

"You don't get to come until I've gotten what I want." Honey's voice is husky, deep, commanding.

"What-" I swallow. "What do you want?" I know the answer, but I can't think straight.

*Football.*

*Broadway musicals.*

*That pothos plant in the kitchen I somehow killed. What idiot can kill a pothos plant?*

"I want you to make me scream."

Leaning forward, I roll my hips into her. I reach around, my chest pressed against her back, and my fingers just barely brush her clit. I continue to play, my cock deep inside her. A high-pitched whimper escapes her, but I can't focus on that, still trying to hold my own release back. My lips trail kisses over her shoulder and up to her neck. When I pull her soft earlobe into my mouth and bite down gently, Honey shudders. Her walls spasm, fluttering around my length. Honey's head falls to the couch while she emits moans like I've never heard. Deep and guttural, I don't know if this means it's more intense or less, but I talk her through it.

"That's it," I whisper. "Fucking use me. Come all over this cock, Honey. Take what you want, I'm yours."

Honey hangs her head as her body relaxes.

"Sit on the couch," she orders. Her breathing is heavy, her voice weak, but the excitement for what comes next is unmistakable.

Pulling myself from her now feels illegal, but I follow her command. Before getting into position, Honey moves the tripod that was behind us so it can get a side view. The tripod on the other side of the couch has just enough height to capture what we need.

Honey kneels before me and that grin on her full, swollen lips makes me shudder. I'm going to hate this.

"Who knew you were so good at this." She reaches for my aching cock.

"And what is *this*?" I ask. It's hard to focus on her words when her fingers find me, using her arousal as lube.

"Being used," she replies, "being a good boy."

Her words send another jolt through me.

"Please. Please let me come now." I squeeze my eyes shut at the same time Honey's fingers tighten around my cock. "Please."

"I like hearing you beg." She lets go and I whimper, letting my head fall back on the couch. Honey traces one finger up my thigh. "I like hearing you desperate."

"Damn it, woman," I growl, trying to reach for her hand to bring it to where I need her touch the most. Honey bats my hand away and my head snaps up, eyes on her.

"Ah, ah, ah," she scolds. "Hands beneath your ass. I don't want you reaching for things you shouldn't."

I glare, but do as she says, rocking on the couch cushion to shove my hands beneath my bare ass. Honey grabs a bottle of lube from the floor and squeezes some into her hands to warm it up. When her fingers brush my cock again, I moan.

"Is this what you want?" she asks.

"I want your mouth."

"But how can I fully appreciate you begging me for relief if I do that?"

Honey's fingers encircle my cock, almost touching around the girth, and I buck my hips. My fingers slip as my arms twitch, but I don't move them from beneath me. Her grip tightens as she works me from base to tip. My stomach tenses and I feel my balls draw upward, so close to that release I've been seeking.

"Please." I can't stop whining and whimpering. "I'll be your good boy. Please, please, please." The repeated word continues to tumble from my lips. "Please, I need to come."

"You belong to me." It's her character, but I wonder if she knows how right she is. "Do you hear me? You belong to me."

"Yes," I agree, nodding quickly. "Yes, I belong to you. Please, Honey." Honey's movements are still slow and I groan when she refuses to speed up, trying to move my hips faster. Honey's hand disappears and I grunt in frustration. "No, please."

"I'm in control here, Lance," she warns.

"Yes, you're in control. Please, touch me. Please, I need to come."

"You need to come?" She mimics me, reaching out once more.

"Yes, please. I belong to you. It's all for you. I'm your good boy and my cum belongs to you." What the fuck am I saying? This wasn't planned.

"All for me?" Honey asks, slowly stroking me once more.

"Yes, all of me." I need her to speed up. Does she want a different answer? "My cum is yours, my cock is yours, please."

"Good boy."

Honey renews her efforts and I continue to whimper, begging for release. I don't know what I'm saying as she focuses on my tip. One swipe in particular has me thrusting my hips forward and I let loose. Honey angles my cock toward me and I shoot warm, sticky ropes up my stomach while she continues to work me. I groan, twitching in her hands, trying to control my breathing.

When no more can be wrung from me, I allow myself to lean down and kiss her then pull back quickly so we don't get into the same dangerous territory as before. Honey sits back on her heels.

"Are you ok?" I ask.

"Yeah, that was amazing." She stands and stops one phone's recording while I balance on unsteady legs to stop the other. "Can you hand me that pack of wipes?" She points to the little table by my backpack.

I hand her the wipes sitting on top and grab one for myself before I quickly find my pants and slip them on.

"Good, I wasn't sure if that worked for you." I hate that she didn't get to come more than once.

"Oh no, I had fun."

When I finish fastening my belt buckle, I stare at her, biting my lip. Honey grabs her top and slips it on before looking for her shorts. Once they're in hand, she stands but doesn't put them on. She meets my gaze and cocks her head.

"Are *you* ok?" She raises one eyebrow.

"Iwannatakeyououtonadate." There's absolutely no break between my words and there's definitely no way she understood what I said.

"'Scuse me?" Honey asks with a smile. It's a kind smile, an amused smile.

I take a breath and try again.

"I'd like to take you out on a date." I try to pronounce each word individually, speaking slowly. "If you're open to that."

Her eyes are wide. Is that shock on her face? Is it anger? No, it can't be anger. I need her to reply, to put me out of my misery.

"Lance, I-"

"Miles," I correct. "If you're going to turn me down, at least use my real name."

Honey smiles at me. It's small at first, just barely playing on her full lips, but then it spreads.

"Is this because you've had so much *fun* with me or do you actually want to date?"

I understand her question. A lot of men like me would probably ask for a date, intending to just become fuck buddies off-camera. But that's not me.

"Honey-"

"Sophie."

I smile and sit on the couch. She slips into her shorts and joins me, facing sideways to look properly into my eyes.

"Sophie, I've seen you on social media. I've seen your TikToks and your silly responses on Twitter. You're funny, you're smart, you're quick, you're kind. I know how hard it is to be authentic, but you make it look easy. I want to get to know you better."

How do I explain that I feel as if I'm being pulled toward her? That she is the sun and I am a planet caught in her orbit, basking in her glow?

First a flower, now a planet. Who have I become? Fucking Shakespeare?

Sophie studies me. It feels like hours, but she likely only takes seconds. Her eyes roam my face as if looking for a sign that I'm lying, that I might hurt her. I don't intend to do any such thing.

"I haven't been in a relationship with someone in the industry." It's not an answer. It's a test.

"I have," I admit. "It didn't end well."

"What makes you think this would be any different?"

The reply tumbles out before I can think.

"You." I swallow hard.

"What if this ends badly? Messy?"

"Do you think it will?" I'm avoiding the question. I don't want to think about an end to my time with her.

"I can't tell the future." She continues to study me. "I don't-" She stops and frowns as if trying to find the words.

"It's ok if-"

"No, I want to say yes." Sophie holds up a hand to stop me from talking, but all I hear is the last word. My heart leaps. "I've been on a couple dates with someone else," she explains. "And I like him. But we haven't- I mean, we haven't discussed-"

"You're not exclusive." I hate that word, but Sophie nods. "I won't ask you to stop seeing him as long as you're upfront if something changes, either with him or me."

More silence. I hate the silence. I hate not knowing what she's thinking. I hate the fact that someone beat me to the punch, but I'm determined to win her over.

"Then yes."

# 16

## Miles

It's been twenty-four hours since ~~Honey~~ Sophie said yes. Twenty-four hours of worrying about how to impress her, how to sweep her off her feet. I have competition. Some dickhead thinks he can take her from me.

"So, what did you decide on?" Brody is sitting at the kitchen island with a sandwich and a beer when I walk out of my room to leave.

"I'm taking her to the rose garden at Exhibition Park."

"That'll be nice." Brody nods slowly before taking a bite of his sandwich.

"Yeah, then I'm going to take her to the brewery."

"Stealing my ideas?" Brody raises an eyebrow.

"I gave you the painting idea. I think I earned this."

"Maybe you jinxed me."

"Maybe you're just a moron," I shoot back. "I just want to show her a fun time. I want her to feel like she can relax with me, not put on a mask like she probably does in public, you know? The brewery seems like a good place for that."

"Ok, not a horrible idea," Brody admits.

I pull my phone out to check the time.

"Gotta run, I'm grabbing flowers for her first."

"Before you go to a rose garden?"

"Yes, shut up. Eat your sandwich."

I skip the flowers. Brody got in my head, the stupid prick. I run a hand through my hair, trying to calm my nerves while waiting at Sophie's front door. It's a different sort of anxiety than filming with someone for the first time. I want co-stars to appreciate my professionalism–when I'm not trying to make out with them. I want Sophie to appreciate... all of me, I suppose.

A nude Sophie is a sight to behold, but in her cut-off shorts and black, cropped tank top, hair flowing over her shoulders in those soft curls, she's perfect. She's a vision, standing there with the door open, waiting.

Waiting for me to speak.

Shit, I didn't hear what she said. I'm not even sure I was breathing.

"You look beautiful."

"Oh, er, thanks." She looks down at her clothes and I realize that this might be her casual look for a first date. I'm awestruck nonetheless.

"Ready?" I ask, stepping back and allowing her to exit the townhouse.

"Absolutely." Her smile is infectious, her lips coated in a dark red that has just a hint of purple. The outfit may be casual, but the lip color adds a bit of sin.

Sophie steps out the door and turns to lock it. But when she spins around to follow me to my car, parked out on the street, I gently grab her wrist and turn her back around to face me. Our chests pressed together, I wrap a gentle arm around her waist and use my other hand to cup her cheek.

"Can I kiss you?" It feels like an odd question, given all we've done. Given how I'm holding her now. The heat between our bodies is already causing mild discomfort in my shorts. Sophie blinks at me as if startled. "I'm playing this by the book."

"No bombarding me, hm?" she asks, but there's a devious twinkle in her brown eyes.

"No sneak attacks." I remove my hand from her cheek and hold up three fingers. "Scout's honor."

"Then I suppose I'll allow it."

Lowering my head, I brush my lips along hers, just a ghost of a touch. I breathe her in, her scent a mixture of florals and citrus. When I press my lips to hers, it takes every ounce of control not to tighten my arm still around her waist, not to roll my hips, not to slip my tongue into her mouth and entangle my fingers in her hair.

Instead, after only a brief moment of contact, I lift my head. Sophie's eyes are closed when I pull away, her lips parted. When her eyes flutter open, there's a look of confusion in those golden brown depths.

"Ready to see some roses?" I ask, my voice husky and deep and far too lustful to be safe.

Sophie swallows and nods, then steps away and out of my embrace. Time to show her that I actually know how to be a gentleman.

The rose garden stays open until dusk and on a Monday evening, it's not overly busy. We stroll along the paths of perfectly manicured grass, stopping along the way to admire a particularly perfect blossom here and there.

"So how long have you been in our line of work?" Sophie asks, straightening after having bent down to smell a beautiful yellow rose.

"About six years." We continue walking.

"Four, for me," she says, not looking over at me. Instead, she turns her head from side to side, eyes focused on the beautiful bushes. "I was solo for a couple of years, then started working with locals for about a year before I was able to travel a little for work."

"Women are lucky," I muse. "Your solo content is much better received than a man's. Not that I'm complaining," I add when Sophie shoots me a look that I can't decipher. "It's just hard to convince people to work with you when you're a new guy."

"I get that." She nods and continues to study the flowers. "I've had to implement some rules on who I work with. A couple bad eggs will ruin the whole thing."

"Don't I know it," I mutter. "I was turned down a lot in the beginning. Most women just don't trust someone who doesn't already have a few collabs under their belt, you know? A few wouldn't even talk to me until I had at least ten thousand followers on my clip site."

"Seriously?" Sophie stops and stares at me in shock. "I mean, I need to see experience, but follower count doesn't mean a damn thing."

"I didn't count you in that group, don't worry." I place a hand gently in the middle of her back, urging her to keep up as we turn a corner down another path. "And I'm not judging the women who do that. If it's what keeps them safe, then I won't question it."

"That's good." Sophie nods, her gaze still on the plants surrounding us. "Out of curiosity, have you had any," she pauses, trying to find the words, "less than savory experiences? I haven't really heard from men about stuff like that."

"Yeah." I sigh and run a hand through my hair. "Like you said, always one or two bad eggs."

Sophie hums and nods, but doesn't push for details. I'm thankful for that. My horror stories would definitely kill the mood, though I'm sure I've got nothing on her.

"Where'd you get your porn name?" It's a question I don't usually ask when I work with someone, but I'm curious. She shrugs.

"I didn't think very hard. Honey is sweet and I'm built like a goddess. Divine." She winks with a crooked grin. "What about you?"

"Well, Lance, because they're long and heavy and could potentially skewer someone."

"That's ridiculous." The laughter that bubbles up from her chest is the most wonderful sound. I want to make her laugh every day.

"And Kixxx," I continue, "like a kickstand." I smirk, certain she knows what I'm referring to. She fixes me with a chastising stare, but it just makes me laugh. "I never said it was clever."

We walk in silence for a few more minutes, enjoying the plants even if the heat is less than ideal.

"What made you think of this place?" she asks.

"My mom used to like to come here before she moved away." The memories flood my mind of spending several afternoons in near silence with her, particularly after my father had died.

"Oh, where is she now?"

"Florida."

"Well, that's a pretty big move, isn't it?"

"Yeah, her sister lives there. My uncle passed two years ago and my aunt can't really live alone anymore. She decided to help."

"Family sticking together," Sophie sighs. She stops to bend over and examine a rose, but then straightens and turns to face me. "I like that. It's nice."

I feel one corner of my mouth lifting into a smile.

"It *is* nice. Where's your family? I saw you're from Oklahoma originally."

"Yeah." Sophie pulls her bottom lip between her teeth and chews for a moment. "It's just my parents. No siblings. They're still in Oklahoma City."

"Do you go back to visit often?"

That strikes a nerve. Sophie's spine goes rigid. My eyes drop to her throat as she swallows, clearly trying to suppress a memory or two.

"Never mind," I mutter, shaking my head and looking away. "Forget I asked." *Foot. In. Mouth.*

"It's fine, they just don't exactly support my work, you know? They thought they raised a good, Christian girl." Her eyes are downcast when mine find her face again. I take her chin between my thumb and index finger, angling her face up toward mine.

"Instead they raised a smart, ambitious young woman who, from what I can tell, doesn't take shit from anyone."

Sophie grins and that, right there, is the look I want to see from her for the rest of my days. I'll do anything she asks if she'll only look at me like that again. Like I can do no wrong.

Oh, I am so done for.

We stay until the sun begins to set. As the garden closes for the evening, walking back to my car, Sophie's arm slips around mine. The heat where we touch is electrifying, reminding me that she's something special. It also reminds me that there's someone else out there I'm competing with.

"You promised me dinner." She hangs just a little bit off of my arm as if it's the most natural thing in the world for her to be holding me like this.

"I did, didn't I?" Laughter is evident in my voice and I look down at her.

The rose garden isn't far from our next stop. As we walk up to the brewery, I notice Sophie smiling.

"What is it?"

"Oh nothing, I just-" she chuckles, "I *just* discovered this place recently."

"Well, then you discovered a gem."

"Oh, I agree. Great sour beer."

There's no wait and we're seated quickly, near the back. Sophie settles into her chair and glances around.

"Looking for someone?" I ask, following her gaze when it stops on the bartender.

"Nope, just studying the place." She looks back at me. "So, what's your go-to here?"

"I'm always happy with any of their burgers."

"I do like a good burger."

"So, did you come here with your roommate?" Or was it a date, I wonder?

"Yeah, someone she worked with told her about it."

"Does she approve of you going out with someone in the industry?" I ask, changing the subject slightly.

"She kind of swore off men recently, so I think she disapproves of me dating *any* men, porn star or not."

A man approaches, wearing the brewery's t-shirt and black jeans.

"Hey guys, I'm Shane. What can I get for you folks?"

I gesture for Sophie to go first.

"I'll take the Spitfire," she says, pointing at the beer on the menu.

"Same." I smile up at Shane who jots down our orders.

"I'll give you guys a few more minutes, but let me know if you have any questions."

"I know we're only halfway through, but I have to ask." I stare at her, waiting for her eyes to fall to mine. "Did I do enough to earn a second date?"

She stares for a moment, weighing the question. I wait, holding my breath. This hasn't been the most mind-blowing date I've taken someone on. It isn't expensive or unique in any way. But it has been relaxing, a way to get to know her without fuss and without cameras.

"Maybe." Her tone is light when she finally speaks. "Depends on how the rest of the evening goes."

"I'll take that."

Our beers arrive and we give our order to Shane before he disappears again.

"How often do you travel for work?" she asks.

"Depends on the time of year, really. I don't plan too far in advance unless there's a big event coming up."

"Makes sense, I guess. I try to do some major travel every couple months or so. Three times a year minimum, as long as it's in the budget."

"I'm awful about that," I chuckle. "Making and sticking to a budget, I mean."

"You should take some tips from my roommate. Natalie is anal about budgeting, even though she makes an obscene amount of money."

"Well, we have that in common. Wealthy roommates," I add when Sophie stares. "At least yours gets out of the house now and then."

"She's a social butterfly, that one."

We spend the evening discussing work and various co-stars, laughing about the more ridiculous things we've seen and commiserating about the less fun experiences. Sophie, it seems, has a bit of a bucket list for her porn.

"There's a lot of stuff I haven't done yet," she muses. "I've been with a couple of women, even had a few threesomes with male-female couples, but never with two men." Her cheeks flush, but I grin.

"I'm sure I could find someone and we could make that happen, if you're up for it," I offer. Sharing a partner has never been something I thought I would enjoy, but if Sophie finds pleasure in it, I'll do anything she wants.

"That would be amazing."

"What else is on that list of yours?" I grin and lean forward, resting my elbows on the table.

"Oh, there's plenty, but I think we might get into trouble if we talk about it in public." I laugh.

"Fair enough. Have you worked on any pro shoots?"

"Not yet, that's one of my goals." She bites her lip before continuing. "I'd actually like to have my own production company one day. Woman-run, focused on making the more intimate, passionate porn, you know?"

"A real boss bitch, huh?" I chuckle. Sophie grins. "Do you have a plan for it yet?"

"No." She looks down at her hands for a moment before meeting my gaze again. "I have some ideas jotted down, but I don't feel like I have the brand recognition yet."

"You don't need that before you start a company, you know. Did you have brand recognition when you started making content?"

"No, but-"

"It's the same thing. As long as you're authentic and treat people right, which I know you will, you'll be amazing."

"I won't argue that. I just don't feel ready."

"Well, don't wait too long. I'd love to see what you can do with that kind of power."

"Yes, sir." She giggles. Glancing around, I know she realizes how late it is. I noticed half an hour ago that the other patrons were beginning to empty out. "We should probably go soon."

"We should."

Neither of us move.

"Are you waiting to see if you earned a second date?"

"Maybe."

"And if I say yes?"

"Then I'll take you home."

Sophie raises an eyebrow, but her lips form a smile.

"So you're saying you'll leave me here if I don't say yes to a second date?"

"Only one way to find out."

"Fine." She rolls her eyes. "Second date, confirmed."

"Fantastic. I'll take you home now."

I park on the street near her place so I can walk her to her front door. When we reach the door, I pull her to my chest, out of view of her doorbell camera, which has a blue ring around it, indicating it's on. I've been planning this move from the moment she said yes to going out with me.

There's a hint of pink creeping into her cheeks, spreading down to her chest. It's adorable. I bend to kiss her lips but pause. Hiding a smirk, I gently kiss her forehead and when I pull back, Sophie's eyes are closed. Her head follows my lips for half a second before she stops. Her eyes snap open.

"That was sneaky." She scolds with a grin.

"I know."

# 17

## Brody

"Just do me a favor."

I don't meet Miles' eyes while I focus on the task he gave me. I hate dicing onions and he knows it. My eyes are already watering and I've only just begun, but I have to follow through. He said he would help me prepare dinner, so he's been instructing me for the last twenty minutes.

"Remind you to use frozen in the future?" Miles asks. I glare at him before returning to the cutting board in front of me.

"I'm not ready to, er, share her," I say slowly. Well, that sounded wrong. "I mean introduce you two. It feels too soon."

"I'll head out for the evening. Maybe see a movie. You need to dice that a little finer." Miles grins like the smug asshole he is while he directs me around the kitchen.

Half an hour later, he's gone and I'm standing in the kitchen, wondering if we turned off the AC for some ungodly reason. Sophie will be here in a few minutes. Miles texted me after he left to say he'll be out of the house until around midnight. Dinner is ready, but I'm not sure I can say the same for me.

I pace back and forth in front of the stove. The contents of the frying pan and the sauce pot are covered and Miles told me they will keep for a while, in case she's late. I want to be ready and focused solely on Sophie when she arrives.

The doorbell chime grates on my nerves. Any other time, it's a mildly annoying sound, but that's probably because I hate answering the door. Tonight it reminds me I'm about to admit something I've only ever discussed with Miles and not at length. He's tried to offer advice, even tips for a time when I might find myself naked in bed with a woman. I've shut him down almost every time.

Opening the door causes the dry heat of another LA August evening to hit me in a wave, but I barely feel it. Sophie is standing there, beautiful as ever in the warm glow of the sky just before sunset. If I didn't know better, I'd say she's dressed to make sure I know what I'm missing if I fuck this up. I know full well, but it doesn't stop me from taking a quick look at those cut-off shorts that are just a tiny bit too short. Or at the neckline of her crop top, the scoop dropping far lower than necessary. Her hair is swept back with just a few curly tendrils framing her face. The final nail in the coffin is the dark red lipstick, standing out from her dusky complexion.

"You came." I don't bother to hide the relief in my voice or on my face. She has to know I had my doubts.

"I want that painting." She flashes a smile and I'll be damned if my heart doesn't skip a beat or five.

I have to clear my throat before speaking again.

"Come on in."

Sophie hesitates before stepping inside, allowing me to close the door behind her.

"Thought you'd never ask."

When I turn, she's eyeing the two paintings near the door.

"My roommate and I did those a few years ago," I explain casually. I allow my eyes to roam down her back while she responds.

"Well, if that's not an excuse to display a couple of mediocre art pieces, I don't know what is." She turns to face me and my gaze snaps back to hers, but she grins. She noticed.

"Mediocre?" I gasp. "How dare you? Those are our best works."

"Please tell me they're your only works." Her musical laughter lightens the mood a little.

"Oh, no, my mom has the really good stuff. First grade is where I peaked."

"Is this where you got the idea for last week?"

"I thought it might impress you." Warmth floods my cheeks and I realize with embarrassment that I'm blushing. That only strengthens the blush. I have to turn away, leading her toward the kitchen.

"It did," Sophie confirms. I hear her footsteps behind me, soft on the hardwood floor. "Renting out a whole event space will have that effect."

I round the kitchen island, but instead of approaching the pans on the stove, I turn back toward her. The island is between us. I lean forward, hands on the cold, white granite, hoping it will ground me.

"I have something to-" she starts, but I speak at the same time.

"About the other night-" I stop, unable to wipe a look of surprise from my face.

"Go ahead," she urges.

There's something in her delicate features that worries me. I want her to go first, to help me delay the inevitable, but maybe it's better to get this over with. I swallow before taking a ragged, stunted breath. She expects an excuse to make up for the fact that I left her alone in a cafe. I'm one hundred percent sure she's not expecting the excuse I'm going to give her, but I hope it's enough.

"I just- I want you to know that the other night." I pause to lick my lips. "I didn't run because of your job."

Sophie cocks her head to one side, studying me. My eyes plead with her, willing her to just read my mind so I don't have to say it, but the only person on the planet capable of that isn't here. I'm not sure I'd want him around for this anyway.

"So why did you leave me there alone?"

I flinch at the harsh tone, but Sophie doesn't back down. Good. Good for her. She's got fire and that's one of the reasons I feel pulled to her.

"There's- I, er-" The struggle is fucking *real* here.

"Breathe." She takes a step around the island, just a little closer, but not close enough to touch just yet.

My tongue darts out to wet my bottom lip and I take another deep breath, this one a little steadier than the last.

"I've always-" I stutter, "I've always been kind of an introvert." *That's an understatement.* I know my words are tumbling out, spilling from my lips almost too fast to understand. But I can't stop now or I'll lose my nerve and then what? Kick her out? "Since high school, middle school," I continue. "Hell, even at recess, I liked to be on my own."

A chuckle escapes me and I hang my head, eyes focusing on my hands where they rest on the counter. I have to work hard to drag my gaze back to Sophie's, those caramel depths pulling me in.

"I didn't date in high school," I continue slowly, never taking my focus from her face. "Or college, for that matter. And when my roommate and I go out, it's..." I swallow, "it's not usually me getting the attention."

"Oh my god." Her whispered words barely register.

"I didn't- I just-"

"You're a v-" she starts and my stomach drops. Part of me is disappointed she pieced it together, but a larger part is relieved. "A vir- God, I hate that word. You're untainted. Ew, no." When she sees my lips parting, my face falling, she waves her hands as if that's enough to dissipate this sinking feeling. "I'm just trying to process. I'm not judging. Please believe me when I say I'm not judging."

"It's ok if you are." My voice is weak, barely audible. I have to give her an out.

"But I'm *not*," she presses, taking another step forward. "Brody, I don't care, trust me. I'm just realizing how much *my* admission last week probably scared you."

I hang my head again, shaking it. With doubt? With relief? I'm not sure.

"This was stupid," I mutter. "I shouldn't have-" I force my head to raise, my eyes to meet hers again. "It's ok if you want to leave. I'll grab your painting."

I hate that my voice cracks with that last word. Two dates. We've been on two dates, not counting this one–and I'm not counting this one.

"What?" She blinks at me, startled.

"I mean I'd understand if-"

Sophie holds up a hand to silence me, circling the rest of the island. I follow her with my eyes, but my body remains stationary. I drop my focus when she gently takes my hand in hers, the heat from her touch radiating down my spine.

"Why in the world would I care about that?" she asks softly, raising my knuckles to brush her cheek.

I turn, reaching out with my free hand to grab her waist and gently pull her to me, our bodies pressed together while I lean to rest my forehead on hers. I just want to stand here like this, holding her close, breathing her in. That scent of citrus and some kind of flower–I'll never be able to identify it in a million years–invading my senses. When she speaks, her breath flutters across my lips and chin.

"I have something I need to tell you," she whispers.

"Something worse than having never had sex at the age of 30?" I ask with a breathy laugh. I guess now that I've admitted it, I can laugh about it. Funny how quickly things can change.

"Maybe."

I lift my head, searching her face for a sign. *Ok, now she'll tell me she's married.*

"No judgment," I say, despite the worry reforming in my stomach. She doesn't speak. "Are you already breaking up with me?" My tone is light, but I know she sees the fear in my eyes.

"No," she says quickly, her grip on my hand tightening. "No, I just need to tell you I'm..." She bites her lip before continuing, her words staggered as they fall from her lips. "I'm seeing someone else. It's not serious, just one date so far. But I needed you to know."

I guess I shouldn't be surprised. How many men ask her out on a daily basis? She could date a new guy every week, hell, every *day* and it would take a lifetime to work through the list. I blink at her, trying to keep my expression blank.

"Oh." I sound like a fucking moron.

She studies me with a frown. I know it's not the response she wanted, but what do I say? What do I do? I admitted my secret and she didn't run. Sophie is worth the fight.

"Oh?"

"So I have competition?" I smirk, trying to remain confident. Her body relaxes in my grip.

"I guess you could say that." A smile creeps across her lips.

"Ok." Telling her I'm up for the challenge would be a lie, but I'll give it my best shot. If nothing else, I'm more determined than ever to make up for last week.

"Well, that was easy."

A nervous laugh escapes her. I drag my hand from her waist up to her cheek, cupping her face. My other hand turns in hers and she grips my wrists.

My lips crash to hers, releasing every bit of pent-up worry and need into this one kiss. It's unlike anything I've shared with anyone before, even her. Frantic and demanding, I decide to take control–something I've been wanting to do since I watched her walk into that brewery just over a week ago. Using my tongue, I part her lips and she complies, allowing me to explore her mouth. She moans into me and the sound causes my dick to instantly perk up. It's not a new feeling–I'm human–but this is the first time I've felt the freedom to act on it.

I move my hands back to grip her hair, holding her tightly to me. I turn us so that her back is against the counter and her hands fall to my waist, to steady herself, to pull me closer. I drop one hand from her hair to caress her neck, her shoulder, her upper arm. I want to feel every single inch of her silky skin beneath my fingers.

When I break the kiss and pull away, we're both panting. I'm still pressed against her and I know she feels what the kiss has done to me pushing gently against her stomach. I'm not sure what she wants, if I should continue to take control. How the fuck do I ask?

"Sophie," I breathe, my lips ghosting over hers before I trail kisses down her chin to her jaw, continuing to the point where it meets her neck. I'm not sure why I do it, but I gently graze my teeth over her skin. Goosebumps erupt beneath my hand on her arm.

"Tell me what you need." Her voice is half whimper and I feel her squirm slightly, but not in an attempt to escape. "What can I do?"

I pull my lips from her skin, dropping my forehead to the crook of her neck. I can't think straight anymore. She's intoxicating.

"Sophie, I-I don't-" A frustrated grunt slips from my throat. I raise my head far enough to see her whole face. Her pupils are dilated, her lips swollen and parted. "I need-" My voice cuts out. "Fuck," I whisper.

Sophie reaches up, gently stroking my temple, running her fingers into my hair. I lean into her touch, closing my eyes momentarily. When I open them again, I see that the fire in her eyes matches exactly what I'm feeling. It alleviates any last shred of doubt–at least for the time being.

"I need you," I choke.

Sophie's grip on my waist tightens.

"Not to put a damper on things," she whispers with a grin. "I want to, but-" She bites her lip and it hits me.

"Testing!" I shout, startling both of us with the volume. We never discussed it, but that has to be what she wants. "Sorry. I, er, yeah. I got tested last week. I can pull up the results."

This is quite possibly the weirdest thing I've ever done. Stopping ourselves from tearing each others' clothes off to pick up our phones and share test results–not something I'd considered having to do. I make a mental note to thank Miles tomorrow for making me go last week.

Satisfied with my results, she shows me her proof, hiding her stage name from me. I wonder if she'll ever let me see her videos. The idea of her being with someone else feels odd, but I suppose it could also be exciting.

"Now that I've sufficiently ruined the mood," she giggles, setting her phone on the counter. I set mine next to it.

"Not at all. Safety first."

Sophie hums in agreement.

"I know you promised me dinner, but I'm..." She bites her lip and rakes her eyes over me. My erection has only grown and there's no hiding it from her gaze, but she keeps her eyes moving. "...not so hungry anymore."

She's in my arms again. Our mouths battle for control, Sophie meeting my movements. Her arms are caught between us. I have one hand on her hip and the other is tangled in her hair again–which is a mess, but a very sexy mess. Her back is facing my bedroom hallway, so I begin to walk her toward it, thankful I left my door open.

Sophie stumbles after a few steps, so I spin us, dragging her backward with me while we're still attached at the lips. I don't want to stop kissing her, worried if we break the spell a second time, I may lose my nerve. She giggles against my lips as we cross the threshold and I flip on the light. Finally pulling my mouth from hers, I let her take a look around the room. It's sparse, with just a few furnishings and some family pictures on the wall above the bed. I run a hand through my hair, trying not to reach out for her.

"You just gonna stand there?" she asks, putting a hand on her hip.

# 18

## Brody

Sophie leads the way, backing up until her knees hit the bed. I reach her and kiss her again, before gently pushing her backwards. She bounces onto the mattress and scoots away with a giggle, her eyes flashing when I follow and crawl toward her. Sophie's legs part for me to get nearer and I kneel between them, running my hands along her shins. More goosebumps follow my touch.

*Now what?* I want to ask the question aloud but Sophie saves me, sitting forward and taking my hands. She slides my fingers up her thighs and then brings them together over the button of her shorts.

"Go at your pace," she assures me, but her voice is deep and husky with need.

"I don't think you want that," I chuckle, shaking my head.

"I can assure you, I do." She giggles and lays back on the pillows, watching me. Waiting.

"Then, I think you're wearing too many clothes," I growl.

Instead of unbuttoning her shorts, I lift her shirt, revealing her stomach. My eyes flick to hers, but there's no hint of hesitation or doubt. Instead, Sophie lifts up to help me pull the top over her head.

"Fuck," I whisper, my eyes on her breasts. I couldn't imagine a more perfect pair. Covered by black lace, I can just glimpse her dark nipples, hard and waiting for attention.

"That good, huh?" she chuckles.

I can't answer. She's stolen my voice. I lean over her using one hand on her stomach to press her down into the bed, the other to support myself above her. Trailing my hand up and over one breast, I pull the lace down to bare her. My eyes can't seem to focus and that nipple is practically crying out to me. I flash a smirk at Sophie and then dip my head, pulling her nipple into my mouth.

I'm not sure if the groan comes from me or her. Possibly both. Her hands tangle into my hair. Holding her breast with my hand, I swirl her nipple in my mouth, sucking and twisting it between my lips. I graze my teeth over the sensitive bud and the tiniest squeak comes from the woman beneath me. I smile against her skin, but I'm nowhere near satisfied.

"That good, huh?" I repeat the words back to her when I pull my mouth off with an immodest sucking sound. Gazing up, I see that her eyes are closed, but she's smiling. A breathy laugh escapes her.

"Just touch me," she moans, not looking down at me.

I laugh, a rumble deep in my chest. When my mouth returns to her nipple, my hands move to unbutton her shorts. Sophie wriggles beneath me as I lower the zipper and then her hands are out of my hair and impatiently pushing the denim down her hips.

There's a severe lack of anything beneath the denim and another curse tumbles from my lips as my hands grasp that bit of skin between her hips and the tops of her thighs. So soft, so malleable, so delicious. Why do I want to bite it?

I raise up, allowing Sophie to lift her hips and maneuver so that she can pull the shorts down completely. Once they're off, I grab them and toss them in the same direction as her shirt. Her legs fall on either side of me once more and she's completely open to my gaze. With one raised eyebrow, she stares at me, not a hint of shyness to be found. The woman's confidence is impressive. Not that she has any reason to be self-conscious.

I move forward, lowering my lips to hers, but after only seconds, I forge a path south, down her neck, across her breast, avoiding her nipple. I kiss the soft flesh of her belly, the attention causing one of her hands to fly into my hair again. Then when I reach the skin between hip and thigh, I do exactly what I've been wanting to. I sink my teeth in, gently, slowly.

Sophie moans and bucks her hips. I file that away for later and trail kisses over the top of her thigh, inhaling the scent of her arousal. It drives me fucking wild. There's a little voice in the back of my mind, asking if I can do this, if I can *really* please her, but I'll never know if I don't try.

I raise my head to make eye contact, silently asking one last time for consent. Sophie's gaze drifts down and even if she didn't nod, I'd know by that fire in her eyes that it's a resounding yes.

I plant kisses across her skin, placing my hands on her knees to widen her legs. She allows the movement and I sink down to get a better angle. I tease with my lips and my tongue, along the outskirts of her absolutely soaking wet pussy.

"Please." It's a hoarse whisper from above me and I grin into her skin with a low chuckle.

"So impatient." I have no idea where my confidence comes from, but Sophie seems to like it because she moans again. "Tell me what to do," I breathe against her. "Tell me what you like."

"I need your mouth." She sounds as desperate as I am. It seems that's all the instruction I'm going to get.

Without giving her any warning, I press my tongue against her entrance and lick my way up until I find her clit. Using one hand to spread her, to give me better access, I begin to suck and tease and swirl my tongue, causing her to squirm. Her hips buck and a string of curses falls from her lips.

"You taste so fucking good." The words tumble out, muffled by her pussy because I refuse to move my mouth even for a second.

"Brody."

Hearing my name on her lips forces a groan from me, the vibrations soaked up by her body.

"Use-" she chokes and then gasps when my teeth graze her clit. "Use your fingers too," she begs. I lift my mouth and she whines.

"Is this what you want?" I slip two fingers inside her, watching in awe as the first knuckles disappear and then the second.

"Fuck." She draws out the word like a sigh. "Yes, now-" she grunts, "curl them upward like this." She shows me what she wants with one hand.

I adjust so I have the right angle and begin to do as she says, watching her face for a reaction. She's so fucking tight around my fingers and her hips move when I crook them upward.

"Like this?" I ask.

"Yes," she whispers. "Just like that, keep going."

I press my thumb to her clit, circling it while curling my fingers inside her. Sophie cries out, arching her back while her hips chase my movements.

"So fucking wet for me." My eyes drop to her pussy as I slide a third finger inside.

"Oh god." With her head thrown back, I can't tell if her eyes are open or closed, but the moans tell me I'm doing something right.

"My name is Brody," I chuckle, "but I'll accept god."

"Shut up," she laughs breathlessly. "But don't shut up. Keep talking."

"You want me to talk to you?" My fingers pick up speed and I growl when I feel her respond. "Want me to tell you how beautiful you look in my bed, with my fingers inside you? How much I enjoy feeling your pussy clench?"

"Fuck, yes."

"I want you to come on my face," I continue, lowering my mouth to her clit while continuing to work my fingers.

The moment my tongue swirls over her, she bucks again, her thighs closing in, but not tight. I don't stop her, keeping my focus on her pleasure and nothing else.

"Brody," she whines. "Please, just-" She grunts, the sound guttural and animalistic. "Fuck!"

Without warning, her thighs close completely like a vice and I can feel her walls fluttering around my fingers. I keep going, keep playing with her while her body convulses above me. One of her hands flies to my hair, pulling hard. Then her body stiffens, no noise coming from her. Her muscles haven't stopped spasming around fingers and I'll be damned if I'm going to cut this short for her.

Seconds tick by and then she's trying to pull my head away.

"Brody," she whimpers. "S-stop. You h-have to st-stop." She gasps every other word, begging, her thighs releasing me.

Before lifting my head, I allow myself one more indulging lick. I crawl forward just a little, settling my chin on her stomach and staring at her. My chest is directly against her wet center and I don't give a damn that she's going to leave a spot on my shirt.

"How was that?" I know the answer. I *felt* the answer. I want an evaluation anyway.

"You sure you've never done that?" she asks breathlessly, still panting. She doesn't look down at me.

"Sounds like a good review."

I move again, kissing my way up her body until I reach her lips. I have no idea if this is appropriate, kissing her when I've just had my face between her legs, but I know she'll stop me if she doesn't like it. Thank goodness she does, her tongue exploring my mouth instead of the other way around. It even darts outward, licking the remnants of her from my chin. She tilts her head to continue what her tongue has done, moving along my jaw and back again.

"I taste so good on your skin," she murmurs before her lips reach mine.

"Can I just stay right here?" I ask, breaking the kiss and shifting back down her body just a bit. "Right here between your thighs?" Sophie grins.

There's a sheen of sweat over much of her body and face. Thin hairs are plastered to her temple and she's panting, trying to regain her breath.

"If that's what you want," she sighs.

"It's absolutely what I want." My tongue pokes out of my mouth to wet my bottom lip as my eyes rake over her face and chest. "But first," I add with a mischievous grin. I move again, lowering myself between Sophie's thighs again. "That's quite the mess I need to clean up."

"Brody," she giggles as I press my lips to her inner thigh. "You don't-" she cuts off with a gasp when I move to her clit again. "That's not-"

"Sophie, do me a favor," I growl, my face still making full contact with her pussy.

"Anything," she sighs.

"Shut up unless you're telling me how to make you come harder."

Her only response is another moan when I slide two fingers inside her.

"Still so wet for me," I muse. "So greedy." I smirk but in the back of my mind, I'm still confused by my own confidence. "Is the guy I'm competing with not giving you what you want?"

I shove my fingers as deep as I can while my chin is in the way and curl them, pulling another whimper from her. I could listen to that sound forever. I could stay here forever. Sophie squirms, her hips writhing, trying to chase my lips, my tongue, my fingers.

"That's it, sweetheart," I hum, feeling her begin to tense around me just before she explodes again. "Come for me again."

A cry rips from her throat, her back arching before she goes still, unable to move as her orgasm takes over. Just like before, I keep sucking, keep working my fingers. I've never felt so exhilarated. I've never felt so utterly satisfied as I do knowing that I can bring a beautiful woman like her so much pleasure. I wonder how many orgasms I can wring from her.

When Sophie begins to relax again, I pull my fingers out and flick my tongue against her clit once more. Breathing heavily, I crawl back up her body, wedging myself between her legs like before, my face just below hers, but raised so I can see her eyes. A bead of sweat runs from her temple into her hair and her eyes are closed while she tries to catch her breath.

When her eyes flutter open, finding me, she reaches down for the fingers that were just inside her. Maintaining eye contact, Sophie pulls them to her mouth and sucks greedily, cleaning them off. I groan when her tongue slides between and around them, letting loose another curse. Sophie grins, allowing my hand to drop to her belly.

"I know that you know what you're doing to me," I groan.

"I know *exactly* what I'm doing," she laughs. She's treading lightly, not asking the question I see in her eyes. Ignoring it, I look down and kiss her stomach before resting my chin on my hand.

"Any notes?" I tease.

"I'm sure I'll think of something when I review this later."

"Oh?" I raise an eyebrow.

"Of course. I'm a classic overthinker, even the good stuff."

"So, it was good." I smirk.

"Adequate." She shrugs. "Are you just going to stay like that all night?"

"Can you blame me?"

"Yes, actually. I've never met someone who was content to stop there."

I reach forward, pulling a stray curl behind her ear.

"I'm starting slow. That ok?"

"Your pace," Sophie reminds me. There's no judgment in her eyes. "What's going through that head of yours?" she asks, reaching a hand so she can tap my forehead with her finger.

I catch her hand and bring it to my lips, kissing her knuckles gently and then brushing my lips across them.

"Just wondering what I have to do to keep you."

# 19

## Miles

Topher Star's apartment is about as nice as any I've been in, especially for a content trade. I've experienced gorgeous sets for larger productions, but for a simple collaboration, this takes the cake.

I run a hand over my face as I sink into his couch with a groan.

"Sore?" Topher laughs at me from the kitchen. I don't really need aftercare for tame scenes like the one we just filmed, but he insists on feeding me.

"I'll be ok." I reach for the bottle of water on the coffee table and feel some of the lube still slick on my ass cheeks. It's going to take a long shower to get everything off–and out–of me.

"Good." Topher nods and reaches into the fridge for the huge bowl of what he calls cowboy caviar–a midwestern name for corn salsa. "Next time, we'll have to switch it up. I think the viewers are getting bored seeing you bottom so much."

"We both know that's not true." I smirk, watching him over the bottle as I take a sip.

Topher joins me on the couch with individual bowls of salsa and a bag of lightly salted tortilla chips. We're both fully clothed in his chilly apartment. I've even drawn a blanket over my legs.

"Anything new with you?" asks Topher. His blue eyes take me in, studying me. If he sees anything different about my demeanor, he doesn't mention it. "I've been talking to some production companies. You're always the first name I recommend."

"I've been told." I moan when I take a bite off the chip in my hand. The salsa is spicy, but not so much that I can't handle eating an entire bowl like it's a meal. The red onion is strong, but that's the way I like it. It's a good thing this is a *post*-shoot snack. "Thanks again, man. I really appreciate it. Some of the companies I've worked with have been really amazing."

"If you sucked, I wouldn't be giving your name to everyone I work with." He waves a hand at me before chowing down on his own chip and salsa combo.

"I do suck." It's a stupid joke, but I'm never going to pass it up.

"You know what I mean," Topher says through a mouthful of food and rolls his eyes.

"Yeah, but I appreciate it. Really. It's hard to find someone you can just vibe with, you know?" I bite into another chip, staring down at the bowl.

"Working with anyone new lately?" He pauses. "Oh, I saw that selfie with... what's her name?" He frowns, trying to think.

"Honey Dee Vine?" I ask. She's the only new partner I've had outside of industry events or pro shoots in several months.

"That's it!" He points at me with a chip. "Yeah, how's she to work with?"

"She's great." She's fucking amazing. "Super fun, very easy to work with. Professional, too."

"She's gorgeous. I haven't worked with a woman in a while. Do you think she'd do a threeway with you and me?"

"Funny you should mention that." I grin. "She literally *just* told me the other day that an MMF threeway is on her bucket list. We'll have to make that happen."

"If you think she'd be up for it, feel free to ask. I'll make time."

"I'll keep that in mind," I reply with a nod, wondering if I should divulge the other bit of information about her. "Have you ever dated anyone in the industry?"

"A couple people, yeah. Sometimes it works out, sometimes it's awful. Depends more on the person, you know? Why? You thinking this latest collab might be something more?"

"I, er," I rub my eyebrow with a thumb, looking away. "We actually already went on a date."

"Shit, man. That's good, right?" He turns a little more toward me, his food forgotten. "Or isn't it? I can't read that expression."

"No, it's good. She's," I groan, "amazing. But how do you keep that kind of thing separate?"

"You've dated other creators before, right? How did you work things out then?"

"I don't think I should use previous experience."

"Maybe not." Topher shakes his head, then takes a deep breath. "Well, clearly I'm not amazing at dating in general. I'm still single, but my advice is to just talk about it with her. Figure out what each of you can and can't accept someone doing. Rules about working with other people, communication. All that good stuff."

"Good advice." I nod, absently. "I guess I just want her to know I want more than sex. I'm worried that she might think it's all I care about."

"Definitely a good thing to worry about. I'm afraid I'm not much help there. Hyper-sexual idiot here." He raises his hand sheepishly and I chuckle. "I'm all about sex on the first, second, third, fiftieth date."

"We didn't fuck after the first date."

"That's good. Leave her wanting more."

I throw my head back and groan.

"I almost want to stop working together until we- until I can-" I'm not sure how to finish the thought.

"Well I don't know why you're talking to me and not her." He shrugs and returns to his snack.

"Super helpful, thanks, man."

I *have* to edit today. I've been putting off cutting new footage together from the last couple of weeks, unable to focus. Motivated by my phone nearly vibrating its way off my desk with responses to my latest post, I plant my ass in front of my computer and pull up some footage from a scene with a local couple from two weeks ago.

In the video, the boyfriend and I used his girlfriend like a toy. It was incredible and I know it'll sell well. As I edit, cutting out discussions about changing positions or the time the woman needed us to pause for a moment, the urge to stroke myself becomes impossible to resist.

I work through the footage, working my cock at the same time. I fucking love this job.

My phone buzzes again with a single notification and I smile. A certain adult actress has commented on my post about editing a new clip.

@HoneyDeeVine replied:
Can't wait to see what you've got cumming out!

She ends her message with a GIF of a woman fanning herself.

I grin and like the message, then return to editing.

It takes three hours to finish the video which ends up being nearly an hour in length. I add my opener to the beginning, my logo as a watermark in the corner, and then export the final product to my external hard drive for safe keeping. Next, I create a thirty-second teaser.

Once the teaser and final video are finished, I set about the tedious task of uploading the video to all of my pages for publication at the beginning of October. Nothing like a slow upload to a clip site to make my dick soft. I don't understand how it takes some sites forever and others just a minute or two to upload a video. *Get it together, people.* On top of that, they have the audacity to take 20-40% from the content creators that use them.

*Fucking thieves.*

---

After Topher and I talked yesterday, I feel even more confused about how to proceed with Sophie. But she asked me to come over to film this afternoon and I'm not about to pass up a chance to have her to myself.

She opens the door before I can knock and I smirk.

"Couldn't wait to see me, hm?"

"Well, we've got work to do." Her amber eyes are sparkling.

Her hair is set in the usual soft curls, framing her face, and she's wearing a simple pair of cotton shorts and a plain black t-shirt. I'd love to see her in one of my T-shirts. The thought of it stretching across her breasts makes my dick twitch.

*Down boy.*

"Oh, we do?" I raise an eyebrow, stepping inside. This time, she leaves me to close and lock the door and immediately heads upstairs.

"Of course. I have some new ideas we can work on." Sophie's still talking when I reach the top of the stairs, hot on her heels. "I was editing our first video and there were some moments I'd like to recreate. I think they'll do really well."

She falls silent when I gently grab her hand, not enough to pull her to a stop, but she does so anyway. I lick my bottom lip when Sophie turns to face me. The amber in her eyes is barely visible, her pupils so dilated.

"I have a question for you." My voice is low and raspy.

"You gonna ask me out again?" Her tone matches mine as she tilts her head to one side. She's still standing a foot away, our arms outstretched slightly between us.

"Yes, but that's not what I want to ask."

I step closer, moving my hand from hers and sliding it up her wrist, her forearm, all the way to her shoulder. My touch drifts across her collarbone and then to her throat before I wrap my hand around the back of her neck, beneath her hair.

"Oh?" Her voice is breathy, barely a whisper.

I smirk, lowering my lips to her ear. She's going to slap me for this.

"Will you... peg me?"

Sophie pulls away, but only far enough to see my face clearly. Her brows are drawn into a frown and she pulls one hand up to playfully slap my shoulder. Ok, not as bad as I expected. She's giggling. We haven't talked about pegging, so I knew the question would throw her off.

"You idiot."

"I'm sorry, that was just too tempting."

"See if I go on another date with you now."

I lower my hand from her neck and take a step back to give her space.

"Oh, you will."

"Your confidence is ridiculous." She snorts and shakes her head, turning again to lead the way to the studio bedroom.

"I do actually have a question."

"Gonna ask me to join an orgy?" she asks, rounding the corner into the room.

"No, but good idea. Let's keep that in mind." I set my backpack down by the bedroom door, watching Sophie as she sits on the bed to face me. "I wondered if we could film something a little different. More voyeuristic."

"How do you mean?"

"We've filmed before, but I want to worship you." There it is again, that husky, velvety tone. I can't hide it from her and I'm not sure I want to anyway. I squat in front of her, having to look up now. Placing my hands on her knees, I continue. "I want to show you how much I appreciate you and not because you're everything I've ever wanted." Wow, ok, so I'm going there. "But because you clearly haven't been properly worshiped before." It was obvious the first time we worked together.

"What makes you think I haven't?" Sophie's throat works hard as she tries to swallow.

I lower myself to my knees properly, keeping my eyes on hers at all times. Softly pressing against her knees, I spread her legs to allow my torso to fit between them. I raise myself up so that I can brush my lips over hers, sharing her breath.

"Because I know damn well I made you come that first time and you were shocked." I kiss her quickly and then sit back on my heels. "So, what do you say?"

"That sounds way better than what I was going to suggest."

"You'll have to tell me what you had in mind. Later, though," I murmur.

She swallows again then clears her throat and averts her gaze, looking to her tripod in the opposite corner of the room.

"Give me your phone." I glance around the room, looking for her device. "I'll set things up. I just want you to get comfortable."

"Miles, are you sure?"

She's biting her lip when my eyes fall upon her face again. The uncertainty in her golden orbs would break me if I thought it was aimed at our intimacy, but that's not possible. No, she has to feel the way I feel–that this connection we have is something special.

"Am I sure I want to drive you absolutely wild?" I chuckle when my words cause her to flush, the rosiness just barely visible in her dusky cheeks.

"My phone is over on the dresser."

I hadn't clocked it, a black brick against the dark dresser. I nod and stand, but hear nothing behind me. No rustling of clothing or sheets. Sophie doesn't move. I feel her eyes on me and when I turn to hand over her phone for her to unlock, she does so without speaking. I find the camera app and set the phone in the tripod.

Continuing the process, I retrieve my own tripod and set my phone up in the same manner. My eyes sweep around the room, not pausing on Sophie who is still sitting on the bed, her legs over the edge. I don't like where the tripods are set. They won't allow Honey's adoring fans to see the ecstasy I plan to force into her expression or the way my tongue swirls around her clit.

Knowing now where her ass will be perched when lying on the bed, I set my tripod half a foot below that point for the right angle. I shorten it so that my phone will be a little above the mattress. I move Sophie's tripod up near the head of the bed, raising it as high as it will go to get the widest view possible.

Satisfied with my work, I hit record on Sophie's phone before rounding the bed to do the same on mine.

"Lay down for me." It's not an order, but a request. Sophie sucks in a deep breath and begins to take off her shirt, but I shake my head. "That's my job."

"I'm not used to this," Sophie whispers, moving to do as I've asked.

She scoots back onto the bed and then leans against the layers of pillows, biting her bottom lip. She can't have any idea what that does to me. Or maybe she does and it's part of her tactic to get me to fall so absolutely for her that I'll do anything she asks of me.

*Already there.*

"Not used to what?" I ask, kneeling on the bed from the end and crawling toward her. She glances at the cameras. "We can mute this." I freeze, my hands just inches from her shins.

"I'm not used to-" She stops, as if unsure of how to continue.

"Being worshipped," I finish, repeating my earlier words. Sophie nods and a thought occurs to me. "That competition of mine," I muse, "how does he treat this body?"

I slide one hand up and down left her shin, over the colorful floral tattoo. The hiss of skin-to-skin contact in the otherwise silent studio is utterly sinful.

"He," Sophie says hoarsely before clearing her throat. "He's good. I don't want to talk about him."

I grin, but inwardly, that single word has begun to chip away at my confidence. *Good.* It's noncommittal when combined with her tone. She doesn't want to talk about him. Fine. I'll make her forget about him. She won't even remember his name when I'm done.

Wrapping my hand around her calf, I lower my lips to the inner side of Sophie's knee. My tongue slips out, tasting her exquisitely soft skin before I start trailing kisses up her thigh. Quiet whimpers leave her throat and one hand tangles itself into my hair as Sophie tries to pull my mouth to where she needs it most.

"So needy already," I breathe against her. "Patience, Honey." Using her porn name feels wrong, but maybe if I think of it as a pet name instead. "We'll get there. First, I need to get these damn clothes off of you."

Crawling up her body without yanking those stupid shorts off of her feels wrong, but I didn't play with her tits last time. I'm determined to fix that mistake. I slide my fingers beneath her shirt, lifting slowly while Sophie rises up to help. She's wearing nothing underneath and I mutter a curse because she's fucking perfect. I knew that already, but it strikes me again anyway.

It's criminal not taking my time while I'm up here, but I want her desperate for me.

"So fucking gorgeous," I whisper as I slide back down her body, hooking my fingers into her shorts while she lies back again. "Lift."

Sophie does as she's told, lifting her ass off of the mattress so I can pull her shorts down. She shivers as her bare pussy is revealed to me. Any man who doesn't take the time to worship at this shrine clearly doesn't understand what true beauty is.

With the shorts off, she's completely naked beneath me. My hands find her feet, gliding up to her ankles, her shins once more, her knees. I can feel the goosebumps as they erupt along her tattooed skin, following my hand as it traces her thighs.

"Why is every part of your body so kissable?" I moan. "So lickable." To emphasize my words, my tongue darts out to taste her again. "So squeezable."

Her supple love handles are one of my favorite things. After my lips trace along one side, my hand massages, squeezing and molding it to my grip. I place kisses across Sophie's belly, following a few stretch marks, slightly darker than the surrounding skin. Her breasts, natural and heavy, fall to the sides a little, but her nipples are hard and stick straight up. I want to draw this out, but I can't. That one dark nipple inches from my face is too inviting.

When I take it into my mouth, the moan that escapes her does things to my dick that no other sound has ever done before—no other woman, either. Her hand, still in my hair, pulls tighter as I swirl my tongue around the pert little bud. Sucking and playing and grazing my teeth over it causes Sophie to writhe beneath me.

"Mi- Lance," she breathes, catching herself before saying my real name. I should've done this off-camera.

I pull my lips from her nipple with a pop.

"That's right Honey, I'm yours." My voice is low, almost a growl. "I'm all yours."

My mouth continues its path up her chest to her throat, her jaw, until I reach her lips. Capturing them with my own, I brace myself on one hand and cup her face with the other, my thumb down below her chin. My mouth devours hers, my tongue slipping inside to explore her as if it were entirely new territory. I allow my touch to drift down again, gliding down her neck and across her breast.

I'm half tempted to stop there, to squeeze and massage as I have been. But I allow my hand to move further south, back across her stomach and over the stretch marks that add to her beauty. Thank god she's not self-conscious about them. I might actually die if she ever hid herself from me.

Rotating my hand, my fingers graze the skin above her pussy, causing Sophie to jump and me to chuckle in response.

"Please." It's a hiss against my lips and I smile.

"Please what? Use those words, Honey."

"I need more." She sounds desperate. Good.

I move my hand just a touch further, brushing lightly across her pussy and feeling how wet she already is.

"More what?"

I know the phones won't pick up my voice and that my fingers are half blocked from view by my hand. It's not good for the video, but I'm beyond caring. My competition, whoever that fuckwad is, doesn't have this career to contend with. I won't let it come between us.

"I need-" She groans in frustration when my hand freezes. "I need you. Please, L-Lance."

I pull my face away. I want to make sure she understands every word.

"I didn't make myself clear," I say a little louder for her and the future viewers. "You're in charge here, Honey. I'm yours to order around. Tell me what you want and I'll obey."

"Fuck." The curse is a reverent whisper as she studies my face. The thought that those words I just spoke may have won her over enters my mind, but only briefly. There's still work to do.

I raise my eyebrows, smirking.

"You want me to fuck you already?"

That breaks her, causing Sophie's full lips to spread into a smile, a giggle bursting forth.

"Use your fingers." Her voice may not sound desperate anymore, but her eyes are frenzied and hungry.

"Yes, ma'am."

I wink and work myself back down her body, spreading her legs a little further so the camera can see what I'm about to do. Settling myself between her thighs, I rub my hand down her, feeling what my words and my mouth on her skin have already done. Licking my lips, I slide two fingers inside Sophie. She gasps at the intrusion and whines my name.

"Is this what you wanted, Honey?" Her stage name is growing on me. "You wanted me to feel how fucking wet you are for me?"

"Yes, I-I- oh!" She writhes her hips, seeking more. "Right there."

"Right here?" I repeat, curling my fingers in just the way that made her gasp moments ago. Sophie moans, her eyes closed as she continues to move, trying to feel more. "You're so fucking beautiful," I breathe, speeding up.

"Keep-keep going."

Her plea or her command, I do as she says. My fingers remain consistent even as the muscles in my forearm tire. I make a mental note to grab a toy for round two, but I want this first orgasm to be my doing entirely.

"Use your mouth." Now *that* sounds like a command, her voice deep and controlling.

"I thought you'd never ask."

I lower my face until I'm level with her pussy, continuing to work my fingers, just inches from the object of my desire. The scent of her arousal makes me absolutely feral with need. I flick my tongue out, tasting her clit, and Sophie emits a tiny squeak. The sound forces a smile onto my lips just before I close them around the sensitive bundle of nerves.

"Lance." My stage name is only a faint whisper.

"That's it." I don't want to take my mouth away from her, so I speak directly to her pussy, sending vibrations through her. "I want you to come for me, Honey."

Sophie's moans grow more desperate, her hips moving faster now as my fingers continue to work. I can feel the fatigue in my arm, but it's not so much that I'll stop. Swirling my tongue around her clit and then down, I continue to work her, trying to bring her closer to the edge.

Her walls begin to flutter around my fingers, the movements not yet what I'm looking for, but I know she's getting close. She moans louder, her movements erratic.

"That's it," I urge. "That's it, let go for me. Just let go and give me what I want."

When her orgasm hits her, Sophie's back arches, her legs stiffening. Her chest stops moving. I keep the momentum, drawing out the waves of pleasure for as long as possible. The sounds of my mouth on her are wet and obscene, sending blood rushing to my dick. Still fully clothed, I'm so hard I can barely stand it.

Sophie whimpers, her muscles slowing around my fingers. I give her one last slow, languid lick and pull my fingers from her. I place a kiss on the flesh just above her pussy before rearing up onto my knees.

Her eyes are closed, her chest heaving. Every few seconds, a spasm wracks her body–an aftershock. I wait for her breathing to slow, just watching her, resting my hands on her legs.

"You," she breathes heavily, "call that," another breath, "worship?"

I laugh, throwing my head back and squeezing her thighs.

"You don't think so?"

Sophie opens her eyes to meet my gaze. She licks her bottom lip before pulling it between her teeth. Her eyes rake over me.

"One orgasm ain't worship."

Keeping eye contact, I lift my hand and suck on the fingers that were just in her pussy, cleaning every last drop from them. Sliding my tongue between my fingers, I grin.

"Who said I was stopping at one?"

# 20

## Sophie

### Sophie

*Swoon.*

I have absolutely no idea what I did to deserve this man. Or Brody, for that matter. I've never had a partner, on- or off-camera, who cared so much about my pleasure. On film, it's always about the man's orgasm. The scene ends when he lets loose. Not that a creampie can't be faked, but it's not something I like to do if I can help it. A woman's pleasure? That can and *will* be faked. I don't know the statistics, but if it's less than 90% of the time in straight porn, I'd be shocked.

Yet, here I am—three orgasms down, covered in sweat despite keeping the place at or below 65 degrees. If the bulge in his pants is any indication, I doubt Miles is even close to done. He's giving me time to come down from this most recent explosion and it truly was an explosion. I'm not sure I'll be able to walk when we're done.

Miles kneels between my legs, sitting back on his heels. He's surrounded by a slew of dildos and a vibrating wand. I open my eyes again and smile with a breathy laugh.

"What's your record?" he chokes. I wonder if it's difficult to keep his eyes on my face when I'm bared to him like this.

"Th-three." I still can't breathe normally.

"That's it?" Miles raises an eyebrow.

"It's solo," I clarify. "My hand gets tired."

"Ok, what's your record *with* someone?" His hands on my thighs are distracting me. I can't think straight. To give myself a moment to think, I swallow and lick my lips.

*Zero* is the word that comes to mind, but then Brody's face looms in my memory and I grin.

"Two." I fell asleep after my second orgasm with Brody the other night and when I woke an hour later, I went straight home. No third O.

"Pathetic," he growls.

I struggle to sit up, bracing myself with my hands behind me.

"In his defense, I think I was his first. So two is admirable."

"He should've kept going." Miles shrugs as if it's simple. He leans forward, placing his hands on either side of me and bringing his face to mine. Our lips are close, so close, but not touching. "Two is pathetic, three is all you can manage on your own, but I told you I'm going to *worship* you and my offerings include a lot more than this." His words cause goosebumps to erupt across my body before he dips his head to kiss my neck.

"Miles." I don't care that I said his real name. I don't even want to release this footage to anyone. This is ours–private intimacy that feels like a secret we shouldn't share with our fans.

"Lance," Miles corrects between kisses down my body. I allow him to take control.

"I'm using your real name."

I swear there's a hint of laughter rumbling from his throat, but it's so soft that I wonder if I imagined it.

"You're in charge, Sophie."

"Then I'm gonna need you to fuck me already."

Miles' head pops up, his brown eyes connecting with mine. The fire there matches the one he's built inside me. His next movements are quick, practically jumping from the bed and frantically removing his clothes. Once naked, he stands before me, allowing me to take him in. I've seen it all before, but his sculpted torso, that V at his hips that makes girls stupid, his impressive cock–it all makes my mouth water.

"So you just want me for my body?" he teases as mischief mixes with the hunger in his eyes.

*And your hands.*

*And your mouth.*

"You caught me."

"Waiting on a command." Miles winks and, despite the flush creeping up my chest and into my cheeks, I'm not exactly embarrassed by my appreciation of his body.

"Get over here."

Miles kneels on the bed, crawling to me and settling between my legs. Bracing his body with one arm, he takes his other hand to position himself against my swollen and needy pussy.

"Please," I hiss just before Miles thrusts inside me, fully seated in one swift motion. "Fuck!" I squeeze my eyes shut. The toys he used on me stretched me, readied me.

"Look at me. Sophie, look at me."

My eyes snap open and find his immediately. He stares intently as he moves above me, grunting softly with each thrust.

"That's it," he breathes. His hand comes up to cup my cheek, fingers sliding into my hair as he moves. "Eyes on me, that's it. You're a fucking goddess, you know that?" he grunts.

"Yes." It's all I can think of to say.

"Of course, you fucking know." He laughs and lowers his lips to mine, pumping into me harder and faster.

I can feel another orgasm building, his cock hitting just the right spot. I reach a hand down between us, but Miles pulls my hand away.

"Let me," he growls against my mouth, swirling circles around my clit.

It's enough to set me off with a cry, my eyes squeezing shut again. My walls clench around Miles' cock, but he keeps moving, keeps thrusting. He leans his head down beside mine and, with my lips next to his ears, I whisper what I want next.

"I want-" I choke, my body still writhing beneath him, "I want you to fuck my ass."

Miles stills, his head jolting up. Jesus, I've never seen anyone look at me the way he is right this very second. His eyes were hungry before, but I have no words for what's staring back at me now.

"Lube," is the only word he seems able to say and I grin.

"Bedside table." I point to the side and, without pulling himself from me, he reaches over to find it in the top drawer.

"Roll over."

We do our little dance so I can get in position, but when I'm on all fours, Miles presses my lower back. I'm forced down to the bed, lying on my stomach, looking back at him while he straddles me. The cold lube makes me hiss, but then I feel Miles' finger sliding through it, spreading it around my puckered hole before he slips a finger inside.

I whimper, my pussy throbbing, jealous of the attention. When I press my ass up, Miles chuckles. He removes his finger.

"Just tell me if I need to stop," he says and I hear him squirting more lube, but it must be on his cock because I don't feel any hitting me.

He presses himself up against me and I whimper again, needing more. I gasp when his head pops all the way in and moan when he keeps going.

"So fucking tight," he groans. "This ass is so fucking tight, so perfect."

The more of him I take, the closer his torso gets to my back until he's practically lying on top of me. When he pulls out and then gently rolls his hips toward my ass, I swear my eyes roll backward. My legs are closed tight and I clench my thighs, getting a tiny amount of pressure on my clit.

"Fuck me," I beg. I know I'm supposed to be in charge, but I need him. I'm desperate for him to speed up.

"As you wish," he whispers before speeding up.

Miles pulls out, thrusting back inside, wringing a cry from my throat each time. His chest is slick with sweat against my back and I can feel his breath in my hair. He's so deep inside me that it feels like he's legitimately rearranging my guts. I wriggle my hips and he hits that sweet spot through the internal barrier once, twice, three times and then I explode.

My legs shake and my whole body tenses. I can't breathe, can't even cry out. My eyes are squeezed shut while Miles keeps fucking me. My muscles once more tighten around him, milking him, wringing a release from him. He thrusts again, completely filling me, whispering my name like a prayer, over and over.

My torso convulses with aftershocks for several minutes after I come down from the high. My eyes flutter open, but Miles is still above me, lying on top of me. He's still twitching inside me and moaning, holding some of his weight so as not to crush me, but I'm not sure I'd care if he did.

When his movements slow, his muscles relaxing, I grin, trying to look back at him. He takes a deep breath, blowing it down into my hair. He presses his lips to my cheek, then pulls out and rolls over and onto the bed next to me. I can't speak, still trying to get my breathing under control. I revel in the deliciously stretched and used feeling. A soft laugh escapes him, sounding almost like one of relief.

"What's so funny?" I reach up to move my hair out of the way and see that he's staring at me.

"I was going to try to last longer."

He doesn't seem embarrassed and I don't see why he would be. Any guy who takes that much time on a woman should be made a saint. I'm reminded that the bar is literally on the floor.

"I don't think I could've taken any more," I chuckle.

"We'll have to test that theory sometime." He rolls onto his side, propping his head up with one hand so he can look down at me while I roll onto my side for a better view of him. His expression is serious. "Look, I don't want to get things confused between us."

"Content versus just us?" I surmise. Miles nods.

"Is there anything you do to set boundaries with other creators?"

"You mean when I'm dating someone?"

"Yeah, to make things clear between us. I don't know if I'm explaining it right."

"I think I understand." I press my lips tightly together, but I do feel like he deserves to know. "I haven't dated since I got to LA," I start slowly. "My ex back in Oklahoma, I-" I take a deep breath because I've only ever admitted this to one other person. "I had to leave. In a hurry," I add quickly, the words tumbling out. "He's the only guy I've been with since I started making content and it didn't end well. I'm not sure I handled things the right way, but even if I did, I don't exactly want to use that relationship as a baseline."

Miles is silent, searching my face with worry in his eyes.

"My dating history track record isn't the best either. That's part of why I wanted to ask. I," he grabs my hand and brings it to his lips, "like you, probably more than I should." He smiles against my knuckles. "Was that too much to admit?"

"It wasn't too much." The words surprise even me, but I suppose it's true. I like him, I feel at ease, safe. "My ex, he... he wanted me to promise not to do certain things with the people I filmed with. Things he wanted to keep for himself, that would make him jealous if I did them with someone else."

"You don't need to relive that," says Miles softly. "We don't need to reopen those wounds. I just want you to know that, even though I'm working with other people, you're the only one I'm thinking about."

I have to smirk at that, arching one eyebrow.

"Even when filming with men?"

Miles chuckles and drops my hand to wrap his arm around my waist. His hand splays across my lower back and he pulls me closer. His face is inches from mine.

"I asked if you'd peg me."

I giggle, hiding my face in my hands. Another blush spreads into my cheeks when I look up at Miles again.

"You did, didn't you?" I sigh. "Let's work up to that one."

"You got it." He leans down to kiss my nose, then my eyelids when I close them, then each of my cheeks. "I meant what I said earlier. I'm all yours."

"This is weird." Natalie sits across from me at the kitchen table, eating her salad while I chow down on my burrito bowl.

"I know."

"No, but this is weird."

"I know," I repeat.

"No dating for like six months and then *BAM*! Two boyfriends."

I snort.

"They're not my boyfriends, they're-" I pause, trying to think of the right thing to say. "In training."

Natalie nearly spits out her salad.

"And are they trainable? Because most men aren't."

"Amen," I mutter before taking another bite. "I'm not gonna lie, I've never been so fucking satisfied."

"In bed, right?" Natalie stares over a forkful of salad.

"Yes," I laugh. "In bed. But they're also just *nice*. And caring. Brody stumbled a little, but he made up for it and Miles has that golden retriever energy you read about in books, but I've never met a guy that I thought fit that description."

"Just be careful he doesn't go chasing after another bone." She motions to me with her salad before stuffing the food into her mouth.

A text comes through on my phone and Natalie's head shoots up.

"Fan, filming, or fuckboi?" asks Natalie, nodding to the device.

"Brody. He wants to see me tomorrow." I stare at my phone with a grin. "His room-mate's out of town all weekend."

"Get it, girl!"

# 21

## Brody

Miles is in the kitchen buttering a piece of toast when I leave my office Friday morning. He's driving to Vegas this afternoon for the long weekend to film and it's going to give me several nights with Sophie with the house to myself.

"Gonna invite your girl over and have a fuck fest this weekend?" Miles waggles his eyebrows before taking a bite of his toast.

"Hello to you too." I can feel the blood rushing to my cheeks.

"Calm down," he chuckles through a mouthful of food. "I'm not asking for details."

"Not much detail to give," I admit, running a hand through my hair. I can't meet his gaze, instead walking over to the dishwasher and beginning to unload it.

"Wait, what?"

"I, er, I mean I haven't- We haven't" I can't continue.

"The fuck have you been doing?"

"Do I have to say it out loud?" I groan, turning to face him with a large mixing bowl in my hands.

"Yeah, you fucking do." Miles' toast lays forgotten on his plate. He crosses his arms and leans sideways against the kitchen island, waiting for an explanation.

"I've only-" I grunt in frustration, trying to find words that don't sound ridiculous. I fail. "I've only eaten her out," I grumble.

"You know there's more to sex than that."

"Excuse me for not diving in head first." I roll my eyes and turn my back to him again, putting the mixing bowl in the upper cabinet.

"You definitely didn't dive in *head* first." I can *hear* the smirk in his voice. "That's adorable." He snorts. "Glad I didn't get you that 'no longer a virgin' cake I was going to."

"What about you? Still keeping it PG with *your* girl?"

"Nah, I really connected with her yesterday. But *I* don't kiss and tell."

"You literally just did."

"Tomato, potato." He pauses and I hear him chewing while I continue with my chore. "Look, just take the weekend to show her a good time. With or without your cock."

"I'm going to smack you."

"My safe word is cucumber."

A few minutes after Miles heads out, my phone buzzes with a text from Mel–a reminder of our standing lunch date. She does it every month and I've never known if it was a test, but I haven't canceled in over nine years. I'm not about to start now.

I take the route I know well, down to Marina del Rey. The restaurant where I meet Mel once a month is nestled inside a luxury hotel. I'm not sure why she prefers this place. I've never asked, but they typically have a good menu with a lot of locally sourced ingredients as well as seasonal cocktails that she enjoys.

When I walk into the restaurant, the hostess glances up at me before continuing to organize the menus in front of her. I've seen her before and she knows Mel and I have a standing reservation. I don't need her help to find my boss in the small, mostly empty restaurant. Mel is sitting with her back to me, facing out over the water. The table is set right up against the threshold of the restaurant, though still inside. When it's nice out, huge windows collapse to the sides to allow an uninterrupted view of the marina. Today it's cloudy, but no rain is expected, so the windows are folded open.

"Punctual as always," Mel says in her velvety tone when I walk past her and pull out the chair to her right. I don't want to obstruct her view and the table seats four.

Her brown hair, tinged naturally with red, is pulled back into her usual tight bun. The front of her hair has some volume to it. Her hazel eyes are striking against her pale skin and her signature deep red lipstick is flawless as is her sleek, black pantsuit.

"Can't be late for lunch with my boss. What are you drinking?" I sit and scoot in my chair. Mel glances down at the cocktail in her manicured hand. It's purple with two edible flowers sitting on top.

"I believe this one is called Purple Mountains Majesty," she says with a smile. "I ordered your usual."

"Would you believe I wanted water today?" I ask, settling in and placing a napkin on my lap.

"Not for a second." She grins and watches while I pick up the menu.

The waiter arrives with my beer and then dashes away when Mel dismisses him. He knows the tip she leaves for excellent service is usually twice what the bill costs and it's always in cash—every server's dream. Mel Ashcroft is probably whispered about in awe, for the tip alone. I only worked as a server in my first two years of college and I remember only getting good tippers once in a blue moon.

"The new client," Mel begins after a few minutes of silence. "The one with all the documents." I set down the menu to meet her gaze. "I may take you off of the project."

"What?" I frown at her. She just gave me the project and it's not as if it's small. She knows it'll take time.

"It's nothing to do with you," she clarifies, absently straightening the silverware in front of her. "I simply think it's a lost cause. The client is difficult." She says the last word as if it's not quite right, but she can't find another to use.

"If you're sure." I watch her carefully. "Is there anything I can do to convince you not to take it away?"

"I thought you didn't want it." Mel studies me. "But no, there's not. I just..." she trails off, pulling both lips between her teeth and biting down for a moment like she isn't sure how to continue. "You know some of what we do is dangerous." I nod. She never involves me in that side of things. I wonder if something made her change her mind. "I think this may cross a line we don't usually cross."

"That's all you have to say." I trust her judgment.

Mel has never put me in harm's way. A policy of Harp Solutions is to keep every department, every individual employee, essentially separate. I don't know a single other person who works for her, but I know there are at least a hundred people on the payroll—which Mel takes care of personally.

"That simple, hm?" she asks, the corner of her mouth pulling upward in a smile.

"You're immovable, Mel. If you made up your mind already, I'm not going to waste my breath trying to change it."

"I knew I liked you."

"So, is that all you wanted to discuss?" I ask, looking down at my menu again. I haven't been able to focus on the words in front of me yet, so I have no idea what to order.

"Unless you accept my offer."

"I don't want to be the CIO," I mutter.

"Because it takes you away from the action," she sighs. "Fine, then I'll just give you another raise. What's the amount that'll make you feel so guilty you *have* to accept?"

"I don't know, how much are you willing to offer?" I tease with a grin.

"You're too good to be a grunt."

"If you had managers, I'd accept that," I shoot back. "Too bad there's so much secrecy."

"I thought you hated people."

"I do."

"I'll speak with payroll."

"*You're* payroll."

She narrows her eyes at me.

"Then I'll speak with myself."

"I like the freedom of being an individual contributor," I chuckle. "Can't you let me have that? At least for a few more years?"

"No."

I roll my eyes. Mel has been trying to promote me to CIO for two years now, asking me at every single monthly lunch. The job description she provided is so simple and boring, it means I'd be retiring. A lot of people would love that–earning an obscene amount of money and doing zero work is the dream. Not mine, of course. I may hate client interactions, but I like the challenges I'm faced with and I like the thrill. I came to terms with what our company does a long time ago.

Mel picks up her cell phone from beside her silverware and taps a few times.

"Your raise will be on your next paycheck."

"You've been trying very hard recently to get me to retire," I muse, setting my menu down again. I'll just order the chicken, any chicken. "What's going on? Is there trouble?"

I can imagine someone upset by their cheating spouse or their scornful parent might want to take their anger out on us. Nothing would ever come of it. Mel is very good at putting people in their place and getting what she wants, but nothing is safe forever. I can also imagine that some of the shadier dealings of Harp Solutions can get dangerous quickly.

"No, nothing like that." She's lying. "I just want to show my appreciation. You've been by my side from the beginning. You've never questioned me or my motives."

"I don't have to know *why* you're doing what you're doing." I shrug.

"Few people have put their trust in me the way you have. Can I not reward loyalty?"

"You can, just not with a forced retirement."

Now it's Mel's turn to roll her eyes, which she does in a very dramatic fashion, parting her lips with a sigh. If you were to look up 'eye roll' in the dictionary, you'd see a picture of her.

"One of these days," she chuckles.

"When you offer me enough."

# 22

## Sophie

### Sophie

I pull the sheets from the bed in the studio while Janey Romper gets dressed. Having just finished a scene, I want to quickly take care of this laundry so I can leave for Brody's on time. I don't want to feel guilty about leaving it for Natalie to deal with tomorrow.

I'm thankful Janey wanted to play the bottom for the scene. I'm not sure I could have taken on that role before seeing Brody tonight. Strap-ons are great, but toys just don't have the same *give* as real dicks. I'm not sure how anyone prefers dildos over the real thing.

Janey pulls on her shorts and wiggles as she yanks them up.

"Hey, do you have any local guys you can recommend for me?" she asks. "I'm looking for new ones to work with."

I pause, my arms full of dirty sheets. We've worked together several times over the last two months, but haven't discussed other co-stars much.

"Well, I just started working with Lance Kixxx," I offer. It shouldn't feel weird to recommend him, but somehow it does. It pulls at something in my gut after our time together yesterday.

"Professional?" She pulls her tank top over her head.

"Yeah. Why don't you reach out and tell him we work together? I'll give you a glowing review." I wink, fighting off the oddly possessive feeling.

"I'll talk to him. Lance Kixxx," she repeats.

"Three x's. I think he said he's out of town for the long weekend, but it sounded like he may be back before Monday."

"Awesome, thanks!" Janey slips on her flipflops and follows me out of the room. I drop the sheets by the washer to take her downstairs. "Let me know if you think of anyone else. I really need some new consistent content partners," she groans as I open the door for her.

"Am I not enough for you?" I feign shock, hand on my chest and mouth agape.

"You're *too much* woman for me," she laughs. I drop my hand and grin.

"I'll have a think. I've worked with a few that I definitely *wouldn't* recommend," I add with a grimace.

"I get it. I appreciate any suggestions. See ya!"

I close the door and practically stomp up the stairs, still not completely sure why I hated suggesting Miles. It's just work. I'm not possessive, I'm not jealous. I never have been. He's very obviously into me. If I doubted that before, yesterday made it perfectly clear.

The memories of his skills are enough to make even me blush while I dump the sheets into the washer and add the detergent. Just as I shut the door and turn around, Natalie leaves her bedroom. Her hair is still damp from her shower as she passes me, headed to the kitchen.

"Axe throwing tomorrow?"

"Yeah, what time is the reservation?" I follow her, but I need to shower as soon as possible.

"Three, I think. I'll double-check. That still work or will you be with one of your guys?"

"God, I hate that you just said that," I groan.

"And I hate that you're dating two men. We can't always get what we want."

"Unless *you're* going to take me off the market, I'm going to have some fun with this. I'm seeing Brody tonight, but Miles is out of town this weekend."

Natalie pulls the kettle from the stove and fills it with water before returning it to a burner. She twists the dial and the open flame sparks to life with a click.

"You talk about it so casually," she mutters, but there's a smile on her lips when she takes a mug from the upper cabinet.

"Is it really so bad that I'm enjoying my time with them?" I don't know how to do this. I'm a completely different person than I was when Caleb and I started dating. I don't know what the norm is anymore. What *my* norm is.

"No," Natalie sighs. She turns to grab a tea bag from her little wooden box on the counter and drops it into the mug. "I just want you to be careful. Men can get jealous."

"As if I don't know that."

Natalie shoots me a look, but then her expression softens.

"I'm sorry. I know you know what they can be like. We both do. I just worry about you."

I step up next to her and put my arm around her waist, then lean my head on her shoulder. She's a couple of inches taller than I am, so I don't have to lean too far.

"I know, Nat. And I love you for it."

Natalie gasps and spins out of my grasp to rush to the side wall enclosing the refrigerator. She picks the calendar up from its hook and grins at me.

"Time to change!" she exclaims, showing me the weird bird calendar. It's full of colorful drawings of birds, very simply done, but with human-looking legs. They're all ridiculous.

"What do we have for September?" I ask as she flips to the current month.

"Oh, look at this!" The drawing is of a yellow bird sitting with its human legs on the side of a bird bath.

"He looks sad."

"That bird is thinking about Shakespeare."

"Ok, but one of the sad Shakespeare plays." I snort.

"I mean, even the comedies were…" Natalie trails off with a look of disgust.

"The comedies are funny," I argue. "I was in a couple in high school." Thinking back, it's rather surprising that an Oklahoma school was allowed to do a play with crossdressing like The Taming of the Shrew.

"Oh," Natalie mocks, "I'm so smart, I read Shakespeare."

"I was in them in high school," I repeat, but Natalie ignores me.

"Look at me, I read Shakespeare for fun."

"I've never read Shakespeare for fun."

"Oh, lah-dee-dah."

I roll my eyes, giving up as Natalie hangs the calendar in its place and rejoins me at the stove.

"Seriously, if one of those boys even looks at you the wrong way, I'm throwing an axe at *him* instead of a wooden target."

I giggle and press a kiss to her cheek.

"Throw one of your crystals at him. That'll do some damage."

"Maybe I'll do a reading for you while you're out tonight. Figure out if either of them even deserve you."

"Sounds perfect." I dash away to hop in the shower, shouting behind me. "Love you!"

"Fuck off!"

I'm frozen to the spot. I've turned to stone. I can't fucking move. My hand is still on the handle of the front door, halfway to pulling it shut, but my eyes are fixed on my windshield. The note isn't from Janey. I watched her walk past my car, her hands full with her things. It wasn't there when she left, which means it was put there in broad fucking daylight and our doorbell camera didn't catch it.

Again.

Attempting to swallow the fear in my throat, I finish closing the door and lock it behind me. It's been over a week and like an idiot, I let myself start to think that maybe it was just a prank. Something a random teenager had left to scare someone they didn't even know.

With a trembling hand, I reach out to pick up the folded note. When I open it, I see one word scrawled in all caps. It's poorly written as if someone—Caleb—used his left hand. His non-dominant hand.

"I'm not his," I whisper to myself, trying to will the tears pricking my eyes not to gather. "I'm not his," I repeat.

*I'm not his.*

I'm not moving again.

I won't uproot my life again.

*Not again.*

Scrunching the note tight into a ball, I take it to the trash and drop it in, brushing my hands off when I'm done. They're still trembling when I slide into the driver's seat and start the car, ready to leave for Brody's.

By the time I reach his house, I'm a little calmer. My breathing has returned to normal, my face has regained its color. I'm not sure what Caleb's endgame is. Is he just trying to scare me? Make me come running back to him for some unknown reason? Does he think that will work? He can't possibly still want me after all the things he said to me. Can he?

Brody answers the door with a warm smile and my heart lifts. *Wow.* The bar isn't just low, it's embedded in the fucking ground. He's happy to see me and that excites me? Not to mention that I haven't even seen this man naked, but I can already feel that burning in my core because I know what he can do with his tongue and his fingers.

"I hope you're hungry," he says, allowing me inside.

*Yeah, for something other than dinner.*

"Of course. I like food," I giggle before his arms slide around my waist.

I let my head fall to one side as Brody's lips connect with the tender skin at the base of my neck. At first, his touch is light, almost tickling, but as his lips trail further up, the pressure grows. I hum in response before turning my head and he captures my lips in a kiss filled with need and desperation–a combination I've come to expect when his mouth is on mine.

Reluctantly breaking contact, Brody pulls me by the waist into the kitchen. He laughs when I shoot a disappointed look toward the bedroom.

"I'm determined to actually feed you this time."

"If you insist," I mutter, a smile playing on my lips.

Brody nods, his hands still on my waist.

"I do. Pizza ok?"

I barely register the two slices I devour or the movie that Brody puts on while we sit on the couch to eat. I can't keep my thoughts focused on anything other than him. Natalie would be so disappointed in me, but what she doesn't know won't hurt me.

When I stand to take my plate to the kitchen, Brody doesn't hesitate to follow. He rinses our plates and dries his hands on the towel beside the sink before turning to me.

"I was thinking about dessert." His voice isn't as light and casual as it was when I arrived.

"Oh?" I squint, studying him while one corner of my mouth lifts in amusement. "What did you have in mind?"

"I'll give you three guesses." He steps forward and, with the towel still in his hands, he brings them up and over my head, then uses it to pull me toward him.

"I'm only going to need one, aren't I?" I giggle, allowing my body to press entirely against his.

In answer, Brody lowers his lips to mine, softly dragging them back and forth with just a hint of contact.

"You just taste so fucking good," he growls. It sends a shiver down my spine, heat already coiling in my center.

"I think that's the pizza," I hear myself murmur against his mouth and feel his lips spread into a smile against mine.

"I didn't mean your mouth."

Before I have a chance to process what is a particularly smooth line, Brody backs me up, dropping the towel that was still holding me to him. His hands slide down my sides, heat exploding at every point of contact. He glances up at me when his fingers hook into the waist of my skirt, silently asking for my consent, and I nod. The fabric is pulled to the floor and I step out of it, hearing Brody groan. I didn't bother with underwear.

"God damn." He leans in, pressing a kiss against the flesh between my thighs.

Readjusting, he lifts his hands to the backs of my legs just above my knees. He hoists me onto the counter in one fluid motion and I gasp. I have to grab his shoulders to keep myself from falling backward onto the raised half of the counter behind me.

"Brody!" I'm not a squeaker, but I have never been lifted onto a counter—and so easily, too. He chuckles, the sound rumbling deep within his chest, as he cages me in. His hands on either side of my thighs, Brody leans forward to place a gentle kiss on my forehead. If I wasn't wet before, I certainly am now. The man is still taller than me by a head while I'm seated on the counter.

"Isn't this a little counterproductive?"

"You think so?" Brody steps between my thighs and I spread them as wide as possible, my skin catching on the smooth granite. He doesn't look down, instead reaching around to grab my ass, massaging the cheeks.

"I do."

Brody hums, sounding satisfied with himself, before slowly dropping to his knees. He presses his hands against the insides of my legs, keeping me open for him. His eyes are zeroed in on the spot where my thighs meet. With the extra weight on my body, my pussy still isn't visible, but I'm sitting just on the edge. All I have to do is-

"Lean back, Sophie," he breathes. When I hesitate, Brody stares up at me, the green of his eyes almost covered by his very dilated pupils. "Please."

That tone, the desperation–I can't react fast enough. The counter is cool beneath my hands as I lean back until I have to rest my elbows on the raised counter behind me. Brody doesn't follow me down, those green eyes staring, studying my body while it's bared before him.

"I know this is the most beautiful sight you've ever laid eyes on, but I need you to touch me."

He crouches and doesn't hesitate to act, his warm breath on my now bare pussy. I can't see if it's his lips or his tongue, but his touch is so light that I whimper, wanting more.

"Patience." Brody's muffled voice floats to my ears and I try to keep still. "We have all night. All weekend if we want."

Another shiver runs down my spine when Brody latches onto my clit. The sensation forces a curse from my lips and he keeps my legs apart while he feasts. He laps at my center like he's starving and I'm his first meal in months. He uses his teeth to rake across the most sensitive areas and I whimper and whine. His grip, tight on my legs, keeps me from moving, despite my efforts to follow his mouth with my hips.

"Brody, please," I beg again. The orgasm is building, but he's purposely keeping it at bay, not giving me what he knows I need to tumble over the edge.

"I could stay here forever," he moans, the vibrations causing that tight sensation in my lower belly to intensify.

He slides a finger inside and I whine, begging once more, but he just laughs, his mouth against me. His tongue slides along my center, drawing a gasp from my throat. It's still not enough. He's teasing me and I groan in protest.

"Keep begging," Brody chuckles. "Beg louder."

"Please." I raise my voice, reaching up to play with one of my breasts. "I n-need," I gasp, "more."

Then his mouth is gone and he's standing over me. He leans forward, his body covering mine. Brushing a hand through my hair, he stares down at me, those green eyes so penetrating. He rolls his hips, his pants and the erection inside them rubbing against my pussy.

"This what you want, sweetheart?" Brody asks, his voice husky with need.

I reach up to grab his shirt collar and pull him closer.

"Absolutely."

He kisses me, hard and aggressive like before. I can hear him unbuckling his belt and unzipping his pants while his mouth devours mine the way it devoured my pussy moments ago.

"I need to get-" He mutters a curse, pulling his lips away, but leaning his forehead against mine.

"No." I shake my head, knowing exactly what he's about to say. "It's fine. I have an IUD, we exchanged tests. I just need you inside me. Please."

Brody raises his head just enough to meet my gaze. He must see what he wants to–consent, enthusiasm, hunger, desire–because he nods and allows me to reach between us to grab him. I want to moan at the size. I've had big, Miles included, and Brody measures up to them in length. It's the girth that's fucking incredible. I can't actually wrap my fingers all the way around him. I wiggle my hips just a little, scooting closer to the edge of the counter. Brody grips my face in both hands while I line him up, rubbing his tip through my wetness before guiding him as he presses his hips forward.

"Fuck." His whispered moan is mirrored in my throat as he takes control, pushing deeper.

My eyes flutter closed and I focus on the sensation of his touch on my face, his cock stretching me. It's fucking incredible and I'm not entirely sure why this feels so different from almost every other man I've been with, but I'm not going to question it. His thighs meet the counter and he pauses. I'm having a hard time breathing through the indecently delightful full feeling.

"Thank you," he whispers.

"We're not done yet."

"I know, but," he swallows, his breathing ragged, "I need to make this last."

I move my hips and Brody *actually* growls. Not a word, a primal sound that makes me clench around him.

"Don't fucking move."

I move my hips again, a wicked smile playing on my lips.

"Oops." I wink when he meets my gaze.

"Brat." He speaks through clenched teeth, but I don't have time to respond.

Brody's lips cover mine and he slowly pulls out before thrusting back in. His movements become furious and somewhere in the back of my mind, I wonder if the counter is going to leave bruises on his legs. He holds the back of my neck with one hand and my hip with the other, squeezing tight. At this angle and with this kind of aggression, he's going to make me come quickly. I can feel it building again, the pressure between my legs about to burst. I don't even need any extra stimulation, I realize, just before the waves take me.

A rush of wetness accompanies the orgasm as my pussy releases a flood around him. I moan and Brody captures it in his mouth. He makes one more hard thrust and freezes, but he's not finished yet. His lips are still against mine when he speaks.

"I-" he chokes.

"Let me down," I breathe just as my muscles finally begin to relax. I need to move fast. "Let me down and lean back against the counter."

He does as I say and I bite back a whimper when he pulls out. Watching me carefully, Brody reaches backward until he finds the island and leans against it, waiting. His erection is sticking straight out, hard as a rock. I wiggle back and forth until I can hop down from the counter. I immediately sink to my knees so that his cock is right at the level of my mouth. I meet his hungry gaze from beneath my lashes and smile. Then I place one hand on his thigh for stability and use the other to gently grasp the base of his cock. He moans when I tease his tip with my tongue, flicking it out to taste myself on him. The air is filled with the scent of me.

When I wrap my lips around his head, he hisses, closing his eyes. One hand sinks into my hair, his grip tight, but not controlling. I slowly bob my head, each time taking more of him into my mouth until he hits the back of my throat. My jaw is going to be tired after this, but when I raise my eyes again, his head is thrown back. The knowledge that he's enjoying this is all I need to keep going. I swirl my tongue as I pull him out of my mouth.

"You can control me," I say softly. His head snaps down, eyes finding mine. I remove my hand from his thigh and place it on his where it's still tangled in my hair. "Here." I press on his hand and then return mine to its perch. "It's ok," I urge, then let my voice drop to a sultry, deep tone. "Fuck my face, Brody."

Brody swallows and nods. Maintaining eye contact, I open my mouth and he presses my head forward. I take him into my mouth again and he slowly puts more and more pressure on my head as I move. Each time he pushes me to take more of him, but then it's my choice to stay pressed forward, gagging myself. Just for a moment. When I pull my mouth off of him, I have to gasp for air before getting back to work. It's a delightful kind of work that I'm more than happy to do. Brody reaches up with his other hand, fully controlling my movements now. I allow him to dominate me, my eyes shut as tears form.

"Sophie," Brody grunts when I reach up to cup his balls. "I'm-"

He tries to pull me off, but I don't let him. Pushing my head forward, I take as much of him as I can and his hands pull my hair hard. He grunts as his cock twitches and I feel him coating my throat. He's so far back, cutting off my air supply, that I can barely taste him. My body convulses in protest, but I don't let up.

When his orgasm subsides, I pull my head back, gasping for air again. I sit back on my heels and lick my lips. Brody let go of my hair at some point while he was coming. I smile up at him, knowing my mascara is probably a wreck. His eyes are closed while he tries to get his breathing under control. I rub one hand gently up and down his thigh.

"You ok?" I ask, licking my lips.

Brody swallows and opens his eyes to look down at me with admiration. He grabs my hand and helps me stand, pulling me forward by my waist so that my body is pressed fully against him.

"I think ok is an understatement," he laughs.

"Great?" I ask with a grin, wrapping my arms around his neck.

"Magnificent, stupendous, amazing, what's another word for all of those?"

"I think you covered it." I stand on my tiptoes to kiss him quickly. "But I mean it. Are you ok?"

"I mean it too. I'm wonderful."

A buzzing fills the room and I realize it's my phone vibrating on the counter. It keeps going and I have to wonder who's calling me. No one *calls me* unless it's scheduled. They always just text.

"Do you need to get that?" asks Brody, nodding toward the phone when he sees my frown.

"I'm sure it's fine."

"Much as I want to keep you here, it's ok if you answer the phone."

I sigh and step out of his embrace, walking around the counter. I'm very much aware of my nakedness and Brody's eyes following me. I frown when I see the name flashing on the screen.

"Natalie?" I ask, holding the phone to my ear. "Are you ok? What's wrong?" I look at Brody and hold my hand over the receiver. "She never calls me."

"Soph, I'm ok, but I think it's Caleb." She sounds shaken. "I think he tried to break in. The doorbell camera keeps cutting out and someone kicked in the front door while I was making dinner." The fact that she's getting the words out is impressive because I'm scared shitless. I doubt I'd be able to talk after that.

"Did he hurt you? Did you call the police? I'm coming home."

"Nothing else happened, Soph. He didn't come inside. I called the police and they're sending someone over so I can file a report." She pauses and I know what's coming next. "Can I please tell them?"

"No." The word is louder than I intended and I wince. "Sorry, but please don't say anything to them."

"Sophie, this is dangerous."

"I'll-I'll deal with it."

"If it happens again-"

"I know." I continue to stare at Brody. The concern is clear on his face. "I'm coming home."

"I'll drive you," says Brody as I hang up. He bends over to grab my skirt and toss it to me.

"No, it's ok. You don't have to." I pull my skirt on and try to wipe some of the mess from my chin and cheeks.

"What happened?" He's fastening his pants as he speaks. "Is your roommate ok?"

"She's fine, but someone tried to break in."

"Jesus, don't you guys have an alarm system or something?"

"We don't usually set it at-" I look at the time on my phone, "seven in the evening." No need to mention the glitching doorbell cam, which I'm sure didn't catch the intruder.

"Fair. I'm still taking you home."

We take my car. Brody offered to order an Uber to get home when he's satisfied that I'm safe. No amount of arguing was going to stop him from coming with me.

Natalie greets us on the driveway, arms folded around herself, and I run to hug her.

"The police already left," she says into my hair, holding onto me tighter than she ever has. "They said there's not much they can do without evidence."

"Fuck, Nat, I'm so sorry," I whisper, though I suspected that would be the case.

Tears prick the backs of my eyes and threaten to slide down my cheeks. I can't believe my past has put her in danger. Of course Caleb would find me. How could I be so naive as to think he wouldn't?

"Hey, I'm Brody." His voice snaps me out of my thoughts.

I step back and let Natalie get a good look at the man I definitely didn't plan on bringing over. She smiles weakly and steps forward to hold out a hand. Natalie takes it, shaking briefly.

"Natalie."

"Lovely to meet you."

"Right back at you." She looks at me. "Let's go inside."

Natalie sits on the sectional, a couple of cushions away from Brody, but I set to work making her favorite calming tea, filling the kettle, and setting it over the lit burner.

"Not to intrude," says Brody slowly, "but you said your doorbell cam isn't working?"

"It's been on the fritz," Natalie says with a nod.

I stay in the kitchen, waiting to hear the kettle whistle. After I grab a mug and the tea bag, I lean against the kitchen counter, in front of the sink, so I can see the two of them.

"Does it just work some of the time?" Brody continues.

Natalie raises an eyebrow at me.

"He's a tech nerd," I say with a shrug.

"To put it simply," Brody chuckles.

"Yeah, we've only noticed a couple times where it cuts out," Natalie says, facing him again. "Do you think it's just the connection or something?"

"Could be," he says slowly, rubbing his chin. "I can take a look if you're both ok with it. I don't want to intrude."

"I think that's a good idea." It's Natalie who responds. I'm a little surprised that she's so comfortable with this, given her evening. Trusting a total stranger with our security after getting our front door kicked in doesn't feel like a Natalie move.

"If one of you can pull up the account on a laptop, I'll head downstairs to take a look at the camera itself first."

When Brody is gone, Natalie turns to me.

"Ok, I know I've had a shit night, but that man looks better than his picture."

I snort. The kettle begins to whistle, so I turn off the burner and pour the hot water into her mug, over the teabag. I add a squirt of honey and then walk the mug over to her.

"You smell like sex," she says before taking the tea. "Slut."

"You caught me," I giggle.

"I *will* be wanting details."

"How can you think about that at a time like this?" I shake my head with a smile.

"Because I'm a slut too." She grins a little too wide and squints. "Think we should reschedule our date tomorrow?"

"Fuck." I completely forgot about axe throwing. "Yeah, I'll call them in the morning. Send me your schedule for next week and I'll get it taken care of."

"Well, I don't see anything wrong on the device," Brody calls up before closing the door and rejoining us upstairs.

"I've got my laptop right here," says Natalie, pulling it from the coffee table and logging in. She opens the website and pulls up the device before handing the laptop to Brody.

He takes it and resumes his seat on the couch.

"If the actual camera is ok, then what do you think the problem is?" I ask.

"Could just be a bug. Maybe an issue with the last update. I haven't heard about any problems with this specific service, but you never know."

He types and clicks around as if he knows exactly what he's doing. I remind myself that I don't really know much about his job. Hell, I barely know *him*.

He frowns and his clicking and tapping slows.

"I don't really see anything wrong here." He licks his lips and looks between Natalie and me. "I can do some digging at home. I have some programs that may give me a better idea of what happened." He clenches his jaw before speaking again. "Would you two want to stay with me for a couple days? Just until the lock can be fixed."

"I don't know," says Natalie.

"I'm sure it feels weird to leave when you can't even lock up your things, but you might be safer."

"I'll be ok, but Sophie, maybe?" She looks at me. "I'll be fine. I'll sleep in the office downstairs if I have to." That room has a separate lock on the door leading to the patio and the one leading into the garage. If we can't lock the front door, that's the only other secure place in the townhouse.

"Nat, I-"

"It's fine. I have my tea, I have Netflix. I'm all good now."

My lips form a tight line as I study her. Either she's a better actress than I gave her credit for or she really is ok. Must be all that feminine rage she channels for her domination sessions. She knows Caleb doesn't care about her. If it *was* Caleb tonight. I find myself hoping so. Otherwise, we might have even bigger problems than an obsessive, abusive ex.

"Yeah." I sigh and turn back to Brody. "Yeah, that might be a good idea."

# 23

## Brody

I don't like that Natalie turned down my offer. I just met her, but Sophie cares about her, so I care about her. I don't like that she can't lock her front door, even if it's just overnight, but she wouldn't be swayed.

I carry Sophie's bag into the house. It feels so bizarre to think about the fact that, just a couple hours ago, Sophie and I were right here in the kitchen, having two more firsts together. I suppose we're about to have another one since she agreed to spend at least one night with me, though I'd prefer it to be under different circumstances.

Setting the bag by the counter, I turn to see Sophie looking around the house as if she's seeing the mostly bare walls for the first time.

"Can I get you anything?"

"No, I'm ok." Her eyes drift to me, but they don't seem to focus.

I close the distance between us slowly, allowing Sophie the chance to step away or stop me. She does neither, instead allowing me to come within inches of her. It forces her to crane her neck to meet my gaze. I reach up to run my fingers through her hair, combing it back and off of her neck. Sophie leans into my touch, closing her eyes and breathing deep as she fits her cheek into my palm.

"I'm ok," she repeats, sounding more like she's trying to convince herself than me.

"Natalie didn't seem that worried." I tread carefully, not wanting to sound accusatory. "Is there something I should know before I look a little deeper?"

Sophie's eyes snap open and I can see the answer there. Yes, there's more, but she doesn't know if she can trust me.

"Brody, I'm just scared," she whispers.

Fuck, are those tears? Her brown eyes swim with them, but she clearly doesn't want them to spill over. I lean down to kiss her.

"Hey," I whisper against her lips, "it's ok. You don't have to say or do anything you don't want to." I pull back again. "I just want you safe."

Sophie sighs, closing her eyes again before turning away from me and out of my grasp. She rubs her hands over her sides, up and down her hips, and then spins to face me again.

"I don't-" She groans and shakes her head. "I don't talk about my ex a lot." Her tongue darts out to wet her lips. "I don't know if it's him," she says hastily when she notices my frown. "But it- Well, it didn't end well with him. I think maybe he's trying to, I don't know, get me back? Scare me?"

She groans again and turns her back, running her hands through her soft curls. I don't move to close the distance between us. I don't want to crowd her. My blood boils at the thought of someone–anyone–scaring her. What if he's done worse in the past? Did she end it or did he? These questions and a million more fly through my head, but I won't ask them. She let me reveal my secret when I was ready. I will to provide her with the same safe space.

"Sophie, it's going to be ok. Let's get ready for bed. Maybe put on a Disney movie or something to lighten the mood."

"Yeah, that sounds good." Her voice breaks on the last word.

---

I make an excuse not to immediately join Sophie in bed, saying I want to do some digging into the doorbell cam before a potential trail goes cold. After watching her snuggle beneath my blankets, I shut the door and head into my office. It only takes a few minutes to get into the system that I know will give me a backdoor into Sophie and Natalie's doorbell cam. It's not the kind of software everyone has access to. I wrote it specifically for Harp Solutions. If it wasn't a matter of safety, I wouldn't be using it outside of work.

Something's wrong. Something's off. There's activity here that shouldn't be there. Someone–and I'd bet my entire bank account that it wasn't the girls–has been logging in and removing footage, altering the notification settings and then returning them to the way they were before. But the changes and alterations are happening within minutes of each other. If it *is* Sophie's ex, he's got help.

Taking a deep breath, I set about putting in some safety measures. Silent notifications to my phone, a way for me to view any and all footage because I'll get sent backups every thirty seconds. Everything I can think of to give the girls the upper hand, I do. It won't be enough, of course. If Sophie has a crazy ex-boyfriend out there trying to scare her, I worry he won't stop until he does something truly drastic.

When I go back to my bedroom, Sophie is lying on her side, facing the door. Her hair is splayed out on the pillow behind her. Her eyes are closed and her breathing is steady. I lean against the doorway, watching her. There's an angel sleeping between my sheets and I can't wait to join her.

---

"That was Nat." Sophie holds up her phone as she walks back into my bedroom, still wearing her cotton pajama shorts and tank top. We've spent the last hour in my bed, relaxing, talking, just being with each other. "The lock is fixed."

"Good." I follow her movements with my eyes, her bare feet sinking into the plush carpet as she approaches. Her hips sway softly with each step. "But I hope you don't think you need to leave right this second."

Sophie giggles and kneels on the bed before crawling to me. She places one arm on my other side so that she's hovering over my torso and slowly lowers her lips to mine. Her nipples brush my bare chest.

"You think I'm gonna run away before I turn into a pumpkin?" she murmurs against my mouth.

I wrap my hands around her waist and pull her down, forcing her breasts up as they squish against me. With a grin, I nuzzle my nose against hers.

"It's ten in the morning."

"And I'm not Cinderella."

"Can I still be Prince Charming?"

She pulls back and giggles.

"That was cheesy. You gotta work on that."

"I'll have my roommate teach me some new jokes."

Just as I lift my head to kiss her, my phone rings. I close my eyes and groan, barely an inch from her lips. I recognize the ringtone.

"Do you have to get that?" Sophie whines.

"It's my sister." While Sophie shifts and lies next to me, I reach for the phone on my bedside table. "Hey, Raegan, everything ok?"

"Everything's fine." She laughs into the receiver. "Why do you think something's wrong every time I call?"

"Because something usually is," I grumble. "Or you need something."

"Good to talk to you too. I do need something." At least she's upfront about it. "Brett and I are at an event up in Ojai. The girls are at a birthday party and Isla was supposed to pick them up, but she had to pick up a last minute-shift at work."

"So you need Uncle Brody to come to the rescue," I surmise with a nod.

"And maybe hang out until we get home?" I can hear the wince in her voice. "Shouldn't be any later than three."

"Wait, who has a birthday party on a Saturday morning? Why not the afternoon?"

"Echo Park parents, apparently," Raegan grumbles.

"Doesn't that include you?"

"Can you help or do I need to call our sitter? I'm not even sure she's in town this weekend."

"No, I'll-" I look over at Sophie who has been pretending not to listen. "I'll take care of it. Just send me the address for the party."

"Thanks. I owe you one. Maybe I can get you a deal on plane tickets for your next trip. Do you have something planned?"

"Not yet. Leave the girls to me."

"Bye, B."

"Toodles."

"Did you really just say toodles?" asks Sophie with a snort when I hang up the phone.

"Someone likes to eavesdrop." I raise an eyebrow, but smile. I set the phone back on the table before rolling back over so we're facing each other. "I have to pick up my nieces from a party in a little bit."

"Oh." Her face falls. "I'll get dressed and-"

"You could come with me." I have no idea where that offer came from, but I'm going to double down. Sophie's eyes widen, her eyebrows raising. Her lips part in surprise.

"I-I-I could?"

"Yeah, I mean if that's ok. I don't know how you feel about kids, but-"

"I like kids," she says quickly but still looks uncertain.

"Then it's settled." I take her hand and kiss her knuckles, then drop our hands between us. "Got something appropriate you can wear?" I tease.

"Is a sundress ok?" She rolls her eyes.

"Depends on how short it is. And how badly it makes me want to," I pull her closer by the waist, "bend you over," I bring my mouth to hers, "and slide inside your tight," my hand drifts down her side and across her body, "wet," I urge her with my hand to lift her leg so I can slide my hand between her thighs, "pussy."

Car seats loaded into the back seat, Sophie and I leave just before noon to go pick up my nieces from the party. It's down south in Echo Park and we arrive just in time for the party to end.

"You wanna come in with me?" I ask Sophie after I park along the residential street. "You don't have to. I think it'll be kind of crazy in there."

"I'll come in." She smiles and slides out of the car to follow me up the sidewalk.

I glance back at her, the sidewalk too narrow to comfortably walk side by side. That damn sundress swishes around her legs in the light breeze while she walks, but I'm glad to see it falls to her knees. Not that she should care what other people think, but I don't want to traumatize a bunch of elementary school kids.

"Oh, I should warn you," I say as we turn to walk up the driveway. "Violet has a speech impediment. She says her k's and similar sounds like t's or d's. Uncle is Untle, cold is told, things like that. If you don't understand something, just look at me."

Sophie nods with a grin.

"That's adorable."

Raegan told me it was ok to just walk into the house, that she had let the parents know I was picking up the girls instead of Isla. When I place my hand on the doorknob and swing it open, pure chaos overwhelms my senses. Streamers hang from just about every door frame and every foot or so along the ceiling of the living room, kitchen, and entryway. Excited screams fill the air, undercut by the heavy thuds of footsteps as children run around, chasing each other.

"Sounds like they've already had cake," I chuckle while Sophie closes the door behind us.

A few parents are visible in the living room, watching the horror unfold. They look unfazed by it all.

"Can I help you?" one of the women asks, stepping forward when she notices our entrance. She looks about my age, maybe a few years older. Her short black hair is perfectly parted on the side and her rosy lipstick is immaculate.

"I'm Brody." I hold out my hand. "Opal and Violet's uncle."

"Oh!" Realization changes the woman's previously cold features. She shakes my hand with a sheepish grin. "Sorry, yes. She said you'd be coming by for the girls. Something about your sister having a last minute work thing."

"Yeah, she couldn't turn it down. Her manager is kind of a d- jerk." I have to watch my language around other kids. Opal and Violet have heard every curse and naughty word under the sun, even if they don't know what they mean. I can't say the same for every kid at the party.

"Well, if you can stop them, you can take them," the woman laughs as Opal speeds past us, following one of the little boys with light-up sneakers.

"Oy!" I shout, holding my hand to the side of my mouth. Opal freezes and turns to face me with a grin. "No love for me?"

"Uncle B!" she squeals and runs at me with open arms.

Despite the chocolate cake on her shirt, I crouch and hold my arms out just in time for her to run into them.

"I missed you, bug."

Her arms are skinny, but still strong enough to strangle me. When she finally lets go and backs away, her eyes fall on Sophie.

"Who's that?" She points blatantly at the woman behind me.

"Opal, this is Sophie. Sophie, this is my niece, Opal."

Sophie holds out a hand, a warm smile on her lips.

"It's very nice to meet you, Opal."

"You're pretty." Opal's back straightens while she shakes Sophie's hand. The little adult.

"Thank you, so are you."

"Where's your sister?" I ask, standing up to search the room and the part of the kitchen visible.

"Iuuh." Opal's version of 'I don't know'. It's the most noncommittal sound someone can make and she does so with a shrug.

"Fat load of help you are, kid," I mutter. Lifting my hand to the side of my mouth again, I shout. "Violet Kincaid, time to go beanie weenie!"

Violet appears, popping out from behind the wall separating the living room from the kitchen. There's chocolate cake smeared on her cheek and she's grinning from ear to ear.

"Untle B!" Her squeal is identical to her sister's.

"'ey!" I hold out my arms but don't crouch. Instead, when Violet reaches me, my hands slip beneath her armpits and I pick her up with ease, swinging her legs up and back before bringing her in so she can wrap her legs partially around me. "Beans, this is Sophie." Violet is already eyeing Sophie with suspicion.

"Is she your dirlfriend?"

"You bet your skinny little butt, she is." I wink as Sophie smiles in response, not a hint of doubt in her eyes.

"Momma says you shouldn't say butt," Violet giggles.

"Yeah, it's a bad word," Opal agrees.

I roll my eyes.

"Well, Momma's not here and snitches get stitches." I grab Opal's hand, still holding Violet in my other arm since she weighs barely thirty pounds. I'm not even sure she weighs that much. The girl is tiny for her age. "You ready to go?"

"Yep!"

"Oh, the goody bags are by the door," shouts the mother of the birthday kid as we head for the exit.

"Thanks!" I call over my shoulder, grabbing two little paper bags from the table by the door.

Sophie follows us and I can feel her eyes on me. Opal glances back every now and then but doesn't say anything.

"Can Sophie help you with your car seat?" I ask Opal as I set Violet in her seat. She nods. "You rock."

"Do *I* rot, Untle B?" asks Violet, staring up at me. Sophie buckles Opal in on the other side of the car.

"You certainly do, beans."

Despite the massive sugar overload, the girls are pleasant, if talkative, on the way back to their house. Raegan and Brett are renting a home in the southernmost part of Echo Park, just a short drive from the house where the party was held. Brett's company has given them a potential date to move overseas. I'll miss the girls like crazy, but such is the nature of my brother-in-law's job.

"Ok, girls, what does Momma usually do for lunch?" I ask as I press my unique code into the keypad on the door. Brett Kincaid is all about the technology. I think they chose this home specifically for this and some of the other tech features. He's a smart guy, but I wouldn't have any of this stuff in my home.

"She lets us eat pizza!" shouts Opal, running inside ahead of me.

"No, she doesn't." Violet frowns, following after her sister at a much slower pace. Opal's stern look–far more impressive given that she's only six–causes her to change her tune. "I mean, yeah. We eat pizza every day."

"Nice try, goobers." I chuckle and close the door behind Sophie. "How about mac n' cheese? Got any boxes?" I glance at Sophie. "You ok with that?" She grins.

"I love mac n' cheese."

"Yay, mat and cheeeeeese!" Violet yells, jumping up and down.

"Do you like pizza?" asks Opal. She comes to a stop by the couch before jumping onto it.

"*Love* pizza," Sophie replies, rolling her eyes backward just a little for emphasis.

"What's your favorite food?" asks Violet, grabbing Sophie's hand and dragging her toward the kitchen.

"Hmm, maybe chocolate cake." She reaches out to take a paper towel from the holder on the counter behind Violet. Then she wets it in the sink and gently wipes some of the cake residue from Violet's face. "Looks like it might be one of your favorites too."

"I lite strawberry better."

"Oh, strawberry's a good one too."

"*I* don't like cake. I like ice cream." Opal pops up from the couch, resting her arms on the back. She's tall for her age and even though I can't see, I have a feeling she's probably only kneeling.

"The chocolate on your shirt would say otherwise." I nod at the bit of chocolate that clearly isn't ice cream. It's a small amount and I'm surprised there isn't more.

"Well, *sometimes* I like cake."

"There we go. Now, you guys grab two boxes of mac while Sophie and I start the water."

Opal and Violet race to the walk-in pantry, their sneakers squeaking on the hardwood floor. Opal is first, swinging the door open wide. I hear things falling, bags of some kind, and a box or two before she and her sister reappear holding two boxes of the organic stuff my sister buys. I grimace at Sophie who has to hide a smile.

Plating up the pasta, along with some cut up vegetables, Sophie and I take seats with the girls at the kitchen table. While they eat, I can see that both pairs of eyelids are beginning to droop. The sugar is wearing off. Maybe that's the reason for the morning party–afternoon naps. I've got to hand it to those parents. That's kind of genius. I'll have to remember that for... Sophie said she likes kids, but I have no idea if she wants any of her own.

*It's still* way *too early for that line of thinking.*

After about three bites of mac and two pieces of bell pepper, Violet begins to push the food around on her plate. Her head is leaning on her hand, elbow resting on the table.

"You not hungry?" I ask. She shakes her head slowly. "Must've been all that cake."

"Can we play a game?" Opal has already had seconds and cleaned her plate of both helpings.

"Take your dishes to the kitchen." I stand to grab mine and Sophie's empty plates, leading the way to the sink. "Then we can play. As long as you don't fall asleep on me."

The girls grab their plates and practically run to the kitchen, shouting a string of games like tag, hide and seek, red light, green light, and some I've never heard of. The last one is the one that catches though.

"Let's play Simon Says!" Opal squeals as she sets her plate on the counter by the sink.

"That sound good to you?" I ask Sophie.

"Yep. Who's gonna be Simon?"

"Me," says Opal confidently.

"You're always Simon," Violet whines.

"Well," Sophie says, crouching down next to Violet as Opal runs to stand behind the couch, "I think you can beat me and your Uncle B, so you'll probably be Simon next."

Violet's eyes shine, her mouth spreading into a wide grin as she looks at Sophie.

"You thint I tan win?" she asks.

"You betcha. I'm terrible at this game."

Opal calls us all to attention, her commanding tone verging on bossy. Sophie and I stand in a line on either side of Violet and I give Opal a wink.

"Ok, Simon says..." she pauses, thinking for a minute. "Touch your nose."

All three of us act.

"Touch your eye."

None of us move. Opal rolls her eyes.

"Simon says hop on one foot."

All three of us begin to hop. Violet is having trouble, but when Opal opens her mouth to mention it, I shake my head just enough for her to see. Glancing between me and Violet, she thinks better of punishing her sister.

"Stop jumping."

Sophie stops and then slaps her forehead.

"Oh, man." She looks at Violet. "You beat me."

Violet grins, still hopping.

"Simon says stop jumping."

Sophie sits at the kitchen table, turning toward us so she can watch.

"Simon says put your hand on your head."

I take the hand touching my nose and place it on my head.

"Ah!" Opal points at me. "I didn't say to stop touching your nose!"

"Guess you win, beans." I groan and look down at Violet who is positively beaming.

"So I det to be Simon?" she asks excitedly.

"You do," says Sophie.

# 24

## Sophie

Sophie

Opal and Violet fade quickly after another two more rounds of the game. I can see the crankiness beginning to rear its ugly head as they squabble over whether each of us is following the rules. Finally, Brody pipes up.

"How about a movie?"

"Momma says we only det movies before bed," says Violet, rubbing her eyes.

"Well, we just won't tell Momma. Or Dad. He can't keep a secret," Brody adds, looking at me.

We settle onto the large couch, Brody and I resting our feet on the ottoman while the girls sit in between us. Within minutes of starting an episode of Bluey, both of the girls are out cold.

"Sorry," says Brody softly.

"For what?" I turn and search his face, my hand absently rubbing the top of Violet's head where it rests on my lap.

"For this." He motions to the TV.

"Oh I'm a Bluey fan," I assure him, keeping my voice low. "It's wholesome, it's relaxing. I'm not bothered by this at all."

"God, you're amazing."

"I know." I wink at him and turn back to the TV.

The sound of the front door unlocking startles us both and it swings open. If I didn't already know this was Brody's sister, I'd have guessed it by looking. The woman who just walked in has similar facial features, the same green eyes, and brown hair which falls just past her shoulders. Her hair has a few streaks of blonde in it, though.

"Hey Brody, thanks f-" She pauses, staring at me for a moment before her eyes focus on Brody.

"Sorry, we can't get up," Brody explains, motioning toward the girls. Opal's head is nuzzled against his side. "This is Sophie. Sophie, this is my sister, Raegan." The man who enters behind Raegan has salt and pepper hair and is a few inches taller than her, though Raegan isn't short by any means. "And that's Brett."

Brett's blue eyes are striking above a slightly crooked nose. His jawline is covered in dark stubble as if his beard hasn't gotten the memo that his hair did. I wonder what the age gap is between them. Brett waves with one hand and a tight-lipped smile.

"Hi Raegan, Brett." I nod to each of them, feeling rude not getting up, but I don't want to disturb the girls. I'll have to eventually, of course, but I want to make this feeling last.

"It's so nice to meet you." Raegan's squeal as she hurries forward to grab my hand and shake it is enough to wake her daughters. "Sorry," she whispers as Violet's eyes flutter open.

"It's nice to meet you too," I laugh as the girls sit up. It gives me the chance to stand and greet Raegan properly. "I hope it's ok that Brody brought me along."

"Oh, it's fine! I don't think he's ever brought a girl around, so you must be special." She winks at me and I hate that it makes me blush. Am I really the first one?

"Nice to meet you," says Brett, approaching a little slower than his wife. "If we'd known it would be more than just Brody, we'd have tidied up."

I raise an eyebrow and look around the home that was basically spotless until we walked in with the girls. Even now, the only things out of place are the dishes in the sink.

"Yeah, the place is a wreck," Brody laughs, standing up from the couch. Opal has finally allowed him his freedom.

"Oh shut it, we're still living out of boxes." Raegan rolls her eyes.

"Where are the boxes?" Brody glances around.

"Basement, mostly," says Brett. "Kinda don't wanna unpack everything if we're gonna up and move in six months."

"Would it really be that soon?" asks Brody, placing his hands on his hips.

"They said six months to a year." Brett nods as the girls drag on their mother's hand, babbling about the party this morning.

"Still thinking Ireland or the UK?"

"I don't think they'd send me anywhere else, but there's been talk of Norway and France."

"The girls are young enough that it should be easy to learn a new language, not to mention up and moving away from their friends."

"Yeah, that's what people keep telling me," Brett sighs. "Kids are resilient and all that."

"They are, man. Just keep me posted. I'll help you move if you want."

"Thanks." Brett smiles at his brother-in-law.

I find myself staring, wishing I'd grown up with siblings. The chance at nieces and nephews, a home full of family, even in-laws. My mind conjures an image of Christmas with Brody and his family, most of whom are still faceless for me. The home is full of laughter and joy and all the things I doubt I'll ever see with my parents again.

Brody already mentioned that he wants children. I used to, but since making adult content full-time, I'm not so sure. How do you raise kids while making porn for a living? People do it, I know they do. Could I? Would Brody want that?

*Getting ahead of yourself, Soph.*

"I think we're gonna go." Brody's eyes catch mine and I know he sees that something's off, that my thoughts are elsewhere.

"Oh yeah, get going. You've been cooped up with the girls long enough." Brett shoos us away.

"It was nice meeting you, Sophie!" Raegan calls as we walk toward the door.

"It was so nice meeting you both." I grin over my shoulder and follow Brody outside.

"So, was-was that ok?" asks Brody once we're safely in his car.

"What, meeting your family? Big step," I admit, trying to keep my tone light. "But it was really nice. I wish I had siblings. Growing up might've been less lonely."

"Well being the only boy wasn't amazing," Brody laughs. "But I'm glad you liked them."

"I really did."

I hadn't planned for more than one night at Brody's, but I hate the idea of leaving. It's been so relaxing being with him, feeling safe with him. When he asks if I'll stay another night, there's no way I'm saying no.

I take my car back to my apartment, noting the new wood along the door frame. The ring around the camera on the doorbell lights up as I approach. It's working, at least for now. As I head up the stairs to pack another change of clothes, I wonder if Brody found anything last night. He didn't mention anything this morning and part of me doesn't want to ask.

I gather a few items, but then, after standing in front of my closet for several more seconds, I grab another sundress too.

"Just in case," I mutter to myself.

"Just in case, what?"

I jump and turn to see Natalie leaning against my door frame, arms crossed and a smile on her face.

"In case I want to stay the whole weekend." There's no point trying to keep the smile off my face.

She laughs, coming to sit on the end of my bed while I pack.

"So things are good?"

"I'm afraid to say yes and jinx it." I chew on my bottom lip, holding the sundress in my hands. "But yeah, things are... great."

"Just be careful." Her tone is far more serious now and I know she's not talking about Brody or Miles before she even says his name. "I've never met Caleb, but if he scared you enough for you to run all the way to LA, I worry what his plan is for you. You should tell the police."

"I can't." My voice comes out softer than I'd like. Weaker. Caleb is a snake and snakes know how to hide. They know when to strike. I know I'm in danger now, but I still can't bring myself to speak to the police.

"Why not, Soph? They could look for him or something."

"Since when do they side with victims in cases like this?" I mutter. "Besides, his brother is a cop. All it would take is a flash of his badge and his cousins in the LAPD would think his brother is innocent."

"Fuck, really? A cop?" Natalie shakes her head.

Why am I talking about this? It's been six months. Natalie promised she wouldn't bring it up, but that was before Caleb started stalking me.

"Did Brody find anything?" she asks tentatively.

"He said it'll take time for some programs to run, whatever that means."

Natalie nods and I place the dress in my bag.

"See you tomorrow?" Natalie asks, standing from the bed.

"Or Monday." I blush again, but she just rolls her eyes and leads the way from the room.

"Ok, ok. The honeymoon phase is in full swing.

I can hear Natalie giggling to herself when I reach the door and I shake my head as I leave. Cold dread stops me in my tracks. The feeling of someone watching me causes the little hairs on the back of my neck to stand up and a shiver to run down my spine.

After checking between the buildings, along the side yard of our place and the neighbors in front of us, and even looking over the fence, I decide it's my imagination. It has to be. Caleb wouldn't be out here watching me in broad daylight. Although, he kicked our door in before the sun was fully down, so maybe I don't know him as well as I used to.

# 25

## Miles

Vegas has been fun, but I'll be glad to get home. The drive is just under five hours unless I hit traffic, so I'm able to make it by late afternoon on Sunday. It's too expensive to stay a full holiday weekend in a place like Las Vegas. I just hope I don't interrupt Brody's fuck fest.

The thought makes me smirk as I pull into the driveway behind a familiar car. I can't place it, but I know I've seen it recently. I'm still trying to figure out *where* I've seen it when I enter the house and freeze.

There's a woman standing at the kitchen sink, her back to me. Her brown hair tumbles down in soft curls, stopping above the middle of her back. Gold streaks are highlighted in the sun coming through the windows along the back of the house. A sundress covered in purple and blue flowers swishes around her legs, mid-thigh, and her tawny skin is covered in black and gray tattoos. There are flashes of color in the ink here and there. I recognize some of them. I recognize *most* of them.

"Sophie?" The word comes out hoarse, but she hears me and spins, her hands still wet.

"M-Miles?" Her eyes are wide with shock.

The sink is still running while she takes me in, looking as if she's short-circuiting. Brody comes striding out from the hallway that leads to his room. The smile on his face drops when he sees the expression on mine.

"Er, Miles, this is Sophie. Sophie, this is Miles." He speaks slowly, carefully, as if one of us might attack him or each other at any moment. While we're silent, he leans over and turns off the faucet behind Sophie.

I swallow the lump in my throat.

Sophie is his girl. Brody is my competition.

Sophie is the woman he's been seeing. Brody is the dick-for-brains I'm trying to make her forget.

*Fuck.*

He has never said her name when talking about her. Why hasn't he ever said her name? Why haven't *I* said her real name when we talk about her?

"We, er-" Sophie turns her head to focus on Brody. I can see the worry on her perfect face. She doesn't want to hurt him and neither do I. "We know each other."

"Oh." It takes him a moment to process, but then his eyes go wide. "Oh, you mean you've worked together?" His cheeks flush, whether from embarrassment or anger or some combination, I'm not sure.

"Brody." Sophie's voice breaks. "Miles and I-"

"We've been on a couple dates," I finish when it's clear Sophie can't find the words.

"Wait." Brody holds up his hands, shaking his head and looking down. "Dates, you mean-?" He stares between us, hands still held high. "Oh, fuck." The curse is a whisper and I pray it's not one of defeat. If I hurt him, I'm not sure what I'll do.

"Brody, I'm sorry." I step toward him, but think better of it. Will he back off, knowing how I feel about Sophie? Should I be the one to give up? Will this even be something our friendship can survive? "I didn't know you two were that she's the one you've been-"

"Miles, stop." His voice is strong, but still low. He shakes his head, blinking slowly. A deep rumble of laughter starts in his chest before ripping from his throat. It's not angry or sad-if anything, it's a little crazed.

"You know, I didn't think this could last." His eyes fall on Sophie. "You're too fucking perfect and there's no way I measure up to the guys you've worked with."

"Woah, hold on." Sophie holds up her hands, shaking her head and scoffing. "Measure up?" she repeats and then angrily, "*Measure up*? Brody, my god, are you serious?"

I watch this unfold with a mix of shock, disbelief, and amusement. I've only seen Brody naked once by accident-he wasn't exactly athletic in high school, so it's not as if we saw each other in the locker room-and even *I'm* impressed with his size. Measuring up will never be an issue for him.

"I-" Brody's eyes flick back and forth between us. "I-I just meant-"

"Regardless of what you meant," says Sophie, "I can promise you that measuring up isn't an issue." She places a wet hand on his upper arm. He brings his opposite hand up to cover hers, still looking at me. "And I had *no* idea about... this." She motions toward me.

"I believe you." Fuck those eyes are sad.

"I don't want to come between you two," Sophie continues. She looks back at me. "Not that I think I could. I just mean-" She takes a deep breath, then mutters while looking at Brody, "Your best friend. I could've handled *good* friends, even neighbors. Best friends." After a heavy sigh, Sophie shakes her head yet again. "I'll get my things and leave."

Brody's hand tightens on hers as she moves, keeping her by his side. Those brown eyes of hers, golden pools I know Brody wants to fall into as badly as I do, are questioning, but she doesn't speak.

"No," he sighs. "No, I'll, er, bow out."

"The fuck you will." The anger, not just in my voice, but in my whole goddamn chest, surprises me. Dating the woman I'm obsessed with doesn't mean he has to back off.

"You guys have a lot more in common," Brody protests. "Why would I- How can I be enough?"

"Shut up, man." I shake my head and take a few more steps closer until I'm able to stand on the opposite side of the counter, my hands on the cold granite while I lean forward. "Sophie," I look at her and she meets my gaze, "I know you can make your own decisions, but Brody clearly cares about you. I'm not letting him end this."

"Excuse me, but your friendship is way more important than me." Her expression is stern.

"Doubtful," says Brody just as I laugh. "No, I'm," he squeezes Sophie's hand again before dropping his, "I'm done."

"Shut up." I slam my hand on the countertop loud enough to get their attention but not hard enough to hurt. My eyes find theirs—emerald and gold staring back at me, waiting for answers I definitely don't have. I run a hand through my hair. It's been a long trip full of making content and I'm exhausted, but this is important. "Look, don't... don't be weird about this, but," I focus on Sophie, "what if we continue like this?"

She frowns.

"Miles," Brody groans.

"This isn't the dark ages." I ignore him. "Polyamory is a thing. I've never tried it, I know *you've* never tried it," I add, looking at Brody, "and I'm guessing it's new for you too." Sophie nods when I meet her eyes. "So it'll be an adventure for all of us." Why the *fuck* do I sound so excited?

"Polyamory," Brody repeats, skeptical. "Is that a big thing in the adult industry?"

"I don't know, fuck the industry. This is about us." I motion between the three of us. "Sophie, I'll give you up if that's what you want, but I really hope it's not because goddamn it, I like you. I'm not asking you to choose between us. I won't put you in that position. Other positions, sure, but not that one."

"Miles, I-" she begins to protest, but I hold up a hand to silence her.

"Let's just try sharing. Brody?"

He swallows, his Adam's apple bobbing with the effort, then looks down at the woman still clutching his arm.

"I'm in."

"Men." Sophie rolls her eyes.

"Is that a yes?" I ask, a hopeful smile on my lips.

"I guess?"

We pass the rest of the week only seeing Sophie one more day each. I start to wonder if she's trying to give us space. I certainly hope not. Brody and I avoid the subject of her unless she's in the room, which only occurs once. On some level, it feels strained, but on another, it feels perfectly normal. If Brody feels weird about the situation, he doesn't let on. He does, however, hide away in his office more than usual.

When Sophie calls me about a party on Friday, I'm shocked to get the invite, but happy to accept. The party is held in Glendale, an area I'm very familiar with, so I offer to drive.

"So, how did you find out about this?"

"I did an interview for Sara Sitwell's podcast when I was in New York last month." She stares out the window as we pass house after house. "She invited me and told me I could bring a plus one." Sophie looks at me. "Is Brody ok that I chose you?"

I snort.

"I don't think Brody would be comfortable at a party like this. Any other time, yeah, he might be jealous."

"Are things... ok between you two?" She bites her lip, waiting for my response.

"He's quiet," I admit, turning onto the last street. I slow down, checking the house numbers on my side. "But so far, he seems ok with the arrangement." That is definitely not the right word.

"Arrangement?" Sophie smirks. "We need to find a better way to say what we're doing here."

"Let's focus on the party tonight." The house comes into view. "Here we are."

The street is lined with cars, but it looks like someone is about to pull out of a space a couple of houses down, so we park there and walk toward the party. As we approach, I can hear music coming from the backyard. A sign on the front door says to head around back. I let Sophie lead the way since she's the invited guest.

When we enter through the gate in the privacy fence, a cacophony of laughter and music meets our ears. The pool, which is being used to its full extent, is filled with other adult performers. A couple of tables sit a few feet from two large grills being manned by two very burly men. Both of the men are shirtless, covered in tattoos, and wearing 'kiss the cook' aprons. There's a bar set directly against the house and it looks like our hostess hired a bartender. Two, I correct myself, as a young woman joins her male counterpart behind the counter, serving drinks to bathing suit-clad guests.

A woman who looks a few years older than me waves at us. Her dark blonde hair is pulled back in a French braid, her pale skin shining with what I can only assume is sunblock–baby oil or something similar would be horrible for that complexion. She's wearing a black, one-piece suit with a slit down the middle that goes most of the way to her belly button. Her eyes are hidden behind huge aviator sunglasses, but she's grinning at us.

"Honey!" she squeals, hurrying over, moving just slowly enough not to spill her drink. "You made it!" She embraces Sophie with one arm, holding her drink away from their bodies with the other hand.

"Thank you so much for inviting me. This is an amazing party. An amazing *place*," Sophie adds as the woman lets go. She motions at me. "This is Lance Kixxx. Lance, this is Sara Sitwell."

"Nice to meet you, Sara." I shake her offered hand and she continues to smile.

"Right back at ya! Hey, if you need local collabs, hit me up on Twitter or something. If Honey brought you, that's all the reference I need."

"Really?" I raise my eyebrows and look over at Sophie.

"Absolutely. Did she tell you she was on my podcast? So much fun. We should do it again." Sara babbles away while I survey the crowd, my sunglasses hiding my wandering eyes. "Maybe you can pop by sometime for an interview too, not just a shoot."

"That would be great. I'll definitely reach out. Thanks again for having us."

"Oh, don't thank me. Just have a good time."

With that, Sara practically dances away to greet someone who walked through the gate after us. The sun is getting low in the sky, but even when it sets, I don't anticipate it'll cool off too much.

Sophie and I grab drinks from the bar and find a couple of chairs around the edge. She doesn't seem too keen to jump into networking, even though that's exactly what this event is for. I don't plan on pushing her. I've seen her come out of her shell and I know she can do it on her own when she's ready.

"Do you know anyone else here?" I ask, looking through the sea of faces

"I don't think so," she says slowly, doing her own surveillance of the crowd. "Some look familiar though. I'm sure I've seen them on my feed somewhere."

"I've seen a few people I've worked with. No one recent," I add, though I'm not sure why. Just as I finish speaking, a woman at the bar waves to get my attention before heading our way.

"Lance!" she calls, a grin on her pale face. Huge sunglasses hide eyes that I know are bright blue.

"Hey, Talia!" I call back when she's still halfway across the yard. "I've worked with her a lot for a pro company," I explain to Sophie. "You'll like her, she's sweet."

In her hot pink string bikini, her blonde hair swinging in a ponytail, she looks every bit the picture-perfect porn star that she is. She was snapped up by a big talent agency within weeks of coming onto the scene as an amateur and she hasn't looked back since. Not that she should.

"What company?" Sophie asks. She's smiling and even though I can't see her eyes behind her sunglasses, I know the smile reaches them. The lack of jealousy is refreshing.

"It's," I pause to chuckle, "it's called Gargantuanal."

"What?" Sophie throws her head back in a fit of giggles. "That's amazing!" I join her in laughing at the ridiculous name. It's not the weirdest I've heard–there are plenty of production companies in the adult industry with names like it.

"I didn't know you were coming," I say, standing and hugging Talia before sitting back down.

"Yeah, Sara and I have worked together a few times." She looks down at Sophie and extends a hand. "I'm Talia Sins."

"Honey Dee Vine." Sophie takes the offered hand and shakes it politely. "Lance was just telling me you've worked together a lot."

"Oh yeah." Talia pulls up a chair from a few feet away to sit opposite us. "The one I've been with a lot recently is focused on anal content, but mostly with those extreme toys that are huge."

"That explains the name," Sophie chuckles.

"He told you?" Talia's voice is full of mirth.

"He couldn't say it fast enough. I love hearing some of these company names. They're just so dumb."

"But they know what they are." Talia motions at us with her cup instead of pointing and I imagine she winks too.

"That, they do," I agree, holding up my own drink in response.

"So," Talia crosses one leg over the other and sits back in her chair, "are you guys going to SpicyCon? I've heard it won't be a huge crowd since it's new."

"I am." I turn to look at Sophie. We haven't talked about the convention next week. It hasn't come up in all of our conversations about work.

"Yeah, I'll be there Thursday to Sunday," she says.

"Sweet! I'll be at the Gargantuanal booth all day Friday, but maybe the three of us can grab dinner or something one night if you have a free evening."

"Sounds good," I say with a grin.

"Oh! I need to go say hi to someone who just walked in. I'll catch you guys later, or at SpicyCon. Whatever." She dashes away and I'm left feeling like a tornado has gone through.

"So, Talia Sins?" Sophie has pulled her sunglasses down to stare at me with those amber eyes and takes a sip of her drink.

"Just a filming history," I chuckle.

"It's fine, I wouldn't judge you if it was more," Sophie giggles. "She seems really nice."

"Ouch." I wince.

"What? She does!"

"It's just, well, I grew up with Brody and his sisters. I've heard some catty comments."

"I'm not trying to be catty." She rolls her eyes before readjusting her sunglasses. "I mean it."

"You really don't get jealous, do you?" I lean away and study her.

"I kind of don't have a right to be jealous, do I?" she asks. "I mean, we both work with other people and..." she trails off, biting her lip and looking away toward the pool.

"And I'm sharing you with Brody," I finish for her. She nods but doesn't turn her head. "Trust me, I know how weird it sounds. And I'm not a cuck or a stag or whatever. I just want you to be happy and if your happiness includes someone else." I shrug.

"So we're ignoring the fact that you wanted to make me forget about the competition?" Sophie raises her eyebrows above her sunglasses.

"Well, I can't compete with my best friend. Not for you, at least." I pat her hand.

Throughout the late afternoon, Sophie and I venture around to meet other creators. I introduce her to a few people I know, helping her to gain more reliable contacts in the industry. It's one thing to meet at an event like this, but it's another thing entirely to have someone introduce you. It's like a reference: I worked with this person and I'm introducing you, so you know that they're one of the good ones.

As the sun sets and the guests get drunker, things get a little louder and more rambunctious. The games of chicken have already begun with squeals of delight and victory echoing around the backyard. The two men who had manned the grills earlier in the evening have either drawn the short straws or the long, depending on how you look at it. The muscular meatheads are the chosen bases for every chicken challenge. Having a woman's thighs wrapped around their head doesn't seem like the worst way they can spend their evening.

"Hey, gorgeous!" One of them calls out to Sophie, waving his arm to join him. "Come on in, let's knock Buddy's gal right off his shoulders!"

"I'm good," Sophie chuckles.

"Aw, you sure? I'll bet your thighs are nice and soft!"

"They are!" she shouts back with a grin. "But they're closed for the event."

"Oh boo!"

He doesn't seem too upset because he finds another woman to hop on his shoulders within minutes. She falls right off as soon as her opponent makes one good shove.

"Looks like you'd have had some real competition," I muse.

"Yeah, I think I would have crushed the poor guy's head trying to stay on."

"You want a go with me? You can crush my head any day." I waggle my eyebrows for emphasis.

"You think you can hold all of this," she motions to her body, "on your shoulders long enough for me to kick some scrawny girl's ass?"

"You betcha." I wink. "Easy."

# 26

## Brody

Caleb Davis. Twenty-eight years old. Barely finished high school. Didn't go to college. Can't hold down a job. Youngest of two children born to Heather Davis. Dated Sophie for over three years.

Since finding out about Sophie's ex, I've discovered quite a lot about the two of them. Police reports that seem to have gone nowhere, past addresses, her high school. Evidence of her relationship with Caleb Davis is everywhere on his social media up until mid-February, when I assume she disappeared. He didn't say anything about it, didn't post about missing her, hell, he didn't even change his relationship status. It still says he's in one.

Coincidentally, his brother is in law enforcement. That explains the lack of follow-through when she called the police on his abusive ass. I don't know what the final straw was or what made her leave, but I'm glad she did.

Building a way into her doorbell cam with backups coming straight to me was the easy part. Caleb isn't staying in LA under his own name, so he must have some semblance of intelligence. I can't find any listing for him anywhere and I can get into just about every hotel database that exists. They're not as airtight as they'd have their guests believe.

Monday morning rolls around again and it's back to the usual grind. I've been trying to make sense of some of the logs Mel sent me weeks ago since she hasn't officially taken it away from me. The information is written in some kind of code that even I can't decipher. I plan to tell her as much later today, but until then, I'm still on the project.

My phone buzzes beside my keyboard and I glance down to see Isla's name.

Isla:

> Hey, buuuuuuddy, can you do
> me a gigantic favor tonight?

I roll my eyes but type out a quick yes and ask if she wants to call me. I hate having long text conversations. Phone calls aren't much better, but Isla isn't the talker our other sisters are.

When the phone rings, I answer it quickly.

"Whatcha need, Isla?" My tone is light. She knows I'd do anything for her.

"I have a date tonight." She's excited, but I can hear something else in her voice. I'm sure it's just nerves.

"Awesome, would I approve of him?"

"Probably not," she snorts. "But all my friends are sorta busy, so they can't do the emergency call. Would you do it?"

"Emergency call? What's that?"

"You know," says Isla, clearly not wanting to take the time to explain. When I'm silent, she does so. "It's when a girl goes on a date, but asks her friend to call her a half hour in or something with an emergency. If the date is going well, the call is ignored. If not, it's answered and uh oh! Gotta go!"

"Does every woman do that?" I wonder aloud, recalling that Sophie got a phone call during our first date and ignored it. It makes me smile to think that's what it was. She was enjoying herself enough to ignore the call.

"Every woman *I've* ever met."

"Right, well, what do I say?"

"You don't even really have to say anything," says Isla. "You can just call and put the phone down and I'll do the rest."

"Well, that's easy."

"I know. So just set an alarm for like 6:36 or something. That way it's not *right at* the half hour mark, you know?"

"You got it."

"Oh and Brody, I'm fucking furious with you."

"For what?"

"Raegan got to meet your new lady friend before I did!" she shouts.

"It wasn't planned," I assure her. "Sophie was helping me with the girls because *you* couldn't."

"Still incredibly rude."

"Yeah, yeah. You want that emergency call or not?"

"I'll just ask Miles," she huffs.

"I'll call you at 6:36."

"Thank you!" she half-sings before hanging up.

I hear Miles messing around in the kitchen and check my watch, only to see that it's past noon. No wonder I'm hungry. I walk out to find my roommate pouring milk over a bowl of cereal.

"What, no sandwich?"

"I kind of just got home." He winces and I realize what he must've been doing until now.

"Ah." I nod and round the island, not sure what I'm going to scrounge up for lunch. "Hey, do all women do that emergency call thing?" I ask, staring into the fridge, willing something to appear that sounds good.

"Pretty sure, yeah," Miles responds through a mouthful of food. "Why?"

"Isla needs me to do that for her tonight. She's got a date."

"You gonna internet stalk him for her?"

"Only if she doesn't answer my call," I laugh, closing the fridge empty-handed. I turn to face him.

"Our little sis is growing up," Miles laughs through another mouthful.

"Yeah, yeah. I think I'm gonna run out for lunch. Text me if you want something."

When I walk back into the house with a bag full of food because Miles did, in fact, text me his very large order, my stomach is growling so loud I think Sophie might hear it at her place. I set the bag on the counter and grab my burrito bowl just as my phone vibrates in my pocket.

It's not a text, but a notification of movement outside Sophie's house. I've gotten them when the girls come and go or when they have people over to film. It's always accompanied by the sound of the front door opening. But when I open up the app to view footage, I know right away this is not normal.

It's hard to make out his grainy face, but I think I recognize the build from his photos online. Caleb walks slowly up the driveway between the front two buildings of the four-building property. There's a folded piece of paper in his hand. I watch as he comes around the cars and slips the paper beneath the windshield wiper before sneaking off.

As he walks away, he pulls a phone from his back pocket, but I can't tell what he's doing. I assume it's a text to his accomplice–the person deleting evidence of his trespassing from the cameras. Not this evidence, though.

Sophie leans against me on the couch, her head on my chest, one hand next to her face. Since September started–spooky season– all she's wanted to watch are horror movies. Tonight's feature is As Above So Below, one of her favorites. I'll admit it's sufficiently terrifying. The thought of running for my life through the miles of catacombs beneath Paris is enough to scare most people, I assume.

I haven't wanted to ask her about the note that I know Caleb left on her car today. She doesn't know how much access I have to her now and I'm not about to scare her off. It's obviously on her mind, though.

"Hey, did you find anything about- about my ex?" Sophie asks softly during one of the most anxiety-inducing parts yet. The cameraman, whose name I forget, is having a panic attack while stuck trying to crawl through a tight tunnel on top of ancient bones. No thanks.

"I, er," I swallow, trying to speak around a lump that has formed in my throat that definitely isn't because of the movie. "I can't find any deleted footage, but I'm still working on it."

"Thanks," she whispers.

I reach down to hook my index finger under her chin and turn her face upward.

"It's nothing," I assure her. "I'd do so much more than that for you." *I am.* I lean down to kiss her nose and she closes her eyes.

Sophie shifts in my arms, giving her the right angle to press her mouth to mine. When she opens her mouth to moan, I slip my tongue between her lips, exploring and taking what I want from her. My hand that had been innocently rubbing her back drifts to her ass, squeezing. She moans again, the sound once more captured by my mouth. Her hand slides down my chest to rub my growing erection through my pants and she smiles against my lips.

"Is Miles here?" she whispers.

"Cam session," I respond between kisses. "In his room. He'll be busy for a while."

"Good."

Her skilled hands work to undo my button and zipper and, before I can protest, her hand is beneath my boxers, palming my cock.

"But-" I try to protest, but she shakes her head.

"You said he's busy," she breathes, kissing her way down my neck before sliding onto the floor in front of me. Settling herself between my legs, she reaches up to pull my cock fully out of my boxers, but hesitates, meeting my gaze. "I'll stop if you're uncomfortable."

I reach forward and slide my fingers into her hair, gripping tight and pulling her forward to kiss her quickly.

"Keep going," I growl.

*Fuck Miles.*

A sinful smile spreads across her lips before she licks them. Sophie wastes no time, spitting on my half-hard length before she begins to stroke me. I let my head fall back against the couch, focusing on the sensations. I inhale sharply and look back down at her when her tongue darts across my tip. Sophie's eyes are on me as she slowly lowers her mouth onto my cock.

"Your mouth feels so fucking good," I groan. With each bob of her head, she takes more of me. "So fucking good."

Her hand reaches down to play with my balls and I utter a string of curses, trying to contain my release as long as possible. It's fucking difficult when she does that thing with her tongue that makes my cock twitch.

Miles clears his throat, startling both of us. Sophie's head pops up, my cock falling from her mouth while my hands fly to cover my erection. It's impossible at this point.

"The fuck, man?" I shout, turning my back to Miles while trying to keep my eyes on him.

"Hey, you were in a communal space!" Miles laughs but turns his back.

I do my best to stuff myself back into my boxers. Sophie stays on her knees, eyeing the two of us and chewing on her bottom lip as if lost in thought.

"What?" I frown at her.

"What?" asks Miles, still facing away from us.

"Not you," I shoot over my shoulder before addressing Sophie. "What are you thinking?"

"I'm not thinking anything," says Miles, rocking forward on the balls of his feet. He's
*definitely* thinking something.

"Shut up," I grumble, glaring at his back before softening my eyes and returning them
once more to Sophie. "Well?"

"Nothing." She shakes her head, letting her lip pop out from between her teeth. "Sorry,
Miles."

"How long were you standing there?" I mutter. Bad question because when Miles
turns, I can see a bit of redness in his cheeks.

"I'm not answering that."

His eyes drop to his pants and mine follow to the evidence of just how much he saw.
Strangely, it doesn't bother me. Now that the initial shock is gone, the idea of Miles
watching me with Sophie might be... exciting. Is that right? Does that mean something's
wrong with me? No, other men enjoy that sort of thing–being watched. Or watching.
Fuck, my mind is scrambled.

"Let's go to your room," Sophie breathes, her voice just as velvety as ever. I'll do
anything she says to feel her mouth on my cock again.

Placing her hands on my thighs, she uses them to guide her body up mine until our lips
touch.

"Unless," I whisper, my mouth dry at the thought of what I'm about to suggest, "you
want him to stay."

Sophie's head jerks back and her eyes widen in shock, one eyebrow popping up. A
smirk plays on her lips, swollen from my kisses and her work between my legs. The silence
that follows my suggestion is enough to cause my anxiety to skyrocket, but the words are
out there. I'm not taking them back. For once in my damn life, I'm going to do what I
want, and what I want, apparently, is a threesome with my girlfriend and my best friend.

"What do you say, honey?" asks Miles. His voice has changed from light and joking to
hoarse and husky.

"Well?" I ask, studying her face.

"Are you sure?" She wants it. It's written all over her face.

"Fuck yes."

# 27

## Brody

I grab the back of her neck and pull her face back to mine.

"What do you want him to do?" she breathes against my lips between kisses.

"I-" I don't fucking know. I didn't get that far. But an idea comes to me. "Get up," I whisper to her. Then I look at Miles. "Sit down."

"Bossy Brody," he laughs. "I like." His words are light, but that tone tells me just how excited he is for whatever is about to happen.

Sophie stands up, allowing me to do the same. I cup her face and kiss her once more before stepping to the side to give her space. Miles takes a seat on the couch, hands on his thighs, and waits.

Now that the time has come for me to make any kind of decision, my brain is broken and my mouth is still dry. I lick my lips and take a deep breath. Sophie places her hand on my arm with an encouraging smile and fire in her amber eyes.

"Actually, Miles," I'm not looking at him, just staring at Sophie with an impish grin, "Simon says sit on the floor, back against the couch."

"Yes, sir." He winks and slides to the floor with a move that borders on ridiculous. "Don't you mean Brody says?"

"Sophie," I whisper, my grin widening, "sweetheart. *Brody* says take that dress off for us and give us a show." I step back to give her some room.

Sophie bites her bottom lip and giggles deep in her throat, a sinful symphony that makes me shudder with need. I take another step back as she crosses her arms and grabs her dress as far down as she can reach without bending. Far slower than I would like, she pulls the flowing cloth up, revealing her thighs and then her lavender lace panties. Miles and I groan in unison at the sight as her breasts are revealed to us, clad in the same pastel lingerie.

"Jesus, sweetheart, move faster," I moan.

"You didn't say Brody says," she teases, pulling the dress over her head as slowly as humanly possible.

"Brody says pull off that damn dress and toss it to the side."

Sophie does so, that same delicious smile on her face. The dress flies over the couch in a flurry of white and floral fabric, landing with a *swish* on the floor out of sight.

"I need to see all of you," Miles chokes. Good to know the sight of this woman does the same things to him as it does to me.

"Well, sweetheart? Brody says take off that bra."

Sophie reaches back to unhook the bra, shimmying out of it and tossing it to Miles with a smirk. Her eyes are still on me.

"Miles, Brody says tell Sophie how perfect her tits look."

"Your tits are so fucking perfect," he moans. "Can I touch her?"

"Nope. Suffer." I wink at him and he grunts his annoyance. "Sophie, Brody says play with those beautiful tits. Massage them and play just the way you like."

"You gonna make me do all the work?" she asks, raising her hands to do as I ordered. She pinches one nipple and moans, her mouth dropping open, eyes closing. I notice the way her thighs squeeze together.

"For now." I'm desperate to feel her suffocating on my dick again, but I'm enjoying this game. I notice Miles' hands creeping toward the zipper of his jeans. "Brody didn't say to move, Miles."

"Fuck, man, this is agony."

"I know." I flash a smirk his way before returning my gaze to Sophie. Her moans are growing louder. "Brody says stop." She drops her hands and her eyes snap open. "I think it's time we give our boy what he wants, don't you?" Her eyes dart to Miles and then back to me. She nods slightly. "Brody says take off those panties and let us see how wet you already are."

Sophie inhales sharply and follows the command, hooking her thumbs into the lace and pulling down. When the fabric passes her knees, I can see the dark spot in the center.

"So fucking wet for us," I murmur as she kicks the panties away. "Now, Brody says come here and give me a kiss."

Sophie takes a couple of steps to reach me, standing on her toes while I lean down. As our lips meet, my hand slides down her side, then across her thigh. With my fingers, I urge her to part her legs just a bit so I can feel the wetness hidden there. Another curse tumbles from my lips and I swirl my middle finger around her clit. She moans into my mouth and then I pull away.

"Brody says," I breathe heavily, "go kneel on the couch with your pussy directly over Miles' face. I want him to taste this." I lift my fingers to her lips and she opens her mouth to taste herself on them. "Good girl."

I give Sophie a quick kiss on the side of the head before she turns to do as I've instructed. Before she gets too far, I take the opportunity to slap her plump ass and she giggles. Miles is grinning ear to ear when Sophie places a foot on either side of him, standing above him before kneeling on the couch. She hesitates, inches from her target, while Miles' head is fully lying back on the couch.

"It's ok," Miles breathes. "Sit all the way down. Smother me with your cunt."

With that, Sophie widens her knees.

"Miles." I address him and he pauses his movements, having been about to reach up to pull Sophie down. "Brody says eat that gorgeous pussy for us. Brody says make her come if you can." My added challenge causes Miles to growl while Sophie continues to lower herself.

Watching Miles' mouth make contact is sweet, sweet heaven and I can't contain myself any longer. I reach into my still undone pants, beneath my boxers, to palm my aching cock. Miles' tongue traces Sophie from back to front before his mouth closes around her clit. Leaning her arms on the back of the couch, Sophie sticks her ass out, her back arching.

"Brody says use your fingers, Miles. Work that pretty pussy."

Miles reaches up and slides two fingers into Sophie with ease. I can see him curling them, flexing his whole hand with each movement. His other hand is holding her thigh, pulling her further down onto his face. That looks like quite the position. I'll have to try it sometime. I firmly believe I could die happy if it was while being smothered by her like that.

"Are you close, sweetheart?" I ask when Sophie's moans turn to high-pitched whines. I take a few steps around the couch so I can see her better. Her face is hidden below the cushion, so I gently grab her hair and pull. Her eyes are having trouble focusing until I squeeze just a bit. "Come on, Sophie. Brody says to tell us when you're close."

"I'm," she whispers, "I'm c-close." She confirms what was obvious by her fluttering eyelids. I smirk.

"Miles, Brody says stop."

Sophie lets out a frustrated groan as Miles stops what he's doing. I have to stifle a laugh when I see her hips trying to grind, to get the friction she so desperately needs.

"Ah, ah. Brody didn't say you could keep going. Brody says lift up for me."

"Fuck, Brody," she whines, but lifts her ass just slightly. I hear Miles softly kissing her—whether it's her pussy or her thighs is irrelevant. It's not what I told him to do.

"Miles," I warn, looking behind Sophie even though all I can see are his feet. I focus on Sophie again. She's watching me intently. "What is it you want, sweetheart?" Sophie licks her lips, her gaze dropping to mine.

"I want you to fuck me," she whispers. I lean down and press my forehead to hers.

"Good girl."

I round the couch again, removing my pants and boxers quickly in the process, and straddle Miles' legs. Sophie's body is still too close for him to move his head away. Enveloped by her scent, I can only imagine how hard he is, aching to be inside her, but it's my turn.

"Please," Sophie begs, wiggling her ass a little. Miles groans beneath her. When my hand lands on her ass, she stops. It's not enough to leave a red mark, but it's definitely going to be a little pink for a few minutes.

"Brody says stay still," I growl, stepping forward and grasping the base of my cock. "Both of you," I add, hearing Miles shift beneath us.

I drag the tip of my leaking cock along Sophie's center, grazing Miles' mouth in the process. Knowing he's at my mercy, right there, so close to both of us has me all the more excited. I smirk as Sophie moans, my teasing making her writhe again. I reach forward and grab her hair, pulling back just hard enough to make her hiss.

"I didn't say to fucking move."

"Please," Sophie whines.

"I second that please," comes Miles' muffled agreement. I have to let out a chuckle at that.

"Ok, I think you earned it." I let go of Sophie's hair and slide into her at the same time, but only an inch or so. When she tries to push back, I grab her ass and hold her in place. "Brody didn't say to move," I remind her. "Brody says stay fucking still so I can use your cunt. You hear me?"

"Yes," she breathes, her forehead dropping to the couch cushion.

"You too, pretty boy," I add, glancing down. I can't see his face. His hands are on his thighs, fingers digging into the denim as he fights the urge to touch himself.

"You got it," he says, still muffled.

Letting go of my cock, I slide my hands over Sophie's ass, grabbing her hips. In one quick thrust, I push all the way inside her, forcing a cry from her throat. I feel my balls slap against Brody's chin and I pull out only to drive home again, hard and fast.

"Now," I pant, "Miles, Brody says to help Sophie come on my cock."

I pull out and begin a rhythm of deep thrusts. Sophie's walls are already choking me, trying to wring a release from me well before I'm ready. Miles is clearly good at what he's doing. Or maybe it's me. Or the combination.

I don't fucking care.

"You're so fucking tight," I grunt. "Taking all of me like a good girl." I can't stop the praise. "You take me so well, so fucking well."

Her muscles tense and Sophie tries to lean forward. I grab a fistful of hair and keep a firm grip on her hip.

"Don't you fucking run." I keep up the rhythm, driving into her fast and deep each time. "You're gonna take this dick like my good girl."

"Y y-yes!" She cries out, trying to do as I say, trying not to pull away from me.

I'm not done with this game, though. After a few more thrusts, I slide out of her. A groan of protest escapes my lips as well as Sophie's, but she stays in place. She's learning. With a light slap on her ass again, I step away.

"Brody says," I pant, "let Miles fucking breathe." I chuckle as Sophie lifts her hips, but Miles stays where he is. It looks like he's learning too. "Miles, Brody says get up and sit on the couch. Pants off."

"You sure, boss?" He doesn't wait for a response. Licking his lips, Miles emerges from between Sophie's thighs and hurries to get in place. When his pants and boxers are off, I have to admit–his cock is beautiful. I'm not sure I'd ever use that word to describe anyone else's, but his? Beautiful is an accurate description. It's thick and almost the length of mine, standing at attention.

"Oh, I'm sure. I want us all to win this little game, don't you?" I raise an eyebrow and meet his gaze, but I know he saw mine wandering.

"Absolutely," he groans, looking sideways at Sophie who's still breathing heavily.

"Sophie," I smooth my hand over one ass cheek and she turns her head so she can see us both. "Brody says sit on Miles' dick."

"Jesus." Miles throws his head back as Sophie shuffles closer and swings a leg over his lap. His hands slide up her thighs, but I slap one of them away. He drops the other. "Sorry," he mutters, lifting his head to glance at me.

Sophie lowers herself with a gasp, her slick pussy sliding easily over Miles' cock. She stares into his eyes and he stares right back, hungry and needy and everything I feel for her too. I run a hand down her back and speak softly.

"Brody says ride that fucking cock."

Miles utters a string of curses as Sophie begins to rock back and forth. I'm not going to correct her movements. Up and down, front to back, I don't care. I just want her to-

"Make yourself feel good," Miles moans. "That's it, honey."

Licking my lips, I gingerly take the next step in my little plan. Setting my foot on the couch, I use the back for stability, standing beside the two of them. My cock is still slick with Sophie's arousal and I use it to stroke myself near her face.

"Miles," I groan, calling his attention to my movements. "Brody says it's your turn to do the work and fuck her from below."

I know he has the strength to keep it up, too. We work out together several times a week. That man lives to make his partners feel good and strength is a big part of that. Miles lifts Sophie's ass and slides them both toward the edge of the couch to give himself leverage. Then with one last glance up at me, his eyes pausing on my cock, he thrusts. Sophie cries out, her head thrown back. While Miles continues, I run a hand over her hair and turn her head toward me as she whimpers.

"Brody says suck my cock, sweetheart."

Without hesitation, Sophie leans to the side and takes me into her mouth. I keep my hand on her head, trying to allow her to control her movements, but I can tell her neck is getting tired from the awkward angle. Even standing as close to Miles as possible, my leg against his arm, it's not enough. I take over, tangling my fingers in her hair, making her choke and gag and sputter when I pull all the way out.

"Fuck," I breathe, my voice cracking, high pitched and full of need. "Fuck, that's it. Sophie, you're so good to me. So fucking good. Good to both of us. Our good fucking girl." *Our?* Yeah, ok, *our* good fucking girl.

"So fucking good," Miles agrees. His words are strained. "Brody, man, I-" He cuts himself off with a grunt.

"You ready to fill her up?" I growl.

"Yes, man, fuck!"

I have to chuckle at that reaction as I pull Sophie toward me, making her take as much of my length as she can. Her eyes shoot up to mine.

"What do you think?" I ask as she gags. "Should we let him fill your cunt?" I pull her mouth off of me and she sputters, gasping for air.

"Yes," she pants, "please." Then she glances down at Miles. "I want you to come inside me," she begs. I turn her head with my hand still in her hair.

"It's not his decision," I growl. "But I think we'll let him have this win. Brody says to put that mouth to work again, sweetheart." I look down at Miles who hasn't ceased his thrusting, though his movements are disjointed now. "Miles," I grunt when Sophie closes her lips around me again, "Brody says fill her the fuck up."

"Fuck." Miles draws out the curse, his hips slamming up and into Sophie while she works my cock with her tongue. A few more thrusts and a heavy groan later, Miles is done, pulling Sophie all the way down onto him.

"Brody says stay right fucking there." I barely get the words out, I'm so close. "Stay right there," I repeat, pulling Sophie by the hair off of me while I stroke myself.

Using her saliva, I come within seconds, painting not only Sophie's face and chest but Miles' too. I groan, my breathing ragged as I finish, squeezing the last drops from the tip. I back up a step and then drop to my knees on the couch, taking in the sight of the two of them, covered in my cum.

Reaching up, I grab Sophie's hair gently and pull her face to mine so I can kiss her. I taste myself on her lips and smile against them.

"I haven't forgotten about you, sweetheart." My chest heaves. "Miles? How do you feel about making her come on your face?" I have my answer in his grin. I'm learning quite a lot about my best friend this evening. "Then Brody says Sophie, lay down on the couch, and Miles?" His eyes snap to mine and I reach out to fist his hair. "Brody says make our girl come."

I let go of them and kneel on the floor for the best view as Sophie and Miles get into position. Watching Miles' cock fall out of her, followed by his thick, white cum, has my own cock twitching again. The things this woman does to me. I've had impure thoughts before, but never like this.

Sophie lays her head near the armrest while Miles settles himself between her thighs, not waiting a moment to dive in. I pull Sophie's nearest leg toward me, opening her up more so I can see his artistry. Miles laps at her, cleaning the evidence of him from every single inch. His tongue is everywhere, touching every place, taking every drop. And when he's cleaned himself off of her, he latches onto her clit once more, wringing a deep moan from Sophie's throat.

"Use your fingers."

"Does Brody say?" Sophie pants and I smirk.

"Yes, sweetheart. Brody says use your fingers, Miles."

He slides two fingers inside and then a third almost immediately, coating them in what's left of his cum, mixed with her arousal. Sophie writhes in front of us, whimpering and whining and begging to come for us.

"Please," her breathy whine is music to my ears.

"Brody says come for us, sweetheart." I move closer to cup her face. Her eyes fall to mine. "Come for us," I repeat.

The lewd sounds of Miles absolutely devouring her become faster and her eyes flutter closed as her body curls inward for a moment. Then all at once, she explodes. Her back arches. She gasps, her mouth open in a silent scream while Miles continues to suck and finger fuck her. Her torso rotates toward me while the pleasure rips through her and I keep my hand on her cheek even though her eyes are closed. She's so fucking beautiful when she comes, even if I'm not the one doing it.

"That's it, baby." My voice is soft and gentle. "He's making you feel so fucking good, isn't he? Making you come so hard on his face."

All Sophie can do is whine in response as her ability to breathe returns. Miles slows his movements, allowing her to recover, but little twitches continue to rock through her.

"That," says Miles, in between licking his fingers, "was hot."

I run my fingers into Sophie's hair and her eyes flutter open. Her chest rises and falls while she tries to control her breathing. I can see clarity returning to those beautiful golden pools.

"It really was," I agree, leaning forward to kiss her softly before settling back on my heels again.

"We need," Sophie pants, "to do that more often."

# 28

## Miles

Brody Motherfucking Torrence.

What a sneaky little pervert. My best friend is way kinkier than I ever would have thought. Not that this is a 10 on a scale of Vanilla to an Everything-but-the-Kitchen-Sink Sundae, but it's more than a 1, which is what I pegged him for. I smirk to myself.

*Pegged*. I wonder what his thoughts are on that. I wonder what his thoughts are on a few things, actually. The man had his balls on my goddamn chin, for crying out loud. Our friendship has withstood a lot, but never anything like *this*. Sharing Sophie with me, dominating us. The thought of what happened just a few minutes ago is enough to send a rush of blood straight back down to my cock.

After Sophie disappears to Brody's bathroom, we find our clothes. I can feel Brody's eyes on me as I zip my jeans and button them. I want to meet his gaze. I want to say something, but I'm at a loss for words, which is un-fucking-usual for me. Taking a deep breath does nothing to slow my thoughts or calm my mind and I absently run a hand through my hair before finally facing Brody. He's chewing his lip, studying me and I'd kill to be able to read his mind right now. Usually, he wears his heart on his sleeve. He's an open book, to me if not to others. His expression right now is indiscernible.

"Say something," I mumble. My tongue feels too big to form words properly. I can still taste the combination of Sophie and my arousal and it's messing with my head, keeping me from thinking straight. Not to mention the fact that I still have his cum on my chest.

"That was," Brody blows out a breath through pursed lips, inflating his cheeks in the process. It might look comical if I wasn't so nervous about what it meant.

"Sorry if I crossed a line." Although it was his idea, I still feel the need to apologize. As if my presence is what forced him to act the way he did, ever the people pleaser.

A crooked grin pulls at the corn of Brody's lips and he rubs the back of his neck, shaking his head.

"No." He seems to have a tough time getting the word out, but his gaze never falters. "No, it was my idea and I enjoyed it."

I smirk, but Brody blushes. He actually fucking blushes.

*What have we done?*

"I should probably leave you to your date." I glance toward the bathroom, but the shower is still running.

"Do you want to join us? The movie-" He takes a deep breath and starts again. "We didn't really pay much attention after a certain point." I can see a little pink flaring in those tanned cheeks and I smile.

"Nah, just pick up where you left off." I shake my head and walk past him toward my bedroom.

I've pushed his boundaries enough for one evening. Letting Sophie cuddle between the two of us while watching a scary movie somehow feels more intimate than what we just did and I'm not sure he's ready for that..

"You sure? Don't you like all that scary stuff?" He doesn't reach out to stop me, but I turn and grin.

"Well yeah, but I try to at least wait until October."

"When it's not still ninety degrees out?" The corner of his mouth lifts into a crooked grin.

"Exactly. Gotta be below eighty-five. Enjoy the movie with Sophie. I'll..." I'll what? Go back to my room and finish editing something? Post some photos to my subscription pages? Make no noise and pretend I don't exist?

Leaving my thought unfinished, I head back to my room just as the bathroom door opens and Sophie emerges, freshly showered. What I wouldn't give to have joined her under the hot water, to bend her over and take her again.

Something tells me things are going to be very different from here on out.

My phone buzzes angrily on my bedside table, waking me up far earlier than I would like. I was dreaming about Sophie's perfect body and Brody sliding his cock-

I groan and slap my hand around without opening my eyes, trying to find the offending object. Unfortunately, my clumsy fingers only succeed in knocking it to the floor. Forced to open my eyes, I practically throw my upper body over the side of the bed, my hand continuing to slap around for the phone.

When I finally find it, I'm even more annoyed to see Isla's face staring up at me with the time across her forehead.

"It's not even six in the morning," I groan into the receiver, holding it to my ear while still hanging over the edge of the bed.

"Sorry," she mutters, but the tremor in her voice shakes me awake. I scramble to sit up and run my hand over my face.

"What's wrong?" My tone is a little kinder now.

"I need you to come get me." She's speaking softly as if trying not to wake someone.

"Where are you?" I listen for anything beyond her voice on the other end, trying to figure out if she's safe.

"I'm- I went home with someone last night and I-I don't know-"

"Drop a pin. I'm getting Brody."

"No, don't bother him."

I frown, pausing my attempts to untangle my legs from the sheets.

"Why?" I growl. I do that a lot lately.

"He," she swallows, "he was supposed to give me an emergency call last night. He must've forgotten."

I have to take a deep breath through my nose so I don't stomp across the house and throttle him. Why Isla asked him and not me, I'll never know. Without an actual alert on his phone, he'd probably forget his own birthday.

"So you went home with a guy because you never got an emergency call?" I ask, finally standing up to find pants.

"Well, no, but," she grunts. "I don't know, I wasn't thinking, ok?"

"Thinking with your dick is more like."

"I *will* slap you."

"Not if I rescue you from Prince Charming."

"Prince Lying Thundercunt is more like it. Just... just come get me, ok?" Her voice is so soft now I can't tease her.

"I'm on my way."

Luckily she's only down near Koreatown, an area I know fairly well. Isla is waiting for me on the curb, her brown hair disheveled and her green eyes look on the verge of tears. I pull up and put my jeep in park, allowing her to hoist herself inside. Even for Sophie, who's a couple of inches taller, it's difficult to climb in and out of this thing. For Isla, it's next to impossible without vaulting herself up.

"What do you need?" I'm not about to ask what happened.

Isla takes a shaky breath and blows it out slowly, the way Brody did last night when trying to think what to say to me after our little game. I hide my smirk at the thought. This isn't the time to be smiling.

"I need a fucking juice cleanse."

I snort.

"Ok, that's not what I expected. A shot, maybe. Eight coffees, sure. But not juice."

"Just," she sighs and looks out the window, "take me to Kreation, ok? I'll buy."

"The fuck you will." I put the jeep in drive and pull away from the curb, into traffic.

"He didn't hurt me or anything," says Isla after several minutes of silence, filled only by the sounds of honking and yelling that accompany rush hour in Los Angeles.

"If he had, I'd break his fucking arms," I mutter without looking. My hands tighten on the steering wheel and I know she hears the low squeak of the leather in my grip.

"I know." She blows out a quick laugh through her nose.

"Isla, I gotta know what happened, kiddo."

"I'm not a kiddo," Isla grumbles, but then deflates. "He was nice. I swear I didn't see any red flags while we were at dinner."

"So you probably wouldn't have answered an emergency call even if Brody *had* remembered?" I offer.

"I don't know. But when I got up this morning, I saw stuff in his place that-" Her voice breaks and she clears her throat. "I think he's married." I can't see the tears that are clearly welling in her eyes, but I can hear them in her voice. "At the very least, he's not fucking single."

"Fucking dick wagon." I glance in my rearview mirror. "Want me to turn around and give him a piece of my mind?" How about my fist?

"No, he's not worth it."

"Jesus, Isla. Where did you meet the fucker?"

"Online." She shrugs, still looking out the window. "Brody seems to be doing just fine with the girl he's dating, so I thought I'd give it a try. I can tell you now, I won't be trying that again any time soon."

I snort. One, because online dating sucks for women. I'd have warned her against it. Two, because yeah, it's going well with Brody and Sophie. *And me.* But Isla doesn't need that information about her older brother.

"So glad you find amusement in my pain."

"I'm not laughing at you, just-" My eyes flick to her and then back to the road. Her arms are crossed over her chest and she's staring at me with one eyebrow raised. "I'll let Brody tell you about Sophie."

"So you've met her too?" Isla's voice rises in pitch and volume and then she groans in frustration. "I swear, I'm gonna kill him."

"I live with him."

"And I live in a studio apartment in the Valley. What's your point?"

"I just see more of him-" *literally*, "-than you do."

"Rude."

"The truth hurts." I round the corner onto a street with plenty of parallel spots next to the curb. It's a short walk to the juice bar from there. "Want me to get you something or do you want to come in with me?"

"You won't get my order right."

---

An hour later, after sitting with our smoothies at Kreation and grabbing a couple of fresh juices to go, Isla is back at her place and I head home. Sophie's car was still in the driveway when I left this morning, but it's gone now, despite the fact that it's stupid early. I'd still be asleep on a normal day.

"Hey, where were you?" Brody calls without looking my way. He's sitting on the couch wearing only a pair of gray sweats when I walk in the door.

"Just went for a drive. Clear my head and all that." The lie doesn't come easily, but Isla is like family to me and if she doesn't want to bother Brody with his broken promise, I won't be the one to fuck it up.

He stands from the couch and turns to face me. Without Sophie distracting me, I'm struck by how much he has changed since we moved in together five years ago. Pushing him to hit the gym with me a few times a week, cooking for both of us regularly–all because he won't let me pay rent, the stubborn ass–seems to have done him some good. I wasn't paying attention last night, but now I have to stop myself from staring.

My phone begins to buzz in my pocket and I remember the scheduled post that probably just went live. It'll have my phone going crazy with notifications–new subscriptions, new purchases, comments, likes, and direct messages are already flooding in. I pull the phone out and turn the ringer off entirely. I can't handle that kind of stimulation right now.

"You want some breakfast? I'm makin' waffles." The Shrek reference goes over Brody's head which means he's far more lost in thought than I realized.

"I'll never say no to waffles," he chuckles, but the smile doesn't meet his eyes. "Are you really ok with last night?"

"Shouldn't *I* be asking *you* that?" I hang my keys on the ring by the door and walk around to the pantry to find the dry ingredients.

"I suppose so. I'm sure nothing we did is new for you, huh?"

"Not at all," I confirm, walking out of the pantry with reusable containers filled with flour, sugar, and baking powder as well as the bottle of homemade vanilla that I've been refilling for lord knows how long. "So that leaves you." I round the corner and set the items down on the island before looking back at Brody. "You've had time to think, so...?"

Fuck, that flush in his cheeks and chest is going to steal my breath. I have to turn back to the task at hand, walking to the fridge to find the milk, eggs, and butter.

"It, er, was fun."

*Understatement.*

"It was," I agree. I remain in front of the open fridge, unable to look at him until he finishes the thought.

He takes a steadying breath and continues.

"I feel like I'm moving really fast," he admits and my heart shatters.

I hadn't even thought about that. It's been a little more than a week since he went *all the way* with Sophie. I've gotta get him to use better language outside the bedroom. Or living room. I mutter a curse under my breath, hoping he can't hear.

"I don't regret it," Brody adds quickly. "But you and I have never- I mean, I know *you've* been with guys, solo too. I don't know-"

"It's ok," I cut him off, closing the double doors so I can see him again. I lean against the cold, stainless steel finish. "It was a spur-of-the-moment thing. It was fun. But if you aren't ready for something like that, I won't push. Sophie definitely won't."

"Yeah." Just the thought of her is enough to bring a smile to each of our faces. He rubs the back of his neck again and looks down. When he eventually looks back at me, those emerald eyes of his seem lighter as if he's gotten a massive weight off of his chest. "Thanks, man."

"Just let me know if you change your mind." I wink, trying to add some levity, and Brody chuckles. "Flavored or plain today?"

"Plain." Brody comes to join me in the kitchen, watching from his usual stool at the kitchen island. "Music?"

"Obviously."

Brody connects his phone to the Bluetooth speaker that sits in the far corner near the sink, pulling up a playlist called *In da Clerrrrb*. It's mine, filled with a bunch of songs I have affectionately taken to calling my 'pump-up jams' because I typically use this playlist in the gym. The music isn't loud, just enough that I can pick out the lyrics.

Humming to myself, I set about grabbing the electric mixer from its spot in one of the bottom cabinets. I pull out three glass mixing bowls in varying sizes.

"Why don't you use the stand mixer?" Brody knows I like it when he asks questions about cooking. He's still not great at it, but he's gotten marginally better in recent years.

"Too much work." I shrug, cracking the eggs and separating the whites from the yolks. The whites go into the medium bowl and the yolks into the small one. "And I can't get everything. It's fine for doughs and things that'll come together easily, but not whisking egg whites. There's always going to be a layer of unwhisked whites in the bottom of the bowl with a stand mixer."

"Interesting." He's silent for a few more minutes while I measure dry ingredients into another bowl, the largest one I pulled out. "And then you have to fold the whites into the batter?"

"Exactly." I continue the process, leaving the whipping of the egg whites until last to keep the structure. "Grab the waffle iron for me. It's in the pantry."

"Magic word?"

"Pleeeeeease?" I grin extra wide and squeeze my eyes shut, earning a snort, but it works and Brody follows the order.

He reappears a minute later, holding the Death Star waffle maker aloft.

"There ya go."

"But I didn't say Miles says," I laugh.

"Very funny." He rolls his eyes and resumes his seat. "That was cheesy, wasn't it?" he groans, dropping his head onto his forearms where they rest on the counter.

"Cheesy," I agree, "but hot." The compliment hangs in the air and I have to change the subject. "Still taking me to the airport Thursday?"

"Yeah, you fly out early this time, right?"

"6:04," I groan, throwing my head back and wincing dramatically. "But if I don't leave that early, I won't get to Miami until super late."

"Yeah, I get it. What time do you want to be there?"

We discuss logistics for a few minutes and then fall silent while he watches me work.

"Hey, watch out for Sophie while you guys are there," says Brody, cutting up the fresh waffle I just set in front of him. "She's been dealing with some stuff and I'm worried about her."

I frown, dying to ask what he's talking about. She seems fine to me. There was a moment at the rose garden where she got spooked, but I think we'd just been in our own little world. Reality startled her.

"Of course, I'll keep an eye on her."

"Don't..." he sighs, "don't tell her I told you."

"I'm not keeping secrets." I've learned the hard way what that can do to a relationship.

"I'm not telling you to lie, just don't tell her I said I was worried. I don't want her spooked."

"We need to have a family meeting," I mutter under my breath. It's going to have to wait until after SpicyCon, though.

# 29

## Sophie

Sophie

**Miles:**
I made a group chat!

**Brody:**
I'm sorry. I couldn't stop him.

**Miles:**
I thought it would help with sharing custody.

**Me:**
Custody?

**Miles:**
Yeah, you know. Brody gets you weekends and holidays, but I get you the rest of the time.

Brody:

Call me crazy, but that doesn't
seem fair.

Brody:

Call me crazy, but that doesn't
seem fair.

"When's the last time we did this?" Natalie asks, grabbing the cooler from the floor behind the driver's seat. I roll my eyes at the group chat with the guys and slip my phone back into my pocket.

"Had a beach day? Fuck, I don't know," I mutter. "Have we done it since my birthday?"

"Don't think so."

"Then about two and a half months."

"We've got to get here more often." She closes the door, holding her wide-brimmed hat to her head so it doesn't blow off in the wind. Cooler in her hand, umbrella under the same arm, she looks ridiculous trying to control it all.

Neither of us feels like swimming today, but we have folding chairs, sandwiches, lavender lemonade, and plenty of sunscreen. Trudging through the sand at Malibu-Zuma beach to get close enough to the water is a workout in itself and I'm glad I didn't try to look cute. No one is going to recognize me and it's not like Natalie cares what I look like.

"This good?" We're close enough to enjoy the sound of the waves while far enough not to have said waves reach our toes.

"Yeah, I'm done walking."

Natalie shoves the cooler into the sand so that it opens toward the ocean while I set up the chairs. When the umbrella is set, covering the cooler and the main parts of our chairs, we settle in. I pull plastic bottles of lemonade from the cooler and hand one to Natalie. Neither of us is hungry yet, so we just sit and enjoy the view and the sounds, sipping on our beverages that are definitely *not* alcoholic.

Days like this, when I can relax and take time off with my best friend, remind me that my hard work is paying off. I get to be creative, choose my schedule, work with people I want to, and avoid those I don't like. I get to be my own boss. This is a job, despite what so many people think, but it's a job I wouldn't trade for anything.

The crash of the waves is soothing, though it's not quite loud enough to drown out the seagulls. I dig my bare feet into the sand, finding the cool layer just below the surface.

There are days it's so windy that, even this far from the water, I can feel the mist and taste it on my lips. It's not quite that strong today, but it's been picking up.

I decide to take a selfie, smiling and holding up a peace sign. Then I flip the camera around and take a photo of my feet in the sand with the waves in the background. I post it online and then take a deep breath.

I'm still trying to process what happened with Brody and Miles. *Together*. Brody *wanted* Miles to join us and Miles did so, not only without hesitation, but with gusto. I never would have guessed that Brody would be comfortable sharing, let alone sharing with his roommate. His best friend. Trading off date nights is one thing, but enjoying each other together isn't something I had expected to experience.

"We had a threesome," I blurt suddenly.

My hand flies to my mouth with a slap and I giggle when Natalie turns to look at me. Out of the corner of my eye, I can see her jaw drop and she pulls her sunglasses down so she can look at me over the top of them.

"You mean with...?"

I nod.

"Yeah."

"Wait, you haven't- that was the first, wasn't it? I mean, with two men."

I bite my bottom lip, trying hard not to smile.

"It was the hottest fucking thing I've ever done," I finally admit, unable to keep the laughter from my voice.

"Sophie, Sophie, Sophie." She shakes her head and settles back into her seat to face the ocean once more. "Ho-lee shit, girl. And Brody, he's- he's like *new*. How did he handle that?"

"It was his idea!" I squeal.

"What the fuck?"

"I know!"

"That kinky motherfucker. Ok, I take back every bad thing I've said about these guys. If it wasn't clear before, it is now. They're good for you." Natalie glances at me again. "*Both* of them are good for you."

"You changed your tune fast."

"You feel safe with Brody?" she asks, not looking at me, but continuing to focus on the waves.

"I really do."

"And Miles, he makes you happy?"

"He does." I smile. His excitement for just about everything he does is infectious in the best way.

"Red flags?"

"I-" I stop. "I mean, probably. Can I keep refusing to see them as red for now? Maybe yellow."

"Yellow is acceptable." Natalie nods and leans her head back against her chair with a grin. "Jesus, *two* boyfriends. And they were roommates," she adds under her breath. I sigh, relaxing in my chair and enjoying the glint of the sun off of the waves.

"I guess best friends who fuck together..." I muse, but don't bother to finish the thought.

"Sorry I can't go with you to Miami," Natalie says, changing the subject. "Just not in the budget this time." She might make way more than me, but she budgets a certain amount for travel each quarter. SpicyCon didn't make the cut.

"It's fine. Miles is actually going to be there."

"At least you'll have someone to venture out with. He'll get you to leave the hotel room for more than just meals and filming."

"I'm paying for tickets, I'm going to attend the events," I laugh, but she's half right. If I were completely alone, I'd inevitably end up skipping some panels, lectures, or events in favor of staying in my room alone.

"What are you most excited for? Besides filming with new people," she adds quickly, knowing that's always my answer.

"There's a demonstration by an industry veteran on rigging."

"You want to be the rigger or the rigged?"

Natalie takes another sip of lemonade before reaching into the cooler for a sandwich. She hands one to me first. We prepared this morning, ordering cold sandwiches from one of our favorite places before heading out and picking them up on the way.

"Rigger." I pull the brown butcher paper away before taking a bite of the turkey sandwich.

"Well, take notes for me."

"You got it, dude. This was a brilliant idea." I hold up my sandwich.

"I know, right?" Natalie's mouth is full of food as she answers and it sends me into a fit of giggles, which she quickly joins.

"I haven't really checked in with you, have I?" I ask, halfway through my sandwich. "I've been so busy with work and the guys. I'm sorry."

"Oh shut up," Natalie snorts. "You've had a lot on your mind."

"I'm still sorry. Got any good sub stories lately?"

"Do you *actually* want to hear what I do to men?"

"I don't know," I giggle. "Do I?"

"Probably not."

"Ok, what about women? I know you've been filming. Has any of it been of the fun sapphic variety?" I waggle my eyebrows suggestively and Natalie grins.

"I've worked with a few lately who've been really fun, but none are local. Just in town for a week or two to film."

"Well, it's a bummer you can't get consistent content with them."

Natalie shrugs. She and I haven't made a video together in a few months, wanting to focus more on working with other people so the content doesn't get stale.

"Most are straight. They travel with their boyfriends or whatever and just take the odd girl-girl scene because they know it'll sell."

I feel a pang of guilt. Minus traveling with a partner, that's me, though I try to have a variety of content available and not just a special scene every now and then.

"I'm not blaming anyone," Natalie assures me. "Even without doing straight porn anymore, I sell a *lot* of content. It's popular stuff."

"I'm aware. Hell, you could afford our place on your own."

"Oh, I definitely could. But you cut my rent in half, so I let ya stay. Gives me extra shopping money, you know?" She pulls her sunglasses down to wink at me and I roll my eyes.

"Because you don't get enough gifts from your adoring fans."

"Bitch, you *just* did an unboxing video with like six packages on your page, didn't you?"

"This is about *you*, not me." I chuckle. Before turning back to my sandwich, I try again. "You made me start dating-"

"You're welcome."

"-so what about you? Got any hot dates?"

Natalie snorts loudly while taking a bite of her sandwich. She takes the time to chew and swallow before answering.

"I'm in my ho phase."

I roll my eyes and we sit in silence except for the waves and the crinkle of the butcher paper around our sandwiches.

"What do you miss about Oklahoma?" Natalie's question startles me. It's not something we talk about often, mostly because of my prompt departure, but she brings it up on occasion. I think it's her way of trying to help me process that I had to flee in a hurry from the place I called home for nearly twenty-eight years.

"Eileen's," I say after a moment's pause. When I catch Natalie's questioning stare, I add, "Cookies. The best damn cookies in the state."

"You have so many things to choose from and you pick cookies?" She shakes her head in disbelief.

"They're *really* good cookies."

I spend most of Wednesday resting, doing laundry, and packing. I know tomorrow is going to be a long travel day and I have so much planned in the short span of time I'll be in Miami. I don't want to risk being exhausted before I even start.

While my laundry is going, I set about editing some content from the New York trip. Other than seasonal videos, I have a lot of clip drops and posts on my subscription pages scheduled two months out. With the holiday season right around the corner, I have to plan out my posts so I don't double-drop. I've gotten good at keeping a backlog in case shoots fall through or I get sick or some other emergency happens to put me off course.

I pull up the raw footage from the shoot with Tony Gerth and layer it over mine. I line up the audios so that the footage is in sync and I can switch between the two layers as needed. Then I start to cut away the excess with about ten seconds on either side of the splits for dissolves or fine-tuning. Before I really start splicing things together and choosing camera angles, I need to figure out which of us has better audio to keep it consistent. I hit play on some of my footage first, listening closely for speech and the various sounds that come from skin-on-skin contact.

"Sounds good," I mutter to myself. It doesn't sound like anything is missing from my footage, so I switch to Tony's. Instantly, I know the audio on his footage is better. It's clearer and catches even the faintest sigh. Well, that makes my job easy.

I spend the next hour interspersing my footage with his, careful to keep the audios matched so they stay in sync.

Just as I stand to check my laundry, a text comes through from Brody and I smile down at my phone.

Brody:

> Hey sweetheart, since I won't see you til you get back from Miami, I want to wish you a safe flight. Enjoy the convention. Send me a selfie of you having fun!

The only issue I have with travel is the amount of *stuff* I have to take. Two enormous suitcases plus a rolling carry-on and a laptop bag are my usual companions and I've gotten pretty good at rolling everything to the check-in counter and away from baggage claim. I still fucking hate it. Thank god for Miles.

He's waiting for me at baggage claim in Miami, the biggest grin on his face like he hasn't seen me in weeks. I roll my carry-on over to him, noting with jealousy that he just has a backpack and one oversized suitcase, and wrap my arms around his neck. Standing on my tiptoes, I place a quick kiss on his lips, but when I try to lower myself to my feet, he tightens his arms around my waist.

Miles deepens the kiss and I can feel my cheeks warming at the public display. He must sense my tension because he lets me go.

"How was the flight?" he asks, gathering our bags together while we wait for the luggage from my flight to start appearing on the metal carousel.

"Fine." I shrug. "I read the whole time."

"The whole time? I slept for the whole first flight."

"Once I'm awake, I find it hard to go back to sleep. But I got halfway through a new book." I nod at my laptop bag sitting on my carry-on.

"What's it about?"

"You don't want to know," I laugh. It's a romance novel and, despite our careers, I doubt he'll care much about the 'porn with a plot', as some people call it.

"Oh, come on. Humor me." He crosses his arms over his chest and grins. "We have time," he adds, raising his eyebrows and jerking his head toward the carousel.

"It's a dark romance," I mutter after a few more moments of hesitation.

"A *dark* romance? What's that?"

"Well, instead of a cute rom-com playing in my head, there's blood and death and 'touch her and die' and all that good stuff."

"And?" he asks with a smirk.

"And hella spice."

Miles chuckles and wraps his arm around my shoulders, pulling me into him and placing a kiss on the top of my head that seriously fucks with my brain chemistry. It's not a forehead kiss, but it's a close second. Good thing I'm already his. That doesn't keep me from melting just a little bit.

"Hella spice," he repeats and I can hear the smile in his voice before looking up at him. He's grinning like he has some ideas. I'll admit that I'm dying to know what they are. "Anything specific?"

"Might tell ya later."

"I'm holding you to that."

*I sure hope you do.*

The heat is one thing here in Miami, but the humidity is suffocating. It's like New York all over again, but with ten percent more 'kill me'. Give me LA heat any day. I feel damp instantly when we leave the airport to wait in the pickup spot for the shuttle to the convention center hotel.

The ride is a bit bumpy in the conversion van that serves as a shuttle, but it's not the worst I've been through. I'm just thankful we're the only two in the van. With our luggage filling up much of the back end, there's barely any room for someone else's.

The driver helps us get everything inside and Miles waits by the group of luggage while I check myself into room 321. The woman behind the counter is polite, but I get the distinct feeling that the event this weekend makes her uncomfortable

I head back to Miles, waving the little paper holder with my key cards with a grin. "Your turn."

I absently play with the zipper on my laptop bag while I watch Miles speak with the same woman. She seems much warmer toward him—no surprise there, of course. He could probably turn any frown upside down with his praise. I bite my lip, thinking about what that praise sounds like in a bedroom setting. Yep, no frowns when Miles Corning is between your legs.

When he rejoins me, waving his key cards like I did mine, I catch a glimpse of his room number and my smile drops.

"What?" He follows my gaze to his hand. "What's wrong?"

"Room 323?"

"Uh, yeah. Why?"

I hold up my hand for him to see the room number scrawled hastily in the given space.

"We're neighbors."

"There *is* a god."

# 30

## Sophie

Present-Sophie is a little frustrated with Past-Sophie for scheduling a collab just hours after flying across the country. But Present-Sophie isn't a little bitch, so once Miles helps me get my luggage into my room, he kisses me on the cheek and tells me to let him know when I'm done–like we're some sort of normal couple and I'm going into a big meeting. It's sickeningly cute.

I take a quick selfie and send it to Brody, then unpack my things. It's my process when traveling. As soon as I arrive in a new hotel room, I hang up costumes or dresses as needed, place other clothing and my toys in drawers, unpack my toiletries, and set the nighttime supplies on a towel on one side of the sink and the morning supplies on a towel on the other side of the sink. The towels are a new development in my process. After my experience with a less-than-clean collab and his sink crusted with soap scum and beard trimmings, I've become a little paranoid about cleanliness.

When I'm happy with the layout, I hop in the shower.

A text comes through while I'm finishing my makeup.

> Steven Drains:
>
> Hey cutie, I should be there in ten.
> Let me know the room number
> and I'll see you soon.

I type out a quick response and set the phone next to my makeup bag. The nerves are back. Miles was the last new person I worked with and I highly doubt this experience with Steven is going to end up the same way. I don't need *three* boyfriends. That's just too much.

I pass the rest of the wait setting up my tripod and ring light, making sure I have the right angle, though I know we'll move things around when he arrives. I pull out the maid costume for the scene we planned out. I didn't realize the room I booked would have a gigantic shower *and* a huge tub with jets, so we may end up changing the blocking we talked about.

The knock on my door makes me jump, but I right myself, pulling my robe sash a little tighter around my waist. I take a deep breath and then let it out quickly. Plastering a smile on my face, I swing the door open.

"I certainly hope you're Steven," I tease, knowing full well that he is. I recognize the tattoos on his tan skin. What is it with me and tattoos lately?

"Only if you're Honey," he replies with a sheepish grin. His brown eyes are warm and beneath the thick, dark beard, I can see a smile on his full lips. He's hesitant to move when I step back to let him in, but I know this little awkward dance well.

"Come on in." I wave my hand and he slips past me.

Steven brought a carry-on similar to mine with all his gear.

"I haven't been to this hotel before." He looks around the room and nods. "It's nice. That bed looks comfy."

"I haven't tested it out yet," I chuckle. "Oh and check out the tub." I jerk my thumb toward the bathroom and Steven pokes his head in to take a peek.

"Oh fuck!"

"I know," I giggle.

"Maybe if you have time later this weekend, we could use that for a scene."

"Unfortunately, I don't think I do."

"Well, that's a bummer." He glances around, as if unsure how to get things started. "Glad you could make it. Miami is expensive."

"Yeah, I'm lucky. A friend of mine is actually right next door." I hook my thumb toward the wall I share with Miles. "Lance Kixxx?"

"I haven't heard of him. Based out in LA like you?"

"Yeah, we've worked together a few times." And we're dating. Oh, and we had a threesome with his roommate. Who I'm also dating.

"Nice." He nods and smiles and I just know he hates the small talk as much as I do.

We take several minutes to cover the legal stuff. Once that's done, Steven takes out his phone and prepares to snap a few selfies with me. We both grin widely and he throws an arm around my shoulders, holding up a peace sign for the camera.

"Send those to me?" I ask as he sets his phone down.

"I'll include it with all the footage." He nods and sets about pulling his tripod and lighting rig from his bag. His is a little different than mine, a large, removable rectangle of individual lights instead of a ring light.

When he pulls out the restraints, I take a deep breath. We talked about this. I gave my consent—enthusiastically, too. The paddle makes me tingle and I'm not entirely sure it's a *good* tingle, but I gave my consent for this too. Steven asked for it every step of the way, with every act we discussed. He doesn't see my expression falter and, by the time he meets my gaze again, the smile is plastered on my lips once more.

"So, I think we'll start with you pretending to make the bed," he says, rehashing what we've already agreed to. "Bending over so we can see that gorgeous ass." He winks. "I'll come out of the bathroom in just a towel and you can apologize and all that. We'll do the whole 'I have something you can clean' thing and then we'll get you tied up. Sound good?"

"Yep." I nod and we make sure the tripods are in place so that the phone cameras won't catch each other.

It's the flurry of movement before we start filming that calms my nerves. This is familiar. This is comfortable. I know how to do *this*. While Steven finishes setting up, I change into the maid costume. It's a short, polyester dress that doesn't even cover my ass. It came with a thong, but that's pointless since it would be swallowed by my cheeks immediately.

We start recording and get to work. I bend over with my butt facing the cameras, pretending to pull the white comforter higher on the bed and fluffing the pillows. Caught first on my camera and then on his, Steven walks into view, a towel around his waist. He pauses for a moment, staring at my ass while I move.

He startles me when he clears his throat and I turn to face him, still holding a pillow to my chest. The man is chiseled. It's the first time I'm seeing him shirtless in person and I have to remember we're filming to keep myself from staring.

I stammer an apology, saying I knocked but no one answered. The scene moves along, starting with oral. When we have several minutes of me on my knees in front of him, he suggests a punishment for coming into his room and disturbing him.

This is the part I'm least excited about. He peels off my little dress for the camera and orders me onto the bed. My heart is pumping and it's not from the usual adrenaline of a scene. Steven slowly circles the bed, holding the leather restraints.

*This is fine.*

When I lay down, he cuffs my wrists, the faux fur on the inside of the cuffs protecting my soft skin from the edges of the leather.

*This is fine.*

Outwardly, I'm smiling wickedly, watching everything he does. On the inside, I'm beginning to panic.

"Roll over," Steven growls. "Ass in the air, pretty little maid."

I do as he says, sticking my backside up while I keep my chest on the bed. I slide my hands between my legs as close to my feet as possible without cutting off my air supply. Steven goes about attaching a metal rod to the chain linking my wrists. He then cuffs my ankles and attaches them to the same rod. It forces my knees up and my hands down, opening me up to him entirely.

*This is fine.*

I take deep breaths, steadying myself as I wait for the real test. To emphasize this punishment for the cameras, Steven sets a couple of leather toys on the bed next to me–a long black paddle with the word 'SLUT' cut into it so that red leather shows from beneath and a whip. The whip is small with soft strips of thin leather less than a foot long. It can still do some damage, though.

*This is fine.*

Steven slides a hand over my ass and up my back, leaning down next to my ear.

"Are you ok?" he whispers.

"Green," I confirm, using the traffic light system we discussed.

Steven nods and then slides his hand back down my body.

"Naughty little maids," he says slowly, "get punished for coming in without permission."

He picks up the paddle and immediately smacks my ass. I know he's only using half his strength, but it still hurts and I cry out. A cold shiver of dread shocks my system along with the pain.

*This is fine.*

*WHACK!*

I cry out again. He smoothes the area with his hand before hitting me in a different spot.

*WHACK!*

*This is fine.*

"Taking your punishment so well."

*WHACK!*

*WHACK!*

*WHACK!*

Every connection forces another scream from me and I'm thankful that at least one of my neighbors won't question it.

*WHACK!*

My hands are trembling and I'm having trouble breathing. *This is fine.*

*WHACK!*

I can't breathe. *This is fine.*

*WHACK!*

Tears begin to prick the backs of my eyes. *This is fine.*

*WHACK!*

I can't breathe. *This is fine.*

*WHACK!*

Those stupid, traitorous tears spill over. *This is fine.*

*WHACK!*

Fuck, I can't breathe. *This is so* not *fine.*

*WHACK!*

"RED!" I scream. The word dissolves into a sob.

Somewhere in the back of my consciousness, I hear Steven drop the paddle and his hands immediately find the fastenings of my restraints, first releasing my wrists, then rolling me over before continuing to undo everything.

"Are you ok?" His voice is full of concern.

I try to stammer a response, but I can't and the tears begin to fall. He hurries to free me and then steps back, unsure what to do. I'm spiraling, sitting up and scooting up the bed, trying to slow my breathing and stop the tears. In a feeble and pointless attempt to cover myself, I pull a pillow across my chest and smother my face with it, as if it'll help force the memories of Caleb from my mind.

"What can I do?" Steven's voice drifts through the fog, but all I can do is shake my head in response.

My chest is tight, my breath comes in short bursts.

His footsteps indicate he's walking away from me before returning to my side moments later. I feel the bed dip with his weight as he sits on the edge and places a hand on my shin. I don't shrink from his touch.

"Honey, drink some water."

When I raise my head, still trembling, still having trouble finding air, he's holding out a fresh bottle of water. He lifts his hand from my shin and twists the lid off. I can't grab it. My arms are locked around the pillow and I can't seem to loosen my grip.

"I c-can't." I can barely make out the words. My jaw is beginning to lock up, the tremors are so bad.

Steven sets the water down and speaks in a calming voice.

"Ok, Sophie." Using my real name clears the fog just the tiniest bit. "Breathe. In through the nose, out through the mouth." He lifts his hands with a demonstrated inhale and lowers them on an exhale.

I try. Really, I do. My breathing is staggered, chaotic. My heart rate is still too fast. I need him to leave, but I can't tell him that. He's being so fucking nice.

"Breathe," Steven repeats.

"I'll-" I have to stop and clear my throat. It takes everything in me to control my voice long enough to speak. "I'll be ok," I choke.

"If you need quiet, I can leave." He's not hurt at all, just concerned for my well-being. "Just nod, you don't have to speak."

I force myself to nod, tears still streaming from my eyes. I can't stop trembling, my jaw is officially locked. This hasn't happened in months. Even the notes and the kicked-in door weren't enough to do *this* to me. It took pain to bring those memories back. Real pain. I hate that Caleb can still do this shit to me. That he turned me into a victim.

*Victim.*

I fucking hate that word.

I stuff my head back into the pillow while Steven packs up his gear, feeling guilty in addition to the overwhelming physical symptoms that are finally beginning to dissipate. My heart is slowing, my chest doesn't feel quite so tight. The tears are still flowing, though.

I vaguely hear the words Steven says before leaving, but I can't process them. The sound of the door opening and closing doesn't make me feel any better, although at least now this embarrassment is only for myself. When there's a knock on my door moments later, I groan inwardly. I can't get up. I can't move. Then the door opens and my head pops up, the fear outweighing the panic.

"Sophie?" Miles' voice is soft.

Steven's last words make a little more sense. When Miles sees my tear-streaked face, he hurries to the bed but doesn't touch me. I can't take my eyes off of him, but I can't speak either.

"What do you need?" He asks the same question and I still don't have an answer. When I don't respond, he asks another. "Can I touch you?"

I force myself to nod. I want his arms around me. I really do. I just can't voice the need.

Miles' movements are achingly slow and I want to scream at him to move faster, but my mouth won't open. He crawls to my opposite side where there's more room and wraps his arm around my shoulders, easing me into him. I let myself be enveloped by his warmth, feeling my muscles finally starting to relax as my legs stretch out.

Instead of speaking, urging me to open up, he holds me in complete silence. Tears continue to leak from my eyes, the fucking traitors, but my breathing is returning to normal. The slow rise and fall of Miles' chest beneath my cheek seems to help me focus. My jaw begins to relax. I'm still holding the pillow between us, half sitting, but turned to my side.

I know he wants to ask what happened, but I'm thankful he resists that urge. He places a kiss on the top of my head and breathes deep. The heat of his exhale makes me shudder in the chill room.

"Can I take the pillow?" he asks softly, careful not to break the calm that seems to have settled over me. I nod and he slowly pulls the squashed pillow from my arms. Once it's gone, they drop, empty. "Come here, you're freezing."

He pulls me closer while scooting toward me and we lay like that for several minutes. Maybe it's an hour. I have no idea how much time has passed when my stomach growls. I haven't eaten since the layover in Denver.

"I'd offer to order room service, but it would end up on your bill," Miles chuckles.

"Think they have good pizza in Florida?" My voice is so small, but being able to speak at all is a step.

"Probably not, but it's worth a try."

While we wait for the pizza—a local place Miles found online—he offers to help me get dressed, but I protest.

"Will you just let me take care of you?" He presses his lips together, but his eyes are soft. "I just want to be able to give you whatever it is you need. Even if all you want is for me to walk right back out that door."

"I don't want that," I whisper. "I don't want you to leave."

I direct him to where I put my pajamas—t-shirts and a couple of pairs of shorts.

Crouching by the bed, Miles helps me swing my legs over the side and prepares one of the leg holes of the shorts. He slips it over my foot and then repeats the process with the other. He pulls them up and when the shorts are past my knees, he grabs one of my hands to help me stand. I take over from there, but then he has my t-shirt. He pulls it over my head, sliding it slowly down my body. When it's in place, he gathers my hair and pulls it through. The whole process is bizarrely intimate, dressing me after an embarrassing panic attack. I can't say I hate it, though. He lets me sit back down on the bed when we're finished.

"Drink some water." Miles nods at the bottle on the bedside table that Steven left for me.

The trembling in my hand hasn't ceased, unlike my other symptoms, but it's steady enough not to spill the water as I lift it to my lips. It's refreshing. I probably haven't hydrated enough today, especially given the air travel.

"Good girl." He winks and the corner of his mouth lifts.

"That's Brody's line." A breath of laughter escapes my nose. I'm starting to feel like myself again.

"There's my girl." Miles finds the remote on the coffee table in front of the sofa and rejoins me on the bed. "Let's find something trashy to watch on TV, huh?"

"As long as it's funny."

"Comedy. Got it." He half-salutes at me and turns on the TV. Immediately, the hotel menu pops up. "Well, *that's* not funny," he mutters, flipping the channel. "News. Never funny." Flip. "More news. More news. Weather. Funny?" He pauses, studying the screen. "Nope." He keeps going until I catch a glimpse of Brendan Fraser on the screen in his classic Rick O'Connell ensemble.

"Stop! Go back!"

Miles returns, knowing exactly what made me shout.

"The Mummy," he muses. "Comedy, action, romance." He moves his eyebrows suggestively and I giggle. "Good choice. Responsible for the bi awakening of a generation."

We haven't missed much. The main characters are on the riverboat, about to be attacked. That means my favorite exchange is coming up.

Miles glances at his phone.

"Hey, the pizza is almost here. You ok if I go down and get it?"

"I'll be fine."

*"Hey, O'Connell!"*

# 31

## Brody

I wonder if Caleb will leave another note while Sophie's out of town. If he does, it would either indicate he wants to scare Natalie too or that he's unaware Sophie isn't here. The latter isn't likely since he's probably stalking her socials and I know she posts updates about her travels. I'm left wondering if he plans to terrorize Miss Weston or if he'll hold off.

Sophie is unaware that he visits often—most days, in fact. Some days all he does is walk up the driveway between the two front buildings, stop and watch for a minute or two, and then walk away.

*What goes through his mind when he just stands there and watches?*

Having given up the new mystery client, my day-to-day at work has returned to the mundane. The latest fiasco is a fifty-year-old woman desperate to see her father's medical records and to know if she's still in the will—if she was ever in the will in the first place. All she cares about is the current version, of course.

It's amazing the access I have to peoples' whole lives. Everything is electronic nowadays—one reason for my filing cabinet in the corner. Everything is kept on paper or in one of several external hard drives, all of which are kept in a fireproof safe in my bedroom. Miles calls it paranoid. I call it being smart in this digital age.

While running an end-of-week report for myself—which will be shredded once I've analyzed it—I decide to try digging a little more into Caleb Davis and his life. Raised by a single mother, one older brother in law enforcement, nothing new or of note. Nothing I haven't seen before.

As I stare at a photo of Caleb and his brother, I start to wonder if the help he has is coming from family. If Jesse Davis has access to certain resources, he might be able to get a back way into the doorbell cam system. Illegal without a warrant, but anything can be faked.

Looks like I'm spending my Friday digging up some dirt on Asshole #2. I don't know Jesse, but I think it's safe to assume that, with a brother like Caleb, he's an asshole.

It's time to reach out to an anonymous contact from Harp Solutions. I have access to a lot, but a backdoor into a government database feels a stretch too far. I hate leaving a trail, even in our secure system, but this is still the safer route. The request takes no time at all to send and now I have no path forward while I wait. I have to find something to distract myself. It could take days to get a response and even longer to get the information or it could be a matter of hours. Every request is different so the response and delivery times vary wildly.

I stomp out of the office to the kitchen and throw open the fridge. Maybe eating something will help. I scan the shelves for several minutes, only half-processing what's in front of me. Nothing sounds good.

The door slams shut harder than I intend, causing one of the heavier magnets to fall to the ground. I gently pick up the gym calendar it was holding to the fridge and then my fingers fall on the thick, ceramic double-decker bus. Isla brought it back for me when she studied abroad in college. The magnet isn't what I focus on.

The gym seems like a good distraction.

The gym is *not* a good distraction.

Starting on the treadmill, I increase my speed and incline until I'm breathing heavily, unable to focus on anything other than not falling off. That lasts for all of five minutes before my mind wanders to the problem of the Davis brothers and what they might be planning.

Weights next. I start with squats. Those are even less distracting, so I switch between various machines. Worse.

I mutter a curse under my breath and lock the plate holding the weights above my body on the leg press machine. The weight is enough to challenge me, but not enough that it causes my muscles to shake. Maybe I should add more. I'm still deciding on my next step when a woman sidles up to me, a towel over her shoulder.

She'd be distracting for any man, but I've got my own problems and my own sexy little distraction on the other side of the country. It's hard to miss the way her leggings hug her hips and thighs below her tight and toned torso. A sports bra covers her breasts and her black hair is pulled back into a ponytail. Wisps of hair stick to her skin where it's shiny with sweat. Her skin is pale and flawless and her brown eyes are full of confidence.

"Almost done with that?" she asks with a glance at the plates, taking a moment to add up the weight in her head. "Impressive, by the way."

"Thanks." I grab my towel from where it's hung over the top of my water bottle and dab it on my forehead. "I'm done. Let me get the plates off."

"I can help." She makes sure to brush past, tits facing me, just close enough to graze my arm. "Sam, by the way." Her touch has nothing on Sophie's.

"Brody," I mutter.

I stack the plates on their racks and give Sam a nod before walking away. In the mirror on my left, I can see that she's annoyed. I'm sure it's my fault, but I'm not going to dwell on it.

I try to finish my leg day workout, glimpsing Sam every now and then, usually on a machine next to me or walking by just close enough to make contact. I grow more and more frustrated until I realize annoyance is at least distracting me from waiting on the information I requested. At least she's been good for something.

Eventually, I have to leave. My workout is done, my legs are jelly, and if I don't drive home now, I'm not sure I'll be able to. As I head out of the locker room, toward the door, Sam darts in front of me. I nearly crash into her.

"Sorry." I grab her arm to steady her but then drop it quickly.

"Oh no, my fault," she chirps. "I just wanted to give you this." She holds out a business card. Great. A realtor. *Great. A realtor.*

"You do this often?" I ask, raising an eyebrow, but taking the card. "Hand out business cards to random guys at the gym?"

"Only the cute ones."

Before I can respond, she dances away and I'm left with my lips parted in mild shock. I have got to get out of here.

My car is on the outer edge of the parking lot, the nearest vehicle a dozen spaces away. I rack my brain for activities that will keep me from going home. A hike won't work because if I try that, my *legs* won't work. If Miles were here, we'd binge-watch trashy movies and eat homemade nachos or some other concoction of his.

My grip on the steering wheel is tight, the veins in my arms popping out. I lean my head back in the seat, closing my eyes. Taking deep breaths through my nose and letting them out in slow, controlled exhales doesn't seem to help. Sophie's face floats through my mind, laughing at something I said during our first date, nervous about telling me what she does for a living on our second date, skeptical on our third before...

I can practically taste her on my lips, feel her clench around my fingers. That familiar warmth forms in my chest, radiating outward into my arms and down to my toes. My hand drops from the steering wheel to palm a rather troublesome bulge growing in my shorts.

My phone buzzes, pulling me from my thoughts. It's a selfie from Sophie. She's wearing a *very* tight, light blue dress. I can't quite tell from the angle, but it looks like it's barely long enough to cover her ass. Her perfect tits are practically falling out of the top. I'm so focused on her cleavage that it takes me a moment to notice my best friend standing beside her. She and Miles are on the convention floor near a booth whose banner I can only see a small part of. They look like they're having the time of their lives. The text along with it just says: *Miss you*.

I type out a quick response and then toss my phone into the cupholder before speeding home.

The shower doesn't help despite using ice-cold water. All I've been able to think about since that stupid selfie–that I asked for, of course–is what Miles and Sophie are doing together *off* of the convention floor. Miles told me they have neighboring rooms and all I can imagine is them *enjoying* each other in their downtime.

I'm not jealous, which is probably the most surprising part about the whole situation. Well, maybe a little, but only because I'd rather be there with them. Joining them. Fucking them. My skin is hot and one hand snakes down my body to find my cock, growing hard thanks to my vivid imagination.

I brace my other hand on the tile beneath the stream of water and hang my head, calling forth images of ~~Simon~~ Brody Says. The way both Miles and Sophie were eager to do as I ordered. The moans Sophie made when Miles ate her sweet cunt, the whimpers when

I fucked her. The whine when Miles came deep inside her and how beautiful they both looked with my cum all over them.

Stroking myself isn't enough and I glance up at the detachable shower head. Keeping the pressure consistent at medium strength and the water ice cold, I pull it out of the holder. Twisting it, I bring it down until the spray hits the underside of my tip and a moan escapes my lips. The cold water does the exact opposite of what I would expect and I feel the tingle all the way down in my toes. Using one hand to cup and massage my balls, I use the water as if it's another hand. Practically stroking with the stream, I angle it up and down the bottom of my shaft and I can feel my release tugging at me.

It doesn't take long before I explode, the jet of water altering the trajectory of my cum as it flies at the wall. Hunching over, I drop the shower head and bring my hand up to squeeze every last drop. Nothing compares to being inside Sophie, of course, but my head is a little clearer when I step out of the shower.

When I return to my computer, not only has the contact responded, but they've sent over an enormous file. I quickly click through so I can gain access to the information. My fingers run through my hair for what feels like the fiftieth time today just as it all finishes downloading. The file on Jesse Davis is larger than I anticipated, but only because he's been involved in *so much*. He's been written up by his superiors for aggression–I didn't know that happened for cops–and has been investigated for his treatment of suspects during their arrests.

For some ungodly reason, though, he's been allowed to train new officers. To mold them to his twisted sense of justice. The system is so fucking flawed, but it's no surprise. Bad apples beget bad apples and the cycle continues.

I lose time clicking through file after file, muttering to myself and shaking my head every now and then. It's vile, baffling that this man still has a job. When I come to the most recent information, my jaw tenses.

Jesse is on administrative leave following his mother's sudden death. It looks like she passed at the end of July after a nasty car accident and I have to wonder when Caleb started showing up at Sophie's front door. Either the loss sent Caleb off the deep end or he realized he has nothing to lose by going all-in, trying to get Sophie back.

Either way, he's more dangerous than ever. I have to tell Mel. I need her help and poor Natalie is innocent in all of this.

I unlock my phone and click Mel's contact. I can't wait for a video call and I don't want to send an email about this. She picks up on the third ring.

"You never call."

"Hello, Mel. Hope you're having a pleasant Friday."

"You too. You never call. What's wrong?"

"I've been seeing someone," I start.

"I know."

*Of course, she does.*

"Her ex is stalking her."

Mel hums and I wait for her to speak.

"I assume adult actors face a higher number of potential stalkers than the rest of us," she muses, speaking casually as if Sophie isn't in danger. I frown.

"I don't have the statistics. You don't have an opinion on me dating a porn star?"

"She's hardly a star." Mel's tone isn't unkind. "She's getting there though."

*Oh god.* I don't want to know the amount of research she's done.

I stammer, trying to find words to change the subject and steer the conversation away from Sophie's job. No fully formed words come out.

"You could have come to me the moment something happened, you know." She sounds... hurt. Why does she sound hurt? "I would have helped."

"You would?"

"Of course. I believe we've cultivated a friendship over the years, don't you?"

"You're still my boss," I remind her. I suppose I do think of her more like another sister. A somewhat cold, distant sister.

"We already work in a gray area. This would at least be on the lighter side."

I take a deep breath.

"I need your help."

"Take the CIO job."

"Are you really going to blackmail me when the woman I love is in danger?" My breath hitches, my heart racing. *Love.* I said that. Out loud. I swear I can *hear* Mel raising an eyebrow. I can definitely see it in my mind.

"Are you really going to gamble with her safety when all it will take is a simple yes?"

"Mel, please," I choke.

"Take the job."

"Fuck, fine. I'll take the damn job."

"Delightful. Now," I hear her typing frantically in the background, "I'm reaching out to my security team. Does Sophie know you're talking to me about this?"

I didn't give Sophie's name, but it's not a shock that Mel knows.

"No. She thinks all I'm doing is digging into a glitch on her doorbell cam. What do you mean, 'security team'?" I haven't heard her talk about that before.

"No need to bother yourself with that. I can have a team install extra cameras at her place."

"Her roommate-"

"They'll do it when Natalie is gone."

Mel obviously checked out everyone Sophie is connected to. Hell, she probably knew about Caleb and Jesse before I did.

Fuck.

"The ex-"

"No record of him staying in the city," she says, cutting me off again. "Or the brother."

"No, they're being smart," I confirm. "If they're planning something, Mel, I-" My voice catches.

"We won't let anything happen." Mel's determination is enough to make me feel more at ease. "Your promotion has already taken effect. Please make sure to transfer any notes regarding current clients back to me by the end of the day so that I can redistribute your clients to other specialists."

"Mel, come on." I guess I should have negotiated for a grace period.

"Brody, this is for your own good."

She hangs up and I'm left to stare at the file on Jesse Davis that scared me so much I accepted a job I don't want–an early retirement I certainly don't need.

Sophie is worth it.

# 32

## Sophie

Sophie

Miles hasn't left my side all day, save for the occasional bathroom break. We attended a panel this morning on sexual assault in the industry, listened to survivors bravely telling their stories and experts talking about how it's far more prevalent than anyone realizes. A burlesque performance after lunch had both of us squirming in our seats.

Now we find ourselves browsing the marketplace and all the amazing booths before it closes for the evening. We take selfies with performers who are representing various brands, production companies, and agencies. A new production company called Exxxess, based out of Las Vegas, has two very familiar faces.

Vera and Penny squeal when they see us, hurrying over to hug me. They're wearing the skimpiest shorts and most revealing tops they could possibly have chosen. I'm desensitized after seeing a well-known porn star wearing nothing but rhinestone pasties and a matching thong.

"We didn't know you'd be here," says Penny, excitedly.

"I never even thought to ask," adds Vera.

"Neither did I." When their eyes fall on the man beside me, I jump. "Oh, this is Lance Kixxx. Lance, this is Penny Pepper and Vera Connor."

"Nice to meet you." Miles holds out a hand and they exchange greetings.

"So, why are you with a Vegas company?" I ask. I don't have any experience with pro shoots yet, so I have no idea how this works.

"Oh, our videos are slated for release later this year," explains Vera. "So we're promoting the company prior to that."

"Come over, we'll introduce you!" Penny grabs my hand and practically pulls my arm from its socket in her attempt to get me to the booth faster.

I recognize the man seated in one of those foldable chairs you see at kids' baseball games—the cloth ones that are next to impossible to get out of and super uncomfortable for my particular shape. Long Ron Wilson has more than ten years of experience in the industry. I've admired him for a while now. He's covered in tattoos, including a few on his face. Nearly every inch of skin below his neck is inked with a variety of designs, none of which seem to flow together. He's tall, probably Miles' height if my judgment is correct. His tousled, nearly too-long, brown hair always seems to look as if he's just been fucked. The flecks of gray in his short beard are new, but then again he might have simply stopped coloring his facial hair.

Penny's grip on my wrist verges on painful, but when we reach Ron, she drops it. He smiles, the corners of his hazel eyes crinkling with the expression.

"Hey, Pen, who've we got here?" He looks me up and down, but only in a way that seems as if he's trying to figure me out. There have been plenty of times I've felt fetishized or objectified by a look like this, but not with this man. With him, it's friendly, even innocent.

"This is Honey Dee Vine," says Penny. "Honey, this is Long Ron Wilson."

"I love your work," I blurt. I have enough sense not to slap my hand over my mouth, but Ron just continues smiling and stands, offering me his hand.

"Thanks, I think I've seen a bit of yours. You worked with these beautiful ladies recently?" He nods at Vera and Penny, shaking my soft hand in his weathered one.

"Yeah, we worked together in New York last month."

"I think I caught a post about it and I took a look. Have you worked with any pro directors?"

"Er, no, not yet."

"Maybe we can change that." His eyes land on Miles and I see him do the most cartoonish double take. "Lance?"

"Hey, man." Miles has been standing silently behind me, patiently waiting to be noticed. He steps forward, placing a hand on my lower back.

"Hey, been a while." Ron folds his arms across his chest and grins. "LA, right?"

"Yeah, Honey and I are based there."

"Right, right." Ron nods as if the memory is coming back to him. "Who did we shoot with?"

"It was an orgy," says Miles. I send him a sideways glance. I guess it doesn't surprise me that he's done that. A lot of men in the industry do group scenes at least once. Some even make a habit of it.

"Oh yeah. Good times." Ron returns his focus to me, reaching into his back pocket to pull out a business card. "Here, take this. Give me a call sometime next week and we'll get you to Vegas for a shoot if you're interested."

"That would be amazing." I accept the card and tuck it into the side of my purse.

"Enjoy the convention. I've heard there are some great performances tomorrow."

Just as Miles and I are leaving the Exxxess booth, I see the huge banner for Gargantu-anal. Directly below it, Talia Sins is standing between two men–clearly fans–who have their arms around her waist on her bare skin, posing for a photo. She's wearing a bright blue string bikini and matching pumps. Her blonde hair is tousled in soft waves and it looks like she's wearing extensions, given her shorter ponytail at the party last week.

When the two fans begin walking away, having gotten their photo with her, Talia's eyes fall on Miles and me. She waves us over, grinning ear to ear.

"You found me."

"We did," Miles chuckles. "Quite the outfit."

"I know, thank goodness it's warm in here."

Before I can pipe up, my phone vibrates in my purse. When I pull it out to check the screen, I see that the number is blocked but there's no warning about a potential scam at the top.

"I'm going to take this," I mutter, finding my way to the edge of the marketplace before Miles or Talia can protest. The Gargantuanal booth is among the outer row, so it's a quick walk. "Hello?" I ask into the receiver when I find a spot. I plug my opposite ear to hear better.

"Sophie."

A chill runs down my spine.

"Caleb." For the second time in as many days, my chest is tight.

"You changed your number, baby." Caleb's voice is soft and menacing–a threat and definitely not an empty one. I remain silent. "What, no love for me? That's all right, baby. Tell your boyfriends I said hi."

He hangs up and my legs shake. My breathing is ragged and shallow. I stagger to the wall and slump against it, trying to remain standing. The familiar threat of tears pricking the back of my eyes forces me to tilt my head back in an attempt to keep them at bay.

The moment I feel Miles' hands on my arms, I know I have to tell him. Brody knows, so my other boyfriend might as well know too. Miles' voice breaks through my racing thoughts, repeating my name, trying to get my attention.

"I'm ok," I finally stammer, meeting his gaze. "I'm ok."

"You are *not* ok. What the fuck is going on?" Despite the forceful language, I hear the concern in his voice.

"N-not now." I can't do this now. I can't fall apart now. "I have to film in a couple of hours."

I make it through my scene with no issues—it's a pretty vanilla video we planned, so there's nothing to trigger me. Showered and dressed, I find myself in Miles' room as we planned. I promised to talk later and it's later. Time to talk.

I pick at the couch cushion beneath me while Miles sits on the far side, giving me space, waiting for me to speak.

"The phone call," he offers in an attempt to help me get started. I breathe out slowly before answering.

"It was my ex." I hate the terror in my voice. "He, er- It-it ended- No." I shake my head and Miles reaches out a hand to pat my knee.

"Take your time."

Another deep breath steadies me and I stare into those golden brown orbs that want so badly for me to trust him.

"My ex wasn't a good guy." My voice is stronger, just a bit louder now, but there's still a wobble to it. "It was ok when we first started dating and I was only making solo content. He liked it. He liked watching me." I pause to swallow and try to keep my breathing consistent.

"A couple of years ago, I got an offer from someone, a creator with a bigger following. He wanted to shoot with me." I cast my eyes down to where Miles' thumb is tracing circles on my skin, making it difficult to concentrate. "I didn't ask before accepting. I just *told* Caleb what I was doing."

"And he didn't like that."

"Exactly," I whisper, raising my eyes to his again. "At first," my body begins to tremble and I can feel my jaw threatening to lock up, "it was just little things. Verbal stuff. Insults."

Miles scoots closer. I know he must feel how my body is reacting, but he continues to keep his hand where it is, touching me nowhere else.

"It-it didn't get bad until a few months before-" my breathing hitches, "before I moved. He h-h-"

"You don't have to keep going. I get the idea."

"I have to," I whisper, but those damn tears are threatening again. *No secrets.* "It got worse and," I take a deep breath, "one morning, he-he held a knife to my throat."

I press my lips together, trying to convince the damn tears to stay back. Reaching my hand up to my neck, I trace the small line, not even two inches long. It's puckered and a shade darker than the surrounding skin. Located on the side of my neck, it isn't overly obvious. If you don't know it's there, you'll miss it.

"What the fuck?" Miles is seething. The switch happened in the blink of an eye–from supportive to furious. He's staring at the spot just above my fingertips, eyebrows pulled down. His breath rushes in and out heavily through his nose as if he's trying to keep himself from saying anything else.

"That was in February. I left when he went to work that day. He thought I was away for a collab, but I took everything I needed and just... never went back."

"Sophie, I-I didn't know," Miles whispers.

He moves closer, raising the hand on my knee up to my face. I lean into his palm, closing my eyes against the pain and terror threatening to overwhelm me. We stay like that for several seconds, the heat from his hand helping to calm my racing heart.

"I'm here for you."

Those four little words release the floodgates and rip a sob from my throat. I hate this fucking feeling–helplessness, terror, a lack of any solution to this stupid fucking problem. It makes me want to scream and cry and rage against the man who turned me into a creature of fear.

Miles is here, though, wrapping his arms around me once more, making me feel as if nothing can touch me. Not even Caleb. That's not true, of course. Brody can't keep me safe either. Even when I tell him everything, the extent of Caleb's violence, he'll still be powerless to stop him.

*Am I going to have to run again?*

# 33

## Sophie

Sophie

The light from the space in the curtains is blinding and I blink as my eyes adjust. Miles must have opened them a little when he got up. The spot beside me is cold and I check the clock to see how late it is. It's not. It's just a few minutes after seven, but I hear the water running in the bathroom.

Sliding out from beneath the sheets, I stand and stretch with a yawn that turns into a satisfied groan. The carpet beneath my feet is anything but soft as I take the necessary steps to reach the bathroom. I open the door a crack but stop when I see that Miles isn't in the shower. He's in the tub, filling it up and leaning back in the hot water as steam rises. His eyes are closed while his head rests on a rolled up towel. His far knee is bent, sticking out of the water, the other leg straight out in front of him. The position gives me the perfect view as he absently strokes his cock. He must've just begun because it's still soft, but he's lazy with his movements. His breathing is even and I hate to interrupt him.

When I start to back out and close the door, he speaks up.

"You could stay." He smirks and I pause. "Enjoy the show."

"Enjoy your bath." I try again to leave, but my feet won't move.

"I'd enjoy it more if you came and joined me." Before I can protest, he adds, "The first panel isn't until ten."

"Even after last night, you want me to join you?" I open the door wider and lean against the frame.

Miles opens his eyes and turns his head slightly to look at me.

"*Especially* after last night." He hasn't stopped stroking himself and I notice he's gotten harder. "I want to show you how," Miles bites his lip as his eyes roam my body, "*supportive* I can be."

I hum deep in my throat and take a step forward. The cold tile sends a shiver up my leg. With the second footstep, the chill works higher up my body, even affecting my nipples, hardening them. I keep walking until I can bend over and lean one hand on the side of the tub. The other reaches out to shut off the water which is now two-thirds of the way up his torso.

"You want to show me your support?" My voice is velvety soft and low and I reach out to run my fingers through his hair. Miles leans into it, his lips parting. His brown eyes are full of the same need I can already feel growing in my lower belly. I drop my hand to grip his chin—not hard, but enough to get his attention. "Use your words."

"Yes." His voice is hoarse and my smile grows. "Please, let me show you." His eyelids droop when my fingers twitch on his jaw. I lean down further until my breath hits his ear.

"Is that what you want?"

"Fuck, Sophie, get in this damn bath," he growls.

I giggle when he grabs me and squeal when he pulls me down into the water.

"Miles! My clothes-"

He shuts me up with his mouth on mine. The cold edge of the tub presses against my calves while he holds my upper body to keep me from sliding down into the water. His tongue plunders my mouth, taking control, but I'm determined to take it right back.

I simultaneously try to keep my lips on his while pulling my legs into the water. Miles does his best to help, but our mouths eventually part and I giggle, trying to dislodge myself. I straddle him, still wearing my shorts and t-shirt. Both are soaked and I know my hardened nipples are pulling focus in spite of the hot water surrounding me. Miles doesn't seem to be able to see anything else until I rock gently, rubbing my covered pussy over his erection.

"Eyes up here, pretty boy."

"Pretty boy?" Miles raises an eyebrow and he's so devastatingly beautiful, I have to look away, instead following the tattoos on his skin with my eyes.

"Still ready to show your support?"

Miles smirks and hums a confirmation.

I stand, slowly so as not to splash too much. Water cascades down my body, the weight pulling on my shorts and making my shirt hug every curve. I take a step back to give Miles the space to see what comes next.

Taking the bottom hem of my shirt in my hands, I lift it as slowly as possible, inching up my stomach. He can't keep his eyes on me as the undersides of my breasts are exposed.

"I'm going to need you to speed up." His voice is low and husky and I feel the corner of my mouth pulling upward into a knowing smile.

"Who said you're calling the shots?"

I pull the shirt all the way off and toss it to the bathroom floor. It lands with a loud, wet splat.

"You want to be in charge?" Miles asks. "Want me to be your good boy?" His throat works hard to swallow before he takes a deep breath. "Tell me what to do. Tell me how to please you," he begs.

His words send a throbbing need straight to my cunt and I have to fight the urge to squeeze my thighs together.

"What are you waiting for? You can't support me while I'm wearing this."

A small laugh escapes Miles' nose, but he twists until he's on his knees. Slowly, his hands rise up the sides of my legs, sending tingles throughout my entire body and ending in my lower belly. Goosebumps follow his touch as he breaches the surface of the water. When his hands brush the bottom hem of my shorts where they stick to my thighs, his gaze flicks to mine.

"Pull them off."

He swallows, his jaw clenching, and he grips the shorts between his fingers. I swat his hand away lightly.

"Ah, ah, ah," I chide, tapping my bottom lip. "With your mouth."

"Sophie," Miles groans, reaching for me again. This time I slap his hand away harder.

"I said use your mouth."

His jaw works like he wants to fight me as they stick to my skin, but the desire to submit wins out. Miles drops his eyes to the bottom of my shorts and leans forward. His tongue makes contact with my thigh first, licking up until it slips beneath the fabric. The move allows him to take it between his teeth.

He pulls slowly, the wet shorts fighting him. He reaches for the other side to help and I swat his hand away again, earning a grunt of frustration. The shorts budge, slipping an inch at a time down my legs until they're too lopsided to keep moving.

Miles lets go of the lower side and raises his head to repeat the process on the other. I watch with a grin. As I'm slowly revealed to him, Miles moans and when the shorts hit the water, I allow him to use his hands again. He leans forward to press his lips to my thighs. My fingers slide into his hair, but I keep my grip gentle to allow him to continue to move.

With the shorts below the water, I step out of them. Miles' hands are on my thighs in the next moment, but I'm unsure of what to do. What to order *him* to do. I rarely take control except on camera and that's planned out in advance.

"Sit on the side of the tub," Miles says softly, offering a suggestion rather than giving a command. "Legs up on the shelves, there."

He indicates indentations in the corners of the tub. I back up another step and sit on the edge, the cold surface sending yet another shiver through me. Once my feet are in place, Miles smiles, waiting.

My confidence is back.

"Crawl to me, pretty boy."

"I don't care what you call me, honey. As long as you let me taste that incredible cunt."

Miles leans forward, approaching me on his hands and knees with his gaze trained on his target. I'm already dripping for him. He stops just short of placing his mouth on me, waiting for explicit instructions.

I run a hand through his curls and grip hard, angling his head up.

"Eat this pussy like it's your last meal," I order. "I want to come all over your face and scream your name doing it. Think you can make that happen?"

"Yes, ma'am." He winks before, quite literally, diving forward to devour me.

"Fuck!" I scream when Miles shoves his tongue as deep as possible.

He licks and laps and sucks and tastes every part of me, the sensations overwhelming. The man likes his worship. Closing his mouth over my clit, he swirls his tongue around it, causing me to twitch as an orgasm hovers just out of reach.

"Use your fingers," I breathe.

It doesn't really sound like an order, but he obeys, using three fingers immediately and forcing another curse from my lips. I let go of his hair to support myself as I throw my head back against the wall, moaning with abandon. The waves of pleasure are closing in, about to drown me. Miles growls into my pussy and the vibrations send me over the cliff with a hoarse cry.

He doesn't stop, continuing to attack with mouth and fingers while my brain absolutely melts inside my head. Even when I begin to come down, he continues until I grab his hair again and pull him off.

"Stop," I pant. "Stop."

He opens his mouth and breathes out a laugh before licking his bottom lip. We both continue to gulp down air and I mirror his laughter. He grips my ankles gently and stares up at me.

"How was I?"

"You were a very," I meet his gaze, "*very* good boy."

"What can I do for you now?"

"You don't think that's enough?"

"I want to break our record." He shakes his head. "And then break it again." He kisses one knee and then the other. "And again. And again."

"Oh boy, you're gonna be trouble this morning, aren't you?"

"Only if you'll let me."

"How can I say no to that?" I grip his chin and pull him up to kiss him, tasting myself on his lips and moaning in approval.

"Please," he whispers against me. "I need you to sit on my face."

I pull back in surprise. The other night, with Brody, I was essentially hovering. My weight fell on my knees on either side of his head, not on his nose and mouth.

"Are you s-?"

He cuts me off with a finger against my lips.

"Don't you ever ask me that again," he growls. "If I ask you to sit on my face, I want you to sit on my fucking face."

"Then I suppose we should move to the bed," I whisper against his finger.

Miles helps me out of the tub, drying me with a towel. While the water still clings to his body, he focuses on wiping every drop from mine. When he's finished focusing on me, he wipes his arms and chest quickly, impatiently.

"You're in charge," he reminds me when I don't lead the way to the bedroom.

This is one of the few times I wish I was skinnier, imagining how it would feel if he could pick me up and just carry me to the damn bed the way the men in romance books do with skinnier heroines. Miles must see my hesitation because he growls out a question that floods me with relief and excitement.

"Do I just need to throw you over my shoulder and take you to the bed?"

"How much can you lift?"

"How much do you weigh?"

"That's not very polite to ask," I shoot back.

"I think polite went out the window three shoots ago."

He studies my face a moment more before grunting and bending over to wrap his arms around my legs. He swings me up and over his shoulder, earning a squeak from me.

"Miles!"

"You didn't give me an order and we don't have all day." He stomps out of the bathroom and over to the bed, throwing me–literally *throwing* me–down onto the mattress. "You ready to smother me?"

"Get down here." My confidence is back, fueled by the fact that *he threw me over his fucking shoulder*.

"Anything you say."

It takes me another hour to make it back to my own hotel room. When I leave Miles' room to get ready, my legs can barely hold me. It's going to be a long day.

Miles and I join the throng waiting outside the hall for the rigging demonstration. Hearing our porn names called, we look back to see Talia heading toward us, wearing a short black skirt and cropped, white tank top. Her Converse are far more practical than the heels she wore yesterday and her hair is pulled back in a ponytail.

"Hey!" she shouts over the din of the crowd as she joins us. "I'm so excited for this demo." She's practically bouncing on her toes.

"Yeah, I've been wanting to get into this kind of thing for a while," I lie.

I've had to force myself just to look at trailers for content involving this fetish, but it's common in the kink community and is becoming popular in porn too. Just the idea of being unable to bend or straighten my arms or legs has my chest feeling tight again. Maybe this demo will help during the rare domination scene when I'm the one giving the orders.

Like this morning, with Miles.

Hiding my grin as the doors open, I take Talia's offered hand and grab Miles' behind me to keep us together. We snake through the crowd to find seats in the fifth row. It's close enough to the action to see details, but far enough that we won't have to crane our necks for a better view of the stage.

The lights dim and screens on either side of the hall light up with live images of the stage. An announcer's voice comes over the speakers.

"Guys, gals, and non-binary pals, please welcome to the stage Scotty Robertson!"

A man who looks to be in his fifties takes the steps up to the stage from the far side of the hall. His head is either shaved or bald, shining in the spotlight. His light gray beard is full, hiding his lips though I can tell from here that he's smiling. He waves as the audience applauds, a mic attached to his ear.

"Thank you!" he shouts with another wave. "Thank you! So," he waits for the applause to die down before he continues. "Some of you know me, but I'm guessing most don't. I've been outta the game for a bit, but I've been in this industry for half my life."

Scotty continues to give us his abbreviated resume before calling forth his assistant. A beautiful woman steps up to the stage, looking a few years younger than Scotty. She's clad in a black, lace bodysuit that hugs her thin frame perfectly. Her black hair is swept back into a bun and she walks toward Scotty on bare feet.

"Before we show you anything, I want to go over the most important thing in any BDSM scene. Safety."

Scotty, aided by his assistant, Georgie, continues to explain the ins and outs of where *not* to tighten ropes that would cut off the important circulation. He gives alternatives, pointing out the right spots on Georgie's body for all to see. When he's satisfied that he's given us a solid foundation, the real fun begins.

I watch, entranced as Scotty and Georgie point out parts of the frame they're going to use for the demonstration. There are different colors of rope to allow the audience to see where specific lengths get connected and knotted.

First, Georgie is seated in a chair beneath the rig so that Scotty can make sure she's bound in the right places before hoisting her up. He explains knot after knot as his hands deftly ensnare his assistant. Georgie breathes calmly throughout this whole process. Her ability to essentially zone out almost makes me want to try.

*Almost.*

By the end of the demonstration, Georgie is hanging sideways with one leg straight out, the other bent with her knee angled down. One arm is tied to her side and the other is bent so that, while her upper arm is at her side, her forearm crosses her chest with her hand pointing toward her shoulder. Her head is supported to take the weight off of her neck and she's grinning as if she could stay there forever.

After another round of applause, the crowd begins to leave the hall while Scotty lowers Georgie to the ground so he can safely untie her.

"That was incredible," says Miles as we break through the doors. Talia nods in agreement.

"I've been tied a few times for scenes, but never by a partner just for shits and giggles," she says. "I haven't found someone whose hands are good enough." She winks at Miles and he grins, running his hand across my lower back at the same time, reminding me that he's mine and Talia is just a colleague. "What about you?" Talia asks me.

"Oh, I don't know if being tied up is for me," I admit. "Maybe as the rigger." I glance at Miles. "Think Brody would be on board?"

"He might not be, but I sure as hell would."

"Who's Brody?" asks Talia as we head toward the large open area where the marketplace is.

"My roommate," says Miles. "We, er," he glances at me. "I guess we're both kind of dating Honey." His ability to easily call me by my porn name in public and my real name in private is impressive.

"Shit, girl," Talia giggles. "Good luck. This idiot's a handful on his own. I can only imagine what someone who lives with him is like." I laugh at that.

"It's pretty new. But I think we're having fun." I flash Miles a grin.

"Oh, we absolutely are."

"You and I are going to have to get together," Talia says to me. "I'm going to need to know how you juggle two men."

"Lots of lube."

---

Miles has a scene in the afternoon so I find myself in another burlesque performance alone this time. This one is aimed at the nerds with themes from all the big franchises—Star Wars, Game of Thrones, and a variety of others. It's ridiculous and fun while still being stupid hot. As a straight woman, I can still appreciate another woman's body.

When I leave the hall, there's a text on my phone from Miles saying he'll meet Talia and me in the hotel lobby to catch a ride together to the restaurant. Talia is already there waiting for me, just inside the front doors. It's way too hot and humid to wait outside until the last minute.

"How was the camera equipment demo?" I ask, knowing Talia has been looking to upgrade her production quality. She talked about it for five minutes straight before we parted ways earlier.

"It was actually really interesting."

Talia babbles on about which camera she likes the most as well as the couple she thinks are in her budget and can get her through the next year or two.

When Miles approaches, she grins but continues speaking for another minute.

"Now that I've been thoroughly bored to death, can we order an Uber?" Miles laughs, pulling out his phone.

"Only if you don't want to hear about tripods," I tease.

"Do you want to?" asks Talia.

"No!" Miles and I practically shout in unison.

"Party poopers." She crosses her arms over her chest, though she doesn't seem too upset.

The steakhouse isn't an overly nice restaurant, but it's far enough from the airport and convention crowd that, even on a Saturday, there isn't a long wait. Soon we're scooting into a booth–Miles and I on one side, Talia on the other.

"So," Talia opens her menu and pretends to look through it while talking, "dating, huh?"

Miles and I share a look before he responds.

"Yep."

"Kinda hard in this industry. How do you guys do it?"

"To be fair, like we said, it's pretty new," I reply.

"God, I fucking hate being single," Talia moans. "But dating is just so hard as a bisexual woman. Men suck, no offense Lance, and women are so intimidating."

"Good to know I'm not alone," I laugh. "Any time I film with a woman, I'm worried I'm gonna fuck something up and accidentally bite her clit." That sends Talia into hysterics and even Miles laughs quietly next to me.

"I can't say I'm worried about *that*. Some people like it," Talia giggles. "Same boat, though." She continues laughing, more to herself now, "The last girl I dated was a normie at the beginning. Didn't even have any nudes on her phone. A month in, I had somehow managed to turn her into an internet whore like me."

"Think Brody would join us on camera?" I nudge Miles' arm as the server approaches.

"I don't think you could pay him enough."

We order a bottle of wine to share and the server disappears.

"Oh, before I forget!" Talia shouts, making me jump. "I'm putting together a Christmas-themed, all-girl thing in December back in LA. Vetting everyone beforehand, but would you be interested?"

"Um, sure. I've mostly done one-on-one scenes, just a few threesomes."

"That's ok. If you just want to be there to experience the vibes, that's fine too. Join when you want. We haven't plotted out the scene or anything," Talia goes on. "But I'm trying to get a variety of women."

"Then, yeah, I guess it couldn't hurt to at least attend."

"Awesome!" Talia claps quickly, a wide grin on her face. "When we connect for details, remind me to ask whether you're a top or bottom. No use telling me now," she adds when I open my mouth. "I won't remember by tomorrow, let alone December." Talia jumps, startling both of us. "We need a picture of us!"

She calls over a passing server and asks him to take our photo with her phone. We lean in and smile, holding up our wine glasses, while he snaps a few and then hands Talia's phone back to her.

"This is a good one!" She holds the phone up for us to see. I hadn't realized Miles' hand was on my shoulder while we leaned in. "I'll send it to you both, but I'm gonna tease my fans that I've got a hot date." She winks.

We chat about various projects we have planned. After several minutes, I ask Talia a question that's been in the back of my mind all day.

"Do you have a plan for after all this?" I wave my hand around as if to indicate the industry.

"After porn?" she asks. "I guess I hadn't really thought about it. I really like what I do."

"So do I," I assure her. "I'm just curious. Looks fade and not all women are lucky enough to break into the MILF category, you know?"

"I've only been doing this a couple years. I've been making good money and I'm investing some to give me some additional passive income."

"That's smart," I reply. "Might need to give me the number for your financial advisor."

"She's good." Talia nods. "Beyond that, I guess I just want to be able to retire comfortably, you know? Maybe with my person, if I find them." She grins, her eyes unfocused for a moment before shaking her head and looking at me once more. "What about you?"

I blush, feeling a bit foolish for my ambition, but give my reply anyway.

"I, er, want to start a production company."

"Really?" Talia perks up.

"Yeah, I mean I don't have a business plan or anything. I'm still getting my feet wet and networking and all that."

"Oh, hush." Talia waves her hand at me. "That's so cool to want to start your own thing. I always trust women-run companies way more than the ones run by men. No offense." She shoots a look at Miles who chuckles.

"None taken." He holds up his hands. "I get it."

"Well when you start it, hit me up. I'll be in your first video."

I smile at her, thankful for the support, even if it's just because of my proximity to Miles.

"Deal."

# 34

*Miles*

## Miles

I'm glad to see Brody when he picks me up from the airport. He greets me as if nothing has changed. As if we didn't both fuck Sophie last week when I'm sure it's been on his mind just as much as it's been on mine. I have to wonder if he's even finished processing it. He's been known to overthink things and that experience is definitely one he would pick apart for days, if not weeks.

As we pull away from the curb, he asks the question I'm sure he's been dying to all weekend. I'm glad he refrained from texting it to me every day.

"Is Sophie ok?"

Flashbacks of the conversation about her ex give me pause, but it's Sophie's story to tell.

"Yeah, she's good. I think she had fun."

"That's not what I meant."

"I know what you meant." My tone is light. "She's fine. How was your weekend?"

"I think I may have driven myself into early retirement," he mutters and I barely catch the words.

"What? I'm gone for all of four days and you retire? What happened?"

"I-" Brody grunts in frustration, focusing on the road as we turn away from the airport. "Mel kind of forced it on me."

"We both know Mel can't force you to do anything." I cross my arms, waiting for a response. Brody owes Mel a lot for his position, his freedom in his job, but he still wouldn't do something he didn't want to.

"I may have asked for help."

"What does that have to do with retiring early?"

Brody spills everything. My jaw drops more and more with every word. When he's done, I'm surprised it's not on the damn floor.

"So, let me get this straight." I hold up a hand, trying to work through what he's just told me. Sarcasm is my first instinct. "You–*poor baby*–were forced to accept a promotion–after *obscene* pay raises, by the way–in order to get Mel to put security cameras into Sophie's place *without her knowledge*?" Brody is silent. "What is wrong with you, man?"

"Miles, her ex is bad, but his brother is worse. And he's a cop. I don't know what his endgame is, but I want her safe."

"So do I, but can't you tell her about this?"

"Not-not yet."

I roll my eyes and let my head fall back on the seat. There's nothing I can say to change his mind, but it's going to come out and when it does, I just know Sophie's going to blame both of us.

"Does her roommate know?"

"What do you think?"

"I'm washing my hands of this." I hold my hands up as if to show they're clean. "You're my friend and I love you, but I'm not going to be a part of *you* stalking her now."

Brody's expression freezes and I realize it never occurred to him to see things that way.

"Fuck." He mutters the curse in defeat. "But what if something happens?"

"Dude, you already hacked-"

"Not hacked."

"-*hacked* into her doorbell cam."

"Not hacked."

"Fine, you built yourself a backdoor so you can see when she and her roommate leave or come home, as well as her ex showing up unannounced. What would you call that?"

"It's already done. Mel has a team trying to track down whatever names they're using at whatever shithole motel they're staying at."

"How do you know they're staying at a motel? Or even anywhere that would have digital records?"

"I guess- I guess I don't."

"You'd make a horrible detective."

———

Neither of us see Sophie over the next couple of days. She has collabs set up for most of the week and claims she's been neglecting her live-stream fans.

Wednesday afternoon, I leave my studio after filming a solo custom video to find Brody napping on the couch. The TV is still on, playing a show he started yesterday morning.

"You have got to find a hobby," I mutter as I pass the couch.

"Leave me alone to die."

"Shut up, Lilo. You have plenty to live for."

"Like you?"

"I would have thought you'd agree that I'm enough after last week." I turn toward the kitchen. "Obviously there's Sophie."

"Obviously."

"You were always working on little side projects in college," I recall. "Contract work or something?"

"I haven't worked on my own programming in a long time. Everything has been for Harp." Brody sighs and sits up, pausing the show, though I doubt he's been paying attention.

"Surely Mel will let you do *something*."

"I had a meeting with her Monday," he says. "Even though I'm the CIO, I don't have access to anyone on the tech side of things. I can review any updates to our systems and I can discuss tech-related issues with Mel during our monthly lunches."

"Is that really it?"

"I don't know why she wanted me out."

"You know I don't have any insight. That shit has always been over my head." I go to the fridge in search of something to eat, but I'm not sure what. Brody's aimlessness is going to be contagious if he doesn't find something to occupy him soon. "What about," I hesitate before asking, "the security stuff for Sophie?"

"I still have access to some of that."

"So our girl is safe?"

"Her ex showed up again on Monday and left another note. Mel even has a team trying to track traffic cams in the area, but there aren't many near her neighborhood, so it's been slow going trying to figure out what car he's even driving."

"Fuck. You know, he called Sophie during the convention. Scared her so bad I thought she was going to pass out."

"She told me." He stands just as I close the fridge doors. I'm glad she told him so quickly. "She told me you had to talk her through more than one panic attack."

"She had a tough time." I run a hand through my hair.

"You were there for her when I couldn't be."

"You're trying to track down her douchebag ex. I think you win."

Brody spends that evening with Sophie, out on the town for a nice dinner and I turn in early. In an attempt to release some pent-up energy and tire myself out, I film a masturbation video before going to bed. It's a good opportunity for content, even if it's short. If the camera wasn't on, Sophie's name would be on my lips the entire time. A wish, a plea, a fucking prayer.

Her name or Brody's.

Hours later, my mind races with thoughts of Sophie dominating me, thoughts of her ex stalking her, and now thoughts of his brother doing even worse things. I can't get it out of my head. Brody has been able to help thanks to his job, even in his semi-retirement. I feel utterly useless.

All of a sudden, the sheet wrapped around me is suffocating, the blanket on top far too warm. I can't lay here any longer, dwelling on impure urges and feelings of helplessness. The combination will be lethal if I let it continue. Fighting with the covers, I finally untangle myself and throw my legs over the side of the bed. I lean over and rest my elbows on my knees, dropping my head into my hands.

Sophie hasn't brought up her ex again with me since we got back from Miami. Brody hasn't given me much of an update except for what he said this afternoon. I'm in the fucking dark.

I'm at the door in a flash, ripping it open and aiming for the kitchen. I've never been one to use any kind of sleep aid and I'm not entirely sure what my goal is. A shot? A midnight snack?

I glimpse the time on the oven.

A two-hours-past-midnight snack?

Movement out of the corner of my eye makes me jump, clutching my bare chest, just inches from barrelling into my roommate. Brody steps away from the kitchen island to come fully into view. The mounted lights beneath the upper kitchen cabinets couldn't reach him where he was standing before.

"You scared the shit out of me." My heart is pounding.

"Sorry," Brody mutters.

"Couldn't sleep?"

"Apparently not. You?"

"Can't shut off the damn brain. How was the date?"

"It was good. I, er, took her home and then left."

"Nothing says 'good date' like a chaste kiss goodnight," I chuckle. Brody smiles half-heartedly. "You're not worried, are you?"

"No, no. Honestly, it was my idea. I don't want her thinking I'm," he sighs, "I'm only after sex."

"Good call." I wink. "Find anything in here to help you sleep?"

"No, got any ideas?"

My perverted mind has a few ideas, but I don't think he'll go for any. Brody catches my look and I follow the bobbing of his throat as he swallows. My eyes flick to his lips when he wets them with his tongue.

He's been my friend since I was twelve. He's off-limits, right? Sharing Sophie with me, *together*, doesn't mean he wants more.

The faint light falling across his face glints off of his green eyes. His pupils are probably only dilated because it's dark. As the silence stretches between us, I begin to wonder if there's something more in those emerald depths.

My mouth is suddenly dry and I don't think I can find the words to say goodnight. This is the closest we've been since our little game, other than the rides to and from the airport. I lick my lips and his eyes drop to follow the movement of my tongue.

"Fuck it," I breathe, grabbing his hips and pulling his body flush with mine.

As my lips tilt upward to reach his, one of his hands snakes up and around my neck to pull me closer. His mouth is hot and hungry on mine, his tongue parting my lips. I moan into him as his other hand glides down my side, but doubt flashes in my mind, sending a chill through me. I pull away, still holding him.

"I'm sorry," I mutter, shaking my head. "I shouldn't have-"

"Shut the fuck up."

Brody grabs my chin and tilts my head up again, returning to where we left off. My hands clutch at his shirt, my body wanting more. Needing more. Needing *him*. He grabs my hair, pulling my head to the side as his lips trail along my jaw and down to my throat. He nibbles the sensitive skin and another moan escapes me. His hips shift and I feel his erection almost flush with my own.

I turn our bodies and back him up so that he's leaning against the counter. He allows the movement and lets go of my hair, but doesn't lift his face to mine. Instead, he pulls back to stare at me, lips swollen and eyes dark.

Silently, I sink to my knees, dragging my hands down Brody's body, feeling the chill of the tile through my thin pajama bottoms. Brody's boxers are the only thing in my way. Keeping my eyes on his, I slide my hands back up his legs to the waist of the offending garment and slowly pull down. Brody chews his bottom lip but doesn't ask me to stop.

*Thank god.*

I tease his boxers down further and come face to face with the proof that Brody wants this as much as I do. I stare at his cock and lick my lips again because fuck, I need to taste him. With one last glance up at Brody's somewhat pained expression, I close one hand around the base of his shaft and then flick my tongue out to ghost over his tip. Brody's hands grasp the edge of the counter as he groans and I smile with him against my lips. I continue to tease him, swirling my tongue around the head of his engorged cock several times before finally opening my lips to take him into my mouth. His salty taste sends a jolt straight to my own dick. Another groan from above makes me move, bobbing slowly at first, hollowing out my cheeks.

Brody wants more. Without saying a word, he lifts his hands from the counter and gently puts them on either side of my head. When I don't speed up, he takes control, urging me to move faster. Pushing off of the counter, Brody moves his hips in time with his hands on my head. More and more of him slides down my throat with each thrust, causing me to gag and choke. I drop one hand into my pants to gently stroke myself for some relief. My other hand follows the movement of my lips.

Brody pulls my head closer, shoving his hips so far forward that I feel my throat stretch to accommodate him and I swear my dick is so hard, I could come right this very moment. My nose meets flesh as my hand drops away to take as much as I can and my body convulses, fighting for air.

"Fuck, you take this dick so well," he breathes just before letting up.

His hips pull backward, his cock falling completely out of my mouth as I sputter and gasp. Saliva and mucus mix on my chin while my hand returns to stroke him. I look up, meeting his gaze, before returning to the task at hand.

"That's it," Brody grunts while I take him deep into my throat again. "Such a good fucking boy."

Jesus, does this man know what he's doing to me? I might come undone before he does if he keeps that up.

I speed up, listening to the moans and grunts from above me and using them as motivation. I want to suck this man's soul out. His hands are on my head, pulling and pushing while his hips piston toward my face. I have to stop stroking myself to focus on him.

His grip is tight in my hair and he pulls my mouth off of him. My chin and chest are a mess from my efforts and I'm panting as he tilts my face up toward him.

"I didn't know how much you wanted this," he growls. "But now that I do... Do you want me to paint your face?"

My god, this man has the filthiest mouth. Talk about making up for lost time. No wonder Sophie fell for him.

"Yes, please." It's an out-of-body experience, as if I'm watching the two of us from afar while I beg him to finish.

"Open that pretty mouth," Brody orders. "Tongue out."

I do as he says without hesitation.

Then, one hand still tight in my hair, he uses his other hand to stroke himself. It only takes moments before his breathing becomes erratic, his body tensing. Sticky, salty, white ropes land on my nose, mouth, and chin. I flinch, my eyes fluttering as each spurt lands on me. He moans, his voice high and pained. I know the feeling–it's the same one Sophie brings out in me.

When Brody sighs and lets go of my hair, it's clear he's done. I use my finger to wipe the cum around my lips while I can stare up at him. I use the same finger to wipe what I can from the rest of my face and lick it clean. Brody curses under his breath as he watches.

"Thank you," I sigh.

Brody seems to come out of the fog of lust, eyes going wide.

"W-w-was that-? I mean is it ok that I-?" He's stammering.

I sit back on my heels.

"Brody, that was more than ok," I assure him. "But if you want it to be our secret, I'm ok with that." Sophie wouldn't hold it against us, but I won't push.

He closes his eyes and shakes his head while I stand. My own erection is still very obvious, even in the dimly lit kitchen. Before I can turn to hide it, Brody's eyes widen.

"Should I-?" He motions with his eyes and I smirk.

"You're not ready for that." I shake my head. "Get some sleep. I'll take care of this." I quickly brush his lips with mine in a gesture I pray isn't too far. Brody's face breaks into a smile.

"Thank you?"

"Is that a question?" I laugh. Now that the tension has lifted and the air is a little lighter, all I want to do is smile.

"Thank you." Now it's a statement.

"Go to bed."

# 35

## Sophie

### Sophie

It's happening more. The little notes that Caleb leaves on my front door, on my windshield, even on the back door by our little patio that's accessed through the office. I don't know what Brody has been doing or if his little programs are helping at all, but Caleb just became bolder.

The note on the driver's seat of my car stares at me while I clutch my purse in fear. I have forty minutes to get to Janey's place, but I'm frozen. If he got into my car, why hasn't he tried harder to get into my home? Kicking down our door and then running was a good scare tactic, but that was weeks ago now.

My mouth is dry as I dial Brody's number. He answers on the first ring as if he's been waiting for me to call.

"Hey, Soph," he answers. I can't speak. "Sophie? Sophie, what's wrong?"

"C-Caleb."

"Is he there?" There are faint keyboard clicks in the background.

"No, he-" I swallow and try again. "He left a note in my car. *In my car*, Brody." Tears well in my eyes, spilling over seconds later.

"Hold on, Soph." He's still typing away.

"What is going on?" I whisper. My voice has all but left me.

"I'm checking something."

"No, Brody, I mean- What-?"

"He's gone," Brody sighs. "Sophie, he left it over an hour ago."

*What the fuck?*

"H-how would you know that?"

"Let me come over. I... I need to explain face to face."

"I have work," I choke out, my mind racing.

"You and I both know you're not in any state to film."

He's right.

"Ok." It's a weak answer, but I feel weak right now.

Fingers trembling, I send a text to Janey, not trusting the strength of my voice any longer. We've filmed together enough that it shouldn't hurt our working relationship. Making the excuse that my one of my boyfriends–which is fucking weird to say–has an emergency, I ask to reschedule for sometime next week. Her response is almost instant, wishing my 'man' well.

When Brody arrives, I'm still standing beside my car. I'm not sure I want him in my home right now. I don't know what he knows, what he sees. I don't know what I can trust him with.

He walks briskly up the driveway, reaching out as he nears me, but I take a step back, pressing my back against my car. Seeing my hesitation, Brody stills, dropping his hands.

"Sophie, please," he begs, his voice hoarse.

"What did you do?" My mind has come up with a thousand ideas in the time it took him to get here. "How did you know Caleb was gone?"

"I haven't..." Brody's face falls, a broken man, begging for a last chance at life. "I haven't told you everything I do for work." His voice cracks halfway through the sentence.

"What does that have to do with any-?"

"The company I work for has... connections."

"Connections?" I shake my head, frowning.

"And I have access to programs and systems most companies couldn't dream of."

"Brody-"

He holds up a hand to stop me.

"Please, let me explain Sophie. I have to get this out. Hate me or forgive me, but you need to hear everything."

My mouth snaps shut, lips forming a thin line while I wait for him to continue.

"Harp Solutions," he goes on, "is focused on security, or anti-security in many cases. We can find our way into virtually any system, any device, any network. That's my branch of the company. When you first told me about Caleb, it was easy to find a back way into that camera system." He points to the doorbell.

"A back way?"

"And I've been able to watch him come and go and leave those stupid notes," his voice grows louder, angrier, "and I haven't been able to do anything about it and it pisses me off because you're so fucking scared." Brody takes a ragged breath.

"Why didn't you just tell me this?"

"That's not all." He drops his gaze and takes a steadying breath before meeting my eyes again. Those green orbs hold a plea—to believe him, to forgive him. "My boss, she- I asked her for help. I wanted to protect you." He falls silent.

"Brody just fucking tell me." I'm not sure how he hears my whisper. I can't tell if I'm trembling with rage or fear or perhaps admiration that someone cares so much about me, crazy as that may be. I haven't had that before.

"Cameras," he whispers. "I- We put up cameras."

My stomach drops, knowing the answer to my question before I ask it.

"In my fucking house?" *That* tremble in my voice is definitely rage. "You put cameras in my fucking house? Where? My bathroom? My bedroom?"

"Your office," Brody replies, speaking over me. "Pointing toward each door. And one above your front door. That's it."

"That's it?" I repeat angrily. "Oh thank you for not putting cameras in my room to watch me sleep." I try to stomp toward my door, but Brody steps in front of me.

"Sophie, I didn't know what else to do. You weren't telling me about the other notes, you weren't-"

"Confiding in you? I barely knew you!" My neighbors are going to hear if I don't calm down. "I *still* barely know you!"

"I know and I violated a trust I never even earned, but please believe me when I say I never intended any harm. I did everything in my power to keep you safe. I even-" He takes a steadying breath. "To convince my boss to help, I basically agreed to retire."

"I don't-"

"She's been trying to get me out of the day-to-day work. I still don't know why, but in order for her to put up those cameras, to help me track Caleb and his brother, I had to agree to take the promotion."

"Promotion? You said retirement."

"I can explain later."

"So I should feel sorry for you? You had to retire early to get your boss to help you spy?"

"It's not spying," he presses. When he takes another step toward me, I take another step back, once more up against my car. "I should've asked, but when you were in Miami, I did some digging. Caleb's brother is an animal, Sophie."

"You think I don't know that?"

"But when I read his file-"

"His file?"

"-I knew I had to do something. Sophie, I lo- I care about you."

My heart breaks. He might as well wave a huge, crimson banner in my face and scream at me not to trust him. But the earnestness in his voice makes me pause. Brody licks his lip, but then falls to his knees, sitting back on his heels, face angled up at me.

I've never had someone give a damn about me like this and I'm not so stupid that I'm going to push him away for loving me. I caught his near slip. He almost said the word.

I sink to my knees in front of him as tears flow down my cheeks once more. His hands are trembling when I take them in mine.

"Sophie, I'm so sorry," he whispers.

I lean forward, pressing my forehead to his and closing my eyes.

"Don't you dare fucking lie to me again." I don't have to finish the threat. He knows he won't get another chance.

"Never," Brody agrees, his voice so soft I can barely hear him, even this close. "Never again."

After kneeling for several minutes together, we make our way upstairs and Brody sets about heating water in the kettle. I direct him around the kitchen and watch his movements, smiling when he pulls out a calming blend that Natalie favors in the evenings.

"So," I take the mug of tea Brody hands me. "Retirement?"

I'm not totally sure I've forgiven him. He can see it in my eyes when he sits next to me on the couch with a mug in his hands. I'm worried he's going to treat me with kid gloves as if I'm some breakable porcelain doll in need of a glass case for safekeeping.

"Long story short, my boss, Mel, has been trying to get me to quiet retire for two years."

"Quiet retire?" I snort.

"Like quiet quitting." He shrugs. "Promote me to CIO and then take all of my day-to-day projects away. I barely do anything now."

"Why?"

"I think she's been planning something she doesn't want me to be a part of."

"Something dangerous?"

"Or illegal." He blows on his tea, seemingly unconcerned by the idea. "Mel has always tried to protect me from the darker parts of the company."

"Darker parts?"

"Despite the promotion, I feel like I know less than before."

"Fuck, Brody, why do you work for her?"

"She's like a sister to me."

"Thought you had enough of those." I allow a small smile to grace my lips and Brody returns the grin.

"Mel recruited me right out of college, said she wanted to build a company that helps people by staying in the dark. It all sounded so cool when I was twenty-one. She said I'd get to create all of our programs, design all of our systems, alongside her. How could I say no?"

"I guess if someone came to me and offered to let me build a production company based on my own vision, I wouldn't be able to say no."

"That's what you want?"

"Some day."

"Got a name for it?"

"Yeah, but I'm keeping it a secret for now." I smile. It's a stupid name, but it makes me giggle and sometimes you can't take yourself seriously.

"Still don't trust me?"

"What if you steal it?" I tease.

"Ah, yes. I know a lot of porn stars wanting to start their own production company. I'd definitely tell them about your brilliant name. You got me." He winks, the expression so casual and easy. "Miles mentioned wanting the same thing once when he was dating..." Brody trails off and shakes his head. "Hasn't said anything about it since."

"A bad relationship can kill dreams easier than most people realize."

I wanted to marry Caleb. Even after the first time he hit me, I still wanted a life with him. I wanted children with him.

"I've seen that." He nods. "My sister doesn't seem to be able to find the right guy. Been trying dating apps for a few years and she dated in college, but-" Brody's eyes widen. "Fuck."

"What?"

"She had a date last week," he groans, setting his tea on the coffee table and running a hand over his face. "I was supposed to give her a call half an hour in, but I forgot."

"Why you?" That's much more rude than I want to sound. "I just mean, instead of a friend or-or one of your sisters."

"Apparently everyone was busy. She's gonna kill me."

I can't help but giggle.

"Well, since she hasn't made you regret it, I doubt she needed the call anyway."

"Do women really do that? Set up those calls?"

"Better than telling a man no when the vibes are off." I nod.

"Given your ex and his brother, I can only imagine."

The front door opens to announce that Natalie is back from her yoga class this morning. When her head pops up above the half wall and she spots Brody, she smiles at me.

"I thought you had a shoot today."

"Last-minute cancellation," I fib.

"Bummer. Hey Brody."

"Hey Natalie, how's it going?"

"Oh, don't mind me. I'm headed straight for a shower and then I gotta leave again."

And with that, she disappears down the hall to her room.

"Think she'll forgive me for the cameras?" he asks when we hear the door shut.

"Let's keep it between us for now."

A week passes with no new notes. Brody told me he'd keep an eye out and tell me if he saw Caleb or his brother on any footage, but there's been nothing. I'm not sure if I should be terrified or relieved.

"Yoohoo! Earth to Soph!"

Natalie waves a hand in front of my face, startling me out of my spiraling thoughts. I shake my head and inhale sharply, meeting her gaze. We've been sitting on the couch watching a movie from our Halloween list. The closer we get to October, the more often we pick one out. The original Poltergeist holds up surprisingly well.

"Sorry," I mutter.

"Been doing that a lot lately," Natalie muses.

"Just a lot on my mind."

"Juggling two men will do that." She nudges me with her elbow and I force a smile as we watch the mother get overly excited about an invisible entity sliding her and her family across their kitchen floor. *Idiot*. It's always fun and games until your daughter is sucked into the spirit realm.

"I think I'm doing pretty well at juggling," I comment with a wink.

"Circus freak," she chuckles.

"Think I should audition for Barnum and Bailey?"

"Only if they'll let you juggle naked."

"Probably not."

"Better skip it, then."

Natalie's phone buzzes and she types out a response. She's been going back and forth with one of her financial subs throughout the movie, draining his account and sending pictures of our television screen instead of herself.

"Lean over here," she says, holding up the phone and taking a quick selfie.

She doesn't need to explain that she's posting on social media, taunting her subs because I get to spend time with her and they don't. I'm sure there's a command to send three hundred dollars or something obscene 'simply for existing'. Once again, I'm reminded that she can afford this apartment four times over on her own.

"How much have you made today?" I ask, knowing she doesn't find the question crass.

"Only six hundred and..." she trails off adding up the remainder in her head, "thirty-five dollars."

"*Only*," I repeat, rolling my eyes. There are days she makes three times that before noon, so I guess it's appropriate. "When's your next trip again?"

"It's on the calendar," Natalie groans.

"I forget to check the calendar." I match her groan.

"I leave a week from Monday and I'll be back Thursday."

"Quick turnaround." I frown. "Driving or flying?"

"Driving. No trips to the airport for you, babygirl."

I throw my arms around her and squeeze. Natalie reaches up to pat my arm, laughing while I squeal.

"You *do* love me."

# 36

## Brody

"Isla, I can't talk right now." My phone is wedged between my ear and my shoulder while I search through footage. I'm not doing anything that Mel's team hasn't already done, not reviewing new footage. I'm fucking impotent.

"What are you doing? You sound like you're working out."

"I'm working," I mutter. I'm going to have to pay more attention to my frustrated grunts.

"Since when did you become a wrestler?"

"What do you need, Isla?"

"Ok, ok, fine. Sheesh! Mom was asking me about your new girlfriend. I guess Raegan raved about her. Do you think you'll still be together by Thanksgiving?"

I freeze. I hadn't thought about holidays. If she's still with us—with *both* of us—how is that going to work? Not to mention that Raegan had barely five minutes with Sophie. I don't know what there was to rave about, other than her beauty.

"I don't know," I answer honestly.

"No help, dude."

"Thanksgiving is still two months away."

"Fine, I'll ask Miles."

*Oh, that'll be a fun conversation.* I hope I'm in the room for that.

She hangs up and I let my phone fall into my lap while my head drops backward against my chair. I need a break. Not from screens, but from this specific footage. It's all the same, boring unmoving background with just the odd entrance or exit by Sophie or Natalie. On occasion, Miles or another performer pops in, but I've reviewed footage going back over a month now. Nothing has helped me to find Caleb and at this point, I'm sure Mel would act before telling me anything.

I've been lost to this woman from the moment she responded to my first message on KinkRink. I wish I could be with her all day, every day. I've never been a fighter, but I already know I'd die for Sophie Larson before I let Caleb get his hands on her. Watching over her from afar is agonizing. I need another distraction.

"Miles!" My voice echoes across the house while I stand in my office doorway.

"What?" His head pokes out from his studio, but when he sees his face, his whole body emerges. "Dude, you look like shit."

I throw my arms up and leave the office, heading for the kitchen.

"I can't *do* anything," I mutter.

"Context." Miles approaches as I stand behind the couch, placing my hands on the back and hanging my head. I feel his hand on my back, an attempt to comfort, and my muscles bunch beneath his touch.

"Can you imagine what Sophie is going through?" I choke out.

"Mel is working on it, though, right?" His hand rubs in circles on my back. It's comforting, like I'm a kid again, beeding comfort for being the shy, quiet one in class. "She'll find him."

I turn and Miles' hand drags across my back and over my side, resting on my hip.

"But I can't help." The pressure in my chest threatens to overwhelm me. "Sophie, she's out there trying to live her life and this- this *asshole*-"

"We'll work on your insults, buddy."

"-is trying to ruin it all for her. This fuckface-"

"Better."

"-is leaving these stupid notes."

"He's a fucking coward."

"But what if he does something worse?" My eyes snap to his.

"What, like break down her door again?"

"No, what if-" I can't breathe. "What if-?" Oh god, I really can't breathe. The air rushes into my lungs too quickly and not quickly enough. My gaze falls to Miles' hand on my waist before it moves to my shoulder. He grips my other arm tightly, trying to shake me out of my panic.

"Hey." He shakes gently and then harder when I can't focus on him. "Hey, hey, hey! Brody. Snap out of it. Brody!"

Suddenly, no more air is forcing itself into my lungs. Miles' lips are on mine, his hands on my cheeks, holding me tightly to him. When my brain finally catches up and I start breathing through my nose, he pulls away. His hands are still on my cheeks, eyes full of concern as they study my face.

"Brody?"

I don't want to speak. My hand flies up to the collar of Miles' shirt and I pull him toward me again, this time with the express intent of thanking the man properly. He smiles against my lips, a grown rumbling from deep in his chest.

"Easy, tiger," he chuckles against my lips. I let my mouth fall away, pressing my forehead to his.

"Sorry." I inhale deeply, letting it out fast.

"I'm with you, Brody," he breathes, the warm air hitting my chin and neck. "I've always been here. It's ok."

I don't know how I didn't see it before. Miles hasn't just been there for me, he's cared for me more than anyone else, protected me when kids in school made fun of me, assured me that nothing was wrong with me. Images flash in my mind of touches and glances and moments alone with him, even before we met Sophie. Before she allowed us to bridge the gap. My reservations crumble.

"Studio?" I don't know how else to ask. I don't know how to do this with him. I want him, but I need help.

"Brody, are you sure?"

"Ask me that again," I growl, gently grabbing his throat and noting that his eyes flash, "and I won't show you how good boys get rewarded."

"Jesus, fuck." Miles begins backing toward the hallway. "I'm taking that as a resounding yes."

I run my hand through my hair and follow Miles to his studio, thankful that the pause doesn't give me second thoughts. Once he crosses the threshold, he turns toward me and I walk him backward to the edge of the bed. Again, I find myself uncertain of the next step, but Miles pulls me in gently with his hand on my side.

My lips find his and they part to allow my tongue to take over, conjuring up the memory of how his mouth felt around my cock. My aching erection is dying to escape. Miles seems to read my mind, dropping his hands to the button of my jeans. I snake my hand up to grab his hair, pulling his head back. He smiles with an open mouth, eyes on me while his fingers work to free me.

"What do you want, Brody?" he asks, his voice husky and low. "You want me to suck your cock? Want to taste mine?" He winks. "Or do you just want me to ride you?"

I let go of his hair and back away, my pants undone but still hanging at my hips. Not wanting to waste time, I strip my shirt and hurry to kick off my pants, while Miles does the same. As his shirt lands near mine, my fingers find the waistband of his boxer briefs and I slip my hand beneath the fabric to palm him. It's the first time I've touched him like this and the need for more drives me forward.

Miles' hand lands on my wrist, to beg me to keep going or to make me stop, I'm not sure. I search his face for an indication either way, my eyes falling to the movement of his inked throat when he swallows whatever he's about to say.

"Where's your lube?" I ask, glancing around the room. He'd be a poor porn star if he didn't keep some on hand.

"Bedside table."

"Grab it."

I've never seen him move so quickly, pulling open a drawer and taking out a half-empty bottle of clear lubricant. His hand extends halfway to me, unsure what my plan is.

"Sit," I order. Miles hurries to comply and I smirk. "Good boy." I like the way he responds to my praise.

I take a step back and bite my lip while I study him. Miles squirms beneath my gaze and I have half a mind to make him sit there longer, but we'll toy with that idea later.

"Pull out your cock." That sounds absolutely filthy. Miles shudders and complies, the waistband slapping his legs once he's free. "Now, I want you to use the lube and stroke yourself. Show me what you like. Keep your eyes on me."

Taking a ragged breath, but remaining otherwise silent, Miles flips open the lube and squeezes some into his palm. He inhales sharply as the cold gel hits his hand and dribbles through his fingers onto his waiting shaft. Tossing the lube back onto the bed, he drops his hand and covers himself, stroking with a groan.

My chest rises and falls a little faster, in time with his movements until he speeds up. He focuses on the head, squeezing as he reaches the end of each stroke.

"What else can I do?" he asks, desperation in his voice.

"Keep going," I urge, taking a step closer. I still can't reach him, so I watch.

"Brody." He sounds pained, eyes closing.

"Look at me."

Those golden orbs snap open and I grin. His hips roll into his hand, his breathing fast and uneven.

"Stop," I order and, though he whimpers, Miles stops, gently holding the base of his cock. "Good boy."

"You're an asshole."

"What, you think you deserve to come already?" I shake my head and take the last few steps to reach him. "You've wanted this for a long time." He doesn't have to respond, the desire obvious as I lean down until our noses almost touch. "Let's see how long we can draw this out."

A curse escapes Miles' lips just before I cover them with mine again. His hands fly to my boxers while my tongue plunders his mouth and I groan when he takes me into his hands, still slick with lube. I shake my head, sucking his bottom lip as I pull my head away. Miles likes doing what he's told. I'm not going to allow myself to feel embarrassed or nervous anymore around this man. He wants me and the feeling is mutual.

"I want your mouth on my cock. It felt *so* good last time," I add with a grin, standing up straight.

"I thought you'd never ask."

Before Miles leans forward, I grab his neck and force him to meet my gaze.

"I wasn't asking," I growl.

"Oh boy," he breathes, just barely audible, and I have to fight a smile.

Miles returns to the big, hard task in front of him, licking his lips while he scoots forward on the bed. He pulls my boxers all the way down, allowing me to kick them off. One hand slides down to cup my balls while his other hand holds my cock steady so that he can give me the attention I need. My fingers tangle into his hair without pulling. When I slip inside Miles' wet and waiting mouth, it's almost too much. I hadn't realized how excited I was, but this ache that's been building forces my head back and my eyes closed. Miles works me, swallowing me, taking me to the back of his throat and gagging. Each convulsion around my tip sends a matching jolt through me. His hand below fondles and I feel his finger sliding backward.

Apprehensive, but excited, I let him continue the exploration while he lazily bobs his head on my cock. When his finger finds my asshole, I hiss and clench. Miles pulls his mouth from me and my head snaps down.

"Stop."

"I'm so-" Miles stammers, but I shake my head.

"Just not this time." I try to catch my breath. "I can't- I need-" I press my lips together, glancing at the mattress behind him.

Rather than speak, Miles grabs my hips to pull me down on top of him. Straddling his waist, I have to admit my cock looks good against the ink on his torso. When I chuckle, Miles raises an eyebrow.

"Something funny?"

"It's too bad you don't have tits."

He snorts.

"We can always call Sophie." He continues when I don't respond to that. "What are you gonna do from up there?"

"Getting impatient already?" I grin. I walk my knees up his sides until my dick is pressing against his jaw. "Open." When he complies, I murmur, "Such a good listener."

I lean forward, placing my hands on the bed above him and slide into his mouth with a groan. Rolling my hips makes him gag, so I do it again. And again. And again. Miles' hands trail up my thighs, but he takes everything I give him. He takes every fucking inch. When he squeezes my ass cheeks, I thrust hard to the back of his throat.

I pull out, allowing Miles to catch his breath.

"Ride my cock." It's a caveman-like order, but I don't care. His mouth, while skilled, just isn't enough. I roll off of Miles and he hesitates, glancing down at my glistening shaft. *Was that too far?* Those golden pools find my face again and my doubts dissipate.

"As you wish," he says with a wink, grabbing the lube.

I groan when it dribbles onto the tip of my cock, but Miles' hands are there in the next instant, warming me. His erection is staring me in the face while he positions me against his asshole. I want to buck, to thrust upward, but I resist, not wanting to hurry him.

Suddenly, Miles' gaze turns wicked, the corner of his mouth twitching into a grin.

"I think," he presses down, but not enough for me to squeeze through the ring of muscle, "you should be the one begging, Brody." I groan and throw my head back, trying to grab for his hips. He bats my hands away.

"Miles," I growl.

"Beg," he repeats. "Beg me to ride your thick cock."

I rise up on my elbows, my eyes dropping to where we're making contact before I look at him again.

"If you don't sit your fine ass down- Fuck," I moan as he does exactly what I want.

My head falls back as he swallows me and he matches my sounds of pleasure. He's stretching to accommodate me, letting me mold him, fill him. It's intoxicating.

"So tight," I groan. "Fuck, Miles, slow down, I can't-"

"Shouldn't-" he grunts, "shouldn't I be the one asking *you* to slow down?"

I can't open my eyes to glare at him. He's still sliding his ass down to squeeze my dick, enveloping it with far more ease than I would have expected. I can't focus on anything other than not coming right this second. In an attempt to gain control, I reach out to grasp his length and he stills. The brief pause allows me to lift my head so I can take stock of what I see before me.

My fingers gently grip Miles, his ass millimeters from my hips, eyes closed like he's struggling just as much as I am. I stroke him, getting his attention and he stares at me, his eyes hooded.

Miles leans down, his muscles around me clenching and forcing a grunt from my throat. His lips meet mine and he lifts up before slamming down my cock. Stars explode across the backs of my eyelids and I move my hand faster, fingers meeting as they encircle his tip. My other hand grips his throat, holding his face to mine while he bounces against me.

"Miles," I whimper. Being in charge doesn't matter right now. I don't want this to stop. "Please. Fuck-" He speeds up.

"Brody Torrence, I want you to fucking fill me."

His words are the final push I need and I gasp, twitching as my release explodes deep inside him. Miles sits fully on my cock while I come, my hand halting its movements on him. When I finally still, he tries to lift, but I grab one hip and keep him in place.

"Oh no," I pant. "You're going to stay right there."

I grab the lube that has rolled next to his foot, needing a refresh, and smirk when it hits his skin, cold and jarring. My hand finds his shaft again and I watch Miles' eyes flutter closed with a whispered curse.

"Brody, please."

"Please what?" I speed up.

"Fuck, I need-"

"You *need*?" I speed up a little more.

"God, Brody, I- Fuck, please."

"I said," my hand freezes, "please what?"

"Please, I need to come," Miles whimpers, still unable to open his eyes. I grin.

"Look at me when you paint my chest," I order and his eyes snap open.

I use both hands this time, the better to grip his full length. He struggles but keeps his eyes on me. His breathing becomes ragged, whimpers escaping his throat. I catch the odd curse here and there and lick my lips.

"Come for me," I urge. "Be a good boy and come for me, Miles."

He grunts, another curse dying on his tongue and I feel the jets of warmth hitting my chest. My hands pull everything from him, not even stopping when he's spent. His body convulses, overstimulated.

"Stop," he begs, curling down and trying to lift his hips, but I have a grip on his cock that he doesn't want to test. I continue the torture. "Please, B-Brody, p-p-please."

With a dark chuckle, I let go of him. Miles sits there for a moment, my soft cock still inside him, before rolling off. My release pours from him onto my hip as he falls and I let my eyes close. I've gotten my breathing under control for the most part and heave a sigh.

"Brody Motherfucking Torrence," Miles laughs. "When did you become so depraved?" I'm too tired to open my eyes to look at him.

"I've been living with you long enough," I shoot back. "You just rubbed off on me."

"That's not all I did." There's movement beside me and when I open one eye to see what he's doing, Miles is propped up on his elbow, staring at me. "When did things change?"

"Kinda deep to ask while my brain is still half-melted," I mutter.

"That's your own fault." He trails a finger through the white mess on my chest. I catch his hand and bring his fingertips to my lips. "Jesus, seriously, when did things change?"

He moans when I pull his finger into my mouth. It won't be the last time I taste him, that much I know. I drop his hand and meet his gaze.

"I don't know. I really don't. Maybe it was a few weeks ago with Sophie, maybe it was a long time ago and I just didn't realize."

"I guess I really shouldn't care *when*," Miles sighs, leaning forward to kiss my shoulder. The gesture is sweet and intimate in a way unlike anything we just did. "I'm just glad you saw the light."

Miles squeezes my shoulder as he rounds the kitchen island on Saturday morning. My oatmeal lies forgotten in front of me, having gone cold while I scroll my phone.

"Whatcha doin'?"

"I'm, er, looking at something." I haven't broached the subject with him yet because I don't even know if finding a house the right size is possible.

"Got that," he snorts, turning on the coffee maker. "Is it secret spy stuff?"

"I'm not a spy." I don't have the energy to roll my eyes. I'm still not sure how I made it to the shower last night without my legs giving out.

"Is it secret, black market stuff?"

I'm looking at houses," I mumble.

"Come again?" He spins.

"Don't have the time for that," I reply with a smirk. "I'm looking for a house."

"One hot love-making session and you're leaving me?" The false hurt in his voice forces my smile to spread.

"I'm just looking. Don't you want more space?"

Miles takes a moment to look down his hallway, then down mine. His eyes roam the living room behind me and then he makes a show of inspecting the kitchen.

"More space?" he repeats with raised eyebrows.

"I just meant it might be nice for Sophie to-"

"You think she'd leave her comfy little townhouse for us?" He shakes his head. "Not likely."

"Like I said, I'm just looking."

"Never let anyone say you're not prepared for every eventuality."

# 37

## Miles

> We're meeting at the usual place at 9. You're on the reservation if you want to join.

Moira's reminder about Sunday brunch goes unanswered for the umpteenth weekend. I haven't been since before Brody's appointment with her. Sophie has taken up every extra thought I have, but I'm going to have to bite the bullet soon. It's not that I don't miss it, but I know I'm gonna catch shit for my absences.

It's been a week since I've physically seen Sophie. Not a day goes by when we don't exchange texts and voice memos, but I haven't held her in my arms in a week. By Sunday, I'm chomping at the bit just to feel her skin on mine.

She suggests doing a live session together.

"This'll be a change."

Sophie steps through the front door with a grin.

"Because we haven't performed live together or because we haven't filmed here?"

"Both." She shrugs and allows me to lead the way. "Where's Brody?"

"Locked in his room."

"Still trying to find my ex?" The guilt is evident in her voice, though it shouldn't be there at all.

"He's worried about you." We come to a stop in front of the open doorway to my studio and I wave her in first. "Here we are. It's not much, but-"

"It's perfect," Sophie interrupts, her eyes sweeping the room while mine take her in. She wore leggings today, despite the heat, and they hug every single curve of her voluptuous body. I cannot wait to get my hands on her.

There's a queen-size bed in the center of the room with black sheets. I have a restraint system beneath the mattress and the cuffs are hanging down at each corner. The frame is black metal, thin enough to attach ropes to, but sturdy enough to steady oneself on. There's an oversized lounge chair in the corner, but it doesn't get used much. Besides those two pieces of furniture, there's a small table on either side of the bed and two huge studio lights sitting to one side, turned off. I haven't moved them because I'm not sure how we're going to set things up just yet. My tripod is extended to its full height next to the lights and a small, foldable TV tray is leaning up against the wall by the door.

Sophie pulls out her laptop since we're using her account for this event and I help her set it up next to the bed so that we can see chats and tips spent as they come through. I set up the webcam on my tripod before Sophie and I decide where the studio lights should go.

After flipping on the second light, I turn to find that Sophie is stripping out of her public-appropriate clothes. A minute later, two light blue scraps of lace are all that cover her breasts and the spot between her legs, but the back of the thong is swallowed by her ass. I want to drop to my knees and beg to taste her, but we've got a job to do and a schedule to keep.

# 38

## Brody

*I'm not going to watch their live session.*

*I'm not going to watch.*

*I'm not.*

That doesn't last long. Their broadcast has only been going for three minutes when I join the event anonymously. I can't tip without revealing my username, though that wouldn't give me away. I watch as Sophie and Miles interact with the viewers who *do* tip and respond verbally to the chat messages.

Miles is only wearing a pair of boxers, but Sophie looks good enough to eat in her pale blue lingerie. She's only just across the house from me, so close and yet so far. This might be the death of me, watching from the other room, knowing what it feels like to touch them both. Thoughts of the other night with Miles fill my head, interspersed with knowing what Sophie's pussy feels like when it grips my cock.

When the tips based on their menu start rolling in, I gently grasp my growing erection through my pants. The screen isn't big enough to do them justice and I find myself wanting to hook up a cable to the television on the opposite side of the room so I can truly appreciate what's happening.

Sitting behind her, Miles pulls one strap of Sophie's bra over her shoulder, kissing her dusky, inked skin following the movement. When both straps are off of her arms, she pulls her hair out of the way to allow Miles to unhook the back of the bra. Feigning shyness,

Sophie holds the lace against her chest with her arms, but Miles turns her head to kiss her while his hand frees the fabric from her grasp.

I want to squeeze those beautiful, natural tits so bad. Her dark nipples are hard in the cold room and, staring at them, I almost miss Miles' hand traveling south to cup her pussy. Sophie moans, their lips still connected, as her hand covers his.

I know the tips are coming in, but I'm not watching the chat.

Miles slowly pulls Sophie's thong down, not that it was hiding much to begin with, and she opens her legs. He rolls over to grab a vibrator from the bedside table and turns it on, dragging it gently over Sophie's clit. She whines and moans, likely for the camera.

Sophie's head falls back and Miles leans down to take her nipple into his mouth, pulling a sigh from her throat. The vibrator in his hand never leaves her and her hips begin to roll and buck.

Before long, Miles glances up at the laptop again and grins against Sophie's tit. He whispers something to her and she takes the vibrator from him while he leans to the side again and pulls out a dildo that looks far too big. In Miles' other hand is a bottle of lube that he squirts onto the toy, spreading it with his hand.

Sophie moves the vibrator away as Miles brings the toy down, pressing it against her entrance. She meets his eyes and the moan when he pushes the toy inside her makes me groan. I wish that was my hand, pushing it deeper.

"Mmm, you like it when I fuck her with this monster cock?" he asks the camera. "You like watching me stretch her like this?" He glances at the laptop and chuckles. "I thought so."

He switches between toys, using each one for several minutes, but none are as big as that first dildo. Every one of them pulls a symphony of moans and whimpers from Sophie. Eventually, he tosses the last toy onto the floor.

Miles smirks at the laptop barely visible on the far side of the screen, then kisses Sophie on the cheek before hopping off of the bed. He unceremoniously yanks off his boxers and reveals his thick, fully erect cock for the viewers.

My mouth goes dry when Miles rejoins Sophie, kneeling further down the bed for a closer view of what's going to happen next. Sophie crawls to him, smirking at the camera before she comes even with Miles. Turning, she looks up at him and I watch in awe as he cups her cheek. If I didn't know already, that look in his eyes would confirm that he's head over heels for this woman.

"Be a good girl," he murmurs softly. "Suck Daddy's cock."

I'm enthralled. I've never watched Sophie's content. I may have put cameras in her home without consent, but I wouldn't view her porn without her giving me the ok. Then again, I'm sitting here watching her on camera. Jesus, I'm fucked up.

Sophie opens her mouth slowly, sticking her tongue out as Miles grasps the base of his cock and slaps the tip against it. She moans and a smile tugs at the near corner of her mouth. Her eyes are still on his when she brings her head closer, her lips closing around him. Miles' head falls back. The sounds of pleasure coming from both of them make me regret having turned this on.

I'm not sure if Sophie continues her work for thirty seconds or thirty minutes. Hell, it could have been hours. I don't even remember blinking when she finally comes up for air, spit glistening on her chin and his cock. Miles grabs her hair and forces her up as he bends down to kiss her.

The tips have stopped so they crawl back up the bed, grinning at each other and lazily kissing when they lie down against the pile of pillows. Miles, who's closer to the laptop, checks the chat every few minutes, but nothing is coming through. Grumbling, I start clicking around to add tokens to my account. I feel ridiculous, like one of their rabid fans, but I also feel the need to see this through.

# 39

## Sophie

### Sophie

The tip comes through and Miles grins.

"How do you want me to devour her?" he asks the tipper, keeping his eyes on me. The hunger in those orbs makes my stomach flip every time I see it.

"Don't mind if I do," I giggle.

Miles slides down the bed. Once he's in position, I swing a leg over his head so that I'm facing the camera. While I place my hands on his chest for stability, his fingers slide up my thighs, squeezing my flesh and pulling a sigh from me.

"Sit on my face, Honey," he urges.

Lowering myself with a grin at our audience, I feel his hot breath on my center. His tongue darts out to taste me and I whimper.

"Sit," he says again, pulling on my thighs. "All the way."

Before the last word is out of his mouth, I plant myself firmly against him. My giggle at his muffled voice turns into a whine as he starts to suck and toy and nip at me. My hips rock, searching for friction, my body yearning for release. Miles' strong hands pull me down in an attempt to smother himself.

"Is this what you wanted?" I ask the camera. The laptop chimes a moment later and it's hard to pull focus from what Miles is doing beneath me.

> **ready4u27**: *Tipped 250 tokens* you're fucking perfect, sweetheart

The pet name sends a shiver down my spine and I close my eyes, imagining that the words are Brody's. I throw my head back with a moan when Miles grazes his teeth over my clit. Everything he does brings me closer to the brink.

> **ready4u27**: *Tipped 250 tokens* tell him he's a good boy

"Good boy," I breathe.

Miles pushes his tongue inside me, pulling another squeak from my throat. I try to ride his face, but his grip keeps me solidly in place. I moan a curse, aching with the need to come.

As if reading my mind, the big tipper sends another message.

> **ready4u27**: *Tipped 1000 tokens - cum for us* soak his face, Honey

"You wanna watch me cum?" I hum, giving Miles direction since he can't see the screen.

I reach up to play with one nipple, my other hand still holding me steady. My hips begin to move faster and faster, seeking the orgasm that is so close. With one more stroke of Miles' tongue, I'm over the edge, crying out. My back arches as my core tightens and Miles continues to lap at me before the pleasure subsides.

His legs bend, but he's still holding me down. I lean forward, placing my hands on his knees, and grin at the camera.

"Thanks for joining us." My voice is velvety, despite the fact that my throat feels raw. "Lance and I are going to finish up without an audience."

I wink and, lifting only slightly off of Miles' face, I reach over to stop the broadcast on the laptop. When I try to lift one leg, Miles pulls me back down and I giggle.

"I have to let you up for air."

"Fuck air." His voice is muffled against my pussy. "I don't need to breathe."

Just as another giggle escapes my lips, the door flies open to reveal Brody. His chest is heaving, his eyes are wild. His belt hangs undone in the loops of his unbuttoned pants and he stands there for a moment, studying the scene before him.

"Soph?" Miles' muffled question makes me gasp.

"H-hi Brody." My voice shakes with anticipation.

"Up," he growls. When I frown, unmoving, he takes a step forward. "Get up."

I scramble off of Miles' face, still on the bed, while Miles props himself up on his elbows. He looks at Brody, one eyebrow raised, half his face still wet with my arousal.

"Hey, buddy." He grins. "Wanna play another game?"

"You," Brody points at Miles, "sit in that chair." His finger swerves to the armchair in the corner.

Miles and I are both curious as to what Brody has planned this time. This dominating nature of his turns me on more than I could have imagined. I've played the sub before in videos, followed orders. This is entirely different.

Miles moves slower than I did, making a show of sitting up and swinging his legs over the edge of the bed. He doesn't move to hide his erection as he stands and walks past the studio lights, turning them off as he goes so that we aren't blinded or overheating. All that's left are the lamps on the bedside table. He makes his way over to the chair and takes a seat, bringing one foot up to rest on the opposite knee with a grin, his hard cock proudly displayed between his legs.

Brody, whose eyes were following Miles, now turns his gaze to me. Removing his clothes, he approaches the bed and I have no time to react as his hand shoots out to grab the back of my neck, pulling my lips to his in a violent kiss that bruises. In return, I pull his lip between my teeth and bite gently. Brody moans into me before pulling away. His eyes flick over to Miles in the chair.

"You're going to watch," he growls. "Watch while I make our girl come."

"Fuck." The word escapes my lips and my pussy aches with desire. "You were watching." How else would he have known when to come in?

"I watched you come on his face." Brody nods. "And I wanted it to be my cock, so I decided to do something about it."

"What, no 'Brody says'?" Miles teases.

"Do you have a gag?" Brody asks. Miles simply closes his lips and pretends to lock them and throw away an imaginary key. It's clear he's trying not to smile and I giggle. "Now, where did I stop you two?"

On his knees above me, Brody reaches down between my thighs and I spread my knees a little more. The moment he slides a finger through my wetness, I whimper. My arm flies up to clutch his inked shoulder, nails digging in to form crescent marks in his skin.

"So needy," he groans before kissing me again. "I'm going to lie down," he says against my lips. "And you're going to sit that sweet cunt down on my cock.

I swallow hard. The last time I was on top, with Miles beneath me on the couch, I didn't have to do much. On a bed, it's a lot harder.

"Brody, I can't-" I whisper. "Being on top," my eyes flick to Miles and then back to Brody's as I pull back to see him clearer, "it's harder for..." *For someone my size*, but I don't say that.

Brody's expression falters, his eyebrows softening. He cups my face and I lean into his hand.

"I'm sorry, I didn't mean to-"

"It's ok, just... bad knees." That's half the problem, but I don't want to get into it now. I've already ruined the mood enough.

Brody's fingers ease into my hair.

"We'll just have to find another position, won't we?" He licks his bottom lip and smiles. "Hands and knees for me, sweetheart. Face Miles."

I inhale sharply but do as I'm told, crawling as far down the bed as possible, to be as close to Miles as I can. Moments later, Brody's cock slides up and down my center, dragging moisture down to my clit and then back. I push my hips into him, trying to urge him to speed up, but he laughs deep in his throat.

"See how desperate she is for me?" He asks Miles whose casual expression has changed. He's watching us intently as if nothing else exists in this world but the two people on the bed before him.

"She needs it," he agrees.

"Should I oblige?"

My toes wiggle as I fight the urge to beg Brody to fuck me already.

"I don't know," Miles muses, but his voice is strained. "The question is... is she desperate *enough*?"

"Please," I whimper.

"What's that?" asks Brody with another swipe. He slaps himself against my clit and I nearly jump out of my skin, earning a chuckle from both men. "Come on, sweetheart, beg for us."

"Fuck." I hang my head, wondering at the fact that there isn't a goddamn river flowing between my legs. The teasing is sweet agony.

"He's not here," Miles laughs. "Go on, beg my best friend to fuck you while I watch. Beg to come on his exquisite dick." My head snaps up.

*Exquisite?*

"Please," I whimper a little louder. "Fuck me, Brody."

He plunges into me forcing a cry from my lips. Grabbing my hips, he fucks me hard and fast, thrusting deep with every stroke.

"Eyes on me, honey," says Miles.

I hadn't realized my eyes had closed, I was so focused on Brody's movements. When I force them open again, Miles has shifted. Both feet are on the ground, legs spread. His elbows rest on his knees and those beautiful, brown eyes are focused on my face while Brody pounds into me. Whimpers and whines spill from me and it takes everything I have to keep my eyes from closing again as my core tightens and my muscles tense.

"That's it. You're taking Brody's cock so fucking well."

When my head starts to fall, Brody's hand leaves my hip and tangles into my hair, forcing my face to remain even with Miles'. He's not pulling hard, but it's enough to set off the explosion of ecstasy. As my body stiffens, my eyes squeeze shut.

"Fuck, Sophie, fuck," Brody grunts, thrusting through my orgasm.

The spasms finally slow and I fall forward, taking him with me. My back is still arched, Brody's hands on the bed on either side of me, his hips still. A sheen of sweat begins to cool on my skin while Brody trails light kisses over one shoulder.

"So," kiss, "fucking," kiss, "perfect."

My face is buried in the sheet beneath me and I have to turn my head to try to gain control over my breathing. When Brody backs away and I'm left empty, a whimper escapes my lips. He leans down to whisper in my ear, his breath tickling the sensitive area.

"I think," though not in my line of sight, I can hear the grin in his voice, "it's time we allowed Miles to join us, don't you? Seems like he has a painful problem you could help with."

I lift my head, my movements stunted. Miles' eyes are hungry, burning, begging to touch me and they're focused directly on my face. He doesn't even bother to look at Brody.

"Y-yes," I whisper.

"Oh, Sophie." Brody pulls the hair away from my ear. "You're going to need to be louder than that, sweetheart. Now," his face is no longer next to mine, "should we let Miles join us?"

"Yes." My voice is stronger, but not by much.

"Yes, what? What do you want Miles to do?"

"I..." I don't know what answer Brody wants. *I want him to fuck me? To choke me with his cock? To utterly devour me with his tongue?* "I want you both." The confident seductress from my videos asserts herself in my voice.

I know something has changed between them. I'm not sure what, but *something* happened. I can't wait to explore it, but not right now. Right now, I want to be the center of attention.

"Good girl." Brody leans back down to kiss my shoulder. "What are you waiting for?" he murmurs, clearly addressing Miles. "Get over here."

Miles practically jumps out of the chair, taking just two long strides to reach the edge of the bed.

"Do you trust me?" asks Brody, taking a finger to my chin and turning me toward him. I search his face, trying to decipher his meaning. Would I be here if I didn't?

"Yes."

"I'm going to lie down," he begins, backing away. "And you're going to get on top." Before I can even open my mouth to protest, Miles takes my chin and turns my face upward, catching my lips in his.

"I think you're going to like this, honey," he assures me when he stands above me once more.

I wet my lips and take a ragged breath, then turn to crawl up the bed toward Brody. The smug smile on his face is so out of character. Maybe that's why it turns me on so much. I'm already slick with arousal, absolutely soaked, but I swear the sight of him lying there, waiting for me to straddle him, causes a tear to roll down my thigh.

My knees on either side of him, Brody reaches between us to guide himself. Before the head of his cock can slip back inside me, his hands grasp my hips and don't allow me to sink down further. His green eyes on me, Brody addresses Miles.

"I think we're going to need to help," he growls. "Don't you want to taste us?"

I try to turn my head to watch as Miles kneels on the bed and lowers his head behind me, but Brody's grip on my hips keeps me facing forward. He moans and I imagine that Miles is *helping* Brody with his mouth. My lips part in shock. I wish I had this on camera—there's no way my imagination is good enough to capture what's happening beneath me.

Miles' head lifts and his hand snakes into my hair, pulling my head back.

"Open your mouth," Brody orders. I immediately comply.

Now directly above me, Miles gathers the saliva in his mouth and slowly lets it fall from his lips onto my tongue.

"Swallow," he breathes.

As soon as he sees my throat finish working to swallow his gift, Miles' lips crash down onto mine. His tongue slips, almost immediately, into my mouth. Brody's hands tighten on my hips and he slides inside me, either with Miles' help or getting the angle perfect on his own. My whimper is captured and consumed by the man behind me.

"I wish you two could see what I see," Brody moans. Miles and I break the kiss to look down at him. "Do you know how-" he chokes on his words, "-how magnificent this looks?"

Miles lets go of my hair and I lean down to kiss Brody. His hands roam my body, his hips still. I feel a second set of hands join moments later and I no longer know which ones belong to which man and I don't fucking care anymore. Someone runs gentle fingers down my back and another hand grasps one breast, squeezing gently until fingers from the same hand pinch the nipple. I moan into Brody's kiss.

I hear the soft snap of a bottle cap opening just before something cold is poured onto my asshole, dripping down to cover the spot where Brody and I are joined.

"Did you plan this?" I giggle against Brody's lips while Miles' fingers spread the lube, bringing warmth back to my skin.

"We just know each other *very* well," he whispers back. "Where do you want him, sweetheart?"

I lift my head and raise an eyebrow.

"I thought you were in charge."

"Only to an extent." Brody trails his fingers over my temple and into my hair. "I know you're more experienced," he breathes. "So it's your choice."

"I need you both, together." My lips find his again and Miles grunts his approval.

"That's what I hoped you'd say."

His thick cock prods at my already stretched pussy, trying to fit himself in next to Brody. After a few slippery mistakes, he begins to squeeze inside. My breath stills in my chest, my eyes closing as I concentrate on all the sensations of pain and pleasure mixing together. An altogether different pain from the kind that would have me cowering in a corner.

"Eyes on me, sweetheart," Brody growls, his hand still in my hair.

"I can't," I whimper as the pressure grows, as Miles pushes further inside me. Had we not used the large dildo during our broadcast, I don't know that I would be able to take both of them at once. My breath keeps catching, gasps escaping me with every other inhale.

"You can," Miles urges. A hand brushes down my side. "I know you can."

I force my eyes to open, finding Brody's green orbs just as Miles stops pushing, fully inside me. I can breathe again, even if it more closely resembles panting.

"So fucking tight," he groans. "Feels so fucking good."

"Miles is going to move," Brody says slowly, his eyes flicking to his friend and then back to me. "He's going to fuck you and you're going to take it and if I don't hear you scream our names when you come on both our cocks, then we'll keep trying until you do. Be a good girl and scream for us."

Brody pulls me back into a kiss while Miles slowly backs out and then plunges deep inside me. He speeds up, soon pistoning in and out so furiously that I can't keep contact with Brody's mouth, instead just keeping my face as close to his as possible. Our noses rub, foreheads brushing each other's, sharing our air while Miles grunts and squeezes my hips.

"Such a good girl," Brody murmurs. "Taking us both so well, so fucking well." The praise doesn't stop and I can feel an orgasm building. "Do you know how perfect you are, sweetheart?" He doesn't wait for my response, not that I could give it anyway. I'm too lost to pleasure, too focused on chasing a high that I know is so close. "I need you to know-" he grunts and I know he's losing control. "Fuck, Sophie, look at me." He takes my chin, lifting my head just enough to bring his face into focus. "I love you."

I open my mouth to speak, but instead, cry out as I tumble over the edge. My core tightens, pulsing around both men inside me. My back arches and Miles removes one hand from my hip to wrap it gently around my throat and hold me to him. Their names, along with a dozen curses, tumble from my lips like a wicked prayer.

Miles' movements stutter, Brody grunts, stiffening beneath me, and I feel the warmth as both releases flood my still spasming-pussy. My body relaxes and Miles lets me fall gently forward onto Brody's chest, our skin slick with sweat. When Miles pulls himself from me, I whimper and then feel their combined releases fall from me as Brody lifts my hips.

He helps me to slide my leg over him so that I can fall with a sigh between the two men. The sigh turns to an exhausted laugh, which Miles and Brody join.

"That was unexpected," I breathe.

The feeling of all of us mixed together, leaking from between my thighs, almost has me wanting to go again.

# 40

## Brody

The room is dark when I wake up next to them. Miles keeps his studio curtains drawn when he films at night. The window faces the back of the house, but we still have neighbors across the fence who would easily be able to see inside with the lights on.

I haven't slept that well in a very, *very* long time. I like waking up with Sophie between Miles and me. I like having her so close during the night and warm beside me in the morning.

I love her.

I love him.

I love *them*.

Miles has been my best friend for years. I'm not sure when I began to see *him* differently, but I feel freer, lighter, having admitted how I feel about Sophie. Can I say the words out loud to him?

If we were in my well-lit room, I'd happily lie here for hours, watching the two of them sleep. Unfortunately, Sophie's ex is still at the forefront of my mind. Without the ability to figure out where the bastard is staying while in LA, he feels more dangerous than ever. What gets me is that he hasn't sent an outright threat to come to her, to hurt her, or to take her. Just insults and acknowledging that he's found her. It doesn't make sense.

I slip from beneath the sheet and thin blanket and leave the studio as quietly as possible. In the back of my mind, I wonder if Miles has ever spent the night in there. He works there, films there, does live sessions there, but I don't think he's ever slept in that bed. First time for everything, I suppose, and I've had a *lot* of firsts since meeting Sophie.

Walking naked through my own house isn't exactly at the top of my list of things I enjoy doing, but I didn't want to wake Miles or Sophie by gathering my clothes. I stop at the pantry for a granola bar and a bottle of water before finding a pair of sweats in my room and then sitting at my desk.

Starting up my laptop seems to take forever, but when I pull up the camera footage from Sophie's place, things are quiet. There's no sound, so I can't hear if Natalie is home. I rewind the footage to the last time stamp I viewed and start watching at three times the speed. Mel has a team of three men watching the feeds, live, in shifts. It's their only job and they do it well, letting me know each time Caleb appears, within seconds. I still like to review it myself.

There's nothing new in the footage and I pass the time staring at the feed from all four cameras—the three we added and the doorbell cam. Other than Sophie leaving yesterday to make her way here, an Amazon package delivery, and Natalie going on some kind of shopping trip, the place is quiet.

A knock on my office door startles me from the footage and I turn to find Sophie opening the door slowly. She's clothed again, damn it, but she's grinning ear to ear.

"Hey." Her voice is soft, deeper than usual from having just woken up.

"Morning." I spin my chair to face her.

"You left us."

"I didn't want to wake you, but I," my hand motions to the monitors, "wanted to review some things."

Sophie steps into the room, her bare feet sinking into the carpet. She glances at the monitors, but otherwise, her eyes stay on me.

"I gotta go."

"Work?" I ask as she bends over to place a kiss on my lips.

"Natalie's leaving for San Francisco in a little bit and I told her I'd see her off."

Sophie stands and makes to turn for the door, but I lean forward and grab her hips and twist, pulling her backward, between my legs. She giggles, her breasts bouncing in my face and, heaven help me, I want to suffocate myself between them. Saint that I am, I resist the urge.

"Come back tonight?" I ask, running one hand down her thigh.

"If you're lucky."

"Oh, I've been *very* lucky lately."

"I have to go," she repeats. "Ask me again in a few hours."

---

A few hours later, I send a text asking Sophie to come by tonight, just as she told me to. She doesn't respond immediately and I assume she's working. Leaving my phone on my desk, I stand to open my office door and call across the house to Miles, who I know is just sitting in his room, editing.

"Mario Kart?" My voice echoes through the house. A few seconds later, his door opens and he pokes his head out.

"Five minutes?" he calls.

I thrust out my hand with a thumbs up and leave my door open. I figure I can fire up the Switch in preparation and get to the game's main screen while I wait. The entire time, I'm listening for my phone to buzz with a response from Sophie.

After several minutes of waiting, I wonder where Miles is. He probably got distracted. I stand from my gaming chair, grumbling, just as he walks slowly to my door. He's staring down at his phone with a look of concern.

"What is it?" I frown and Miles opens his mouth to speak, but no words come out. "Miles?"

"Yeah." He shakes his head as if to clear it and looks up at me. "Yeah, sorry, it's Natalie."

"Sophie's roommate? You have her number?"

"No, she... she reached out to me on Twitter. Said Sophie was supposed to be home in time to see her off, but wasn't."

"Sophie said that's why she had to leave."

"Natalie never saw her." Miles takes a step into my office and turns his phone to show me the messages, but continues to explain. "Natalie didn't think anything weird was happening til she stopped for gas and didn't have any messages from Sophie. I haven't heard from her since she left, have you?"

"I-" I glance at my phone on my desk, dread forming a knot in my stomach. "No." Before Miles makes his suggestion, I'm back at my computer.

We're both thinking the same thing. There's no need to say it out loud.

*Caleb.*

When reviewing the footage this morning, I didn't fully catch up, ending a few hours early. I skip to the timeframe when Sophie left, speeding through footage until I see Natalie packing her car. I watch her speedy little black-and-white form waiting on her friend. She sends a text, but doesn't seem to receive a response, and finally leaves.

Within minutes, I've caught up to now–two thirty-three in the afternoon.

"She never made it home." My choked whisper barely makes it out of my throat as my fingers reach for my phone. "I'm calling Mel."

She picks up quickly.

"Mel, please, you have to help." I don't like having to ask again so soon, but I have no choice.

"What's wrong?" The genuine concern in her voice does little to thaw the cold fear in my chest.

"It's Sophie, she's- She left a few hours ago, but she never made it home. I'm not-" My breathing is coming so quickly, I can't control it now. Miles steps up to take my phone and put it on speaker while I try to calm down. I run my hands into my hair and drop my elbows to rest on my thighs, my head hanging low.

"Mel, it's Miles. Sophie was headed straight home." The fear in his voice matches mine, but it's not crippling him the way it is me. "Her roommate said she never made it and now she's not responding to anyone's texts. Brody needs access to your systems again."

"No need, I'll get a team on it."

"Mel," my voice breaks as I lift my head, "I need to help. I need to find her."

"We'll find her, Brody."

# 41

## Sophie

### Sophie

*What the fuck happened?*

The surface beneath my right arm is hard and rough with what feels like little bits of gravel digging into my skin. My head hangs awkwardly to one side. I'm clearly not in my bed. When I open my eyes to darkness, my pulse quickens. *Did I go blind too?* No, wait. My eyelashes brush against some kind of cloth. I'm blindfolded. My heartbeat is like a painful drum in my head, concentrated in one spot on the left side. I try to raise my hand to feel what I expect is a cartoonish lump, but something tightens around my wrists. It's rough, burning when I turn my hands. Rope?

*Seriously, what the fuck happened?*

Since I can't physically do it, I focus through the pounding ache in my head to mentally examine the rest of my body. My ankles must be bound too, likely by the same rough material. I can't straighten my legs. Something must be connecting my wrists and ankles. Using my elbow to push myself, I roll onto my back, bringing my hands to rest on my stomach and pulling my ankles up.

"Sooophie."

Caleb might as well have doused me in ice water for the cold fear that takes hold of me. The elongated pronunciation of my name breaks through the fog of pain in an instant.

"Sophie."

This one is short and quick.

*Of fucking course.*

"We were worried you'd sleep all day."

Jesse's here too, I gather.

"Nothing to say?" asks Caleb.

My mouth is dry, but even if I *could* speak, I wouldn't give him the satisfaction. I won't scream. I won't beg. I'm fucking terrified, there's no denying that. Caleb has proven he's a dangerous man and his brother is worse, but I refuse to wither in his clutches.

"I came to find you, baby." His tone is overly sweet and my stomach churns. "You've been gone so long. I've been so lonely."

Even as I steel myself, questions race through my mind.

Did Natalie realize something was wrong when I didn't come home to see her off? It's not weird that I didn't come home, given where she knew I'd be all night.

Will Brody and Miles hate me for disappearing? Will they think I freaked out after last night and ghosted them? Will they search for me?

My best guess is Caleb plans to return me to Oklahoma, maybe keep me locked up like that girl in *Room*. He's lost his goddamn mind if he thinks I won't scratch his eyes out the first chance I get.

My blood boils at the thought of leaving Natalie and the guys–*my* guys–to wonder about my fate. How fucking dare Caleb do this? How dare he threaten the life I worked so hard to build? I could fucking kill him.

Cold fear is replaced by burning rage, taking hold in my chest and radiating to my limbs. He won't break me. I won't let him. He forced me to put up walls around my heart, but Brody and Miles already tore those down, brick by brick. I've never been cared for–*loved*–the way I am by them. Caleb Cunt Rag Davis has no right to take me from them.

A foot connects with my side and I cry out in pain, despite my promise to myself to keep silent.

"She *does* have a voice," Jesse snickers. If he was within reach, I'd jam my thumbs in his beady little eyeballs.

"Does your boyfriend know what you are?" asks Caleb.

"Which one?" The words are out of my mouth before I can stop them.

Caleb sneers.

"I'm gonna enjoy punishing you, you know that? You ran from me. That's not what good girlfriends do."

*I'm not your fucking girlfriend.*

Rough hands grip my chin and I hear someone spit just before a wet splat lands on my nose and cheek. I wonder if he was aiming for my mouth. *Dumbass.*

"You got any idea how long I've been looking for you, bitch?" Caleb snarls when I don't respond, "I'm talking to you." His hand collides with my cheek, my face turning abruptly to the side. It doesn't help my headache. "I'll teach you to respect me."

*Fat chance of that.* Disrespect is all he's ever getting from me again.

"Say something." Caleb smacks me again. My teeth slice into my lower lip and the taste of blood fills my mouth. I right my head but remain silent. "Let's get her in the chair."

Two sets of hands grab my upper arms to haul me off of the floor. I'm forced to crouch on the balls of my feet until the tether connecting my wrists and ankles is released. The sound of a knife sawing through the rope precedes a final snap and I'm able to stand, though I still need steadying.

Rather than free my ankles, the brothers drag me backward and throw me in a chair. Cold metal almost stings my skin where my shirt has ridden up in the back. I hiss at the contact.

The blindfold is removed from my eyes, allowing me to examine my prison cell. We're surrounded by what looks like an unfinished construction site. It clearly hasn't been touched in years. Past Caleb, a good fifteen feet in front of me, is a large window spray-painted with colorful graffiti. I can't see through the paint. For all I know, we could be on the second or the twenty-second floor. Above the graffiti, the sun is setting. The sky to the left is already purple near the top of the window.

To my right is a folding table and two matching chairs. On the other side of the cheap furniture is a closed, white door.

My eyes focus on Caleb when he squats in front of me. He sneers like he's some evil genius who's just revealed a grand plot twist in a superhero movie. I haven't forgotten his beady, little brown eyes, just a little too close together. His nose is crooked. It's been broken more times than even he probably knows, mostly by his brother. His gym bro build is about his only redeeming physical quality, but it looks like he hasn't found the time to work out as much lately. Probably something to do with stalking me for two months.

They can't have been staying here. This place is obviously abandoned—they'd have no running water or facilities. I want to ask, but I don't want to make it seem like I care, like it's been driving me mad not knowing when he'd attack. I *don't* care. They could have been staying here or in a five-star hotel. It wouldn't make any difference to me.

Caleb reaches out to brush his fingers over my knee and when I flinch, he takes it in his grasp and squeezes. He studies me while his fingers tighten, but all I do is swallow and maintain eye contact. His jaw clenches, the side of his nose twitching with anger when I don't react again, even though his grip is beginning to hurt.

"Guess I should be grateful you finally learned to shut your whore mouth." The back of his other hand makes contact with my cheek before wrapping around my throat when I turn my eyes back to him. "Did the notes scare you?" he asks, clearly trying to *sound* scary.

"Quit talking," Jesse grumbles from behind me. I had almost forgotten he was here. "I wanna play." Caleb's hand drops from my throat, the other loosening its grip on my knee.

The way he says that word—*play*—as if it means something far more sinister sends a shiver through me. My anger from before has started to cool, despite staring at the man who made me flee my home. Who made me feel weak. Who made me feel less than.

"You told me we'd have fun with her."

I close my eyes against Jesse's words. These fucking brothers. Ruining my goddamn life even after I ran halfway across the country to leave Caleb's violent ass. I want to scream. I want to rage and break things and push Caleb and his cunt of a brother off the goddamn roof.

When I open my eyes again, Caleb is grinning. He obviously believes he finally got a reaction from me. He has to know that it was Jesse who did it, though. Has to know that it was *Jesse's* words that forced a response.

Jesse's hand falls on my shoulder, but I don't look at it. I focus my eyes on the graffiti on the window, memorizing it like it's a beautiful piece of art in a museum. The hand on my shoulder slides toward my neck, leaving a trail of decidedly creepy goosebumps in its wake. When he reaches the back of my neck, Jesse moves quickly, fisting my hair, his grip tight. He yanks backward and I hiss, squeezing my eyes shut against the pain.

"Look at me, you worthless bitch."

*No.* I refuse.

"I fucking said *look* at me."

Jesse's fingers begin to pry open one of my eyelids. Caleb laughs in front of me and I give in, opening my eyes to avoid further pain or worse. Jesse stares down at me, grimacing—or maybe smiling? With him, it's hard to tell. He looks like his brother, only several inches taller. His muscular build doesn't seem to have suffered during their stay in LA and I wonder if Jesse has been here the whole time or if that's what Caleb was waiting for. Maybe that's why it took him so long to act. He needed his guard dog.

"I dunno what my brother ever saw in you," Jesse mutters, studying me. I notice his eyes stray to my tank top.

"She was a good little slut for me," Caleb muses. I can't look at him with Jesse's hand still stuck in my hair. "Until she started fucking other people."

"That was for *work*," I snarl. Fuck being silent. I supported his chronically unemployed ass.

"Don't lie." Jess pulls harder on my hair. "You liked it. You wanted to make a fool of my brother."

"Shut up, Jesse."

"I don't think your brother likes that," I sneer. It earns my hair another tug. If Jesse doesn't let up, he's going to rip it out in chunks, but I can't stop now. "Are you just gonna keep insulting me all day?"

Jesse finally lets go of my hair.

"Still too early to start the real fun," says Caleb, glancing out the window.

The blindfold descends over my eyes and then a ball gag is being shoved into my mouth, forcing my jaw open. It's buckled behind my head and then I'm left alone. Whether the Davis brothers actually leave or simply remain silent over the next few hours, I'm not sure. It gives me time to swing between rage and despair. Rage at Caleb for ruining a life I worked hard to construct and despair that I'll never again feel Miles' hands on my face or Brody's arms around me.

# 42

## Brody

"Well?" Miles paces my office. He hasn't left since we spoke with Mel earlier.

She refused to grant me access to our systems again, giving me no way to help or even follow her team's footsteps in tracking down Sophie.

I shush Miles with a wave of my hand, and switch to speakerphone, setting the phone on the desk.

"These brothers are a piece of work," says Mel.

"We knew that," I mutter, frustrated. "Mel, please. It's been hours." There's no point trying to keep the desperation from my voice.

"We found her car at a coffee shop near her apartment. I have someone driving it over to your place."

"She wasn't in it?" I demand.

"Brody." Mel sighs and my stomach drops. My mouth goes dry. Is that a good sigh or a bad sigh?

"What is it?"

"My team thinks they've found her." Mel is quiet and I wonder, yet again, who this team is that she assigned Sophie's safety to. "I have someone heading to you. He's ex-military."

"What? Why is he coming here?" I frown at the phone.

"Because," she sighs again, "I know that if I don't make him take you two idiots, you'll find a way to get there first and get yourselves hurt or worse."

She's not wrong. She has to know that I've been trying for hours to get back into Harp's systems, but I built the security well. I never thought I'd have to break in, so I didn't give myself a way to do so.

"Thank you."

"Just don't get yourselves hurt. Those two are dangerous men."

"So his brother is here too?" asks Miles, stepping toward the phone.

"Unfortunately," Mel mutters. "Booker should be there soon."

She hangs up and Miles looks at me in confusion.

"Do you know anything about this Booker?"

"He's news to me."

The waiting is the hardest part. Knowing what Caleb and his brother are capable of, knowing Sophie has been with them for hours. I'm losing my mind. Miles returns to pacing even once we move to the living room to wait for Booker.

"It's going to be ok." I feel like I have to be the voice of reason here even though I'm dangerously close to falling off the edge into insanity. "Mel only works with the best." That's true, at least. "Booker will find her."

"Brody, I didn't-" A choked sob cuts off his words. The only time I've ever seen him like this is when his father died. "Never mind."

The doorbell rings and Miles freezes, staring at the front door, leaving me to answer it.

The man on our doorstep may not be as tall as I am, but he's wide, filling the doorway with his huge frame. His long-sleeve, black shirt is tight enough, making it look like his muscles have muscles. The sleeves are pushed up to reveal one arm covered in black ink. Or rather, the darkest gray with black tattooed over it in geometric designs. The other arm has more colorful artwork. More tattoos with jewel tones snake up from beneath the neck of his shirt and up his head, disappearing beneath jet-black hair which is shaved on the sides. I stare at the artwork for a moment, forgetting that I should probably speak.

"Booker," I say, by way of greeting. My voice is hoarse.

"You must be Brody," he grunts, then looks past me at Miles. "Fucking civilians. If I tell you to hide or shut up or run, you fucking do it. Understood?"

"Understood." I nod and Miles echoes his agreement.

"Let's go get your girl."

# 43

## Sophie

"You know, we planned something special for you." It's the first time Caleb has addressed me in a while, maybe hours.

The ball gag keeps me from doing anything other than moaning an 'oh goody'.

"What was that?" Jesse teases. Without warning, my chair tilts back and my arms and legs jerk, but I have nothing to grab onto. My ankles and wrists are still bound. "I'm having trouble understanding you."

*Fuck you and the horse you rode in on, you cow-fucking, cum-guzzling butt-monkeys.* Natalie's knack for creative insults must be rubbing off on me.

They spin my chair and drag me for several feet before coming to a stop, spinning me again, and setting the front two legs back on the ground. I've lost all sense of direction, unsure if I'm by the closed door from earlier or the big, graffitied window–are they going to throw me off of it?

"Take the blindfold off," Caleb orders. "I want her to watch as we put together her *set*."

*The fuck?*

Jesse takes off the blindfold, but not the gag. My jaw aches and I've been drooling so bad that saliva has dripped from my chin down onto my tank top. The sight that greets me makes my stomach churn.

The white door that was on the other side of the table is open now and I'm much closer, sitting just a couple of feet in front of the doorway. A heavy-duty, metal saw horse is visible in the center of the room. Set up on either side are large, halogen work lights. Last, on the far side of the room, angled at the saw horse, is a tripod with a camera attached to it.

They're going to film their abuse, the sick fucks. This has to be Jesse's idea. Caleb was never this twisted.

Any words I'd speak to save myself would be lost to the gag, but words won't work on these two anyway. The only language they speak is violence.

Jesse and Caleb each grab an arm and haul me up. Something inside me snaps and I fight, flailing my bound hands and screaming around the ball in my mouth. Tears squeeze from my eyes as the brothers tighten their grip on my arms.

"Now you react. Fucking cow!" Jesse yells in my ear. "We're gonna teach you a fucking lesson. Act like a slut, get treated like a slut."

"Not that we'll have time to test you on the material before-" He's silenced, likely by a look from his brother.

Caleb's words make me stop, my head whipping around to look at him, but he doesn't meet my gaze. When I'm a foot from the saw horse, they drop me and I grunt. Jesse takes a knife and holds it against my throat, bringing his face even with mine.

"I'm going to undo these," he growls. "But if you try to get away, it's going to be so much worse for you. Understand?" The blade pushes into my skin, pricking it, drawing blood.

*Oh, goody*–a scar to match the one his brother gave me.

I nod, readying myself to do exactly what I'm not supposed to do.

He cuts through the ropes around my ankles and I remain still, breathing heavily through my nose. Jesse saws through the ropes around my wrists. The moment I feel the last threads break, I bring up my foot and send it crashing into his chest. I don't watch him tumble away. Scrambling to my feet, I stumble toward the door.

I barely make it three steps before something hits my head and I go down. My chin scrapes the concrete floor while my hands take the bulk of my weight, sending pain shooting through my wrists. My ears ring and the world goes all fuzzy as someone straddles me. I kick my feet, trying to scream around the gag that I would've taken off if I'd gotten any further. My thighs scrape on the rough concrete floor and I reach back, trying to claw whichever brother is on top of me.

"You fucking bitch." Jesse's voice is further away, grunting in pain.

"Can't believe you trusted her," Caleb mutters, letting all of his weight settle onto my ass. "Get over here and help me."

He hisses when I reach back with both hands and dig my nails into his legs. If I go down, I'm getting DNA evidence.

"That fucking hurt, man," Jesse complains.

"Of course it did. Get over here."

Caleb lifts his weight, but before I can react, two pairs of hands grab me once more. They drag me back to the saw horse and Jesse holds me while I continue to flail. Caleb rips my leggings down and off. I try to kick him in the face, but he dodges my foot. Jesse pulls my arms painfully backward for that move. I try to throw my head back into his mouth or nose or *something*, but I don't make contact.

"Nice try, bitch," he growls in my ear. "I can't wait to watch you cry. You'll be begging for fucking mercy."

They leave my tank top in place and force one of my legs over the saw horse. The corners are sharp, digging into my tender areas. I'm forced face down so that my sternum rests directly on the cold metal. The bar only reaches from my collarbone to somewhere beneath my stomach. One good thing about the extra weight on my body is that it relieves the pressure on the sensitive skin below my hips.

While Caleb ties my ankles and knees in place against the supports, Jesse ties my arms down. I'm bound in the shape of the sawhorse with my limbs stretched out. Jesse's ropes are tight and I don't know if it's the stress or if they're genuinely cutting off the circulation to my hands, but my fingers feel tingly. My limbs are restless and I flex my fingers to try to keep the blood flowing. My chest is tight, the anxiety of being unable to move is already stealing my ability to breathe. The rage from earlier—that blood-boiling, scream-inducing rage—isn't enough to quell the panic.

The brothers' hands disappear and I catch a glimpse of Caleb pulling on a black ski mask before he goes to start the recording on the camera. He walks over and pinches my chin, turning my head toward the lens.

"Say hi, Honey." He laughs. "Oh wait, you can't." He turns his head to the camera. "You see, we're going to have some fun with you, our unwilling whore." He glances back at me and then his attention is on the camera once more when he drops my chin. "And then we have the ultimate surprise."

"But we'll save that for later," Jesse chimes in. "Don't want to spoil it for Honey, here."

*WHACK!*

I cry out when something makes contact with my ass. I'm able to twist my head just enough to see that Jesse is holding a long piece of wood, an off-cut as if from a construction site. I have enough brain power to wonder if that's where all of this came from. The building we're in can't have housed it, so it's clear this equipment is missing from somewhere.

*WHACK!*

Another smack brings me out of my thoughts and I squeeze my eyes shut against the pain. My hands are trembling, my breathing coming in ragged and short.

"This wouldn't have happened if you'd just listened to me. If you'd *stayed* with me," Caleb says as Jesse hits me again, in the same spot as the first two times. "If you weren't such a disgusting *slut*."

I used to like pain. Not to this extent, but I used to like rough sex and choking and all of that stuff, but now...

*WHACK!*

Tears prick the backs of my eyes, whether from the stinging and throbbing of my buttcheeks or the situation, I'm not sure. Those tears begin to well, threatening to spill over and if they do, I don't know how much longer I'll last. Caleb intends to break me. I want it to be difficult, but my body might have other ideas.

*WHACK!*

I cry out, muffled by the gag, and my eyes start leaking.

"Are those tears?" Caleb's tone is mocking as he walks away.

When he returns, my head is hanging to take the weight off of my neck, but I can see the black riding crop in his hand. It's obviously a tool specifically made for kink. I steel myself against the oncoming pain, squeezing my eyes and tensing my body.

The board lands another blow just as the crop finds my back.

"I think she should count," Jesse grunts from behind me.

"Did you hear that, slut?" Caleb drags the crop down my back before swatting me again. "Count while we punish you."

*WHACK!*

I remain silent. *I can't, you fucking idiot.* The gag remains in my mouth. Do they want me to grunt?

"I said *count*." Caleb ends the sentence with another blow, followed closely by the board in Jesse's hand.

He steps around in front of me and grips my chin tight, angling my neck so that I'm forced to look at him.

"Count, you stupid cunt," he orders. "I don't care if you have to drool through every goddamn word. Count or I'll give you a real excuse."

I can't help. I really can't help it. My eyes roll when he tries to sound intimidating by grabbing his crotch. The back of his hand strikes my face.

"Maybe when we're done with you, we'll send the video to your boyfriends." He drops my chin and steps over to my side. "Make them watch," he smacks me, "while we bruise your ass." Jesse and Caleb land blows at the same time. "Listen to you scream and cry whine like a bitch while I fuck that asshole dry."

*WHACK!*

"You're a fucking whore," Caleb continues. "Say it!"

*WHACK!*

"Say it," he repeats through gritted teeth.

Tears continue to fall from my eyes, rolling up my face before falling into my hair. Each blow lands in a different spot now and I know my whole body will be black and blue and purple beneath angry red welts tomorrow. I remain silent.

Clearly giving up the idea of making me gargle the gag, Caleb attacks my arms and back while the board in Jesse's hands collides with my calves, my thighs, my ass.

"You're mine," Caleb snarls. "Mine to mark, mine to play with, my whore, fucking *mine.*"

He drops the riding crop and crouches in front of me. His hand tangles in my hair, yanking my head up so that he can hold a knife directly before my face.

"Don't worry," he chuckles darkly. "I'll leave your face pretty."

He swipes the knife along my upper arm and I cry out again around the gag, squeezing my eyes shut. Another slice on my opposite forearm sends pain radiating through my body while Jesse's board continues to make contact.

"I don't think she likes this, Jesse."

*No shit, Sherlock.* I open my eyes when I realize the blade hasn't cut me a third time.

"Maybe she'll like phase two," Jesse retorts.

The board clatters to the floor, imitating the drop of my stomach at his words. I'm pretty sure I know what phase two is.

Caleb's hand tightens in my hair and he shakes me to ensure he has my attention. He brushes the end of the knife along my cheek, not enough pressure to break the skin.

"I'm going to take this gag off." He taps the ball between my teeth with the blade. "You can scream all you want... while your mouth is free." He smirks and my chest goes cold.

"Won't be free for long."

Fingers—I think it's fingers—swipe through my very dry pussy as Caleb undoes the buckle behind my head and lets the gag fall to the ground. I work my jaw, moving it side to side, then in a circle, trying to ignore what's being done behind me.

Fuck, my jaw hurts. Now I know what some of Natalie's subs feel like during her longer sessions. I want nothing more than to let my mouth just hang open and relax, but I know that's not what's about to happen. I think I knew from the moment I woke up on that floor what their plan was. I just didn't want to admit it to myself.

Caleb mutters something about teaching me a lesson while he unzips his pants, but then his brother speaks up.

"I thought you wanted her snatch first."

*I hate that word.* It's a ridiculous thought, but it's the one that breaks through the pain radiating through my entire body.

"Fuckin' right, I do." Caleb looks like a toddler walking away, his pants sliding down further with each step. He trades places with his brother.

I want to squeeze my eyes shut, but I will *not* give in to the fear. I will not react. This time, I'll remain silent as the fucking grave.

"And I," Jesse says, standing in front of me, "get to fuck this pretty little mouth." He squeezes my chin and forces my head back and up as far as it will go so that I can see his eyes through the holes in the ski mask. The same beady, brown eyes as his brother's. "And then we're gonna cut your slut throat and dump your body where no one is ever gonna fucking find you."

My jaw clenches. *That* is Jesse's idea. This sick, twisted fuck doesn't like that I made his brother look weak and him too, by extension.

Jesse pulls down his boxers to reveal a rather pathetically small dick. Even if I didn't make porn and stare at well-endowed men all the time, this guy would be considered small. Talk about an inferiority complex. These two should be studied.

If Natalie were here, she'd launch into a slew of insults like she does with her subs. I've heard her in action. It's a thing of beauty. Instead, all I can make out through pinched cheeks are two words.

"How cute." My voice is low, but Jesse catches my insult nonetheless.

The back of his hand makes contact with my cheek as he drops my chin and my world spins, my ears ringing once more. He grabs my jaw again and I'm forced to look at his face.

"What was that, bitch?"

*Oh my, Jesse, what an inadequate dick you have there.*

I remain silent and Jesse sneers. I don't know what Caleb has been waiting for. There's no barrier between his cock and my entrance. When Jesse takes a step forward, bringing himself that much closer to my face, I clamp my mouth closed. If he ever gets between my lips, I'll bite his dick off, I swear.

My whole body is trembling, my chest still tight. The only thing in my line of sight seems to be the smaller-than-average erection in front of me.

A loud bang rings through the space, echoing in the tiny room. My eyes shut on instinct and I hear a thud behind me. Another bang and the ringing in my ears, which hasn't stopped since the last slap across my cheek, grows louder. My jaw is free. I hear a similar thud in front of me. When I open my eyes, Jesse is crumpled to the ground, dick on display, a gaping hole in his chest. I think I can see one of his ribs poking through. His eyes stare absently at the ceiling as blood pools beneath him.

A sob rips from me as tears stream freely down my face. Trying to breathe feels overwhelming, the air choking me as I attempt to gulp it down. The pressure of the metal becomes too much, my immobile limbs bringing me closer to the brink of a meltdown. The panic attack finally strikes and I breathe faster, hyperventilating.

A warm touch lands on my ankles and I scream, trying to kick, but instead I barely move. My torso wiggles on the sawhorse, the edges digging into my skin. Someone's trying to shush me, to shut me up, but I won't be quieted. I continue to scream, even when my first leg is freed, kicking out at whoever it is. I won't go down without a fight.

I won't.

I won't.

*I won't.*

"Sophie." It's a voice I don't recognize so I continue to try to battle.

My second leg is freed and I lash out again, rubbing my sensitive skin raw on the metal. For some reason, this person doesn't seem to care. I don't make contact so maybe they're just not worried I'll hurt them. My aim obviously needs work.

"Get away!" I cry when they crouch next to my arm, cutting through the rope around my wrist.

"Sophie, it's ok." The heavily tattooed man doesn't exactly look friendly, but his voice is soft. He focuses on what he's doing, careful not to slice my skin as he frees my right arm before moving to my left side.

My screaming has stopped, my throat raw. I'm not sure when, but I stopped fighting.

"I'm going to help you off of there," he says gently, as he cuts the last of my bonds. "I want you to keep your eyes on me. I'm getting you out of here. Can I touch you?"

My entire body is trembling, but what choice do I have? I nod. He stands as he reaches for the soft spots beneath my arms. I cry out when he hauls me up, the relief of the pressure on my sternum and stomach verging on pain. My leg drags clumsily over the sawhorse and I collapse into his arms.

When I try to look around, his large hand shields my eyes.

"Just look at me," he reminds me.

My legs are weak, but I find just enough strength to walk from the room with his help. The stranger lowers me into a chair, the freezing metal shocking my system when it hits my bruised and battered body.

"I'm going to put your pants on."

I hadn't realized he was holding my leggings. I'm surprised Caleb and his brother didn't cut them off.

*Caleb.*

*Jesse.*

I know Jesse's fate, but when I turn to look and find out Caleb's, the stranger places his hand on the side of my face again to keep me from turning. He shakes his head and then readies the first side of my leggings, scrunching it up and holding it out so I can put my foot inside. I'm reminded of when Miles helped me dress back in Miami. It feels like a lifetime ago.

When my second leg is in, he holds out a hand and helps me stand while he pulls the leggings up to my waist. He's careful with me, his hands soft, his movements slow.

"We're going to leave. Brody and Miles are waiting downstairs."

Their names bring fresh tears.

They came for me.

# 44

## Miles

Sophie appears in the stairwell, clutching Booker. Her jaw is beginning to bruise and there are red rings around her wrists and marks on her arms. The blood coming from a long cut on each arm seems to have stopped flowing. The only thing keeping me from going back upstairs and tearing the Davises limb from limb is the woman approaching me who looks like she's been through hell and then some.

Brody and I rush forward and Booker gently lets her go when we reach them. She falls into our arms and the three of us sink to the ground. One of Brody's arms is around Sophie's back, the other around mine. I cradle Sophie's head against my neck and chest, listening to her cry while my eyes find Booker's.

"What did you do with them?" I sound a lot less dangerous than I feel right now, holding the woman I love while she weeps in pain and relief.

"They won't hurt her again," Booker assures us.

Brody nods, but I stare. I'm not sure Brody or I could've done what that man did. Another of many reasons to be thankful for Mel Ashcroft and her shady-as-fuck company. I've never liked her more than I do right now.

"Let's get you home," I whisper into Sophie's hair.

*Are there flowers that say thanks for saving the love of my life?*

She lifts her head, her eyes shifting between Brody and me. They're red from crying, her makeup all but gone by now, more than twenty-four hours after we started our cam session.

"I can't be home alone," she whispers and fuck if my heart doesn't break all over again.

"No," I agree.

"Home with us," says Brody.

I want to take her to a hospital. Brody wants to take her to a hospital. Booker drives us home instead. He helps us get her into the house, into my bed, lying on her stomach, before beckoning us to follow him from the room.

"Miss Ashcroft is sending someone," he grunts. "She doesn't want messy questions."

"Sending someone?" I repeat in confusion.

"To see to her."

"The fuck does that mean?" Brody asks, frowning.

"Are *you* going to stitch up those wounds?" Booker pauses at the end of the hallway, crossing his arms when he turns to face us. "Check to make sure nothing worse has been done?"

"You could've just said doctor," I mutter. "What the fuck happened?" My voice cracks, my mind going into overdrive, thinking of the depraved things that could have been done to her.

"I can't be sure." Booker shakes his head, his tone a little softer. "I have to make a call about the bodies." He slips his phone from his pocket to check his messages. "The doctor will be here soon. She'll be ok." He tries to sound convincing when he looks back at us, but I know it's going to take more than just a few stitches and some ice on those bruises.

---

The older woman who arrives just a few minutes after Booker departs looks like a funeral director, but her long-sleeve, black dress hugs her body from her neck to her waist. Brody lets her in while I sit with Sophie and the two of us watch, helpless, while she examines Sophie's body.

"It's all right, love." She speaks softly as her gloved hands hover over Sophie's arm. "I'm Caroline. I'm here to help." Caroline looks over at the two of us. "Hot water," she orders, snapping open her ancient-looking leather bag. "And clean washcloths."

Brody hurries to comply while I kneel on the floor on the opposite side of the bed. I watch while Caroline uses medical scissors to cut one side of the leggings from Sophie's body, slowly revealing angry red marks with hues of blue and purple.

"Can you tell me anything about what happened?"

Why is she making Sophie relive this nightmare? I want to tell her to stop asking questions and get to work, but she's doing us a favor. I bite my tongue.

"They hit me." Sophie's whisper is barely audible, facing away from me and toward Caroline.

"Do you know what they used?"

"B-board," Sophie croaks. "C-c-crop." Her voice is getting weaker. I'm surprised Caroline can hear her.

"I see." Caroline nods and lifts Sophie's hand to examine the cut on her forearm.

Brody reappears with a steaming bowl and a handful of clean washcloths. He sets it on the table beside the bed and then steps back, as if unsure what to do.

"Sophie, I'm going to clean this cut first," Caroline explains, reaching for a cloth and dipping it into the water. "Then you're going to need stitches," she continues. Sophie hisses and flinches when the cloth makes contact. "It's ok. Hush, it's ok."

While Caroline works, we move the armchair from my studio into my bedroom. We situate it as close to the end of the bed as possible so as not to crowd the doctor–she hasn't called herself that, but Booker didn't correct me earlier. Brody takes the armchair and I pull my desk chair beside him.

Once Sophie's arm is clean, Caroline takes supplies from her bag to begin stitching the wound. At Sophie's first flinch, my hand shoots out to find Brody's. His other hand covers me and he squeezes.

"She's going to be ok." His words are soft, spoken like his throat is constricting.

"She is," Caroline confirms without taking her eyes off of her work.

When she's finished with the cut on Sophie's forearm, Caroline stands and circles the bed to focus her attention on the other knife wound. This one in Sophie's bicep is longer but looks shallower.

Caroline cleans and stitches the second wound before returning her focus to Sophie's legs. She finishes cutting off the leggings and I have to look away from the marks. I'd love to get my hands on the fuckers who did this, but since I'm not a necromancer, I have to be content knowing they're dead. The world is better off.

I force myself to look back at Sophie. Caroline has cut through her shirt, revealing thinner marks on her back. I can tell which instrument was used where, imagine just how hard Caleb and Jesse hit her, and I taste bile in the back of my throat. This isn't impact play, this isn't kink. They wanted her to suffer because they were absolute psychopaths bent on revenge.

Caroline stands and I have to look away again when she reaches between Sophie's legs. It feels indecent, somehow, to watch her examination. When I turn back, Caroline's hands are prodding gently at Sophie's legs, trying not to press directly onto any of the darkened and red spots.

"Her skin isn't broken," Caroline explains, reaching for a new cloth to gently clean the areas she just examined. I realize she's speaking to us. "I recommend icing the worst spots," she continues. "But there's not much to be done for bruises."

*Bruises*. Such a simple, everyday word for the sadistic, violent marks on Sophie's body.

"Keep her on her stomach as much as possible. You may need to help her use the facilities and to bathe. It'll take more than a week until she can sit comfortably again."

Caroline closes her bag and meets Brody's gaze first, then mine as she pulls off her gloves.

"Make sure she drinks plenty of fluids. Leafy greens like spinach will help as will citrus. Miss Ashcroft has my number should you need anything else."

"I'll walk you out." I stand and we leave Brody alone with Sophie. Her eyes are closed, her breathing even. The last thing I see is Brody reaching out to place a gentle hand on her unmarked foot.

"It's going to take some time," says Caroline while we walk. "Not just physically," she adds and I nod.

"I can't- I can't imagine what-"

"Don't do that to yourself." Caroline places a hand on my arm and we come to a stop a few feet from the front door. Her blue eyes flicker between the hallway and my face.

Caroline leaves and as I turn away from the door, my phone rings in my pocket. I never turn on the ringer, in case someone calls or texts during a session or shoot. I turned it on earlier in the hopes that Sophie would call me. Natalie's name stares back at me on the screen.

Before I can say hello, she practically yells into the phone.

"WHAT THE FUCK IS GOING ON?"

"Natalie, we've got her." The words tumble out.

"I should've been your first motherfucking call. What happened? Where was she? Was it Caleb?"

I wait for her to take a breath before I speak.

"It was Caleb," I confirm, but then bite my lip, unsure how much I should tell her. "She, er... Natalie, they hurt her." My voice breaks.

"I'm gonna fucking kill them." Her voice is low, dangerous, and I admire her commitment to her friend.

"No need. They're gone."

"How is she? What can I do? I'm leaving now."

"Stay in San Francisco," I urge. Sophie wouldn't forgive herself if Natalie cut short a work trip for her. "We'll take care of her, I promise. I'll send you the address and you can come by after your trip."

"Fuck that, I'm coming home *now*."

"You can't do anything for her. She's here, she's resting, we'll give her everything she needs."

Silence greets my words and I wait while Natalie processes. Or decides what to do. I'm not sure what's happening in her brain.

"If she asks for me, I'm coming home early."

"Yes, ma'am."

"I'll see you Thursday afternoon."

*It could have been worse.*

The thought bounces around my brain as sunlight floods through the window. Booker didn't tell us how he found Sophie. He didn't tell us the state she was in when he saved her.

*It could have been worse.*

Brody is asleep in the armchair, his head leaning back, mouth open while he snores. I haven't been able to shut my eyes. I tried, an hour or so after Caroline left, but all I could think about was what Caleb and Jesse did to Sophie. What they might have done if Booker hadn't arrived when he did.

Sophie's back rises and falls beneath the blanket. Her body clearly needs the rest. We never bothered to pull her ruined clothes from beneath her, not wanting to disturb her until she's ready.

"Miles." Her voice is so soft, I almost miss it. "Brody."

I scurry to her, practically falling out of the chair in my haste, and kneel beside the bed. My movements wake Brody and he follows suit. I place my hand on hers and try to smile.

"Hey," I whisper. I can feel the sting of tears in my eyes as relief washes over me. Her eyes are open and clear while she looks between us. "Hey, Sophie. We're here." I rub my thumb over her knuckles.

"Sophie," Brody breathes. "You're safe, it's ok."

"Caleb?" she asks.

"He's not going to hurt you again," Brody says through clenched teeth. "*Never* again."

Sophie sighs, closing her eyes. I want to wrap my arms around her, to hold her and tell her I'm never letting her out of my sight again. I have to settle for holding her hand.

I remember what Caroline said and leave Brody to get water for her. I wonder how long it's been since she's eaten, but food can wait. Grabbing a reusable straw that bends at an angle two-thirds of the way up, I shove it in the glass of ice water before returning to my room.

Brody helps Sophie to lift her head just enough to take a few sips and I set the glass on the nightstand.

It's going to be a long road to recovery, but we'll give her anything she needs.

# 45

## Sophie

I haven't filmed, haven't posted, haven't interacted with customers in over a week. I gave Miles all of my login information and he made excuses when someone ordered a custom or wanted a session with me. Other than that, my pages have been silent. Natalie has come by every day since she got back from her trip. I'm glad Miles told her not to cut it short. I don't need the guilt of ruining a shoot on top of everything else.

The guys have been taking care of my every need, feeding me, helping me walk around the house when I get restless, bathing me. More than once, Brody has muttered something about needing a bigger tub for an Epsom salt bath, but I wouldn't have been able to sit down anyway.

Miles and Brody have been careful not to let me put any pressure on my backside. I haven't been left alone since they brought me home with them.

*Home.*

It feels like home, being in this house with the two of them.

Waking up the second Thursday after everything happened, I try to roll over. Gently, I lift my hand until it's level with my shoulder, then press down. I allow myself to turn and the arm beneath me sinks into the mattress pad. This soft memory foam pad is as good a place as any to try this, softer than a couch cushion or a bar stool.

I hiss when I flop onto my back, but the pain isn't as bad as I expected.

"Careful." Brody lifts his head from the armchair. I'm not sure if he was sleeping or watching me the whole time. He stands and comes closer to sit on the bed beside me. "How does that feel?"

"Hurts like a bitch," I groan. "I want to sit up."

"I'll help."

Brody grasps one arm but lets me use my hands to push myself up. My ass sinks further into the bed, making it difficult for me to remain seated with my legs out in front of me. Keeping a hand on my arm, Brody stands.

"Swing your legs over. Be careful."

My movements are slow as my skin rubs the sheet. The pain is similar to someone rubbing a sunburn. A sunburn that also happens to be on top of a bruise. I scoot forward until my feet can touch the floor and sigh.

"Good," Brody breathes. "Good job."

"You can call me a good girl." I grin. "I wouldn't hate that."

Brody leans down to kiss my lips gently, then murmurs against them.

"You're my good fucking girl."

He backs away, letting me have some space while I sit there, on the edge of the bed.

"Hey, breakfast is ready if-" Miles stops when he reaches the open doorway and sees me sitting up. "How do you feel?"

"Well, everything hurts, but I'm not dying."

Miles chuckles and comes over to kneel in front of me. His hands gently reach for my cheek and I'm surprised to see tears forming in his eyes. He swallows, searching my face.

"I love you." His whispered words send a flood of warmth through my chest and I lean forward to rest my forehead against his with a smile. "I fucking love you."

"I love you too." I can't cry. I've cried enough over the last week and a half. I lift my head to look at Brody. "You too," I whisper. "I love you too. I love you both so much. So fucking much." So much, it hurts, if I'm honest.

I didn't get to say it before Caleb took me. When Brody said it first, I was too overwhelmed by pleasure to respond, but I knew it then. I've known for a while now.

It takes two weeks for me to want to go home. Caleb and Jesse didn't take me from my house, but Caleb's messages, his threats, desecrated the place for me. I'll never feel safe again, walking through that front door again. Even with Brody and Miles at my side, my body trembles when I cross the threshold.

I should hate Caleb for it. I should curse him day and night. But I don't. He's dead. Jesse and Caleb Davis died in an abandoned construction site–an apartment building that never got to house anyone. They died and they disappeared and no one came looking for them. No one came to ask me questions as Caleb's ex. No one cares that they're gone.

That should concern me. It should cause alarm bells to sound in my head. Brody works for a company that can make people disappear so completely that it's as if they were never there. Where a normal person would be terrified, I'm just thankful.

If I had died in that building, if I had disappeared without a trace, at least I would have been missed. By Natalie, by Miles, by Brody. They would have looked for me. They would have cared. They would have grieved my loss.

I still think about Caleb and Jesse. I still have nightmares that force me awake at night. I still reach out for Brody and Miles, who have traded off sleeping in Miles' bed with me. Sometimes it even takes me a minute to figure out that I'm not back on that sawhorse. The men who care for me, all but rock me back to sleep, whispering words of comfort, words of love.

After two weeks of Brody and Miles and Natalie tiptoeing around me, not bringing up Caleb or his brother, I can finally attempt to get home, even if it doesn't feel like home anymore.

Someone from Brody's company found my car at the coffee shop where I was taken in broad daylight. The drinks were still sitting in my cup holder. I had stopped to get Natalie her usual hot tea and an iced coffee for myself when I was taken. My keys were on the floor of the driver's side where I must have dropped them after getting bashed in the head. Miraculously, no one broke in to steal the laptop sitting on the passenger seat.

I haven't driven in the two weeks since the *incident*. I refuse to call what happened to me a kidnapping. It makes me feel like a victim. Miles drove the car over last week. Seeing it sitting in the driveway is odd.

Brody and Miles walk behind me as if waiting for me to turn and run. Natalie stands in the doorway, leaning against the frame in a long, flowing, floral maxi dress. Seeing her calms my nerves a little.

The cameras have been taken down. Brody had it done before Natalie returned from San Francisco. That doesn't keep me from scanning for one just inside the front door.

Natalie lets me lead the way upstairs and a shiver runs down my spine when I reach the top. I'm home. Natalie and the guys are with me. I'm safe.

The old dining room table has been cleared off. The tablecloth is even gone. This is weird. That table is *never* empty.

"What's going on?" I frown and turn as Natalie reaches the top stair, followed closely by Brody and Miles.

"We had an idea," Brody explains.

"It was *my* idea," Miles chimes in. "Before you give him all the credit." He hooks his thumb at his friend.

"Are you going to tell me or argue about which one of you is the smart one?" I cross my arms and back away to give them all space to join me.

"Sit down." Natalie motions to the table using her Domme voice and, after squinting skeptically at her for a moment, I comply. I take the chair at the opposite end of the table. "Good girl."

She winks and sits at the far end. Brody and Miles sit on either side of me.

"*Now* are you going to tell me what you're planning?"

"For the record," Natalie begins, "I'm not fully on board."

"Thanks for the support," Miles mutters under his breath. I gently kick him under the table and he at least has the sense to look sorry.

"We want you to move in with us," Brody blurts.

"You- what?" My head swivels between the two before I look at Natalie. "I would think you'd want to get rid of me."

"And have my rent double? No, thanks." She sighs and leans forward in her chair. "I like these idiots, but you don't *really* know them."

I think my brain is malfunctioning. I'm trying to process. Brody and Miles want me to move in. Natalie doesn't like the idea. She thinks they're good for me, but it's too soon. For her.

"You're right." I look at Natalie when I speak. Miles sags. "I haven't known them for very long."

"See?" Natalie asks, looking first at Miles and then at Brody. "You can't move in with someone after a Disney relationship."

"Disney relationship?" Brody frowns.

"You know," she says with a wave of her hand. "When a princess marries a prince after knowing him for three days." I snort.

"I haven't known them for very long," I repeat. "But I can't say I hate the idea. I-" I bite my lip. "I actually like it."

"Really?" Miles nearly jumps out of his seat. "You do?" He grabs my hand excitedly. Brody beams and then looks over at my roommate.

"Is it really so bad?" I ask her.

"Fine, go to the dark side." She rolls her eyes, fighting a smile.

"I'll call a realtor," says Brody.

"A realtor?" I frown.

"Yeah, you and Miles need studios, right?" he asks, then looks across the table at Miles. "We don't have the space at the current place."

"So, what, you're just to *buy a new house*?" I ask, sarcastically. Brody's expression doesn't change when he meets my gaze and my lips part in shock. "You're just going to *buy a new house*?"

"This asshole could buy three new houses before the end of the week," Miles laughs. "Don't underestimate his bank account."

"Fuck," I breathe. What do I even say to that?

"I'm calling a realtor tomorrow," says Brody, ignoring the discussion of his finances.

"Tomorrow?" Natalie asks dejectedly.

"It's going to take time to find a place," Brody assures her. "You won't lose your roommate for a while."

"Something tells me I already have."

A thought occurs to me and I groan, throwing my head back.

"What?" Miles' tone is full of concern and I quickly lift my head to meet his gaze. "Second thoughts?" I swear I can see the bucket of ice water hit him.

"No," I'm quick to say. "No, I just hate packing."

"We'll cover it," says Brody with a shrug.

"What does that mean?"

"We're not making you pack and unpack all your stuff after what you've been through," he explains as if I should know that.

"So you're going to pack for me?" I ask skeptically, raising an eyebrow.

"I'm *paying* someone to do it for you."

Apparently, I hit the jackpot.

Brody:

Been working hard, Soph?

Miles:

Get that bag, girl!

Me:

Been editing all day

Miles:

Can I get your opinion on
some pics I wanna post?

Brody:

Are you sure you want me
weighing in?

Miles:

So you're saying you don't
want to see my cock?

Brody:

Dear god

Miles:

Don't bring him into this. I
don't think he'd appreciate it

I spend my first day at home editing and attempting to get a handle on everything I missed. The group chat is a constant source of delight, keeping me from going insane.

The next couple of nights without Miles or Brody beside me are rough, to say the least. I've come to expect that I'll have them to reach out for when I wake up terrified. Without their comforting presence, it takes longer for my breathing to return to normal and my pulse to slow.

We spend our days looking at homes all over the valley and further west. Every single one is obscenely expensive. Miles doesn't seem to have a problem letting Brody do all the financial lifting. I, on the other hand, am having a tough time wrapping my head around the idea.

After one particularly long day of house hunting, the guys bring me back to their place for dinner.

"So!" Brody shouts, heading for the kitchen as Miles closes the door behind us. "I have it all planned out." He waves his hands at the kitchen as a whole. "Miles has everything for nachos, we added a couple more subscription packages to the Roku so that we can watch anything you want, and I mean *anything*. There's beer and wine in the fridge and-"

"Brody," Miles interrupts with a laugh. "Let her breathe, man."

Brody mutters an apology, but I make my way over to him and wrap my arms around his neck. His hands fall to my waist as he lowers his lips to mine. I don't let him deepen the kiss and to my surprise, he doesn't argue when I pull away.

"Before we do that," I look over at Miles, "I want to know what you two have been up to."

"You mean when we're not trying to find the perfect home?" Brody frowns, but Miles knows exactly what I mean.

"I think," he says slowly, dragging his gaze to his friend, "she's asking what we do when she's not here."

"Wha- oh." Brody's eyebrows shoot up, his eyes wide with realization. Then the corner of his mouth draws up into a crooked grin. The change is almost comical and I have to fight the laugh in my throat.

"You mean you want to see what I do for Brody," Miles says, not looking back at me.

"Only if you want." I'm suddenly nervous.

"I think we can give her a show." Miles closes the distance between us and reaches out to gently run his hand through my hair. "You want to watch me suck our boyfriend's cock, honey," he smirks and I wonder when Brody became *our* boyfriend, "is that it?"

*Fuck yes, I do.*

I'm not sure if it's the exhaustion from seeing six houses today or just the feeling that things are finally becoming normal. This is the first time I've felt any semblance of a sex drive since the incident.

I bite my lip and nod, stepping away. Miles looks at Brody.

"My room or yours?" He smirks.

Without answering, Brody's hand shoots out to wrap about the back of Miles' neck. He pulls his friend forward and I watch with awe when their mouths collide hungry and wild. I'm not sure I've ever seen anything more mesmerizing and perfect.

"Fuck," I sigh because I have no other words. Miles pulls away from Brody, breathing heavily.

"Did you say something?"

"Forgetting about me already?" I laugh.

"Never," Brody growls, grabbing my wrist and yanking me toward them so hard that I yelp.

My cry turns into a giggle when both of their mouths find the sides of my neck at different points, kissing and nipping at my skin.

"This isn't about me," I try to protest. "I told you what I want."

"Who put you in charge?" Brody's question is muffled against my neck.

"I did," I retort. "Just now."

Brody lifts his head to stare down at me.

"Can we vote on that?"

"Nope. It's my turn to call the shots."

"I like her ideas," says Miles, lifting his head too. "She'd have my vote anyway."

"Fine," Brody grumbles.

"What are you angry about? You two are about to get the attention here."

"Good point. Miles?"

"Yes, good sir?"

"You guys are fucking weird," I giggle.

Brody wraps his hand around Miles' throat and when he growls, I have to clench my thighs together to try to get some relief.

"Be a good boy and suck my cock."

# 46

## Miles

This man knows *exactly* what he does to me. There's no way he's oblivious. Not now. Not anymore. The growl, the praise. My cock already aches.

I sink to my knees without a word, Brody's hand dropping away. Maintaining eye contact, I make quick work of his belt and the fastening of his pants. Brody's already half-hard when I pull him from the boxers that are barely containing him. My mouth waters at the sight.

Feeling Sophie's eyes on us, I flash her a grin before leaning forward to lick the salty bead that has already escaped the tip of Brody's dick. He groans when I grasp the base of his shaft and swipe my tongue along the underside. I part my lips and pull just his head into my mouth, swirling my tongue around it and his hand fists in my hair.

He wants to take control. I can feel it in his grip on my curls, but he hesitates, so I decide to toy with him. I don't let him any further into my mouth, though his hips buck when my tongue does its little dance again.

"What are you waiting for, Brody?" Sophie's voice cuts through the tension and seems to shatter whatever has been holding Brody back.

"Since you put it that way," he growls, pulling my head forward.

I give up control, letting him shove his growing cock as far down my throat as possible before starting a rhythm. I grip his hip in one hand and use my other to stroke him in time with my mouth. Brody isn't rough with his pushing and pulling, but the harder he grows, the more he chokes off my air supply.

I glance up to see Sophie has raised up on her toes to meet Brody's lips. Saliva drips down my chin while I gag and suck. My own cock is dying to be touched and my hand drops from his thigh to palm my erection.

"This is a lovely show," Sophie muses, looking down at me, "but I think poor Miles is feeling a little frustrated."

Brody pulls my head back and I gulp for air, staring up at him.

"Is that right?" Brody asks with a smirk. "Do you need some attention?"

*Oh fuck.* That look in his eyes is doing something naughty to my insides.

"I think we need to find a bed for what I have in mind," he continues.

I'm not sure how we get there, but within minutes, the three of us have shed our clothing and are standing in my studio. Brody pulls Sophie between us, her chest against him while he kisses her. I'm left to trail my lips over her shoulder and up the side of her neck. I make a path down her back, which is still marked by the beating she took from her ex and his brother. The bruises are now a mottled green and yellow. She doesn't flinch. They seem to bother her less and less each day.

I slowly sink to my knees, grazing my teeth over the fading bruises on her ass. When I find an unmarked spot, I sink my teeth in, earning a squeal from above me. Immediately, I press a kiss to her skin. Placing a hand on her hip, I urge her to turn toward me. Brody lets her, still hugging her to him while I kiss her thigh.

"Think you can balance on one foot for me, honey?" I look up at her with my bottom lip trailing on her skin.

Sophie bites her lip, hesitating.

"I'll help," says Brody.

His hands wrap around her while I lift one leg, placing her thigh on my shoulder. She's fucking glistening. I'd love to know just how much of it is from my performance in the kitchen. I take a deep breath through my nose, filling my lungs with her scent before I lean forward.

Tasting her by running my tongue along her entrance, I moan into her pussy. Sophie mirrors my sound as she leans back against Brody's chest. I feel her leg on my shoulder twitch while I feast. If she were lying down, I'm sure she'd be writhing beneath me. Instead, Brody holds her still.

That just won't do.

My chin wet with her arousal, I pull away. Sophie whimpers, her hips trying to follow me.

"I think we're going to need you on the bed, honey."

Something sparks in Brody's eyes and he leans down to whisper in Sophie's ear. I can't hear it, but she closes her eyes and moans a 'yes'. The sound sends a jolt straight to my cock which is already aching for more.

"We definitely need her on the bed," Brody agrees. "I want you to fuck her."

"Twist my arm," I chuckle, gently lowering Sophie's leg.

She reaches the mattress and I follow her down onto the bed, settling myself between her legs. While I reach down to guide myself to her, Sophie reaches up to run a hand through my curls.

"I love you," she whispers.

I turn my face and kiss her hand before she drops it.

"I love you too. I love you so fucking much," I breathe, staring down at her. "Every day, I'm thankful for your existence."

I ease inside her and Sophie's eyes close. We moan together as I slide forward, stretching her, molding her to me.

"You look so good taking his dick," Brody breathes, closer than I realized.

His hand caresses my shoulder, sliding down my back. He kneels on the bed behind me, his lips on the side of my neck. I can't concentrate on anything. My movements falter and if he doesn't stop, I might explode too soon.

"Fuck," I grunt, rolling my hips into Sophie.

"That's exactly what I'm going to do," Brody growls.

Heat floods my chest and cheeks. I hear the snap of a lid being opened. A lid like the one on a bottle of lube. But when I try to turn my head to find him, Brody snakes his fingers into my hair and turns my head forward and down.

"Ah, ah, ah," he chides. "Just keep fucking our girl. Make her moan for us."

"Miles," Sophie pants beneath me. Her hand finds the spot where we're joined and I watch as she plays with her clit, moaning my name again.

I try to concentrate on Sophie, on moving my hips. I lose the ability to function when Brody's slick fingers find my asshole, rubbing before he slips one inside. I groan, but he just laughs and leans to put his lips to my ear.

"Do you want this?" He's asking for consent, I know that's the point, but my god if it's not fucking hot.

"Yes," I breathe. "Fuck yes."

"Want what?" asks Sophie, but she's only half focused on the question.

She clenches around me and I know she did it on purpose, trying to draw my attention to her. That grin on her face tells me everything. I need Brody to hurry up or else she's going to make me come before he makes it inside me.

Brody's cock presses against my asshole and I lean further down over Sophie to give him better access, halting my movements. He grabs my hip and pushes, stretching, until the head of his cock slips inside me. A curse tumbles from my lips and my hips buck, but Brody continues to push.

"Why did you stop?" Sophie whines, her eyes flutter open. She tries to take in the scene above her, but I'm not sure what she can see from her angle. Brody's lips are by my ear.

"I'm fucking Miles while he fucks you, sweetheart. Filling his ass," he spanks one cheek, "while he fills your sweet cunt." He spanks the other cheek.

For a man who hadn't been with *anyone* two months ago, he's fucking amazing at dirty talk.

"Finally," Sophie laughs as if she's known all along that this is where we were headed.

"Aren't you going to thank me?" Brody asks, wrapping one hand, still slick with lube, around my throat while the other grips my hip.

"Thank you," I moan.

He's fully inside me now and I'm not sure how long I'll be able to contain myself with him in my ass while my cock is inside Sophie. This is a first for me, which is rare in my line of work. It's overwhelming.

"Good boy. Now, move." He pulls out just a little and I follow him so I can start a rhythm, fucking the woman beneath me while I fuck my ass on Brody's dick. The moans escaping the three of us mix together to form a devilish symphony and Sophie is the first to erupt.

"That's it, honey," I urge with a grunt while Brody showers her with praise of his own.

"Such a good girl, coming all over his dick."

She cries out as her walls contract around me, nails digging into my shoulder. That, combined with Brody's pressure inside me, sends me over the edge. Not wanting to end her orgasm too soon, I keep thrusting, filling her while I moan her name and Brody's along with a few curses.

It seems that's enough to finish Brody as well. He pulls out while I'm still twitching inside Sophie and I feel his warm cum cover my back.

Panting, I pull away from Sophie's warmth. With it, comes a white flood and I'm tempted to clean her up like I did that first time the three of us were together. But I can barely hold myself up, so instead, I fall to one side. Brody does the same on the other, sandwiching Sophie between us.

Too exhausted to move, we lay still for a while, enjoying just being there together.

I've never been happier in my life.

# 47

## Sophie

### Sophie

**Miles:**

We're headed to you, honey!

**Brody:**

Ready for another round?

**Me:**

You're talking about house hunting, right?

**Miles:**

Of course he is. Unless you have other ideas.

**Me:**

What's your ETA?

Miles:

30 minutes

29

28

I'm insanely excited about the house we're seeing today. I've been flipping through the photos on the realty site while waiting for the guys to pick me up.

Miles' numbered texts continue to come through, but stop at four, just moments before my doorbell rings. I race around to grab my purse and slip on my shoes before meeting him at the front door.

"You're early."

"Ok, so it takes twenty-six minutes," he replies with a shrug, walking with me to Brody's car. He's parked in the center strip between the front two townhouses on the property. "Maybe it's this maniac's driving."

I roll my eyes, sliding into the front seat, even though I've told Miles several times that the back is perfectly fine.

Our realtor, Sam, takes us to a home in Echo Park the next day. She lets us enter first and my jaw drops. The photos didn't do it justice. It's all jewel tones and dark wood and looks like a turn-of-the-century home that has been restored.

"Like it?" asks Sam, arms crossed as she follows us around. Her heels make that satisfying clicky sound when she walks.

"It's beautiful," I breathe, walking further into the home to look at the kitchen.

"Built in 1909," she goes on as the guys follow me further in. "It's been restored with as much of the original woodwork as possible. Some of it had to be replaced, but it's all solid wood." She taps a perfectly manicured nail on the ornate frame of the front door. "You'd never know the difference."

"How many bedrooms?" asks Miles, walking backward into the living room while staring at the light fixture on the ceiling. It's a small chandelier that fits perfectly with the rest of the aesthetic.

"Six," Sam answers, following us. "Plus a separate office space. Four bathrooms and a two-car garage. Plenty of backyard space, too. Good for pets or kids."

"What do you think, Sophie?" asks Brody, sidling up behind me and wrapping his arms around my waist.

"It's perfect," I giggle. "Miles?"

"If Sophie's happy, I'm happy."

Halloween passes quietly. Natalie and I spend the evening running through our annual rewatch of *Stranger Things*. Not many kids ring the doorbell, given that we're at the back of our property. I'll say one thing for Brody–our doorbell cam hasn't malfunctioned since the *incident*.

With a week left until we officially move in, the guys invite me over for dinner.

"A real dinner," says Miles over the phone. "No distractions."

It makes me giggle because I know damn well those two get distracted easily, whether I'm there or not. I've seen the way they look at each other, seen the way they touch each other when we're together, even fully clothed. I was happy with each of them before, but I'm happier than ever knowing they have each other in the way that they do.

When I arrive, I still have half a mind to do some distracting. Miles is bouncing on the balls of his feet when he answers the door, like a puppy excited that his human has come home from work.

"You know we aren't moving in for another week," I point out as he leads me inside.

"Yeah, yeah. That's exciting. But Brody and I have something else we've been talking about."

I frown as he leads me to the kitchen island where a manila folder is sitting on the nearest corner. There's nothing to indicate what's inside, other than the thickness.

"Do I get to open this?" I ask, looking between them. Brody is standing by the fridge while Miles sits at one of the bar stools next to me.

"Please do," says Brody, waving his hand with a hint of a smile on his face.

"It's a bunch of... paperwork. Thanks." I don't sound grateful, just confused. There's mention of an LLC. A few papers later is a business plan with the words 'rough draft' along the top. I look back up at them, my head turning back and forth to meet each gaze, green and gold. "What is this?"

"It's the beginning of a production company," Miles explains.

"You haven't talked a lot about what you would want to see in a production company if you owned one," Brody goes on, "but we put this together to show you it's possible.

Much sooner than I think you realize. This isn't set in stone, nothing is signed. It's more symbolic."

"If you want, Brody will provide the funding and act as a silent partner," says Miles. "You'll be CEO and I'll be... I don't know, your henchman or something."

Brody takes a few steps around the island to stand on my other side.

"It's going to take some time to put together a proper business plan," he says. "I'm not just *giving* you the money. I want to make sure you'll succeed. But I believe in you." He cups my cheek and tears sting as they gather in my eyes.

"This *is* something you want, right?" asks Miles and my head whips around to face him.

"Yes," I whisper. It was an idea years ago, but I never took steps to make it a reality. I've never gotten past the general idea stage because what's the point? I'm not ready for that.

I *wasn't* ready for that. Not until them.

"Got a name for it?" asks Brody. I snort.

"I don't think you'll like it."

"Try us," Miles pushes.

"Mattress Testers."

"I love it." Miles' reaction is instantaneous and I'm not sure he actually heard the words. Brody chuckles.

"Brilliant."

"How long have you been planning this?" I frown, flipping through the pages again.

"Long enough to have put all of that together," says Miles. "Pretty much since we asked you to move in with us."

"And you hid this from me?"

"Only so we could surprise you," says Brody.

"Sophie, we're in this with you for the long haul," says Miles, placing his hand on mine. "You want to start a company? We'll be your grunts-"

"And funding," Brody chimes in.

"-and do what you say," Miles continues, his concentration unbroken. "You want to leave California in six months for New York or Chicago or," he shudders, "Texas? We'll do it. We'll complain if it's Texas, but we'll do it." I giggle. "Hell, want to live on the moon? Brody will find a way to do it."

"Being with you," Brody adds, suppressing a chuckle, "feels like... How do I say this without sounding corny?"

"Lean into it," Miles urges with a grin.

"Living with my best friend the last few years has been amazing." Brody glances at the man in question. "It's easy. Miles is a great roommate-"

"Aw, shucks."

"-but something was obviously missing."

"Rude," Miles mutters.

"You, Sophie." His green eyes are begging me to believe him, but there's no need. "You were the missing piece, but you showed me," he places his hand on Miles' where it covers mine, "that I was missing something else."

"You complete us, is what he's saying." Miles shrugs. He's got that big, dopey grin, knowing exactly how ridiculous he sounds.

Brody groans and covers his face with his free hand.

"God, you guys are weird." I shake my head, a thousand thoughts running through my mind. There's only one I want to voice. "I love you both." The tears finally spill over, running down my cheeks. "Like, a lot."

"Love you, too, sweetheart." Brody embraces me and kisses the top of my head.

"Love you," says Miles as he pulls me away from Brody to brush his lips over mine. "Now we can eat."

# Epilogue

## Brody

## 3 Weeks Later

Miles stretches next to me with a groan.

"Good morning." I've been awake for an hour. Sophie's movements woke me while she muttered something about needing to make a last-minute post.

"Happy Friendsgiving," Miles replies with a lazy smile. His eyes are still half-closed and he takes a deep breath before blowing it out slowly. "What time is it?"

"Just after nine."

"Sophie already freaking out?" The corner of Miles' mouth tugs upward into a crooked grin.

"Not yet, but there's still time." I reach out and run a hand through Miles' dark curls before leaning close to his face. "Brush your teeth," I laugh when he closes his eyes in anticipation.

"Wow, ok. Aren't we supposed to be showing each other how thankful we are?" he asks when I sit back up but he still stands and shuffles to the en suite bathroom.

"I'm thankful for toothpaste."

The scent of coffee wafts through the open door, indicating Sophie has finished what-ever she wanted to post. Miles emerges from the bathroom, inhaling deeply through his nose. He pauses, shooting me a look.

"What?" I raise an eyebrow.

"Well, I'm debating what's more important. Coffee or sex."

"Coffee can wait. Get your ass over here."

Like an excited puppy, Miles practically jumps onto the bed before crawling forward and pressing his lips to mine. I slide my fingers into his hair while he straddles me. His fingers trail down my throat, over my chest, and find the hem of my shirt, helping me to pull it off quickly. I do the same with his before reaching into his sweats and grasping his erection. Miles groans a curse into my mouth before breaking the kiss and leaning his forehead against mine. I stroke, lazily because of the fabric in the way, chuckling when he grunts in frustration.

"Get these off, *now*," I order.

Miles is quick to comply, scrambling off of me and stripping away the last article of clothing while I slowly do the same with my boxers. He tries to resume his place on my lap, but I shake my head, pushing him onto his back, into the mattress.

"Brody," he chokes softly.

"You said we should be showing our thanks," I murmur, crawling up his body to kiss him quickly. "So let me show you just how *thankful* I am."

"Fucking Christ."

"Christmas is next month," I chuckle. "I have something special planned for that."

I smile against his skin as I kiss and lick and nibble my way down his inked torso. His hips roll as my lips trail over his navel and I lick a long line back up to his sternum. Miles' throat works while he swallows and his eyes are closed.

"Eyes on me, pretty boy."

"We really need to talk about that nickname," he mutters when his brown eyes snap open to find mine.

"I like it," I shoot back with a grin, moving back down. My face is so close to my goal that the tip of his cock drags up my throat. When it's in front of me, I smirk. "It's very fitting."

I maintain eye contact and open my mouth, lowering my face and letting him slide between my lips.

"Oh, fuck." Miles' hips buck, his tip hitting the roof of my mouth, but his eyes remain focused on my face.

His fingers find my hair, gently tangling into the longer strands on top. I pull my mouth off, having just barely teased him. He groans in frustration and I resume my task. Holding the base of his shaft with one hand, I start to move, taking more of him into my mouth. I told him I want to show him how thankful I am for him, for his presence in my life, and that's exactly what I intend to do.

I let my hand fall to his balls, gently rolling and massaging them. Miles can't keep his eyes open and his head falls back in pleasure while I work. I relax my jaw as much as possible, taking him further and further down my throat with each bob of my head. My eyes water every time I gag, my tongue toying with the underside of his cock. It's taken time for use to get here, for me to feel comfortable with every aspect of our heightened relationship. But in the weeks since we moved in with Sophie, I've come to love even more about him—including the way he tastes.

Miles' hand fists in my hair and I can see his torso tightening, so I pull my mouth away again. He whimpers.

"No, please," he pants. His eyes open to meet mine. "Please, don't-" he swallows, "don't stop." Miles' gaze flicks to the side, glimpsing at something behind me. Without looking, I know what that something is, but I still have to look at the woman who made this entire situation possible.

Sophie is leaning against the door frame, wearing only a thin, short robe. Tattoos peek out from beneath the hem and her sleeves. I'd like to trace the ink with my tongue, but first...

"Come here, sweetheart." I lift my hand and curl my finger, motioning for her to approach.

"I was enjoying the show." Sophie pushes off of the door frame and undoes the sash of her robe while she walks.

"I need your help." I smile up at her and she leans down to kiss me. I look to Miles again. "Sit up, let Sophie in behind you."

"What are you planning this time?" Miles asks without moving.

"I told you." I shrug. "I'm very thankful for *both* of you. But you're first." I wink.

Miles sits and Sophie drops her robe before crawling onto the bed and sitting behind him. He leans back against her chest and I watch as her fingers find his curls. Miles closes his eyes, savoring her touch. Without waiting for instruction, Sophie uses her other hand to slide up Miles' torso until her thumb flits over one nipple.

"Think you can focus on me?" I ask, leaning back down to focus on Miles' cock again.

"I'm always up for a challenge," Miles grunts. He stares at me while Sophie begins to toy with both nipples, her lips against his neck.

"Maybe I want your focus on me," she murmurs against his skin.

He groans when I swipe my tongue over his tip to collect the salty bead that has appeared. I don't hesitate to lower my mouth back over him. He hits the back of my throat and stretches it with every movement, making me gag. My own erection is aching for attention, but I know we'll get there.

"You like what he's doing?" asks Sophie. "Isn't he talented?"

"So fucking talented," Miles grunts in agreement. "Fuck, he's so-" he grunts again, "so good."

"Is he better than me?" Sophie grins, knowing the answer is no. I'm still in training and she's had years of practice.

"He's-he's getting there." The words come out half-chuckle, half-groan. Sophie hums.

"One day, I'll watch you fuck his face," she says as one hand glides over his chest. "Today, I just want you to fill his throat. Can you do that for me?" She rakes her nails over his skin. "Can you be a good boy and fill our boyfriend's throat with your cum?"

Miles whimpers a curse. I catch a glimpse of Sophie sinking her teeth softly into his neck and, at the same time, shove my face down so far that his flesh is pressed against my nose. Miles grunts and bucks while I remain in place, my hand fondling his balls the way I know he likes. I taste him, flooding my throat while he comes. He convulses and whimpers and his fingers drop to dig into Sophie's thighs beside him. My body fights for air, but he's not done and I'm not letting up until he is.

"Brody," Miles whimpers and I finally pull away, gasping for air but grinning. His head has fallen back onto Sophie's shoulder and she's grinning at us.

"Hands and knees," I order, backing up to give him room.

"Can't I take a moment to-"

Sophie sinks her fingers into his hair and pulls his head back to kiss him and cut off his words.

"Come on, Miles," she urges sweetly. "Be a good boy for us."

"I-" His words are cut off again by Sophie's lips and I grin at the interaction. She has learned to embrace her dominant side with him in the two weeks since we moved in together. I love watching it. I love watching her come alive like this.

"Hands and knees," I order again, pulling gently at Miles' legs.

He complies, rolling over and getting into position so that he faces Sophie. She grabs the bottle of lube from the bedside table—at this point, every bedroom in the house has a bottle—and tosses it to me. While I squirt some into my hand, Sophie slides down to give him the perfect view of her glistening cunt. It still amazes how much she's turned on by watching the two of us.

I rub one finger between his cheeks and he backs into me when I swipe over his hole. I grin at Sophie and nod, watching her fingers tangle into his hair to pull his face down to where she needs his mouth. She gasps when he makes contact and I watch for a moment. The two of them together are truly a sight to behold. One of Sophie's hands is at her breast, massaging it and pinching her nipple while her head is thrown back.

"You two are fucking perfect," I breathe.

I can't take it anymore. I have to join the fun. Raising up, I align myself with him and he pushes back again. I chuckle and press against the puckered opening, watching as my tip slips in.

"So fucking tight," I groan. The sight alone would be enough to excite me, but feeling him swallow my thick cock is absolute heaven. It's a wonder I can do this without exploding right away. "Such a good boy, taking my cock like this." Miles groans, his mouth focused on Sophie.

"So good for us," she agrees with a sigh. Sophie gasps. "Right there." Her voice is a whine now.

"Use your fingers, Miles," I grunt as my dick fills him. "Make her cum while I fuck your sweet ass."

Miles mumbles something into Sophie's pussy, but I can't hear it. I grip his hips and pull out slowly before pushing back in. I want him to feel every fucking inch of me. Out and back in, out and in.

"Look at you," I pant. "Taking my cock so well. Taking every fucking inch." Sophie's breathing quickens.

"You're doing," she pants, "so well. Making us both-" she gasps, unable to finish her thought.

"That's it, make her scream, pretty boy."

I pick up speed, pistoning into him while Sophie whines and whimpers in front of us. The sight, the sounds, the fucking feel of him squeezing my cock with his ass. It's all too much. With a roar, I push deep, filling him while Sophie cries out in front of us. My fingers dig into his flesh while my dick twitches inside him, releasing every drop.

My breathing ragged, my body finally relaxes and I slide my hand up Miles' back and into his hair. Sophie is panting and lying back while she tries to catch her breath. I pull on Miles' hair, making him rear up until his back is against my chest with my lips next to his ear. I roll my hips, still deep inside him, and he whines.

"I'm very, *very* thankful for you." I glance up at Sophie, though I know she probably won't register my words. "For both of you."

Leaving Sophie and Miles in bed is always the most difficult part of my morning. And afternoon. And evening. And night. But someone has to let the caterers in to set up. Since we're still organizing and living half out of boxes, I knew there would be no way for us to host a Friendsgiving without help. The team is still setting up when Isla arrives, early as promised, with a huge jug of something red and glittery.

"Here," she shoves the jug into my arms and I'm thankful for my reflexes. "It's a mix between a bramble, a French 75, and hard cider," Isla explains, shrugging off her jacket and hanging it in the enormous coat closet by the door."

"Nice to see you too." I lead the way into the kitchen.

"Yes, now where's my *favorite* brother?" Isla looks around.

"I'm right here." I step into her line of sight, but she simply looks past me and I hear the footsteps on the stairs just out of view.

"Is that Isla?" Miles shouts.

"Yo!" she replies, just as loud, and rushes over to hug him as if they haven't seen each other every day for the last two weeks. Isla has already been here nearly every day since we moved in. At first, it was with the excuse of finally meeting Sophie. She figured out our little dynamic immediately, detective that she is, and was genuinely happy. I even heard her mutter something about Miles and I *finally* figuring it out.

"Hey, kiddo, ready to stuff ourselves into a coma?" Miles slaps her roughly on the back while I set the cocktail jug on the counter for the bartender to take care of when he arrives.

"Obviously," Isla snorts. "Where is Sophie? And why is it so quiet?"

"Well, it's not quiet now that you're here," I point out. "Seriously, you walk in the door and the decibel level shoots up."

"And stays up," Miles adds with a laugh.

"Not my fault you guys are boring." Isla shrugs and leads the way into the living room where the antique record player is set up.

"Queue up the music, kiddo." Miles grins.

Isla hums to herself, searching through the albums on the shelf until she finds the one she's looking for. I don't have to see which one she picks out to know what's about to start playing. When *Twist And Shout* by the Beatles fills the living room, my lips spread into a grin.

I hover on the edge of the room, watching the two of them act like utter goofballs, singing and dancing to a song that Miles' father always loved. The record player was his. Every once in a while, after dinner, they would fire it up and dance around to the classic with their plates still on the table. Their own little party of three. Isla never saw it with her own eyes, but when Miles' dad died, she took it upon herself to keep music in Miles' life. Her taste in tunes always aligned much more with his than mine did. They've been concert buddies for years, but this holiday pre-meal tradition holds more love than I can possibly say.

When the song dies, Isla is quick to steal Miles' phone and connect it to the Bluetooth speaker. The playlist starts with a Shania Twain classic and I decide it's time to focus on the festivities.

Most of the guests arrive over the next half hour and the bartender does his job well, supplying them with drinks while we wait for our meal to be ready. For our Friendsgiving. Miles and Sophie invited some people they know in the industry who weren't planning to leave for the holiday. Natalie hangs out near the collection of cocktails, wine, and beer. Moira has her engaged in a very animated conversation, though I can't hear what it's about.

The front door opens and Mel appears just as a Thanksgiving rap plays over the speakers. If I didn't know better, I'd say my boss looks timid. Other than our monthly lunches, I haven't seen her in public in years. Her usual black pantsuit has been swapped out for a short, maroon dress with cap sleeves and a gold chain around the waist. Her hazel eyes sweep the scene in front of her until they land on me.

"You came!" I shout, approaching her and closing the door behind her. Though it's not something we usually do, I pull Mel into a hug. She grunts when her chest meets mine.

"I did." Her gaze returns to the room behind me. "You have a lovely home."

"Thanks! We're still getting settled." I place my hand on her upper back and help propel her forward. "There's booze over here," I point to the counter near Natalie and Moira, "and dinner should be ready in a few minutes. Can I get you anything?"

When I turn back to face Mel, her gaze has fallen on Natalie. The expression on her face is hard to decipher. Perhaps shock? Did she not expect to see people from the industry? At the very least, she should have expected Natalie.

"Everything ok?" I ask.

"Yes." Mel shakes her head and looks up at me with a grin. "I'll take a glass of white wine."

"Chardonnay ok?" I ask, stepping forward to grab a glass.

"Perfect."

"Can I introduce you to a few people?" I fill the glass halfway and hand it to her.

"I'll, er-"

"Come on." I motion for Mel to follow, which she does reluctantly. "This is Moira Hall and Natalie Weston." I gesture at the women before us who have stopped conversing. "Moira, Nat, this is my boss, Mel."

Natalie gasps, her eyes wide.

"Mel?" she repeats with obvious reverence. "Oh my god, *you're* Mel!" Without spilling a drop of her cocktail, Natalie wraps Mel in a tight hug. I fight the urge to laugh at Mel's shock when she goes rigid in Natalie's grasp. "You're seriously my hero." Natalie pulls back and then yells off toward the living room. "SOPHIE!"

"YEAH!" Sophie isn't visible, around the corner, but she *is* audible.

"MEL IS HERE!"

Sophie appears within seconds, her mouth hanging open.

"Oh my god, Mel." Her brown eyes swim with tears and she hurries forward to hug Mel who doesn't seem to have recovered from Natalie's embrace. "Thank you," she whispers.

With Mel's back now facing me, I can meet Sophie's gaze. I smile, showing my support. I don't really care that Mel hates hugs and affection. She saved Sophie's life, she help us get her back. Sophie hasn't had the chance to show her appreciation until now.

Mel clears her throat and Sophie finally lets go.

"It was nothing," Mel assures the group. Moira knows some of what happened but is otherwise in the dark. It seems Miles gets talkative when he's had a few mimosas.

"It was *not* nothing," says Natalie.

"I know you can probably get anything you want and all that," says Sophie with a wave, trying to recover from the emotional moment, "but if there's ever anything I can do for you, just say the word."

Mel smiles–a genuine smile, if small–and nods. She brings the glass of wine to her lips and I nod at Sophie.

"Hey, Moira, why don't we hound Miles about what he's wearing for the awards show in January." She slips her arm around Moira's shoulders and steers her back into the other room.

"I'm sorry," I say to Mel when they disappear. Natalie is far less animated, having expressed her gratitude. "You should be able to get through dinner without having to hug anyone else, but I can't make any promises about afterward."

"It's fine," says Mel. She takes another sip of wine. "I'm glad she's all right. I worried about her state of mind when you told me." She glances at Natalie, then back to me, "what happened."

"She's doing ok." I nod, picking up my cocktail from the bar where I left it when she arrived.

"She's strong," says Natalie, raising her glass. "Sophie has been through a lot, but the woman is resilient."

"I'm glad." Mel nods and I catch looking quickly at Natalie again.

"I'd like it if you got to know her a little. Maybe dinner with the three of us or something."

"Isn't that what we're doing tonight?" she asks with a grin. I'm glad to see she's warming up.

"I meant *just* us." I shake my head.

"What am I, chopped liver?" Natalie snorts.

"You telling me you wouldn't find that boring?" I raise an eyebrow over my glass as I take a sip.

"Dinner with my best friend, her idiot boyfriends, and a beautiful woman? How could that be boring?"

# Acknowledgements

I want to specifically thank my friend who inspired the character of Sapphic Emerald. She was my muse and my biggest cheerleader while I worked on the first book in this series. She even got to read the *trash* that was the first draft where not all of the characters had the same names, the spicy scenes weren't that good or that *detailed*, and the vibes were off. Honestly, it was a lot, but she stuck with it. So thanks, Sapphy.

A quick thanks to my friend GM (I didn't think you wanted your actual name in here) for being the partial inspo for Miles, including the line "every day, I'm thankful for your existence".

Third, thank you so much to Gemma Rakia for the amazing cover art and chapter inserts. The artwork is beautiful and she sent me the very first look on November 5, 2024–election day. Ya girl needed a win and her message brought some very happy tears to my eyes. The final product turned out so much better than I ever could have anticipated, so thank you for bringing my characters to life in full.

Next the BookTok community with whom I've interacted since spring of 2024. You guys have inspired me to really get back to writing. I've always loved it, but due to some health issues, I wasn't able to do anything I enjoyed most of this year. Inspiration from the community of authors I follow, some of whom are mutuals, has been a huge help in getting me back to work.

Speaking of back to work... Even though I know they'll never see this, I want to thank my doctors who worked hard this year to fix me. I started the year with mono. *Mono.* At the age of 34. Like... who does that? Who catches mono for the first time at the age of 34? Me, that's who.

Mono was mild compared to what really took me out of commission this year. After literal months of pain and failed treatments–and a primary care physician who refused to listen to me or my physical therapist–I finally got a much-needed surgery for a herniated disc. Prior to the surgery, I was bedridden (couch-ridden since I couldn't actually get to my own bed) and unable to take care of myself. December 1st, 2024 is just over 5 months after the surgery and I feel like a real human again.

So from mono to surgery for a herniated disc, this year has been a wild, mostly horrible ride. But I'm ending it with a bang (somewhat literally) by releasing my first book as Sara Sitwell.

Here's to 2025 and a slew of new books to come.

# About the Author

Sara Sitwell is a writer who also happens to be an amateur adult performer. She lives in Syracuse, NY, but is originally from the Kansas City area. Some day, she'd like to live in Ireland or Scotland, so if you're a tatted baddie from one of those two places, call her. She's also pansexual.

Sara has been making adult videos since early 2019, but it has been sporadic due to mental and physical health issues along the way. She was a pre-COVID spicy accountant. Not to hate on the people who jumped on that trend in 2020. You do what you gotta do. In March 2019, she jumped into the world of financial domination, but that wasn't fully satisfying, so she expanded her offerings after a few months and the rest is history. Over the years, she has become skilled in video editing, marketing, audio editing, script writing, and directing.

In her personal life, Sara has already been published under her legal name four times. However, knowing that her romance novels would likely make her family blush, she decided to publish under her stage name. She has taken her knowledge and experiences and used them to paint some *very* detailed pictures for her readers.

You're welcome.

You may have noticed a character named Sara Sitwell in this book. That character is, indeed, meant to be this author. However, she does not live in LA or have an amazing podcast called Hide the Sausage where she tries different meats with her guests. It's really a disappointment, so if someone out there wants to sponsor that podcast, make sure to reach out. She'd make it happen.

Sara intends to continue this series with a sapphic novel in 2025. Keep your eyes peeled for a book all about Natalie Weston and a certain boss lady.

More queer romances to come soon.

www.ingramcontent.com/pod-product-compliance
Lightning Source LLC
Chambersburg PA
CBHW070836260626
47170CB00007B/2392